Heirs to the Kingdom

Book Seven

THE BRIDGE OF SEQUANA

Robin John Morgan

www.heirstothekingdom.com

First published (Paperback) in the UK in 2016 by Violet Circle Publishing.

Manchester, England, UK.

Print ISBN: 978-1-910299-17-3
Digital ISBN: 978-1-910299-20-3

British Library Cataloguing in Publication Data.
A catalogue record for this book is available from the British Library.

All papers used in the production of this book are sourced only from wood grown in sustainable forests.

www.violetcirclepublishing.co.uk

To my Specialists.

For all of you who walked my road and inspired me.

Rune's eyes opened wide and she felt frightened. "Tell me Grandmother what will happen to me? Why have I been chosen when my sister is older?" Her eyes began to fill with violet.

"Calm yourself daughter of the woods, you will have your time with your woodsman and his children, and their children's children, and you will also know the joy of life in every form."

Rune began to cry. "Grandmother please tell me I will not have to endure three lives without Robbie, because I cannot bear the thought of that. I love him and want only to be with him, do not tell me that I will have to see him die and live on." Rune fell to her knees and wept bitterly.

The lady in white knelt down beside her. "Rune please you must not upset yourself; please listen to my words, for you have no choice in what has been preordained for you. It was not my choice and it was not your woodsman's choice, but everyone has a purpose, and yours could be such joy if you would open yourself to it." Her grandmother placed a hand on her shoulder. "Calm yourself my child; do you not know who you are?"

Rune hung her head as the tears slowly stopped dripping to the floor, where a wide carpet of violets now grew. "I am you, I am Nature."

The white lady softly stroked her hair. "You are the flowers in the morning and the wind in the trees, you are summer berries and the late sunset breeze, all of the world that grows will be your domain, because your life will be theirs, you will be the mother of all the Lord Hearne creates."

Rune looked up at the white hood, from which, in just a single moment blue flashed across. Rune rose slowly to her feet and looked at the white hood. Slowly she raised her hands and took hold of it. Rune slid the hood back to reveal the face of her grandmother.

Her grandmother smiled. "See my child you will bring life to the world." Rune stared at her own face beneath the white hood. The golden red hair and the sapphire blue eyes were hers in every likeness, she pulled the hood back up over her grandmother, and her arms dropped by her side.

Her grandmother took her hand. "Runestone there is hope in this world and in others, do not despair for you have so much more to gain, not everything will be as it seems, please trust me, for you will one day understand everything fully."

(Taken from the Violet Journals 2038)

CHAPTER ONE

FALLEN ARROWS

Time breaks all circles; stretch it out across all time,
Lay it down in the void, a broken circle, or a line.
Return to the blind, cross the boundary you make shine,
Build a bridge of intention; take the circle to the line.

It was a cold and chilly night, considering it was the middle of July, in the year of 2069. The wind howled across the sea and over the land, whistling in the valleys and dropping from the high rocks on to the weary guards. Those who watched the pass with their cloaks pulled tight and their collars raised, tried to retain the little heat they had left in their bodies, as the longest night of their watch dragged on.

The captain of the guard walked his watch, checking his sentry's, and noting the low morale of the men as they waited for the inevitable to start. The armies of the Dragon and Raven had multiplied over the years, and now the whole host sat just ten miles up the valley, ready to attack the last defence of the resistance, before destroying the long high defensive wall, and taking the Isle of Iona as their own. He halted as he reached the sergeant of the watch, who was a portly and normally upbeat sort of man, and looked back at the men all attentively watching the darkness. "How are they holding up, they seem low tonight?" The Sergeant turned from the wall.

"They are fatigued, they need more rest and we could use more men, with each passing moment it gets harder, we can only hope the power of the shield holds em out a little longer, the rumours are the queen is tired and weak and cannot keep it up for very much longer."

"It's just rumours, we will hold, we have to, she is busy tonight with the last of the council, tell the men to have faith, she has never failed us yet."

It was easy to say, but then he knew that deep down inside all the generals were being briefed, and the power of the Fae was dwindling, as the dark sorceress Raven Merle constantly attacked, and weakened them with each violent outburst. In secret everyone was hoping that the queen would finally find the power to help her mother escape from her imprisonment of thirty years. There was little hope, as the gossip spoke of her unwillingness to fight and free herself, the rumours spoke of her broken heart at the death of the Hooded Man, and many said it was a wound from which she would never recover.

The land was lost, most of it had become a wasteland of concrete and stone, as Mason Knox had taken everything and killed it. Loxley was surrounded by a huge stone wall where no one could enter or leave, and the gossips talked of how they were riddled with disease, and dying of starvation, and how he had encircled it, just so he could destroy it when the rest of the country was finally his. Avalon was sealed again, but this time by the queen of the realm, and everything else had fallen to stone. The Violet Isle was the last bastion of protection, and most of those who guarded it, knew it would not survive the week. It was a bleak night turned bleaker as the rain began, and it fell in torrents driven in from the sea by the savage wind.

The wind had changed unexpectedly, and as the soldiers stood their guard on the towering wall built to seal off the whole of the coast and Ross of Mull to protect the Violet Isle, deep down inside the castle, a lone waiting figure with eyes of the deepest violet, turned her thoughts to her last hope, and the tall circle of waiting stones at Callanish.

Inside the small stone cottage on the headland below the stones, all was quiet. The small room with the white pot sink under the window, and the heavy wooden dresser lined with small models and figures made by a young girl from clay, was bathed in the fine light of a blue moon that had found the small gap in the tatty curtains. Across the room in the blackened stone built chimney, the embers of a daylong fire glowed red, casting a faint sheen on the polished legs of the small table, with a large vase of flowers, which was set in the centre of the room.

Lit by the moon in the middle of the night, as the wind prowled outside banging the old white wooden gate, it no longer felt like the happy home it had been all those years ago, when Melanie lived out her solitude with her two small children. Behind one of the two doors on the far wall opposite the chimney, came the sad mournful moans of the lady of the house, as she wrestled in her sleep with memories too bitter for any one soul to carry. Her words filled with pain screamed out alone in the darkness. "No.... Please no.... Not him, take me but not him." The wind howled loudly banging the gate, and for a moment her words of fear were taken from the room.

From the room next to it came movement, and a tapping and shuffling noise came slowly to the door, it creaked in the darkness as the tapping followed by the shuffle of soft slippers, came into the room to the faint glow of the moonlight. Judith Hargreaves tapped her cane, as her white sightless eyes remained in a fixed stare, and she sensed her way out of her own room, and over to the door, behind which the night terrors took her friend and guide in life.

The latch clicked, and Judith shuffled slowly into the sparse room, where a long thin bow leaned on the wall next to a shabby looking dresser. Her cane tapped as she slowly walked across the room to the solid wooden bed, where below the covers, the hot sweating sleeping figure of Sapphire of Callanish, fought once again with the battle to live with the pain of her loss. Judith sat carefully onto the chair at the side of her friend, and ran her hand along the bed, to rest the long cane on the wall at her side. She turned and slid her hand across the covers, searching for the moaning figure caught in the same dream that had haunted her for thirty years. She felt carefully across the covers and found the face of her greatest friend, and with love and care, softly she stroked her cheek. "Shush... It's alright I am here Saff... Shush you are fine, none of this is real go back to sleep."

But it was real, and Judith knew it, Sapphire's eyes flickered under her eyelids, and as Judith moved her hand across Sapphire face, the connection made between them in the circle at Avalon joined with her. Judith went rigid, and sat upright and stiffened, she shook as the power of the memory connected from her to Sapphire, and inside her head the pictures flowed and Judith tried to fight the overwhelming power of her centre, and avoid sharing the pictures that she had kept from her for over thirty years.

Her breathing gave a start as the images flooded her mind, and suddenly she felt she no longer sat in the chair beside her dreaming friend, but she stood in woodland in front of a stone archway set on the edge of the trees, as the young sleek blonde haired figure of Lance Knox walked impatiently up and down. "You are quite sure this is going to work? I mean after all your plans for some time has been a disaster, let's face it Grandmother, that witch has shown powers no one expected."

Judith turned as she heard the cold voice of Morgan le Fey to her left; the dark clothed, white cold faced woman scowled at Lance with malicious red eyes, her tone was one Judy remembered well, as it showed her suppressed anger. "Yes it will work; I have planned this for years!"

Her words snapped out and she realised, and tried to alter her tone. "It has taken a long time Lance, but believe me, this is fool proof, even our little flower girl will not see it coming, they think they have won, and in their stupidity, they took in everything I wanted them to believe, and now they think they have completed their task and freed Avalon, they will walk right into my trap." Lance gave a nod, his blue eyes as cold as her red.

"I hope so, we have too much at stake and with that bumbling old monk fouling things up at Lincoln, we really need to take the power back and use it with brutal force." Morgan le Fey walked over to the side of the archway where she examined her work.

"It is fine, they will walk freely into the passage, and when they step out at the top of the Tor, they will not even feel the change where their path ends and my tunnel starts. Two strides will bring them ten miles to you, and in the blink of an eye they will be yours." She ran her hand across the stone archway admiring her work. "It is almost time, get your men ready; I shall have to return to Avalon and wait under the veil."

The Dark One bent down and lifted a white robe off the floor, and Judith turned at the sound of weapons being drawn behind her. The ring of trees was suddenly filled with tall heavily built men in black bibs bearing the crest of a red dragon. From the look of the boots and slim canvas black pants she knew instantly they were her father's personal Cutter Brigade, and they were the most brutal and sadistic of all of them, trained by none other than Ivor Walters.

There was a flash and she turned back to see Lance standing alone, he pulled out his sword and waited at the side of the archway. "Well come on and get in position like we have planned a hundred times, do I have to constantly tell you everything?"

It reminded her very much of when she was small, and he would shout at her and push her around, she thought little had changed, except maybe he had grown colder and crueller.

It was only a few short minutes before she saw the archway flicker; Lance prepared and began shouting at the men. "Get ready you all know the drill, do not let them get their weapons, the archway will glow red as each one is coming, snatch them hard and with force, and get them tied up as quickly as possible." The tall Cutters moved in close, as the archway began to flicker much more rapidly, and then it went a deep burgundy red.

Judy gave a gasp as she saw Bear appear, within seconds the Cutters snatched him and beat him to the floor, he was caught off guard and tried to fight, but he was overwhelmed and was dragged out of the way as more Cutters took their place, and prepared for the next Specialist.

Tears formed in her eyes, as she watched the scene with horror, as each member of the Specialists were grabbed and beaten to the ground, Blades wriggled and squirmed on the floor thrashing like a wild cat, and she almost broke free, until one of the Cutters pulled out his knife and drilled it into her chest, she went limp with a look of sadness on her face, her wide soft blue eyes staring into space.

Unable to move and caught in Sapphire's power, her vision of events forced itself to play in her mind, Judith wept as one by one, the group including William, were all gagged and tied by their hands and suspended from the trees, a huge wave of grief and emotion crashed through her as she felt the power of Sapphire, and as Judith turned she saw herself grabbed by a Cutter and dragged to the floor, she like Blades wriggled and screamed and tried to get away from the filthy hands that groped and held her down, and her heart broke as she knew what was coming.

Robbie stepped out wearing a contented happy smile; it had been thirty years since she had last seen him, and the love and affection she had found in her heart over her time with him flooded back into her. It was almost without thinking that she saw herself wriggle free and scream out the same words as she had that day to him. "Robbie run it's a trap."

Before he could understand, she had been smashed in the face, and Robbie had gone for his sword, but he was not fast enough. Five soldiers pounced on him and dragged him to the floor beating him with clubs, he fought back hard, but there was nothing he could do, and he soon found himself tied and bound, and being pulled up to dangle with the rest of his men.

Judith fell to her knees, she had lived this moment once and had blocked it from her mind, she gave a deep bitter painful sob as she did not want to live it again, she saw herself gagged and tied to the tree trunk as her cold malicious brother sneered at her. "Grandmother always said you were weak, well look at you running around all woodland and happy, and defying our father. I will enjoy this little sister, as you see the true power you left for these leaf loving fools."

Her tears streamed, as Lance turned and walked to where Robbie hung by his hands, and yet he still tried to wriggle and free himself, his eyes burned with hate from his gagged bloodied face, as Lance approached him. Lance sneered at him and smiled a cold arrogant smile; he lifted up his long golden sword and held it up in front of Robbie.

"I take it you remember this? It was my brothers until you cut it from his hand. I believe it was black until it met you, well let's see if I can bring about another change." With power and determination, he rammed the sword into Robbie's stomach with brute force; Robbie braced and then jerked on the rope, and all around came the muffled screams and wails of hatred from below the rest of the group's gags. Robbie gave a gasp as the blood ran down his legs and dripped off his boots, Judith clutched her heart in pain as she trembled on the floor, trapped in her vision and being forced into watching her own nightmare all over again.

Lance left the sword sticking right through Robbie; he gave a smile as he turned to his men. "No change, who would have thought?"

He lifted the Sword of Destiny out of Robbie's scabbard and dropped it into his own. "I needed a new one."

The Cutters jeered and laughed, as Judith saw the tears forming in the eyes of the Specialists, there was no longer anything they could do as their symbol of hope hung with his head on his chest, the blade of Dunnottar sticking right through him, their Hooded Man was no more.

Lance returned to his sister as she was dragged up from the floor and tied to a tree. "You have seen too much little sister, watching father build his empire, and then running off to your woodland friends to spill it all, well may this be your lesson. They will all die today, all of them except you, oh you will watch them die and then I shall leave you here to rot. Your precious Violet Witch is already our prisoner, so we shall see if anyone of your remaining friends will come and get you before the wild animals in these parts smell the dead and come to feed."

Lance turned to the Cutters stood waiting. "Kill them, and bring me the Swords of those two, and tie that boy to my horse, he has business with my mother and she wants him alive." Lance gave a cold stare at the others hanging from the trees. "I am disappointed that his general is not here, I wanted to personally despatch Rowan of Loxley and take his sword, it's a shame, I did want the set."

Judith was bound to the tree, and could see as her brother smiled, behind him the Cutters began to stab and slash at the Specialists, and the people she loved so dearly were slain in an evil and brutal fashion. Lance enjoyed the spectacle, and began to laugh with glee as Judith screamed as she saw Harry and Maggs cut and slashed, followed by Jay and Hawk, her heart splintered as they beat William violently, and then dragged his bloody unconscious body over to the waiting horse. He was lifted up and roughly tossed over the saddle, and tied on with thick rope where he hung motionless. Caught in her vision unable to move, she watched the men carry the glowing pan of coals towards Lance, he gave a broad smile as he turned back to her.

"Seen enough have we? Make the most of it, because it will remain in your eyes forever, this is what happens to those who watch and tell." Lance lifted the glowing knife out of the coals; his face looked wild and happy as he forced Judith's face to one side.

She had to sit on the floor and listen to herself scream wildly in her head, as Lance slowly slid the glowing point of the knife towards her wide open pupil, it hissed as it touched, and her head rang in agony as the memory of such a terrible pain returned and clawed at her insides.

Judith felt dizzy and sick, her mind reeled and turned in on itself as everything went dark, somewhere in the back of her mind, her own screams of agony yelled in her head as the knife touched her other eye, and her brother laughed almost hysterically, and then around her she felt the overwhelming feeling of Sapphire.

Judith gave a deep sob, and felt the bed at the side of her, the wind outside rattled the gate as she became aware of Sapphire holding her tight and rocking her. "Oh Judy I am so sorry, I have told you again and again, I cannot stop these dreams or block them out, you must do as I have shown you to block them yourself." She felt Saff move back and then her hand touched her face and wiped away her tears.

"Please forgive me; I am cursed with these images. It is bad enough I have to see them over and over, please Judy, you must protect yourself around me, I want none of this for you, you have suffered too much already."

Sapphire sat on the edge of her bed, and held the weeping figure of Judy as close to her as she could, her hair hung down to the floor like thousands of strands of auburn and white silk, and her blue eyes shone out of a face that looked lined with worry and the weariness of her tortured gifts of sight. The lines of the Fae were known for their good looks of youthfulness, but the burden carried within Sapphire showed, and she looked aged and worn from her endless search to put right the wrongs of the past. Over the last thirty years she had become a very powerful force within the White Circle, but she had chosen a path of isolation, and had travelled far and wide with her only companion, the blinded daughter of the man she fought, Judith Hargreaves Knox.

Sapphire stood up and took Judy by the hand. "Come on and grab your cane, I will make us a tea, there is no way I am going to sleep now, and we do have a long day tomorrow, so we might as well make an early start." Judy stood up and felt for her cane.

"Thanks Saff." Sapphire smiled as she slid her hand round her waist, and walked her through the door toward the kitchen. Judy felt her way along the edge of the table and found her usual seat. Saff pulled apart the curtains and looked at the moonlit sky as the mists rolled in from the coast. "All these years and still more questions, will we ever be rid of it all?" Her voice was soft, and yet the keen ears of Judy heard them, and she gave a gentle nod as if understanding the massive burden on her centre's shoulders.

Sapphire made the tea and sat at the table staring at the window; Judy was starting to calm down and was lost in her own thoughts. Sapphire's mind wandered the past as she tried for the millionth time, to find something she knew was there and so obvious to her, and yet even now after all of the years, she could not figure it out. Her mind replayed the events over again as she searched for the answers, she had awoken abruptly having slept from the exhaustion of forming the Circle of Sight, and Opal was in a panic, as she too had felt the massive surge of power released by Runestone.

Opal's voice sounded in her head as she repeatedly told Saff to go to Robbie, but she could not feel him and thought he was still in Avalon, then came the second pulse of power and Opal was torn, as she then understood what was happening and the Lord Hearne was also in danger. Opal had turned to run into the forest and been blown backward through the trees into her circle as a giant red wall of light began to grow out of the floor, Opal seized her roughly and pushed her finger into her forehead and with a flash of brilliant white, Opal screamed for her to leave; she had seen the blue light and left without at first realising.

Sapphire shuddered, as again she relived the moment of finding the dead Specialists, she had no idea how she had arrived there, and just assumed that Opal had done it, and the feelings of pain at seeing Keith hanging dead, and then Robbie's limp body with the sword still sticking out of him tore her apart. She had fallen to her knees and screamed with grief, and had not at first heard the moans of the semi conscious Judy, the only one to live, with a burned red swollen face.

How the Dark One had done it she had not been sure until this night, when finally, Judith had allowed her to probe deep inside her mind, and unlock all of the memories that she had closed in her head. She did not blame Judy for locking away the wealth of pain she had hidden for so long, but now Sapphire had a better understanding of what really happened. She was not sure how it would help, but it was yet another small part of a badly needed jigsaw that would reveal all, and provide her with much needed answers. Sapphire came out of her thoughts and looked at Judy who sat looking paler than she normally did. "I want to go to Loxley; I need to talk with Steph and Jessica Sapphire." Judy gave a slight nod.

"Can you not talk from here?"

"I can, but I want to make sure all of them are safe, Steph needs us after Pete's death, I think it will help her, she has not seen anyone for some time now, I think we are needed there."

"Will you lift your veil?"

"Not yet, it's better for everyone if I walk hidden, I will not give them false hope where there is none." Judy slid her hand across the table to where Saff clutched her mug.

"I ona misses you, so does Jade, it worries me that you have hidden away from everything, Saff you need to see them and feel their love." Saff slid her hands back from Judy's.

"Not yet, we will both see them soon, and I have all the love I need here with you, I am not sure I would have come this far without you. It's enough for me Judy, I want you to stay in Loxley for a few days while I check some things out, try and do what you can to help Alice and Steph." Judy felt saddened that Saff still refused to listen to her, but she gave a smile and nodded.

"OK Saff, I will do what I can, I will go and pack some things ready for us to leave."

For a moment Sapphire stared out of the window as she heard the chair scrape back on the stone floor, and then the tapping of Judith's cane, as she made her way into her room, she gave a sigh, she had not wanted Judith to relive those terrible moments, but for the first time in thirty years she realised she now had the full picture, as finally she understood the link between Judith and her family. Judith had been able to tap in and see all of the events that happened that fateful night, which had been far more than Sapphire's memories had ever been able to show her. It felt like a new lead, and she hoped that it would give her another part of the complex puzzle to work things out.

Just off the coast, a small blue boat moored up and dropped a small rowboat into the water. Under the cover of darkness, the lone figure sat with Terry in the boat, as it made its way under the small archway, and up to the safe private jetty deep within the centre of the fortress of the Fae. The dark haired figure lifted his bag and thanked Terry, and then with a guard to escort him, he made his way up the steps and along the corridors to the main sitting room of the Queen of the Fae.

The doors swung open, and a woman dressed in green with long blonde curly hair turned and smiled, just behind her a taller woman dressed in the brightest of white with a golden belt of violet flowers, stopped talking to a grey haired distinguished looking man, and gave a bright white smile. Her deep violet eyes sparkled, as she walked toward him and lifted her hand and her voice was soft and warm. "Lord Mackintosh, I am so pleased that you were able to make it. Please come inside and warm yourself by the fire, most of us are here so let me introduce you." She turned to the other guests. "Everybody this is Forbes Mackintosh, he is the son of Grace and has travelled from the outskirts of Dunnottar to be with us." She turned to the distinguished grey haired older man. "Lord Mackintosh, this is General Rowan of Loxley."

Rowan took his hand as the woman in green came up to his side. "Hi I am Jade; it's nice to have you here safely." He shook her hand as her green eyes danced below her fringe. Jade had all the qualities of the Green Circle, whereas Rowan had aged naturally and looked his age as he approached his fiftieth year, Jade looked like she was not a day over thirty, with time and age her true beauty had surfaced, and there was more than a little likeness to her sister. Jade took his hand as she turned to some of the others. "Come, I will show you off to everyone." In the corner holding a glass, sat a shabby looking general dressed in uniform and looking very tired. "That's Rafe, I am sure you have heard much of his adventures, he fought in many of the battles on the borders with your mother."

Forbes gave a very respectful nod, as Rafe smiled and lifted his glass; he had indeed heard many stories of the wild general and his howling band of elite fighters. "This is my daughter Yvee, and that is her brother Frayne." Both of them took his hand and shook it warmly. She crossed the room to where a large man with bright blue eyes warmed himself by the fire, his long dark slightly wavy ponytail swung down his back as he rubbed his hands together, Jade gave him a bright and beautiful smile.

"This is my God Son, Lord Thorn, who I know needs little introduction." Forbes took his hand and shook it with excitement.

"My Lord it is an honour, I have heard so many things about you and your efforts to defeat Mason Knox, I truly am pleased to meet you." Halbert gave a smile similar to his father, as he saw the adoration of the new guest.

"I am not alone My Lord, I have heard many stories of your courage and skill at your mother's side in battle. I believe you have become quite the tactician? I will look forward to many hours of discussion with you, I am indeed sure between the two of us; we can still find a way to push Mason back into the sea."

"I am honoured Lord Thorn, and would be most pleased to discuss some of my ideas with you." Jade gave a giggle.

"I think for now that is enough, we will have other matters to attend shortly. Right Forbes, help yourself to a drink and make yourself at home, we have quite a few guests waiting, many of them stuffy old generals, although the Lady Vivian has yet to come down. She has travelled the long distance from Avalon with word from her mother, so as soon as she arrives, I believe we shall begin."

CHAPTER TWO

DARK DEALINGS, HIDDEN HOPE

At the top of the ridge, which looked out on the wide flat plain of grey stone below, a small platform had been erected to house the commanders. It was a bleak place, high up on the rough chiselled rock above the valley, which stretched for miles to the huge protected fortress of stone that barred the way onto the Violet Isle. There was little protection from the strong coastal wind, and only the wide wooden roof and three enclosed sides, gave any shelter from the endless misery of the constant rain. Two guards in black worked at a wood burning stove, which was the primary source of heat, and a place to cook and provide warm drinks, they hurriedly stoked the fire to full heat, and hung the long black cloak on a coat hanger at the side of the warm stove to dry out.

The tall figure in black stood motionless and completely unaware of their presence, as he viewed the lights of the fortress in the far distance, the smooth cold features of his face showed no emotion, as he watched the rows of men below heaving on the trailers to pull them into position, and begin the construction of his latest new weapons in his fight against the Queen of the Fae. His hair had shortened with age, and his eyes had become colder over the years, Lance was very much the double of his father, and yet there was a coldness to him that chilled a person deeper when in his presence.

This for Lance was the end of a long fight, for him this would be the defining moment of his life, as he finally defeated every one of his enemies in one final swipe of his hand. Mason had not been too worried, and had stepped down from the long military campaign to focus on other things, in his mind with the imprisonment of Hearne and the capture of the Violet Witch, alongside the death of the Hooded Man, he had watched the Woodland Realm crumble and bend to his will. To Lance, this all felt very personal, Mason had left the rest of the job to him whilst he moved across to France and furthered his campaign for domination; he had stamped out an uprising German power, and had most of Europe to himself. For a short time he had been joined by his mother who had been keen to revisit places from her Saxon past to find old trinkets of value to her magic. Raven Merle who had grown into a figure of tremendously cold beauty, had occupied her time flitting between her brother and father, and had become very preoccupied with the destruction of Avalon, where she yearned to retake the Star of the Merle from its resting place in secret.

Lance had shown determination to an almost obsession in routing out and killing everyone connected to the woodland realm. The rabble at Dunnottar he knew would fall quickly, but Queen Iona had proven to be his greatest challenge, he had devoted the last ten years of his life, to the sole purpose of doing everything he could to kill her. The Hooded Man's daughter and son had proven hard and finally after months of moving mile by mile, he sat on her doorstep with a massive army, and prepared as the men below fitted together his super cannons. In a little over a few days he intended to pound her and the rest of the Fae into the earth, he would settle for nothing less than the complete and utter removal of the fortress and the island of the Violet Isle.

Dressed in the thick heavy uniform of the combined forces of the Dragon and Raven's Commander in Chief, his cold unfeeling eyes stared out into the darkness. It was as if he was unaware of the driving rain or biting wind, he bore the look of a man who felt little of the triumph that had grown inside him, as he witnessed the siege of the fortress surrounded by his camps of men, and watched as the light flashed half way up the valley when his guns exploded with another volley, to blow away the rocks that surrounded the impregnable fortress.

"Father?" He blinked, and then looked to the path, which led up from the plateaux below. A tall heavy built man in black waved to him as he walked briskly up the path, his face was square and chiselled, and his eyes burned in the darkest of black below his thick eyebrows, the long thick black hair hung wet round his shoulders. He waved again, and Lance gave a small smirk not unlike his grandmother. "Father how long have you been here?" He hurried closer to get out of the rain and wind and talk with his adopted father. Lance turned to greet him, his voice contained little warmth, but considering his manner to those who observed, this was possibly the warmest he had ever appeared.

"I have been here an hour." His son walked up to his father and stood at his side to look out on the view of the battle, there was little contact between them, and yet it was apparent there was some bond between them, as Lance softened a little in his presence.

"You have done well Victor to get the cannons all the way up here, I was sure there would have been more problems with the old road." Victor gave a satisfied smile.

"It was hard, but we were not going to let it hold up the fight." Lance gave a look of approval.

"How long will it take to get them built and in place? I must admit I will enjoy watching this last hurdle be smashed into the sea forever." Victor gave a sniff and wiped his nose on his handkerchief.

"Within a few days we should be ready, there is still much to do, but I will have everything in order well within your schedule." He gave a smile, and Lance nodded as he watched out. Victor was the son of his wife Nadia; she had been raped by Billy under the possession of Mordred, and had conceived a son to the line of Knox. He had a great deal of Mason in his attitude and spirit, and was often heard bellowing out his thunderous laugh, although his humour was dry and never far from the surface, like his grandfather he could also be cold and brutal. Unlike Billy, he was dark haired and dark eyed, which often gave Lance a great deal of thought, for it had only been the spirit of Mordred that had possessed Billy, and yet Victor had many of the physical attributes of Mordred, his hard facial features and dark bushy eyebrows certainly gave him a look of the Dark One's first born.

"Your mother wishes to see you, she is pleased with the cabin you had built for her stay and has settled in amicably, she wishes you join us for breakfast, she has missed you and wants to see that you are well cared for here." Victor gave a smile.

"I am fine, I quite like it up here, I think the mountains suit me."

"Really? I find them bleak and tiresome, everything up here takes an age, you should go and visit your grandfather in Austria, he too has found an unnatural liking for high wet places and snow." For a moment Lance looked as if he had suffered some momentary pain, such was the distaste he felt at the idea of being happy in such a remote barren wilderness. Victor gave a happy smile; he knew how uncomfortable his father was away from the lowlands and warm sun.

"How is he, Raven told me he was in pain again?" Lance gave a shrug.

"Like us all he is getting older, the wound he suffered from that heathen's sword never really healed. It comes in bursts and each time it's worse than before. I visited him last week to update him, I must admit he looks older and sicker than I have ever seen him, no one really knows how long he has left."

"What about great grandmother?" Lance gave a snort.

"That old hag will outlive us all, as long as she does not meddle in my affairs, I am happy to let her cook up her spells to torture the Violet Witch until the end of eternity if she pleases. Raven is her favourite and that suits me, I am too old to bother with her tantrums these days, I let the old hag deal with her." Victor gave a hearty laugh, and for a slight second Lance almost smiled.

"I miss Raven Father; it will be nice to see her again." Lance raised his eyebrows.

"You have always been far too tolerant of her whims and fancy's, she is very powerful Victor, I would even say she has gone well beyond my grandmother, you be wary around her, one day this empire that I have built with my father will be yours, just you make sure she knows you are the one to rule, never forget we have the means to clip her wings if she steps out of line. I know the power of the line runs strongest in the female, but never forget this empire was built by the men of this line, and it will be our place to rule it."

Lance turned as the guard walked up with his dry and warmed cloak; he looked sternly at his son as he took it from the guard and cast it round his shoulders. "I am very serious Victor, you have done a great deal for this realm, do not let her charms and deviousness creep up and trick you. It's about time you started to think of the future, you need a female heir to put our little Raven back in her box."

He gave a smile and nodded his head; he knew it was a subject his father would continue with until he finally appeared with a suitable female. "I understand you father, I have told you, I have plans for the future, but first I have a few goals of my own. In a few days we will have the victory we have long dreamed of, and then I will attend to a few of my own ambitions. When it comes to Raven, I have told you before that you worry too much, I know my place and what I can allow her to get away with." Lance gave a nod.

"She will be here sometime in the next few days, as with all things around her, she will arrive when she pleases. Let's hope this time she has done her homework, and can remove that shield down there, if not I fear I will have to ask my grandmother, and that at the moment is not an option I wish to use." Lance took his son's hand in both of his. "Tell your commanders I am pleased with their progress, and they shall be rewarded when that fortress is flat. I shall ensure all of them are decorated, and I think a few weeks rest with a trip to the orphanage could be arranged, after all we need to create more men of substance for this army, and we have just found an isolated community living near Canterbury, and I believe there are a large number of single women being shipped over to us now."

He pulled his cloak tight and stepped off the edge of the decking onto the shale path. "I shall see you for breakfast, you will find white roses in your room, bring them for your mother, you know how she loves them when you visit?"

"See you in the morning father, and give mother my love." Lance raised a ring covered hand to wave, and walked out of sight behind the large wooden platform containing the hut. Victor heard the dull clunk of the car door, and smiled as he turned to the guards. "Is there a hot drink ready yet?" The guard snapped into action, and grabbed the tall pot off the stove, and poured it out into a large stone cup. Victor took it and turned to view the progress of his men, the guns in the distance continued to fire, and the shield of violet light flared, as the rounds exploded without harm or danger to those inside who kept the vigil through the night for the land of the Fae.

It had taken Judy several hours to prepare and pack what she needed for her journey, as Sapphire sat in deep thought looking out of the window. She had never seen the full version of Robbie's death in such detail, and although once again she felt the stirring of pain deep within her, her mind had drifted from Robbie to Rune and then to Opal. Trying to figure everything out was as always complicated and difficult. Rune had been taken by the Dark One disguised as Opal, and she had instantly left for the Hidden Realm, Hearne had been sucked down into the Dark One's Castle, and as she knew from her own experience, Opal had been trapped in her own circle. Somehow the three were connected, but she was not at all sure why, Rune was her prisoner, and yet in thirty years, she had not been able to kill or drain Rune of her powers, and she did not understand why. Her voice was almost a whisper as she thought deeply. "What did happen to Una? Is she connected to all of this, is she the link to the three of them? I wonder... what was the task set by my grandfather, and why have we not seen or heard from her since?"

Judith stood at the door as she gave a small sigh. "I'm going alone again aren't I?" Saff broke form her thoughts and Judith shrugged at her. "I said you are going to send me alone again, aren't you? It's OK; I am getting to know the farmhouse quite well." Sapphire gave a chuckle.

"I think you know me better than I do, but no I am still going to Loxley, it's just I will only be there for a short while, I want you to stay and wait, I do have a few things to do, but I will pick you up on the way back. If I am right, we will finally be visiting Iona and Hal, I feel I need to work fast, so if you don't mind, I will travel on with Jessie for a spell." Judith understood, but also was a little disappointed.

"It's OK, it will be nice to see how everyone is, it's been a long time since I could spend some time with Alice, and we have a lot of catching up to do." Sapphire got up from her seat. "One last trip to check the stones, and then we leave, OK?"

Inside the long ancient room of the castle, set deep within the Hidden Realm, all was silent as the candles flickered, and the fire in the huge hearth spat as the logs cracked and split. The Dark One was away from home working in Austria, as she uncovered more secrets of her family line and the source of their powerful abilities. One of the large double doors creaked open slowly, and the slender figure of a young woman dressed in all black stepped inside. She wore a light blouse laced at the neck with tight fitting satin trousers and thigh length boots of dull leather. Her hair which stroked her waist, shone in the dim light, with a slight tinge of blue mixed within the folds of raven black, she looked very Jett like with her fringe sharply cut just below her dark eyes, which peered in and around the room in search for her object of the visit.

Raven Merle noted the long glass case set on four golden stands, and gave a thin smile to herself, then let the door close softly behind her, as she walked quietly into the room past the fire with two tattered old chairs of red, and down towards the glass case.

Runestone lay still and pale, dressed in her long violet top and skirt, her head was propped on a soft cushion of violet velvet, and her hair that now reached level with her knees, was combed and laid with great reverence down each side. Her eyes were closed and her soft golden and red eyelashes rested gently on her snow white cheeks, her arms were crossed, revealing the rings on her fingers, and one in particular seemed to shine brightly creating a bluish essence that bathed her, making her look as if she slept in the moonlight.

It seemed odd to have her enclosed in her case with such care, and yet the Dark One had insisted that she be cared for, and shown nothing but the highest respect. In many ways even though her capture had brought her the greatest prize she could ever possess, she also admired and respected the young violet sorceress for her constant ability to overcome all of the trials she had created for her. There had been many occasions where Runestone had shown her great ability to overcome and fight back with great skill, none more than when she had been confronted with the Star of the Merle, and in her last moments of weakness, had found the courage and strength to draw down more power, and attack back bringing the Dark One to her knees. Morgan le Fey would never publicly admit it, but that one moment in a desperate fight, had earned Runestone huge respect from her adversary.

Raven Merle walked slowly round the glass case as she looked upon Runestone, the power of life itself encased in a sleeping human form, and held captive in her glass box. She smirked as she ran her fingers along the top of the glass; her voice was whimsical and carried a note of dry humour. "Not so powerful here are you? Look at you, sealed in a box like a doll on a child's dresser, and they all thought you were oh so powerful."

She gave a soft harsh chuckle as she came level with Runestone's sleeping face. "You sleep here while your spirit walks like a zombie in whatever state you left it, wielding the little power left to you from the Violet lines. You have not beaten me witch, I will find a way to crack open your world and take back the jewel you hide. It is rightfully mine, and was taken out of the heavens by my grandmother, to add to my crown when I rule this world you fought so pathetically to defend."

She stood in the dim light staring at the face of pure white below the glass, as she mocked and ridiculed her captive. "It would take but a moment of cracked glass, and I could hold up your broken heart for the world to see, and then who would come to save you? Not that any have, they used you to hide behind, and now they cower in the shadows of the Isle you placed so much worth in. Know this Runestone Sapphire of the Violet lines, tonight I will travel to that Isle, and as you slumber here in your broken hearted oblivion, I will strike at the heart of your daughters realm, and crush her with all of those who you held in such high regard. Tonight, will be the moment when I alone walk victorious out of the shadows, and claim everything my grandfather has built as my own."

She gave a cackle as she enjoyed her moment alone with her captive. "When the Isle of Violet is crushed and swept into the sea, nothing you did there will help you, for Loxley will lose its protection, and I will personally burn it out of existence forever."

The door gave a creak and Raven's eyes snapped to the silhouette stood framed in the light. "Lady Raven, I was attending to Lord Hesketh and was not aware you were here, my mistress left no word you would be visiting." Ursula walked down the room towards her. "Can I be of assistance to you?"

Raven stepped away from the glass case and the candles flared brighter as Ursula waved her hand in the air, Raven blinked in the sudden brightness and scowled at Ursula. "I am heading to Scotland and thought to visit; I had forgotten my grandmother was away, I shall not be staying long." Ursula smiled.

"As you wish Lady Raven, but if there is anything at all you require whilst here, I will be at my desk finishing transcribing the notes left by your grandmother, feel free to ask me."

Raven gave a brisk nod and looked back to the case. "Why is she here? I thought grandmother wanted her kept in the dungeons with the old man of sticks." Ursula sat at her seat behind her desk littered with old pieces of parchment and looked up.

"My mistress wishes she be kept here close to hand where she can observe her and ensure she is protected."

Raven turned back not quite understanding; her black eyes flickered with a hint of dark red. "Protected from what?" Ursula gave a smile.

"There are those who would profit from seeing her dead, for the time being she has value to my mistress, and so she keeps her well guarded here whilst she works."

The comment stung, and Raven felt the bitter taste in her mouth, knowing her grandmother was still very much on the ball, and had guessed her motives. She felt her anger rise as she spat back her comment. "Like who?" Ursula remained pleasant, but Raven was more than aware her comments were directed at herself.

"I cannot say Lady Raven, it is my mistress's wishes and therefore I obey, all that I know is that protections have been placed on the case that will only allow my mistress to open it, any other who tried would suffer a great deal from curses that even I could not cast." Ursula gave a small smile as she saw the displeasure cross the face of the young dark sorceress; Raven gave a sinister glance at the glass box and walked quickly away up the hall, her gaze set on the doors and avoiding the eyes of Ursula.

"Tell her I will return here when I have finished with Lord Knox in Scotland, I may need her help at Avalon, there has been more protection than even she thought, and that bitch of the moon is making it difficult. Tell her I need the use of her precious book and soon." The door slammed stirring the dust up from the floor, Ursula gave a smile and lifted her quill, and she turned over a parchment and began to write.

Raven's impatience was not unsimilar to that exhibited by Morgan as a young woman being trained by Merlin. She too had fallen into the trap of being too impulsive and not listening to her teacher, a lesson that had been hard learned when she imprisoned Merlin in the Age of Sleep, which resulted in the whole of Avalon rising up against her and chasing her out. Morgan le Fey had lived a very long extended life, and her experience of trying to defeat Gwendolyn had served her a good lesson. Runestone remained intact, as somehow, she had managed to protect her essence of life, and in doing so the Dark One had failed every attempt to take her powers from her, it was a source of great frustration, and the primary reason why she had left to visit the sites long preserved by her ancestors. As Runestone lay asleep and preserved below the glass, the Dark One sifted through piles of papers trying to understand the riddle of why she could not touch her captive.

Sapphire knew that Runestone was alive and untouched. Rune was her centre and Sapphire could still feel her power, although she felt it lacked that essential personality of Rune. Through her constant connection she was sure that there was a clue as to how to help Rune, but the more she tried to find the answer, the less confident she became, and over time she had begun to lose trust in her own instincts.

Sapphire opened her window and delivered Judith safely to the farm in Loxley where she left her with Alice and a very old looking Jon Lox, and made her way down Hawthorn Lane and on to the main street comprising of fourteen stone built cottages. It had been quite some time since her last visit, and the changes to the town were very obvious indeed. Contrary to rumour, the farm was still functioning quite well, and there were still a lot of people around, although it was a stark drop compared to the thousands that had moved there during the conflict of 2039. Most of the shops were still open and trading, although number twelve was shuttered and closed, Sapphire expected that with the recent death of Pete, Steph would not be up to trading, and she slipped round the back of the houses to the gate, and knocked gently on the backdoor.

The door was unlocked, and after several minutes she entered the kitchen to search for Steph. The house was untidy and it was quite a surprise for Saff, as she had never known the house in all of her years not to be as clean as a new pin. She called out loud for Steph but to no avail, and made her way quietly up the stairs.

Steph was asleep on her bed as Saff stepped in. She was curled up tight clutching a brightly coloured scarf, and by the look of the dark circles and red swollen eyelids, it was clear she had cried herself to sleep. Her hair was loose and unbrushed, and her clothes looked shabby and dirty, it was not at all the sight she expected to find. Steph was half Whiteline and half Green Circle, and like all of those if her line, she looked much younger than her actual age, considering she was now close to her seventies, she looked only in her late forties. Her eyes showed the lines of the hardship all of them had faced since a wall had been built in a one mile outer radius to that of the stockade at Loxley, sealing them all inside.

Rousing her took several delicate minutes, and Sapphire felt uncomfortable having to do so, what followed was hard for Saff, as Steph woke and burst into tears as she hugged her, it took well over an hour of sobbing before Sapphire finally got her downstairs in the kitchen with a hot tea and calm enough to talk.

"Steph I really need your help, I am sure that there is a connection between the taking of Rune and Lord Hearne, and the imprisonment of Opal in the Hidden Realm, I am sure there is something that happened or that passed between them that the Dark One knew about, and that is why she attacked all three at the same time, is there anything that you can think of or remember that could help?" Steph filled up and wiped her eyes.

"They are all my family and I have lost them forever, she hated them Saff, what other reason could she have?" She tried to swallow her tears, and held the handkerchief to her face. "I am sorry." Saff gently held her hand.

"I am sorry Steph, I know how hard things are, and if there was some way I could wait, then I would, but you are the only one left with the full history of that time, you deciphered the notes of your father, so I just thought there must be something that you may remember, I hate having to ask at this really difficult time." Steph got up from her chair and walked over to the kitchen dresser.

"I am not sure if this will help, I have always found it odd, so maybe it will have some meaning to you." Steph crouched down and opened the dresser's lower cupboard door and lifted out an old cotton black bag, Saff instantly recognised it as Rune's bag from her travels. Steph placed it carefully on the table and opened it. "Most of what is in here is her usual stuff, her brush and sewing kit, some letters from Robbie and her arrow cleaning kit, but I have always thought this was unusual." Steph lifted out a small box made of white crystal; it was delicate and very finely made, with a thin lid that had been worked very carefully to ensure it was airtight. At first it was difficult to open, and Steph had to push her fingernail carefully into the crease at the top before she could prize it open. The lid came off with a gentle pop, and Steph tilted the box for Saff to see its contents.

Inside was a perfectly preserved white daisy flower, and underneath it was a violet pendant on a silver chain, and Sapphire recognised it the moment Steph lifted it out.

"Her talisman, I don't understand, why did she take it off? That is what connected all of the Violet Circle." Saff reached into her top and pulled out hers bearing the symbol of a golden butterfly, which now bore the symbol of the Table of Sight on the back. "I have never taken mine off, except for when I use it as my table." Steph reached into her own top and lifted hers from amongst the other chains.

"I have always thought it was odd myself, you see the flower is the symbol of my mother, she chose a flower because it was the most simplest symbol of life, her talisman as you know has the runic stone on it. I suppose you could not get a more positive symbol for Rune or my mother than these." Saff nodded.

"The fact she took it off makes no sense at all, although it does also symbolise Eve as the gift that was given to her in Avalon, do you think that is the connection?"

Steph sat down looking as if many things were going through her mind at the same time. "Eve created the runes, to match the sounds that Hearne spoke, I remember my mother telling me that Eve struggled at first with the new language, and she brought about the runes so that she could learn the words, whether or not that links Rune with Hearne, Eve and Opal I am not sure, although to be honest I always thought that the Dark One didn't know my mother was there in the Hidden Realm." Sapphire looked at her.

"If that is true then how did she find out?"

"That is pretty simple; it had to be the connection of power."

"You lost me Steph, how was the power connected?" Steph smiled.

"Two circles meeting, you see in order for my mother to create your table, she connected with the most powerful stone circle of all of them, and that leaves a signature of the power. All the Dark One had to do was follow it back, and it would have taken her straight to the glade in the Hidden Realm. I am not sure if you know this, but underneath is the stone plinth once used as the stand for a very large wooden table of power, it was hidden there long before anyone knew the Dark One had gone to live there. It was placed for extra protection within a circle of standing stones sunken below the surface; the actual table of stone is about twenty odd feet below the surface." Sapphire understood.

"I saw them; they came up out of the ground when Opal took me to Rune in Avalon."

"I think that is your answer Saff, which is why my mother was caught. She must have known it would create a signature, so it must have been very important that your circle was completed quickly, but unless she is freed, I am not sure anyone but her will be able to help you." Saff gave a long sigh.

"For thirty years I have hit brick wall after brick wall trying to understand what the rush was for, Opal seemed adamant it had to be done there and then, she really got in a panic about it. Look what happened, I was helpless to prevent anything at all, none of it makes sense we should have waited longer."

Steph slid the box across the table. "Listen to me Sapphire; neither my mother or Rune never did anything that did not have a deeper hidden purpose. If I know anything at all, I would say there was a very important reason for setting up the table of sight and it's up to you now to figure it out and find out what they intended." Sapphire looked at the box.

"I have no idea at all where to start, everything is always in riddles and that I am sorry to say is my grandmother's speciality, it has never been mine at all."

"So why not ask her?" Sapphire looked at Steph who shrugged and gave her a smile. "You are her granddaughter, who I might add she chose for this task. I think it is no coincidence that you are the centre of a table concerning sight, I mean come on Saff, if you cannot look back or forward to solve this, then who exactly can?"

"But she has gone; there has been no trace of her since the crypt at Hope."

"Well yes she is a fairy and they can be very unpredictable when they want to be, Gwendolyn was secretive at the best of times, but I just cannot help feeling that she has left you some clue about what you are meant to be doing, have you been to Carnac and checked out her table there?"

"I was there about fifteen years ago, but I could not get in, Treen was supposed to be the heir of that table, so I just figured it would remain closed without her being present." Steph shook her head.

"No you visited with Treen when you got the crystal dagger, one thing I do know is that tables have memories of those who touch them, that table knows who you are, you must go back and look again, think of your grandmother and Treen as you search for an opening. If Gwendolyn wants you in there then you can bet your last bit she has a way of getting you inside, try it before you try anything else."

Sapphire spent most of the afternoon talking to Steph and trying to keep her up beat, but as the time for her leaving drew closer, the tears flowed again and there really was very little Saff could do, she held her tightly for an age after Steph promised to go up to the farm and spend some time with Judith. The moment arrived and she hugged Steph one more time, and then with a flash of bright blue she walked into her window and was gone.

Sapphire came out of her window at the farm where Alice stood smiling looking a lot fatter and very Beth like, she stood with a beautiful woman who had long golden curled hair streaked with brown, and the brightest pale blue eyes. As Saff stepped out through the window, the woman gave a big and beautiful smile and pulled her into a loving embrace. "Hello Jessie, I have missed you so much, I am happy to know you will accompany me for a while."

"Oh Sapphire it has been far too long, seeing you in person is so much better than talking in the darkness."

"I am sorry Jessie, it is important I remain hidden from everything until such time as I can reveal where I am, and yes it is nicer being able to pull you close and hug you in person. I am sorry, I have not been here as often as I should." Alice gave a sniffle as Saff hugged her and took Jessie's bag off her.

"We shall not be long, take care of Judy for me, I will miss her and worry about her being alone. I have seen Steph and told her to come up here later, if you can try and keep her up here for a while that house is filled with too many memories, and I am not sure it's good for her." Alice smiled.

"I will, don't worry about her I am watching her, and it will be nice having Judy stay for a while, we have a lot of catching up to do."

"Alright then take care and look after yourself, I will be back with news as quick as I can." Sapphire turned and her window opened again, Jessie stepped through and Sapphire followed, and Alice gave a wave as the blue orb closed in front of her. She turned and walked back to the cottage, where she knew Judy was sat at the table in the kitchen peeling the potatoes for supper.

Jessie stood in the waist high long grass as the sun slipped through the sky towards late evening, and looked round at the tall stones poking up above the grass. "Where are we?"

Sapphire came through and looked around as she tried to gain her bearings, her long greying haired lifted in the cool breeze, as she looked at the grass that covered almost everything. "This is Carnac, wow it's grown a bit since I was last here. It's not going to be easy finding what we need, still while it's still twilight we best make the most of it."

Jessie looked round. "What exactly are we looking for?"

"The grave of Maurice Du Luc, I need to find it so that I can get my bearings and find what I need." Jessie gave a smile as she looked to the floor.

"OK what shape is it?"

Sapphire turned. "I am not exactly sure, it was placed a little while after I was here at his funeral, so to be honest I have never actually seen it, Rune had it made for Maddy and sent it over here, so I am assuming its stone like those at Loxley."

"Ok then let's get going most of these are standing stones, so I don't suppose it will be that hard to find.

"Yeah, they are all ten feet high Jessie, I would assume the one we want is a lot smaller, and this could take hours. We need to hurry it's already starting to darken; I think we better get on and fast. I really don't fancy being in a lonely graveyard at midnight."

CHAPTER THREE

UNCOVERED PUZZLES

In the main hall at the heart of the large fortress of Fae, the air was filled with louder than normal voices. In the heart of the hall serviced by a huge roaring fire, the long oak table set with glasses of wine, was surrounded by the last of the resistance generals, and all those now charged with the command of the last fight of the realm. Members of every surviving force had been collected by Iona, and brought to the table to look at their options for survival, and the debate at times was heated.

Iona watched as Rowan banged his hand down on the table, his hair puffed up like white smoke with the force, and his grey eyes shone in his old lined chiselled face. "That is not what I am saying, but whether you like it or not Loxley is still the centre of all we have done, and I will be buggered if you think for one moment, I will not return to protect the place." Jade slid her hand from her seat at the side of him, and rested it gently onto his.

"Rowan calm down, shouting will achieve nothing." His eyes glared at the southern general who still continued to argue that London should once again be attacked and taken to show Mason the war was not over yet, his comment that the Hooded Man was dead and Loxley no longer was a priority infuriated Rowan. He crashed back into his seat as Jade squeezed his hand. "They do not understand, they were never with him."

Rowan felt the pain in his chest as the overwhelming grief rose to the surface inside him again. "I will not let them forget him, it was he alone who took the fight to Mason, I will not let them brush away his memory for the sake of a golden crown that none of them are fit to wear." He turned back to the stout faced young general. "Your love of power has clouded your judgement McKay, this was never about fighting for a throne, that is Mason's cause, we fought by the side of Robert of Loxley for the honour he gave us by fighting for those who could not defend themselves. That was the cause of Loxley, and while I still command the entire army of this campaign it will remain the cause of this fight."

General McKay gave a frustrated sigh and sat back in his chair. "Then we are doomed, because we need to strike hard at his centre and soon, it is the only way you will get him off your doorstep." A small dark haired woman who had been quiet for most of the session leaned forward to look at Rowan.

"I believe you are right General Loxley, I have fought around the south for many years, and as you all know it was hard and difficult, Lance Knox has fortified everything, so in order to get anywhere close will cost you thousands of men, something we no longer have since the execution of the Master Sage and his fighters." Rowan gave a courteous nod.

"Thank you, I am sorry I have not been given your name yet, but at least there is one person here who understands."

She gave a smile as General McKay gave yet another snort. "She is the daughter of that bloody pirate Val Andre."

Her eyes burned as she looked back across the table at him. "My name is Augustine Val Andre, and my father was no pirate, it was his men from Carnac that founded the fleet at Captain's Cove with Wilbur and Toby, and they did a lot of good sinking the ships of Mason's fleet. Your men did well by the goods they dropped off, or did you sell them as you have the rest of your values?"

Iona stood up at the far end of the table. "This is getting us nowhere, do we really need to sit here until the bombs come through my ceiling, before we can all make a decision of what we will do to save what little is left? I say we break for a rest and something to eat before we continue." Chairs slid back from the table as the members got up to stretch their legs, Rowan was still angry and Jade tried her best to calm him down.

"Rowan forget him, he is one man, who has no idea of the past." Rowan shook his head.

"I cannot Jade, alive or dead no man will show him disrespect in my presence, I failed him once, it will not happen again. I will preserve what is left of Loxley and I will never fail another single member of that family." His voice cracked a little as his tone softened. "It was their home, how can I let anyone else defile what they built there? I know it Jade, he is still there waiting for her, and if he needs more time before she can find her way to him, then by hell I will not fail him, if it's the last thing I do he will walk on that grass in spirit or other with her once more." Jade put her arms round him and pulled him closer.

"Ok Rowan, we will fight together to ensure it is done, now please do not upset yourself again, you have carried this for so long, please just calm down and let me help you find a way."

Iona came up at his side and slipped her arm round him. "Uncle, you know that I would never let Loxley fall, it is also my home remember, and it has all the protection of Fae, my mother was clever to scatter the blessings she collected at my birth all over the town, believe me Uncle, no member of the Knox family will ever walk on that soil and live." Rowan smiled.

"Your powers are weakened of late; you hold Knox back single handed, and

I can see how much it has taken from you, let me return and help find a way to preserve what they built and ease the burden you carry." She leaned forward and softly kissed his cheek.

"I love you my precious Uncle, but for now we can hold back the tide that threatens us, I have Halbert and Frayne at my side, and Yvee still seeks contact with Sapphire, I feel her occasionally and I know she seeks the answers that will aid all of us, ignore what the generals say, they have no knowledge of what my father inspired in all of you." Rowan's eyes glistened as he felt the tears rise.

"If only you could have known him as I did, it is wrong that they were taken when you were so new to the world, they loved you so much and it should have been they who watched you grow. I know that one day your mother will find a way to free herself, I just fear she will not be in time." Iona felt the pain within him; after all of the years she had grown by his side, she was saddened to see the pain was still as strong as it had been in her youth.

"We must not lose hope in our darkest hours; never forget that the magic weaves in a curious way, even as queen with all the gifts that the Fae bring, we can never really see much further than the moment at which we struggle. We must hope that aid will come when we least expect it." He gave a gentle nod, and she brushed back his white hair from his face. "Rest a while and eat, you need to build up your strength, for I will have need of your wisdom in the coming days."

The love between them was very deep, Rowan had carried the body of Robbie back to Loxley with the aid of Sapphire, and from that moment he had honoured his friends deepest request, and Jade and he had taken Iona and Halbert and raised them as their own in their house across the woodland from Robbie's Mere. There had been many times over the years where Rowan had played the part of proud parent to his nephew and niece, as he watched them grow into the two forces of power for the good of all. Iona had much of her mother's qualities, but in times of need, he always thought he felt the presence of his brother and greatest friend surface within her.

As the days drew on under the shadow of darkness, Rowan was now looking to find ways of protecting the family that had been the focus of his life, if the Violet Isle fell, Iona would be in great peril, and he worried for her, and wanted to give her one safe haven where he knew she would be free from the evil of the Dark One. In his mind there was only one place he could do that, for it had protected all of them in the past, and Rowan's mind turned to the preservation of Loxley as the last bastion of hope to protect the future.

As the light diminished in Carnac, Sapphire turned on the path in the dim light. "Quick hide there are others coming." She grabbed Jessie's hand and pulled her into the long grass behind a large stone. "It's the light from the doorway, you

have no idea how many times it shines too bright, and has got me in trouble."
They ducked down as four soldiers walked along the path holding up large glass
lanterns, to try and find out who was lurking in the forbidden area. Saff watched as
they stopped a little way off and held their lamps as high as they could.

"It was round about here, was it?" The black clad soldier looked grotesque as
the light reflected off just the top of his face.

"I think so?"

"Well did you or didn't you see blue flashing lights? I will tell you now, I ain't
doing no paperwork if you ain't sure, so what is it then?" The soldier shrugged in
the darkness.

"I am not one hundred percent, it was just for a second, it could have been
anything, but I thought I saw a blue light flash in the sky."

"Well that bloody does it then. If you ain't that sure then bugger it. Oi you two...
Any signs or what?"

"There's nought bloody here, I told you he is seeing stuff, I mean none of us saw
it did we?"

"Right, that does it then, let's get the hell out of this place, it gives me the creeps
it does, let's say nothing happened and we didn't come looking, at least that saves
an hour with all the bloody paperwork." The lights moved back, and began to slip
slowly down the path towards a hut in the distance, where the soldiers guarded the
field of large stones; Saff gave a sigh of relief.

"Ok they are gone, come on I think it must be somewhere over there." Together
they crept between the stones, as Saff tried to remember the night when she
watched Treen bury her father. Scanning the tall stones, she looked for the one
she had stood near in her thoughts and tried to compare her vision with the real
thing. It was not long before she recognised the stones surrounding her, and
parting the grass she found the slab, that Rune had placed over the grave. "Here
it is, ok we head this way and slightly to the left, that should put us close to the site
where the entrance opens."

"Saff, what does this mean?"

"What have you found?"

"It's Treen's grave, look at the verse on it." Saff crawled over the grave of
Maurice Du Luc and looked down on the large white marble slab, which bore a
five pointed star of deep red. Jessie wiped her hand across the stone and silver
letters appeared below the star.

Houses made from old trees, circles join on a lakeside breeze.
Flower from the meadow sweet, on a garden pond, old friends will greet.
Crystal cut without a knife, hide the keys and a secret life.

"It means that someone wanted a member of the Circle of Sight to find this, and if I am not mistaken it looks like it's one of Gwendolyn's riddles." She gave a deep sigh. "I hate bloody riddles, why they have to do this I will never know, I mean the bloody thing can only be seen by us, why complicate things more?" She slipped her hand inside her bag and pulled a fine stick of charcoal and a piece of folded paper. "Right wipe your hand across it again." It took several swipes in the fading light before she had it word for word, Jessie puzzled over it as Saff wrote.

"What do you think it all means?" Saff stuffed her charcoal and paper back into her bag; she swept her hair back out of her face.

"To be honest Jessie I have no idea at all. What I do think though is this, there are only two houses I know of that are made from old trees and could have answers, one of them is empty in Loxley, the other belongs to Fagan, so I think we should check out Fagan first and see what he has to offer, and if he cannot help, then the answer must lie in Loxley." Jessie thought it made good sense.

"Ok let's go and see this Fagan then, I must admit I have heard a lot about him, it will be nice to see the man who Aunt Jade thinks is the coolest." Sapphire gave a smile.

"No offence but your Aunt Jade can be a little flaky at times, she was very close to Harry in her time and if you had met him, then you would understand your Aunt more." She gave a giggle. "Come on take my hand, I want to do this quick."

Jessie took Saff's hand and a bright blue orb opened on the floor, the two of them dropped right through it, and landed on a wide path cut through some of the biggest trees either of them had ever seen, it was quite dark as the sun began to set. Sapphire looked around in the darkness.

"Great bloody huge forest and no map, which way do you reckon?"

"Well, ye could wander down that way, but them briar trees has a touch of spite like a nettle in an old hat, or ye could go that way, but them sulphur pits will choke ye faster than bindweed and that's a bugger of a plant that is." Jessie gave a giggle.

"And which way would ye be going Master Keeper? You sound exactly like Aunt Jade said you do." Fagan stepped out of the trees and gave a very royal and courteous bow to Sapphire.

"I was wondering when the good lady of many eyes would wander in my forest, and yes little green eyes has many nymph like qualities, of which I believe the gift of copy cats is one of them. Well my sweet little nymph of the looking touch, I will be going that way, for that way leads to sesame bread and fresh poppy tea." His eyebrows twitched with glee as the soft breeze stroked through his wild white hair. Sapphire gave a polite bow.

"If you would care for company Master Keeper, we would be delighted to walk with you."

"Then we all is agreed, sesame bread and tea it is." With a twist of his hips, and a twitch from his eyebrows, he turned and led the way, and Sapphire and Jessie followed down the long woodland road past the moonlight meadows, and down the path to the wide glade that housed the long wooden house that was home to Fagan. As they walked up the steps towards the slightly open door Fagan gave a call.

"Set two more for tea Allwood, tis been some time since we had guests." Sapphire looked up at the old man in surprise.

"Do you mean Woody? Woody of the Outlaws?"

The door swung open and there he stood looking a little taller and much stockier than Sapphire had remembered him, and for once he looked a lot less nervous than he had been all those years ago. Sapphire looked round the room in hope. "Is Una here as well?" The door closed and Fagan waved them to sit at the table.

"The Lady Una was set a task, and alas to date she has not returned." Sapphire felt her heart sink; just for one moment she had felt a massive burst of excitement. They both sat down in the old kitchen, as an owl landed on the open window sill and gave a hoot, and Woody smiled as he placed the bread and tea in front of them, he walked round the table and sat facing Sapphire.

"She left in the boat and has not returned, I go there every week to check, but the house is empty." Saff gave a sigh.

"I have spent so much time trying to find her, and find out what she was sent to do, just for a moment I thought she would be able to piece the puzzle together with me." Woody gave a nod of understanding.

"I told her I would wait here and return at the start of each week, she took the boat towards the tomb and the entrance to the valley that is shrouded, I wanted to go with her but she said it was her task alone, and I was to wait for her, so here I am."

"So you have no idea what the task set for her was?" He shook his head.

"What little I heard or saw to be honest was over my head, I didn't really understand a lot of it, she promised she would come back and we would marry and live in the old cottage of her father." Sapphire coughed and choked on her tea.

"Marry?" He gave a bright smile and his cheeks reddened making him look like a slightly older version of the Woody that she had known back then.

"Yes... well you know we were there for a while and nothing to do but... Ah! Oh dear, you know talk and stuff." Jessie gave a giggle and Sapphire found herself smiling more out of surprise, she took another drink and then looked at the very red faced Woody.

"I think that is very sweet, my aunt has spent a lot of time alone, I am happy for you both, I think you will both find a new lease of life."

"Well he has look at him, I tell ye when he came back he was walking and standing like the Oak that stole the light he was. Proper man of the trees he is now, not flopping about like wilted sweet peas any more. I will tell ye, done him good to throw some seed on sweet grass it has." Woody turned a deeper shade of red, and Sapphire gave a giggle. It was obvious that Fagan knew little of the meaning of tact; she leaned forward and took his hands in hers.

"I think it's wonderful Woody, now if I can ask you a big favour?" He gave a nod looking more than a little embarrassed.

"If I can help I will." Sapphire's bright blue eyes fixed on his as she focused her thoughts.

"Jessie has a special gift, she can look into your mind and read what you have seen, heard, and experienced." He looked more than a little worried, she suddenly understood what he was thinking and she squeezed his hands tight. "Oh... err... Hearne no not that Woody, what I want to see is things that you did not understand, there may be something you saw or heard that might help give me a clue as to what Una had to do. The thing is Woody that for a long time I have wondered if we did not share some part of the same task, it is why it is so important for me to learn as much as I can about what she had to do."

He understood and was a little relieved, for a moment he had thought that Saff wanted to look into his more private moments with Una, he gave a deep swallow.

"Will it help bring her back?" Sapphire shook her head.

"To be honest until we look, I will have no idea, but if there is a way to ensure she returns safely, then you have my word, I will do everything I can to help you."

Fagan watched fascinated as Woody agreed and Jessica stood up and he nervously turned towards her. She placed her hands onto his head with her thumbs covering his eyes, and then her eyes began to flicker with a soft white light. Sapphire's eyes flashed blue as she connected with Jessie, and took a peep into the life of Woody and Una.

Like playing a film at high speed Jessie flashed through their time together riding across the sandy hills of the Whispering Dunes, to the little cottage on the edge of the Briar Wood. Together they watched their time of talk and living in the cottage as they flicked through two days of long happy talking. It felt really odd for Sapphire as she peeped into Woody and Una's life, and she saw a part of her aunt she had never seen before. It felt very much like they both shared a great deal in common. As they came to the evening of their second day in the cottage, where Una cooked a large meal and set a table with candles and flowers, it almost felt like violation as the pictures flowed and Jessie suddenly understanding where it was leading to jumped ahead and Sapphire got to see the morning of Una's departure.

Una woke very early as the mist thickened around the house. She slid out of bed leaving Woody sleeping and dressed quickly, it was as if she was in a hurry. Una opened the door to the cottage and the mist swept into the house, she stepped out and walked through the mist down to the jetty. Half shrouded by the thick mist

Sapphire saw Una bow to a figure robed in a long tatty looking black hooded robe, he spoke and she listened to him, although Sapphire could not hear the words. After a few minutes Una bowed again and returned to the house, she grabbed a book from the shelf and opened the inside cover, and there inscribed was a small passage, Sapphire tried to read it but it was not easy. Una took the book and slid it into the bag on the floor next to Woody's sleeping figure, and then with great affection she leaned over and kissed him, she returned to the table and wrote him a note. Una turned and left the house, she went down to the jetty where a small boat was tied up, she climbed in and sailed off into the mists. Jessie opened her eyes and Sapphire sat back in her chair. Woody gave a deep sigh of relief and looked very relaxed; Fagan looked at all three of them.

"Well would ye like to share what it is ye all saw?" Sapphire came out of her thoughts and smiled at Woody.

"Thanks for that, I am not sure how it will help but there must be something in there." He seemed happy to help and got up from the table.

"I brought the book back if you want to look at it?" Sapphire turned to him.

"It's here? Yes, I would love to see it." He reached up, and slid the old book down from the shelf, Fagan gave a broad smile.

"Twas me mother's that twas, her herb lore, she took it everywhere with her." Sapphire took the book and opened it at the first page, and there was the scruffy handwriting from Woody's memory. She read carefully to get an understanding of the words and writing and then read them again.

Into the valley with a staff as a guide, lines of gold, does an old friend hide.
Boat across the lake, the golden tomb, down deep dark steps to an open room.
Table sat in an oval light, bridge of stars at the sound of midnight.
Star of light, star of lines, sleep in the grass and relive old times.

Jessica leaned over her shoulder and looked at it. "Well at least it's the same hand writing." Sapphire looked up at her.

"How do you mean Jess?" Jessie pointed at the page.

"It's the same as Treen's grave, look at the word 'lines' it has the same wavy L as those on the grave." Fagan leaned in.

"Well, it's me mother's book alright, but that ain't her writing, she was as neat as a bed of Poppies she was." Sapphire was starting to understand; she lifted her bag and took out the parchment, and then copied the verse down.

"This must have been Gwendolyn's writing, after all Treen was her sole heir, who else would have marked her grave with a stone?" Fagan read both of the verses that Sapphire had.

"Well if ye are looking for a garden pool where old friends greet, I would have to say that it sounds like the Mirror Pool in Eve's garden, she often talked

to Rhiannon and the Lord of the Whitelines in it, tis the only place I know of."
Sapphire looked up at him.

"I did not know she used one, I had thought it might be the Mere at Loxley."
Fagan gave a shrug.

"Well, I ain't heard of that one, for me here in this forest, her pond is the only
one I ever heard of." Sapphire gave a smile.

"Don't suppose you could show me could you?" His ear gave a little wiggle as
he lifted his hand and scratched the mass of white hair growing out of his head at
every angle.

"Well, I suppose I could take ye, but it's best left till the morn, and if ye don't
mind I won't go in, she was special ye know, not sure I am ready for seeing it
without her yet." He gave a big smile and slapped his hands together. "Well if ye is
going to be guests, sesame ain't going to fill ye, I say we get the pan out and does a
little woodland cooking."

Jessie smiled loving every moment watching the old man that her aunt Jade had
told her of so many times growing up. With Fagan in charge there was a lot of
laughter and happiness, as they all sat round the table of the cottage deep inside
the Forest of Time, and ate a hearty meal. Sapphire had not realised how hungry
she was, and all of them were very surprised that for a woman so slender, she
could out eat all of them. Fagan joked as he told her she had the appetite of a
willow, he leaned over to Jessie who giggled as he winked. "They eats' and drinks
more than any tree I know, and yet they are fine and slender and elegant always,
except from when they get the wind up em. Oh ye should hear em carry on then,
makes hell of a din they do."

Jessie smiled feeling happy and excited, and she had to admit her Aunt Jade was
right, five minutes in his company and you just loved him dearly.

CHAPTER FOUR

ANSWERED PRAYERS

The night spent in the house of Fagan was for once very restful for Sapphire. There was a strange calm over the forest, and she felt relaxed and at ease, as she slept deeply and vision free for the first time in years. After a good breakfast made for her by Woody, she waited outside on the grass for Fagan to get ready to take her to the mirrored pool of Eve. Woody was planning to return to the cottage, and so Fagan took Jessica under his wing, and offered to stay with her while Sapphire went to the garden, which he told her was something she should do alone, as it was a place only the centre of a circle could enter.

As the morning slipped past, Woody with his packhorse and the rest of the group made their way along the long woodland track, and finally came to the split in the paths, where Woody said his goodbyes to Sapphire. She pulled him close and hugged him, in many ways it had been so nice to find out that one more member of the Specialists had survived. "Take care and when my aunt returns, watch over her for me."

He had changed so much over the years, and although he was now in his late fifties, she could see how the influence of Fagan had helped him to gain a better understanding of who he was. Woody was far more confident and much less nervous than she had remembered him, and her hopes now lay in him finding Una, and hopefully bringing her back safely to all of them.

After walking deeper into the woodland, they came to a halt at yet another fork in the path, Fagan pointed along the long path between the rows of fruit laden trees. "Follow the path, and ye will find what ye seek, I will wait here with my young company, and when ye are finished return to us."

Jessie gave Saff a hug, and watched as she lifted her bag and turned toward the long path, her mind now posing endless questions as she spoke the lines of the riddle to herself, trying to understand what she could realistically achieve. It was a longer walk than she realised, and lost in thought, she came to the end of the tree lined path and walked out into the garden created by Eve.

Sapphire looked slowly round the rows of lush green plants, with the small narrow grass paths that ran through it. In front of her the cliff loomed up high above her, where the water fell from a great height, down into the smooth clear pool below. Across to her left, the vines had grown to cover the wooden bower under which Eve had rested in her youth, but what surprised her the most from what she had perceived to be a garden of wonder, was the complete lack of a single flowering bloom.

She walked onto the thin path that wove through the tall green leaves of the masses of closely planted plants, and made her way to the edge of the water and discovered a small white stone bench. Sitting down she gave a soft sigh, her blue eyes watching from dark undersides, as she stared into the clear water. "What must I do to save what little we have left?" Her voice was soft, and yet it gave her a sense of isolation in the setting of quiet peace, and the loneliness she had felt for thirty years washed over her and added to her melancholy.

Sapphire sat for some time as she lost herself in thought, before she began to realise why she was there. The lines of words moved into her thoughts, and she opened her bag and took out the white crystal box. When she opened it, the pendant and the white flower were revealed and shone in the light. Was her instinct right? She knew this was a place Eve had used to communicate with others, but now she had gone, was there enough power to still use the pool?

Thinking of Opal, hesitantly she lifted the flower and let it fall onto the water, the surface of the water flashed white, as the flower hit it, and for a few seconds the water turned cloudy. Sapphire leaned forward on the bench, as she watched the clouds of white swirling slowly back as they cleared, revealing the lush green of the grass somewhere she did not at first recognise. As the picture expanded her heart gave a jolt, as the old white face of Opal looked down at her and gave a smile.

Opal watched the water in her basin. "Finally, you have found your way back to us, for a moment my child I was sure you had lost yourself forever, it is so nice to see you have read the signs correctly." Sapphire's eyes clouded with tears.

"I have been so afraid and alone, I am trying so hard to be strong, but it has not been easy." Opal gave her a kindly smile.

"You are doing fine My Child; remember the rules of the magic that weaves around you, only when the moment is right will it reveal its truths." Sapphire wiped her eyes.

"I am trying to work out the lines of the riddle, it feels like I have heard it all my life, but nothing seems to make sense to me. Gwendolyn was good at riddles, but I am not can you help me?"

"I will try Child, for I believe there is much we must do, if I am right as I thought I was when the end came, your centre has given you the tools to understand, and she will bring you aid."

"But how can Rune help me, she is trapped inside your realm in that horrible castle?" Opal gave a soft shake of her head.

"There is a part of Rune that sleeps in her lair, but believe me Sapphire, she is there with you I can feel her."

"But how can that be? I am alone here in the garden made by Eve, if Rune was with me I would feel her, and all I have felt for years is an empty void where she once was."

"Listen to me and trust me Child, for the essence which has escaped the Dark One's grasp all these years is right beside you. It is now up to you to awaken her, look to Iona and she will help you, she has two very important items that will be needed to help Rune rise up again, you must reveal yourself now to all, for you are the key and your quest is reaching its climax. I believe your grandmother has given you the power to help everyone. I am convinced that Gwendolyn was shown how to hide the gifts of her teacher inside you, and in doing so I finally understand how she could also pass the gifts of the Fae to Runestone in order to mix them with the union of Robbie, and create the new queen of the Fae." Sapphire was unsure as to whether or not she fully understood what Opal was telling her, and her thoughts became the question.

"Who was Gwendolyn's teacher? I thought she learned from her mother Bridge?" Opal nodded her head.

"She learned much from her mother, but Gwendolyn was also taught a great deal by one of the most powerful seers the Fae has ever known, and I believe now that it was through her she discovered how to see further than any of us. I am convinced that Gwendolyn saw this moment and prepared for it."

"So who taught her?"

"Her teacher was Fagan's mother Sequana, and although many dismiss her claims to have found a bridge to other realms, I think it is very evident she was telling the truth. Gwendolyn knew of it and passed the ability to you, Sapphire my child you must understand that this is deep Fae magic and I cannot be sure, but Iona is the queen and her table can give you better answers, you must go to her and let her help you open the Bridge of Intention." She nodded to Opal as she listened.

"But what about Runestone, how can I release her from her prison?"

"Use the one thing that Runestone needs at this moment, take her pendant to the circle of Avalon and leave it there in the centre, for it is edged with water, and that is the source of all life, it will magnify her power and help to recover her essence and escape. Go now and return immediately to me to talk more."

Sapphire looked at the pendant in the box and lifted it out to examine it, as she did she noticed the ground where the masses of heart shaped green leaves appeared to vibrate. From the centre of the plant a small violet flower began to expand and open, she felt her heart skip several beats, as she turned, she saw single flowers bloom across the garden. Opal gave a bright smile. "Do you feel her now, for she surrounds you, and as you can see the power of life is all around? Go Child, go to the centre of the circle and take the moment to awaken all that was lost."

There was a bright flash of blue, and Sapphire stepped out of her window into the centre of the large stone circle in Avalon, she looked to the floor and crouched down, and then pushed the pendant into the ground. Standing up she looked round at the thick lush woodland that surrounded the circle, it was so much nicer than her last visit when her circle formed, and with a surge of happiness she turned and stepped back into her window and it snapped closed behind her.

Miles away in Scotland as the members gathered for another day of debate, Iona stopped before she sat down and her eyes gave a faint flicker of violet. She looked around the table where she saw the expression on Jade's face slightly change. "Gentlemen and Ladies, please could you excuse me for a moment, Aunt Jade may I borrow you a second?" Jade looked up with a confused look and then shrugged.

"Yeah no problem." She got up from her seat as Rowan watched carefully, he was sure Jade's eyes had just flashed green.

Sapphire looked back into the pool where Opal was waiting. "It is done, what do I do now?"

"You have begun a chain of events that will help all of us, go now to Iona and help her, you have begun to solve the riddle, and she will help you find all the answers you need." Sapphire gave a nod.

"But what about you, you are trapped also, what can I do to help get you free?"

Opal shook her head. "Have no fear, Runestone will come to my aid, you have solved the first part of your riddle, it is now up to you to seek the answers with the Queen of Fae, and if I am right, I think your goal will be to return the Sword of Truth to its rightful place, for believe me Sapphire you have the means."

Iona hurried through the door, leaving the meeting behind her as Jade followed feeling a little confused. As she came in behind Iona, the door closed behind her, and she looked up at the tall oval shaped tower with a high glass roof containing a central round glass pane, it looked almost like a giant eye above her, through which she saw the blackness of the stars. Iona walked quickly across the room to a large round table, and she looked excitedly at Jade. "Did you feel it, I know it was only weak, but you of all people must have felt it?"

Jade felt a little unsure, it was true something familiar had stirred inside her, but in many ways she was afraid to hope, she shook her head nervously. "I am not sure, my stomach is so full of butterflies and I want to believe, it's just..." Iona moved from the table and pulled Jade into a big hug as her eyes filled with tears.

"Oh Auntie you must believe, I felt her and for me it was strong, I know it is true and I know you do to."

Jade trembled slightly, it was a moment she had dreamed of, yet now she had felt something she was terrified of being wrong. Iona stepped back smiling as the tears ran down her cheeks, Jade saw them and as hard as she tried to hold them in, she could not help but let them fall, and her own tears welled in her eyes and rolled onto her cheeks. Iona smiled and just for a moment she looked so like Rune it shook Jade and she burst into masses of tears, and Iona pulled her close as she too allowed her tears of joy to fall. "All my life I have waited, all my life Auntie, I have wanted this and I have tried so hard to find a way to help her, she has done it, and all I want is to hold her in my arms."

Jade pulled her tight and found she could not speak, she simply stood trembling and crying as thirty years of heartache and pain finally welled up inside her and came out. It was several minutes before Iona gave a huge sniffle and leaned back to wipe her face.

"Sapphire, I must talk to her, I felt her hand in this the moment it happened." She let go of Jade, as Jade wiped her eyes and watched as Iona went back to her table and quickly swiped her hands across the smooth white surface. Instantly the table coloured and an image of a huge golden tree set on a violet background came to the surface. Around the edge of the table was a ring of twelve bright blue small stars. Iona watched as images began to rise out of the table and form as moving pictures, she gave a happy chirp as she saw the face of her old teacher for the first time in over eight years.

"Greetings my teacher, I have missed you." Jade stared at the image of her friend and was shocked to see the worn aged face and grey streaked hair. Sapphire smiled as she saw Iona in the mirrored pool.

"My Queen, it has been long since we spoke, I am happy to see you are well and safe."

"Sapphire where are you, why have you hidden from me? I was so worried about you and I have tried so hard to find you."

"I am sorry My Queen, but I have searched long and hard for answers to the questions we all have asked, and I have worn the veil of protection to keep prying eyes from knowing what I was doing. Forgive me, but it was a necessity of my task." Iona understood and smiled with happiness.

"Is it true, does she live?" Sapphire felt the urgency in Iona's words, and she gave a gentle nod.

"Her essence is free to return to her, although as far as I know she is still held captive, My Queen you know what to do, we have spoken of this, and I now believe you are right about the Sword of Truth. I am in the Forest of Time, but I will come to you soon, gather all of those concerned and I will be with you as soon as I can, but remember once they are there, none of them must leave, there is still much we must do and we must have everyone present." Iona gave a nod.

"It is already done my teacher, they are all here except for Jessica and Judith, I was led to believe they are with you." Sapphire felt a huge weight lift from her shoulders.

"They are, and it is good that they are there, keep them in and prepare as we agreed." The picture faded and Iona turned to Jade. "There is much to do, we must prepare and Auntie I must ask a very big favour of you, and one you will not take kindly too."

Jade was still slightly in shock from seeing Sapphire. "What can I do?" Iona came round the table to face her.

"I must ask that you speak of this to no one, not even Uncle Rowan." It was quite a surprise, and she did not quite know what to say.

"But...But he will be hurt if he finds out... you know how hard he has tried to find a way to help her, he will feel betrayed if he finds out we know and he doesn't." Iona looked saddened.

"I know how much he desires to free her, but she is not yet free and I cannot give him false hope, please Auntie, just keep this between just us for a while longer until we know that she truly walks free." Jade understood but did not feel very good about it, but seeing the face of her niece, she understood.

"Ok I will keep it between us for now." Iona hugged her.

"Thanks Auntie, I promise as soon as I know for sure, I will let you tell him before anyone else. Now come we have things to prepare, go back into the meeting and try and stall them from any agreements, I will be there in a little while."

For a few quiet moments alone, Iona felt the pumping of her heart, like Jade this was a moment she had yearned for, and she took a long deep breath before turning to the wall where two portraits drawn shortly before her birth by Steph hung. Both of them were framed in highly polished silver frames decorated with flowers, and depicted her mother in one and her father in the other, on the wall between them set on a bracket of gold was the highly decorated Sword of Knowledge.

The sword of power and the belt of golden violets were the only possessions that Iona had of her mother's, the belt she had worn every day since her fourteenth birthday, and the sword hung in her keep, as she had become the guardian until her mother was free again to wield it. Taking a deep breath, Iona made the first of her preparations; she lifted the large golden sword off the wall and looked at the intricate carved runes on the blade. With a soft smile she turned and walked back to her table, and laid the sword down on the cool surface. "You will feel a familiar grip on your hilt soon, but for now I need you to guide me."

Iona slipped her hand into her deep pocket and withdrew a bangle of soft white, she felt great fondness for the possession of her father, and her heart felt a little joy as she slipped it carefully on to the hilt. "Again, in this life these tokens will reunite you both and release the love you held for each other." Iona gave a satisfied smile and closed her eyes as she summoned the powers of the Fae and her line of life.

"Hear me Mother."

Sapphire stood up next to the bench and felt the wind blow through her hair, it felt cool and fresh and she felt a pulse of life surge through her, almost as if just knowing had changed everything. Down the long path Fagan felt the breeze as he stood on the grass with Jessie; he gave a broad happy smile as he looked up to the trees. For a moment he listened carefully as Jessica Sapphire watched him. He took a long deep breath of the air and then gave a large smile.

"Oh that is a reward beyond all the fruit of the forest, do ye feel that stirring through ye branches and leaves?" Jessie looked at him unsure of who he was talking to, as he tilted back his arms and gave a howling laugh of great joy and shouted into the air. "Can ye not feel her footsteps above ye roots? Oh my, I feel the thrill of fresh bluebells laughing in the dew I does, welcome home my sweet little Redstone, ye is most welcome to come for tea with an old happy man of the trees."

Jessie was unsure, she had not felt any other presence than that of Fagan, she watched as he looked down with huge swollen tears in his eyes. "Ye have no idea how lonely they have been without her; I have spent many a day hugging them to make up for it." He pulled out a huge cloth and blew his nose, which sounded like a very loud trumpet; the trees above him gave a shudder, and few leaves floated down out of the canopy.

Jessie was not at all sure what was going on, when she turned to see Sapphire waving madly as she ran down the path towards them. "It's in bloom.... All of it, and it is beautiful." She came running up and threw her arms round Jessie and squeezed her tightly; Fagan who was completely overwhelmed gave a large belly laugh and snatched both of them together into his wide arms.

"They know ye know, I knew it, I knew they would know and get their best coats on for her, they would never be so rude as to greet her in green." He squeezed hard, and Jessie almost felt her lungs explode from lack of breath, she gave a gasp and Fagan released them back to the floor. Sapphire was in tears and Fagan was in tears as Jessie watched them both thinking they had gone mad. Sapphire turned smiling to her.

"Can you feel it yet?" Jessie shook her head.

"Feel what? To be honest I have no idea what you two are shouting about, please tell me." Sapphire wiped her face and gave a broad smile as more tears rolled on to her cheeks.

"She is coming... Jessie she is coming home to all of us."

Deep down in the castle at the centre of the Hidden Realm, Ursula scratched on her parchment with her black stained nib, a small chink echoed in the room, and she looked up. All was as silent as the grave as she lifted her head, for a moment the candle gave a slight flicker catching her eye, she watched as it steadied and returned back to normal. She peered over the piles of papers stacked on the table, and a mass of red hair shot up from the floor. A hand on the end of a violet sleeve shot out and grabbed her by the throat, the room exploded in violet light and she squealed with fright, as the two bright sapphire coloured eyes burned with life across the desk into hers. "Got you witch, where is that hag you call your mistress?"

The day passed into yet another long drawn out evening, and the view from the gates of Loxley was bleak, across the valley where there had once been hills festooned with dense woodlands and meadows, was a sea of green that crashed up against the monstrous wall of dark stone that towered into the air blocking out a great deal of the sunlight. Within the stockade many of the well tended fields were brown with tough rough grass, and most of the wooden cabins that had lined the walls sat empty and quiet, their doors open wide and swaying softly in the breeze. Above the gates a few solitary soldiers watched the road, but they knew that nothing would be coming their way; the great wall had prevented anything from entering the wooden town.

The Mere remained unchanged, as the power of the Fae was strongest there, and as the new moon reflected in the still waters of the Mere, it was easy to think that Robbie and Rune were still there asleep in their beds. The silent trees that surrounded the wooden house were older and taller, they had thickened over the years and little of the moonlight passed down through the canopy, to light the paths as they wove through the trees towards the centre of the woodland realm, and the Sacred Oak of Loxley.

Steph knelt in front of the ancient tree, and gave her silent thanks to the green world that had aided their life in the dark times that they all had lived through, she silently asked that her husband who had died of illness with the many, be guided safely to the other realm, and her tears dripped from her face onto the old wedding platform built by Robert for his son's wedding.

She gave a deep sob, as her dirty hands gripped the floor, and gasped her words through her tears. "Oh Dad where are you now I need you? I cannot contact mother and Rune is lost with Jade." She took a huge gulp of air, and her pain wailed out with her large sobs of anguish and loneliness. "Everything is lost and I cannot continue like this, we are trapped and I need you, please come back to me, without Pete I am nothing..." She fell on the floor and wailed into the smooth grey wooden floor, as years of holding everyone together alone exploded out of her, and her gasps and sobs mixed with her tears rapidly expanding on the surface of the wooden deck.

In the silent darkness she lay on the floor and shook as her grief at the loss of her husband tore at her soul and ripped out of her, and as she whimpered and cried a soft breeze rose up out of the grass, and fluttered across the tops of the flowers, towards the woodland and the sacred tree at its centre. Steph lost to her grief did not feel it at first, but as exhaustion took her and she settled, lay on the floor of the decking she felt it tug at her fringe, and lifted her head as the coolness of it swept across her hot face. Her vision was blurred from her tears, and it was getting very dark, but just for a moment she had thought she had heard a voice.

She watched the grass and the roots of the trees as she lay there still, and breathed in the cool air. There was a faint shimmer of light through the trees and she stiffened, it was hard to tell what it was, she thought the voice was just her mind playing tricks, as she slowly sat up and looked to where the light had flickered. Steph sat motionless and blinked to clear her eyes; there was no mistake as the voice sounded louder in her mind. "Mother is that you? Oh... help me he is wounded."

She stood up in a flash as she recognised the voice, not daring to believe it was true. "Runestone?" Without hesitation she was off across the grass between the trees, as she headed to the source of the light, her heart pounded inside her chest, as she sprinted as fast as her legs would carry her towards the figure that staggered in the trees in front of her. Rune staggered into a small open space, and the moon came out from behind a cloud and illuminated her, as she strained under the burden of the limp tree like figure that she had draped over one of her shoulders. "RUNESTONE!"

Steph crashed through the trees, bumping off the trunks as she hurtled into the opening and threw her arms around her daughter, and she staggered and fell backward with a thump, still clinging to the injured form of Hearne. As the old man lay on the grass and breathed heavily, Rune put her arms around her wailing mother and squeezed her tight. "I am home Mum, I am safe, please don't cry. Mother I need you; our lord is injured and we have to attend to him, please there is no time, we must get him back to the house and tend his wounds, time is not on our side and he must regain some of his strength, the Woodland Realm will need him."

Steph looked up with renewed tears in her eyes, she looked at the resting figure of the old man and then back at Rune as she smiled. "In all my years never has a prayer been answered in such a perfect way, oh sweetheart your timing is just perfect." She pulled Rune close and kissed her cheek, Rune smiled almost unchanged from her sleep of thirty years, she stroked her mother's face and wiped away her tears.

"It's nice to be home, but we have so much to do, and there is so little time, come on we must hurry."

Hearne was heavy, and between them they staggered across the glade and up the steps to the house, the thought of the stairs was just too much, and so Steph suggested they make him a bed up on the long couch by the glass windows. It was some time before the old lord laid resting and breathing a little easier. Steph knelt on the floor next to Rune, as they bandaged his cuts and wounds, he was still very weak and Rune gave Steph a tall bottle of pink liquid. "Mother I cannot stay for long, I have much to do and I need you to help him, he must drink all of this and recover his strength, for there will be need of him before the day is out, and it is vitally important that all of the powers of this realm are ready when the time comes."

Rune handed her the tall bottle. "I must leave now, do not fear I will return soon, you are the guardian of the Whitelines, and whether or not you know it, you and you alone have the power to heal our woodland lord, stay with him here, under no circumstances must you tell anyone you have seen me, or leave this house, do you understand Mother?"

Steph gave a nod, a frightened look on her face. "Are we in danger?" Rune smiled.

"You are safe here do not fear, I shall return as soon as I can, do not fear for all will be fine, just help him heal quickly, it is more important than you realise." Before Steph could answer, Rune picked up the long bag she had carried, the room flashed violet and she was gone, and she was alone with the old lord of the woodland. She grabbed the bottle and lifted his head upwards softly.

"Come My Lord, you must drink, whatever she is up to she will need all of us as fit as we can be." Hearne gave a soft smile and began to take in the liquid, and from the second it touched his lips, he felt the power of violet, and his strength began to slowly creep back into his limbs.

On the western outskirts of the stockade, deep inside the woodland of rowan trees was the old cemetery. Across the wide open area surrounded with a neat wooden fence, many new fresh mounds of earth had been dug, the loss of life for the Woodland Realm had been very high. At the northern end of the cemetery was the large plot dedicated to the family of Lox, Rune stood silently in front of the neat line of graves bearing the name of Jessica, Robert, Jake and Beth. All of them were well tended and had small posies of wild flowers on them; it was obvious that Alice had visited them many times.

Set back with a large shield bearing the crest of a wolf's head was Robbie's grave. Rune slowly walked round and knelt at the foot of the grave, and her voice trembled as she quietly spoke. "Robbie I am here, please forgive me for letting you down, I tried so hard and yet I could not get through to help you. Avalon sealed and I was trapped, please forgive me I never deserted you." Her tears dripped onto the soil and violets sprung up and ran onto the grave, as she silently released the huge wave of her grief. Alone in the dark, the pain in her heart came out as she shook with the loss she felt. Her words of love became garbled as they flooded out between her hands, as she held them to her face and wept bitterly.

"Runestone Sapphire." Rune sniffled as she heard the soft loving voice, and turned to the direction from where it had come from. Stood in the trees lit partially by the moonlight was a figure in a hooded cloak, her tears flowed faster as she saw him, and she swallowed hard to contain the pain she felt. "Come to me, I have waited a long time for this moment."

Her sobs exploded as she jumped to her feet, and raced across the grass toward him. Robbie opened his arms and she flew into them. "Oh Robbie I have missed you so much, I was so alone and lost without you, I have wanted so badly to be with you."

His shadowy figure hugged her tightly and she wept in his arms. "Rune your time here is still important, there is much to do in order to undo all that has happened, you must let me go and save our children. I will wait in the other realm with my father until the time comes, and then as I vowed, we will never be parted." She pushed herself deeper into his chest.

"But I don't want you to go, stay with me here Robbie, life without you is painful and terrible, with each passing moment I fracture more, please stay here or let me come with you." Robbie softly stroked her long hair down her back as she cried into him.

"You know I cannot allow you to end everything Rune, you must finish what we started together, Halbert has struggled under the mantle of Lord of Loxley, and he needs his mother to guide him as she did me. Please Rune, you must let me go for a short time, you cannot allow the age of dreams to end in a nightmare."

She cried deep bitter sobs and clung to his tunic, his voice was soft and caring. "You know I am right, and that I could never truly leave you, I am in your heart and your dreams as you are mine, and no matter which realm we walk, we can never truly be parted for we are bound by the power of violet." He pulled her gently away and looked down at her tear streaked face, she was so pale and yet her hair shimmered in the moonlight like fire, he smiled and she felt the love he held wash through her. "I love you Runestone, as you love me, and that can never leave me can it now?" She gave a sniffle and smiled.

"I love you too, you know that, but I miss you so much it is hard to do anything without thinking of you." He lifted his hand and wiped away her tears.

"Runestone Sapphire you are the life in the heart of everything, and at this moment in time the realm needs you. You must say goodbye for a short time and go and do what is destined for you. I have the rest of eternity to be with you, so say goodbye for now and walk to the aid of your remaining sisters of the circle. Our children need you, go to them." He leaned down and kissed her softly on the lips, her eyes exploded with violet light, as she stood frozen held tightly in the love that surrounded her, and Robbie lifted his hood and turned as the mist rolled out of the trees and took him finally into the Other Realm.

Violets grew all around her as she stood motionless, and watched him fade away and leave her until her time here was done; she stood for several minutes staring at the empty trees in the moonlight, as her tears dripped to the floor. "Goodbye my love." Her soft whisper followed him into the trees and beyond, and was gone.

Rune walked slowly back to his grave and knelt down. From inside her cloak she drew out a broken arrow with a blackened, tattered white feathered end, and gently scraped away some of the earth. Placing it gently into the small dug out hole she looked at the headstone. "The first arrow of my life with you, and the last of this woodland realm that contained you, I place it in your keep my love, for when I return to retrieve it, I will be on my way to meet you again, guard it well Robert of Loxley, my husband and the Hooded Man, for in this lies all of the power we hold together. Rest now until I return my love." She patted the earth and the violets spread to cover and protect the spot, and then wiping the tears from her eyes, she lifted her bag, and with a flash of bright violet she was gone.

CHAPTER FIVE

RETURN OF THE CIRCLE

The drizzle of the day had finally begun to ease, and as darkness descended, the camp was set up and the fire blazed. The meal had been sparse compared to other days, but in the driving rain hunting had not been as easy. The wood popped and split, shooting sparks out of the fire, as the damp wood smoked with the surrounding heat. Jett sat back from the camp under the dryer protection of the large sprawling Cedar like tree, as all around the water dripped and bounced off the carpet of dry needles, as it ran down the branches looking for a place to drop free of the wood and dampen the earth below.

She sat with her back to the trunk staring out from under her fringe, the hood of her long black cloak over her head to keep off the damp, and hold in the warmth. Below the folds of her cloak, she fingered her pendant, as she stared at the strange curious group that she had somehow become allied to, in a bid to survive a land that was foreign and alien to her. Her mind wandered as she watched the flames flicker, and pictures of Rafe and Ruby wandered through her thoughts, deep in her heart the pain of separation burned as it had with each day since her strange arrival, and in the gloom of the most miserable day since she had arrived, she felt more homesick than ever before.

The black suited figure got up from the fire; she hardly noticed the movement as he came toward her with a metal cup containing the strange aromatic tea of their land. She hardly moved as he bent down to her and spoke quietly. "Jember?"

She blinked as her dark eyes twitched, and then looked up at him; he offered the cup and smiled. Her cloak moved as it parted and two streams of water ran off it, and from below the folds, her pale hand slid out revealing the tattered lilac cuff of her black jacket.

"Thanks Jariden." He gave her a smile, and understanding she liked to be left with her thoughts, he turned and walked back to the warmth of the fire. Jett warmed her hands on the cup and lifted it to her lips, the steam clouded in front of her face as she breathed out, and it lifted from the steaming cup. The whites of her eyes gave a small pulse of blue and then the feeling inside exploded. Jett jumped, dropping the cup and startled by the huge wave of feeling that pulsed through her, just for an instant her mind flashed with pictures of bright blue eyes, which stared into her head with intensity like she had never known. The tea cup clattered across the roots of the tree, as Jett leapt to her feet and looked wildly round, but the moment had passed as she steadied her breath and heart, and tried for the thousandth time to focus her mind. *"Rune... Rune is that you girl?"* There was nothing and she gave a sorrowful sigh.

Jett looked back at the camp where all the others were watching her. "What?" Her eyes flickered with intense blue. "Drink your tea." She lifted the cup which was almost empty and slumped back to the floor, pulling her cloak back round her, and settled back against the trunk half her mind alert in hope that there might be another chance to connect, but she knew deep down that it was not going to happen again tonight, and she felt the misery build inside her. The sound of heavier rain above her, just added to the gloom, as she snuggled deeper down under the thick fabric. "Oh great... God I hate this place, doesn't anyone here drink coffee?"

In the darkest corner, deep within the fortress away from the prying eyes of the guards, the palest of blue lights flickered for a brief moment. The swish of fabric quietly touched the air, as through the shadow cast by the tall wall, a silent single figure moved quickly. A little way behind her two other figures walked closely, as one was aiding the other, their faces were hidden beneath large hoods, as they made their way down toward the heavy double doors that greeted the entrance chambers to the large hall within, where around the long oval table the leaders of the realm sat discussing their options to resist for as long as possible.

Out of the darkness, and silently into the light of the blazing torches, the shadowy figured stepped, and the guards jumped to attention as they pointed their long spears at the rapidly advancing hooded figure, who was wearing the brightest of deep royal blue cloaks.

"HALT!" The figure slowed and lifted her pale hand out from under the cloak and dropped her hood, where a mane of long auburn and grey streaked hair fell out, and down past her waist, revealing her pale white face with dark heavily lined eyes, which shone with the brightest of sapphire blue. The guard was wary as he looked at the stranger, and then across to his partner to ensure he was covered. "Name yourself, and state your business here." His voice was stern, and yet showed a little of the surprise from the sudden appearance in a fortress protected by the queen of the Fae.

The figure stopped ten feet from the guard, and as her cloak opened, he could see the slender figure of a woman aged around her late fifties, her face looked lined and tired as if she had not slept in weeks, her voice was soft and quiet, as she gave a nod to the guard and waited. "I am the Lady of Callanish, and I have come with urgent news for Lord Loxley and Lord Thorn, and would seek an audience with your queen and my old student Iona Violet."

The guard blinked not recognising her at first, but as he stared across the stone in the flickering light of the torches, he realised that she had aged much since he had last seen her in the court of the queen. The surprise of recognising her reverberated in his words. "Lady Sapphire is that really you? We all thought you were dead." She gave a small smile, and took a step toward him, as he lowered his spear.

"There have been days Mr Thomas when I wished I was, but no, as you can see, I am very much alive and have very urgent business that could make a huge difference if I could be given an audience." The whole manner of the guard changed as he gave a large wide smile.

"I am sure such a revered guest as the old teacher and advisor of our queen will be granted entry with open arms Lady Sapphire, it has been many years since you left, and I am sure that your insight in such dark times will be of great counsel to our queen. Please come with me, I shall escort you myself." He gestured to her to pass, and she turned back to the dark shadow cast by the wall and waved.

"I have two of my apprentices with me, one of whom has no earthly sight." He gave a nod as Jessie guided the blinded figure of Judith into the flickering light of the torches. Mr Thomas agreed, and the two girls crossed the yard and walked behind Sapphire, as they entered the doorway and walked down the corridor, where their escort chatted happily, and walked merrily along at Sapphire's side as if she was an old friend. Sapphire slipped her yellow wooden bow down from inside her cloak and hurried through the large oak doors into the high entrance hall, with Thomas chatting at her side. "Well, I must say My Lady it's nice having you home, how long has it been, it must be at least six or seven years at the most?"

Sapphire hurried through the hallway toward the red polished doors of the large hall. "It has been a little over eight."

"That long? Well, I must say it's gone so fast it hardly feels like it's six."

"No, definitely eight, tell me is Lord Thorn still here?"

"He is My Lady, he stayed back long enough to attend the meeting, but he will be leaving tonight with Lord Loxley, they are hoping to make it back to Loxley to try and find a way of rescuing those trapped behind the tall walls." Sapphire gave a sigh of relief.

"Good, then I am not too late."

It had been a long day of discussion, and some of the members in the meeting were feeling tired, as Iona looked to her brother who had the eyes of everyone at the table. "You have the right to claim that land, are you still set on returning to Loxley to protect those now trapped and isolated from all of us?"

Halbert Thorn rose from his seat; it was uncanny how like his father he had become, except for the bright burning intense blue of his eyes, which bore the same resilient and determined look of his mother.

"I vowed when I was young to protect my father's land and home, I have not changed my opinion with age, my uncle has always had my sword behind him."

The double doors at the bottom of the hall burst open, and the old voice of the blue clad figure screamed into the gathering. "NO... YOU MUST NOT!"

A few of the group jumped, as all heads turned to the old figure dressed in blue, as she hurried up the long hall toward them shaking her bow in the air. "My Queen forgive me, but the Lord Thorn must not leave, all of you must remain here for I have finally found the answers to my search, and I bring hope to all of you in your hour of need. My Queen I beg you, let no one leave, especially Lord Thorn."

Sapphire came hurriedly up the long room, and made her way to the head of the table, as many of the guests stared, irritated by the interruption. Rowan was on his feet and wore a huge smile as she passed him and walked into Iona's open arms. "Forgive me My Queen, for my journey has been long and I have worn the veil, but not a day has passed that you have not been in my thoughts." Iona squeezed her tightly as her eyes sparkled.

"Sapphire, my teacher of so much, you are always welcome in my home, and likewise my thoughts have been with you every day since you left." Sapphire turned to the two girls behind her.

"We have travelled far and we are very tired, I have Jessica Sapphire and...."

"JUDITH!" Jade ran round the table as Judy dropped her long hood, and flung herself into her arms. Iona smiled as she saw the happiness of both of their faces as the two old friends greeted for the first time in over twenty years. Jessica gave a curtsy to Iona and Iona gave a chuckle.

"We do not stand on formality in family." She embraced her cousin warmly. "Tell me how is your mother, I hope she is well?" Jessica gave her a big hug.

"She is fine, you know mum, she fights on always and she sends her love, and told me to tell you that she misses you."

Rowan joined Jade and hugged Judy and then Jessica, it was quite a reunion as the others looked on not entirely sure if the meeting was to be adjourned. Iona turned to the table. "Gentlemen and Ladies, with your permission we shall take a short break for refreshments while I organise our new guests." They all rose and bowed, and then broke from the table, as Hal and Yvee joined in with Frayne as they greeted Jessie and Judith. Rowan stepped up to Sapphire with a smile, she turned with tears in her eyes, and he pulled her into a warm embrace and spoke quietly.

"I cannot tell you of the joy I feel to see you are still alive, I have been so worried about you Saff." She gave a huge sob and buried her head in his shoulder.

"Oh Rowan, I am so sorry, I failed them when they needed me most." He held her tighter as the memory of the moment she arrived in Avalon to ask for help returned to his thoughts; he turned his head and spoke quietly to her.

"I said it then, and I will say again, there is no blame here Saff, he warned us, and we let our guard down and paid the highest price possible, but as long as we remain, we shall honour his life and fight on his behalf. Hush now and know of the joy we feel knowing you too are with us."

Outside the guns blazed and pounded the protective shield set up by Iona. Through the high windows, bright orange flashed onto the white walls, and the explosions boomed in the air. It was almost an hour later when the new guests were seated at the table having been given food and warm drinks. Iona gave the floor to Sapphire, who now sat at her side, and Sapphire rose looking tired and old to address the group; she lifted her glass and took a long drink.

"I have searched now for eight years driven by my instincts and the gifts of sight given to me through my line. We all know the history of suffering at the rise of Mason Knox these past thirty years, but I come here tonight to ask all of you to be patient and not act rash in this the most difficult of times. I have come here to tell you all that I have found what I have sought, and with the aid of My Queen, I intend to use the only way we can defeat the army of the Dragon and the Raven. You all should know that the Sword of Truth shall return to fight amongst you all again."

There was a loud rumble as a chair slid backward somewhere at the end of the table. Sapphire gently turned and smiled as she saw the look of hope in the soft pale brown eyes of the grey haired scruffy general, who had risen from his chair, and watched with hope for the first time in thirty years, Sapphire gave a nod. "Yes Rafe, she is safe, and I am bringing her home to you." He flopped into the chair almost as if he no longer had the use of his legs and wept, pulling his hands to his old lined unshaven face.

Rowan watched her carefully unable to believe her words. "How is this possible Saff? Jett was cast into a realm that even Runestone could not detect her in." Sapphire gave a nod.

"Rune did try to find her, she even asked my brother to help, and it is true that neither of them were successful, let me just say that there are certain paths and secrets known only to the Fae, and some of those are only even known within the White Circle. But please believe me when I tell you all, that on this day the tide for good has turned, and I will use the bridge referred to in old tales to collect Jett Amber and return her to you all."

"But the bridge is a myth, I heard my grandfather talk of it loads of times, there were many in his time who tried to find it and failed, I heard him a thousand times deny it ever existed." Jade's voice was soft and quiet, for a moment her whole insides had squirmed and twisted at the thought of her closest friend being returned to her.

"Your grandfather knew of it, but he like Fagan kept the secret. I have just returned from the Forest of Time, where I have spoken with Fagan, and I can assure you Jade that not only does it exist, but Fagan helped your grandfather learn its secrets, and he used it."

"How could he have used it, all the legends state that it was discovered by Sequana the Seer, and she disappeared never to be seen again? I also was in Avalon when my grandfather died fighting the Dark One, both my mother and Rune were connected to him when he died." Sapphire shook her head.

"No Jade that is wrong... Like Opal it was time for your grandfather to leave and pass on the guardianship to his heir, he used the moment to fool the Dark One into false hope, to try and hide the fact that he knew that the redstone would be passed to your sister, he left his staff in Rune's care to pass on, and he did take the Bridge of Sequana to leave this realm forever." Jade looked round the room at the others.

"But it does not make sense; we needed him, why would he leave us when we needed him most?" Rowan took her hand as Iona turned to her aunt.

"His time was over, it was decided by the Ruling Council at the start of time, that each member at a pre given point would leave to take on other tasks. The Whitelines has vast realms, and he chose to walk in those furthest from us, just as Opal decided to live in the Hidden Realm and work with diminished powers for the good of these realms, their time was over Aunt Jade, and they were instructed to leave." It was hard for Jade to fully understand, Merlin had not said goodbye to her, he left letting her believe he was dead, Sapphire felt her feelings.

"Jade he loved you, maybe he could not say goodbye because of the pain it would cause him. Merlin was a man who loved his family more than anything, so it was probably easier for him to fake his death and slip away." Rowan understood, and he knew the feelings inside Jade, for he had known of the pain she had carried for many years at losing so many of her family.

"Sapphire if this thing is really possible, and Jett can be returned, what hope will that truly give us, for here we have sat for two days now trying to find a way to overcome the might of the Knox Empire, and to date we have found little that can help us."

"If we do not do this, as the centre to the circle of sight I can tell all of you, that within the week you will all be dead and the fight for the Green Realm will be lost forever." Rowan sat up straight in his seat as he thought for a moment, he turned and looked round the table at the solemn looks on the faces of his family and his friends.

"OK so tell me what we do to achieve this." Iona gave a nod to Sapphire and she took a deep breath.

"This country is not in as bad a shape as you have been led to believe, but travel is difficult and little news can be passed around. There are large areas that are creating problems, but without aid from here they will fail. Canterbury is still very much a green zone; once again every attempt by the Dark One to kill it has failed. The magic invoked by Robbie through Hearne has proved more powerful than any of us ever expected, and the trees are growing and spreading. Mason has placed many walls around it, and all have fallen to its power, the woodland has grown so vast that it now threatens London."

There were smiles and murmurs round the table, as the thought of a little more resistance to Mason gave them hope. Sapphire took another drink as she watched Rowan as he thought deeply about what she had said, he turned to look at her, and she gave a slight nod to allow him his question.

"This vast forest, does it have men who can fight within it?" She smiled noting the wisdom of his thinking.

"Until recently yes, the Master Sage has kept many faithful to the Hooded Man, it is a sad twist of fate that he was caught six months ago and was executed in London, it was the reason I returned to Loxley. I am sorry Rowan, but after his capture the army of Knox led by Lance, entered the woodland and slaughtered all faithful to him. The only resistance left now is those who fight under the command of Grace Mackintosh and her son, who I see present, and those few left hiding in the forests of Caerleon, under the command of Louisa who has assumed control after the death of Phillip. Neither have enough numbers to lead reinforcements here, everywhere else now is under stone and ruled by Mason the so called, King of this land."

A stocky dark haired man bearing the Caerleon crest shook his head slowly. "This is grim news indeed, my mother has spoken often of her time with the Sage fighting for London, she will be saddened to hear such news, as she holds him in the highest esteem, he was one of very few men she really respects."

"Louisa saved his life, and I believe there was a deep bond between them, for I know she loved him deeply for what he did for the woodland realm. He did much to aid my circle and his loss has lessened it." Sapphire turned back to the others.

"It is very bleak indeed, but the fight has not been lost yet, Avalon still defies the forces of Raven Merle, and the realm is shut tight and cannot be breached from outside, Amethyst has proven herself to be all of the forces of her line, and the realm is safe. Raven Merle desires the return of the black star, as she claims it belongs to her, but even with greatly superior powers than her grandmother, she cannot break into Avalon to recover the stone. I was there a year ago and spoke with Amethyst, and it will not crumble easily. I see the Lady Vivian has made it here, and I am sure that you can speak with her to confirm this."

Vivian gave a nod to the others. "It is true, my mother has and will continue to hold off the darkness, Avalon once suffered at the hands of that family, and my mother has vowed it will never happen again. I have come at this time on her behalf to offer all of you safe haven should things turn to the worst."

"Well, it's nice to hear the first constructive comment of the week, let's face it we all know Mason has brought in bigger guns; it cannot be much longer now." Rowan scowled at General McKay, and turned back to Sapphire.

"These secrets and powers of the Fae, if there are of such importance, how is it you can reveal them to us now, and how can you be so sure they are right?" Iona gave a smile.

"Sapphire you arrived telling us of the bridge and its existence, would you like to explain to those here who are unaware of something the Fae have guarded for a long time. I think a little more detail of this ancient secret will prove your case to some of our guests." Sapphire again composed herself and prepared to tell her story.

"Sequana was the mother of Fagan the Maker of the town of Avalonia, and advisor to the Queen Rhiannon. She was held in great esteem as being the most gifted seer and mystic of all the Fae. In the days when the Ruling Council took the empty garment from Tideguyde, and used it to make two copies to become the Fae of earth and moon, it was said that a small part of Tideguyde had been caught within the garment, and it passed into the line of one of the Fae. It is believed that Sequana was the Fae member who in time inherited it, and she held a connection that was linked directly to Tideguyde, which would explain her superior power." Sapphire looked round to ensure all of them understood what she was telling them, and when it appeared they did, she continued.

"Sequana was aware of where the moon goddess went to, and through her connection with her, she found that she had left a thread joining her to this world, as she travelled to meet with Erathome and build other worlds. This thread she called the bridge of intention, and she used all of her powers to try and find it, to such a point that it became an obsession, and the people of the town said she was going mad, and ridiculed her. Eventually believing she was right, she secretly took a trip and entered into the vast Forest of Time to seek it out, rumour has it she found it and returned to her son and told him the secret of the bridge, and where exactly it could be found, but she swore him to secrecy."

Sapphire took a breath and relaxed for a moment, everyone was listening, and some of them nodded understanding as they had heard of the myth of the bridge. Sapphire took a long drink.

"A year later the Dark One struck killing firstly Eleanor, and then Eve, a short time after that Gwendolyn confronted her and was very badly wounded, her daughter Una requested the aid of Rhiannon, and Gwendolyn was hidden in the forest. It was at this time that Rhiannon decided to clear and seal the realm of Avalon, Sequana left her service and disappeared never to be seen again. Fagan begged Rhiannon to leave him behind in the forest as Keeper, and most people said it was because his mother had not found the bridge, but was living in a cave and he was helping her.

Merlin discovered that Fagan had become the guardian of the bridge, and had sworn to hide its whereabouts forever, he would not even talk to his old friend Merlin about where it lay, but he did leave clues to see if the old wizard could find it alone, and in which case he would be true to the promise he made to his mother. Not long after, Gwendolyn was captured in battle with the Dark One. I have spoken with Fagan, and he believes that his mother returned and met with Gwendolyn before her capture, and I am convinced it was Sequana who showed Gwendolyn how to place part of her line into the line of another, as she did with Opal to ensure Runestone would bring forth her successor as Queen. I think she showed Gwendolyn how to do it by taking a small part of the gifts of Tideguyde from within herself, and placing them into Gwendolyn knowing that this moment would one day come, after all she saw further and deeper into the future than any of the other Council." Jade gave a nod.

"Gwendolyn was clever at hiding her core in my sister to give to Iona, but who did she give this gift to, and who should we look to in order to know the truth?"

Iona understood deeper than any of them, and she sat forward with a smile. "A gift of such value would only go to where it would be used to its greatest advantage, now I truly understand everything, this gift could only be placed in the centre of the Circle of Sight, where all the circles would benefit and aid the lines of Fae, am I not right my teacher? Did it not guide you in the teaching of a young king and the next queen of Fae?"

Sapphire gave a small embarrassed smile. "You have great wisdom My Queen."

Rafe sat up in his chair, he was a simple woodsman and man of fighting, this all felt a little too fantastical to him. "Sorry Saff, but I do not understand, even if this bridge does exist and you can use it, how can Jett and her sword help win this? We only have Honour and Knowledge in our midst, Destiny, Courage, and Justice, have been taken by Knox, we would need all five to defeat him, which is why we have been at war for the last thirty years. Any fool can see that without all the swords he is unbeatable."

"That is easy Rafe. Tideguyde was fearful of losing her way if she could not find Erathome, so she asked for the aid of the most powerful member of the council to help her construct the bridge, she asked the holder of the whitelines of time." Rafe looked a little blank and she smiled. "The bridge will reunite all the swords again, and new days will follow, I will travel to Merlin using Cal my spirit guide, and will send Jett back to her guide in this realm, who will be Una as she has the staff, and will complete her final task for Merlin. The swords will reunite and fight to save everyone, and with hope we shall be victorious.”

It was obvious that a great deal of them did not fully understand, but Jade and Iona had grasped all of what Sapphire meant, Iona rose from her chair.

“This will take great power and only the table of a Fae queen can wield that much power, all of you will reside here tonight, as I feel dawn will begin the change of all things, we shall gather later around my table. I will send for you all when I am prepared, Sapphire, Aunt Jade, come with me now, for we must prepare and soon we shall begin the return of our red queen at last.”

As Iona and Sapphire left the room to prepare with Jade, higher up the valley in the darkness, as the army commanded by Victor worked through the night to assemble the large new guns, Lance sat alone at his desk in his study while Nadia slept upstairs in her bed. Impatient and unable to sleep, Lance cast his eyes over the details of the army encamped on Iona's doorstep. He shuffled through the papers reading the many reports made for him by his son as his eyes grew tired. Engrossed in his papers he did not notice the faint shimmer from the other room.

Rune stood in the doorway, and watched him as he planned his victory, and yearned for the power and freedom it would bring to finally achieve his goal. Thirty years had passed since he had killed the man she loved by trapping him, and then killing him when he was defenceless, and for thirty years he had worn Destiny on his hip as a prize to be worshiped as the man who had slain the hooded man. He leaned back in his chair as he yawned and stretched, and then froze as his eyes met with the bright sapphire blue that shone in the dim light from the doorway.

Slowly he lowered his arms to the rests of his chair; his hand slipping slowly and casually towards the finely made sword on his belt, Rune took a step forward into the room. “That gem on your belt will not aid your hand this night son of the snake, there is only one hand that can wield that with honour, and as we know, honour is not your strongest quality, is it?”

He felt the cold trickle down his spine, as she took another step closer to him; fear was building in him as he tried to remain cool headed. “You do not frighten me Witch, one word and my guards will take you screaming back to your glass box.”

Rune looked behind her, and then back to him, she gave a slight smile. “There are no guards here I can assure you, one click of my fingers and they all sank into a deep sleep, as for glass boxes, it appears mine is a little full at the moment, and will keep your grandmother busy for some time as she tries to free her little assistant. So, as it appears, we are quite alone and will not be disturbed for some time.”

He swallowed hard as his brain raced to find some way he could escape, he thought of the lower drawer that contained the heavy old pistol, Rune shrugged. "No bullets, they rusted away and returned to nature the moment I stepped in through the door, you may check if you wish."

He physically shrank in his seat, as Rune watched him begin to unravel, the glow of violet pulsating all around her.

"All I have is the sword, my grandmother has the others, if that is all you want then take it, your people will die whether or not I have it." Rune lifted her hood up over her face.

"You have more than the sword, and I will take everything before I leave this night." His voice rose as he arrogantly scoffed at her, as his cool blue eyes fixed on her, his lip curled showing his arrogance.

"What else do I have that an old witch like you could use?" She could see his leg shaking as he tried to push it into the floor.

"You have nothing of use, but you do have something I want young snake." His eyes scanned the desk trying to determine what it was exactly she wanted.

"What on earth could you possibly want from me?" Rune gave a small smile.

"I will take back what is rightfully my husband's, and then I shall take your wife and your life for payment against the life you stole from me."

He shot up from his seat. "WHAT... Who the bloody hell do you think you are? Breaking in here in the middle of the night making ridiculous demands, are you insane?"

Rune gave her fingers a loud snap, upstairs Nadia screamed out in pain, his head snapped to the open doorway and the stairs up to the bedroom, panic crossed his face as it reddened and sweat began to form on his brow, his bright blue eyes opened wide in panic as Nadia screamed out again.

"No... Stop this... I will give you anything, just spare her, she has a son, please I beg you take me if you must, but spare her she is innocent in all this." Lance looked terrified as he begged Rune to stop and the wails of agony screamed down the stairs for him. Rune snapped her fingers, and wails above abruptly ceased.

"Fine... Although the lives of my children meant nothing to you when you drove your sword through a tied up father, but I will agree to the terms, your life will be mine in payment, but know Lance of the line of Knox, your line will end here, for the life of your son will be matched to that of the time that you held the sword of my husband, for every second you have held it he will have life, and at the moment I take it from your dead corpse this night, the clock will stop and his life will return to me. Your empire will crumble by my hand, and your son will never see his thirtieth year. I am the Runestone, the Violetline and Lady of Life, and all will know I have been here this night for you."

He shook as he stood before her, the fear coursing through his veins, and his eyes widened as Rune lifted her arm and it began to glow violet. He felt his chest tighten and his breathing restrict as Rune pulled at his life force, her bright blue eyes shone with menace, fixed on the terror in his, she did not rush as he fought for breath, the pain in his chest increasing. Finally with agony coursing through his body, he screamed like a child and gasped out a retched gurgle, and thrust his arms to his chest, as his face contorted with the agony, Rune did not blink.

"There is no honour in what I do to you Snake, as there was none in the way you took the glory for the death of my husband, although I have faced you in person and alone, something you never had the courage to do yourself. You chose a coward's way to earn your victory and a good man of honour died, and so you will struggle and cling to your painful life until the very last second. I hope you think of that as your heart takes its last beat."

His shirt tore open, and his heart shot out in a stream of blood, and flopped onto the papers scattered across the table, his legs buckled, and he fell to his knees shaking violently as his life seeped away with the blood. The eyes of Lance were level with the table and fixed on his own heart, and as it spluttered before him, it gave one final huge spasm and stopped, he crashed forward onto the desk, a look of horror fixed on his face.

Rune walked slowly round the desk, and knelt down as she undid the Sword of Destiny from his belt; she stood up and folded the blade within the folds of her cloak, then turned and left the room.

Upstairs the soft moans of Nadia could be heard as she called in pain to her husband, Rune stopped at the door and turned, she gave another loud click of her fingers, and violets shot out of the floor and spread across the carpet back to Lance's study, she opened the door and walked out into the cold night air. There was a flash of violet light and all was still, except for the creeping carpet of violets that covered the floor of the whole ground level of the house. In the distance the guns roared, as the bombardment of the defences of Iona in the fortress held for a little while longer.

Under the trees of Robbie's Mere, the lights of the house burned brightly. Inside the old lord of the woodland was sat up, and recovering his strength quickly now he was back in the Woodland Realm. He still looked tired, and on his right leg there was a large black angry looking wound, Steph cleaned it as best she could, using Witch-hazel and bound it tightly, the old man smiled as he watched her apply such care. "That will help a great deal, I have used a little of Alice's arnica ointment, it has powerful properties so with luck you should find it will heal perfectly."

He lifted his hand and placed it on her shoulder, his long twig like fingers gave a slight squeeze. "You have suffered greatly in my cause Granddaughter." She stopped and looked up into his dark caring eyes, and saw the love he held with his sorrow, she gave a little smile.

"You have never called me granddaughter before; I like the way it sounds." His hand slid to cup her cheek, and she felt the tears in her eyes well up. "Grandfather I feel lost and alone, what should I do because I am losing the fight, and I just cannot let all we have built fall?" Hearne reached down and pulled her up to him, and like a frightened child she pushed her arms around him and nestled into his chest as he folded his large powerful arms around her. Feeling safe for the first time in a long time, she let out her pain and cried.

"There little Moonstone. Let out all the darkness that is trapped within you, for you soon will need the power of light. It saddens me that we must lose so many who we love, but know this my little Moonstone, he has not deserted you, and although he has a high seat in my house, Peter watches over you and wills his love back to you." He softly patted her back and began to rock her in his arms feeling the comfort it brought her. "Shush My Child and settle, for you are safe within the arms of your family, be still a moment and know we are with you."

Outside in the dense trees close to the large wall of sunken trunks, a bright burst of violet coloured the damp wood of the trees. Rune stepped out of the light cradling the wrapped section of the cloak close to her heart. For a moment she stood silent as the violet archway behind her faded away, and then holding the sword up she fell to her knees and pressed the hilt close to her cheek. It was the symbol of everything Robbie had stood for, it had been carried by his side, and wielded in his hand, and it was all she had left of him. With her hood over her face, and pressed against the sword as she knelt in the woodland he had loved the most, the bitter pain inside her flowed out as she grieved for the loss of her only love.

Set back from her in the trees, obscured from the moon, a tall hooded figure in a tattered black robe watched, as he respected the private moment that Runestone used to release her deep bitter loss. Holding onto the sword she cried alone in the darkness, hidden below her rich violet cloak until all she could do was gasp out dry silent sobs. Rune quietly stirred as she lifted her hand and wiped her eyes, and took long deep breaths to clear her head, knowing she had to finish what he had started. She lifted her head and slid back her hood, and her red swollen eyes noticed the silent figure, he took a step towards her.

"Greetings Little Redstone. You have grown in your years of sleep, and used the time well to master the forces within you. The honour you show to your Hooded Man is beyond measure, we all feel the pain you hold at his loss, but I think you know that now is the time to turn the tide, for there is a moment looming when all will gather to seek out the hidden paths." Rune sniffled as she tried to compose herself.

"My Lord, I am ready, I have been able to release my grandmother from her trap, and she has spoken of the things that occurred. As we speak I feel my grandfather of the woodland growing in strength." Albanlin gave a nod and the rain shook from his hood.

"The Mortal le Fey has discovered her box, and she is aware that you will strike hard, she has seen how you have dealt with her line, and as we speak she moves the small raven to sacred ground to protect her. There is much to do Little Redstone, your powers are returning and growing strong, and soon others will have great need of your gifts, for our star of blue will walk into oblivion on a quest of great danger to undo all the evil of past deeds. Go to your table, for now is the time for you to take the control destined always for you, and become the one circle to which all circles will join. Your table awaits, but you will not be alone, for I have a friend who has sat by my side to keep you company." Albanlin snapped his fingers, and through the trees came a very familiar growl.

Rune gave a smile and swallowed hard on her tears as she saw the large proud tiger walk into the woodland from a white door of light. He sniffed the air and gave a whimper, and then bounded through the trees toward her. Rune gave a gasp of delight and went back down on her knees as the old tiger ran up and nuzzled into her, she flung her arms around him and clung to him with great love to him. "Oh my big baby boy I am so pleased to see you." The tiger whimpered and nuzzled his large head onto her as Rune gave a happy laugh. Albanlin turned in the trees.

"You have much to do Little Redstone... Go and take the fight of your Hooded Man to her, bring back the Sword of Truth and gather the five swords together with the Sceptre, for they too are keys to the doorway of the Bridge of Intention, the final gathering has begun, go and be the stone that all has been written on, and use your intention to guide them." Rune looked up as his shape turned to white light and rose up into the trees like a shooting star.

"Thank you, My Lord, I will not fail you." His voice came softly through the trees.

"I have never thought for one moment you would, remember my Little Redstone, I will always be with you." Furry Face gave a little whine as he watched the light shoot through the sky and fade, and Rune stood back up and scratched the back of his head.

"Come on baby, my daughter and sisters have need of me."

The tiger gave a happy yelp and bounded off into the trees, and Rune waited for a moment and took a very deep breath. "For you my love." Pulling her hood back up she took her first step forward, and began the task of completing Robbie's work, the fight for the Woodland Realm was back on track

CHAPTER SIX

LOOKING BACKWARD

Iona looked deeply into her table as she sought the answers to her questions, the colours swirled as she gleaned every bit of help she could, to try and determine what the past could reveal about the coming hours. As she watched her table with a troubled mind and lost in thought, Sapphire sat with Jade across the room and they spoke quietly to each other. Jade stroked Sapphire grey streaked hair back from her face and smiled warmly at her; she was worried about Sapphire, as she looked tired and sick.

"You must take better care of yourself, you have lost so much weight you are almost skin and bone Saff." Her bright green eyes showed her concern, and Sapphire felt the warmth of her hands, and felt a little relief knowing one of her oldest friends was there with her.

"Oh Jade I am so tired, you have no idea how hard it has been, I have felt the pressure of trying to use all my strength to find the bridge." She closed her eyes and leant back against the wall. "I could sleep for a year if only I could turn off my mind."

Jade understood the curse of visions flowing through her mind, she had seen how scared Jessie Sapphire had been when the visions first came to her, and even Rune at times had been startled by some of the visions she had dreamt of as a small girl.

"We have time Saff, just rest for a while here while you are safe with us." Jade felt more concerned as she saw the heavy dark bags under Saff's eyes and the pale colour of her skin, most of the sisters of the circle had remained relatively youthful, but Saff looked older than all of them, she looked back to Iona who was busy watching the table and trying to understand the pictures she saw.

Saff remained still her eyes closed and resting, even though it was only for a few moments it felt like heaven. Jade placed her hand on Saff's tummy and closed her eyes, for a moment green light flashed across her cheeks, and her hand began to glow with a faint green light, Saff felt the warmth radiate inside her and she gave a soft sigh of relief, as she felt the energy of Jade pulsate into her giving her more strength.

Jade opened her eyes and saw the smiling face of Sapphire watching her; she gave an embarrassed sort of grin. "I kinda thought it would help, you know, top your energy up a little before you go, I mean, no one really knows what will happen, I just figured a little extra strength won't hurt."

Sapphire took her hand and squeezed it. "Thanks Jade." Her face changed to one of being very solemn. "I will not fail you all again... I promise." Jade frowned.

"You have never failed us, why would you say that Saff?"

"I should have seen it.... I should have been there to protect him, but I got all tied up with the Sage and Rafe, and I did not understand the signs. I failed him Jade and all of you." Tears welled into her eyes. "Jade I was the one chosen to see for all of you, I was blinded by my own foolish confusion and did not respond fast enough, if I had done things differently, he would be alive and none of this would be as it is."

Jade took her hand and squeezed it hard; as she watched the tears run down Sapphire's face. "We all let him down Saff, you cannot blame it all on yourself, we did the one thing he always warned us about, and we got complacent. Every one of us has suffered the pain of losing him, you cannot blame it all on yourself, Avalon was hard on everyone, and we were so relieved that we had made it and were on our way home, that we dropped our guard. You must not suffer with this alone Saff, you have found the key to undo what we all have carried in our hearts, you alone have fought for everything he believed in, so dry your eyes and put the pain behind you. Tonight, we must fight one more time to turn this around and make his dream for this land live again."

Sapphire gave a tearful sob and nodded as she tried to smile, Jade squeezed her hand tighter, and Sapphire tried to push back the huge wave of sadness that had engulfed her, no words were said, but the understanding between the two of them deepened as Sapphire wiped her eyes and Jade smiled to reassure her.

Iona lifted her head from the table. "It will soon be time to start the gathering, the moon is hidden, but it is moving in the sky and the powers of the Fae are growing stronger now, come we must prepare, for within the next twenty four hours the powers of this Isle will rise with the moon, then we shall summon the force we require."

Jade helped Sapphire up, and together they crossed the room to the edge of the large round table where many pictures swirled around in a white mist on the smooth surface, Jade was unsure at what it was she was looking at and looked to Iona for guidance. Iona gave her a smile.

"Everything you see is what my table predicts the bridge will appear as, and as you can see, it looks like it will appear different to everyone, to Sequana it was a valley of white stone that was decorated with bright flowers, into which she walked through to the other side, for Merlin it was a long tunnel, Jett it seems was unconscious, and yet in her mind she felt like she was floating through darkness. The last time it was opened from the Violet Isle, it was Robbie and you who travelled through it to the Hidden Realm, and that looks like it was a tunnel that spun you out of control, which can only mean that it works with the power of the mind, and projects what you feel at the time." Jade looked surprised, but Sapphire looked more surprised.

"How did Robbie and Jade use it? I was there and helped Merlin." Iona gave a warm smile.

"I think Sapphire you did more than help him, I think he knew you were the key and he used your powers to open it."
"But that's not possible; I didn't know it existed back then."

"Remember Sapphire, he did, Merlin had known of the bridge for a long time, he knew you were destined for the centre of the table of sight at birth, which is why you could not be the centre of the table of knowledge. I think at that time, and if my table is right, he felt that Gwendolyn had passed something to you, but he was not sure for certain it had anything to do with the bridge. According to this table, shortly after you were born, he went to visit Fagan and stayed there for several months working alone in the forest. I think it was at that time he realised that the gift you received, had been placed there by Gwendolyn on the wishes of Sequana. It was a gift for a time of our greatest need, Merlin knew when the hidden realm was closed, that the Dark One had no knowledge of the bridge, and so with you at his side, all he needed to do was unlock it inside you, and use it to get Robbie and Jade in undetected." Sapphire and Jade glanced at each other and then down at the many pictures floating around on the surface of the table, Jade gave a big sigh.

"You know nothing has ever been simple with my lot, why on earth they have to hide everything, and talk in code has never made any sense at all, it's why with Rowan I always talk straight. At least he knows what I know and can understand what is going on, I mean let's be honest, if they had all sat down with a cup and had a chat, things might have been so much easier." She gave a small giggle. "It's a wizard thing I am sure, Rune was the same, I never understood half of the things she told me." Sapphire gave a small giggle.

Iona watched the pictures of Merlin and Opal swirl round with Robbie and Jade, as Gwendolyn stood alone in the forest waiting for something to come out of the trees. "I think Sapphire that if you think back to that time, you will probably understand that it was at that time the restless feelings within you began to grow, I think in unlocking the bridge Merlin awoke your true gifts, and it is from that moment onwards your destiny with the table of sight began." She paused for a short moment and thought; her voice seemed lost and far away as she spoke. "He must have known about this time, I know Gwendolyn said she had never seen these events and she spoke with Sequana, I wonder.... Yes he must have... I mean how else could he have known? The sight was never his to wield, but time... The Whitelines... Could he have?"

She blinked as the two women watched her, and she waved her hands across the table as if looking for something else, Iona was deep in thought and no longer aware of the others, as she tried to puzzle out the questions forming in her mind. Her bright violet eyes shone below her hanging fringe of brown, streaked with copper and blonde, as she quietly voiced her thoughts. "He was there when she received the stone, he watched over her and ensured Opal went to Billy on the moors, he took her from the cave to hide her in the Merle. Oh what did you do, and what were you up to, he was your guardian, did you tell him?"

Jade shrugged as Sapphire watched mesmerised not really understanding the thousands of pictures that streamed into the table, it was obvious that Iona understood something, it was just that she was so involved with whatever it was she was looking for that Sapphire did not want to interrupt her. Iona suddenly straightened up and turned to Jade, her eyes blazed with violet light and Jade jumped with surprise. "Jade you must leave for a short while; there are things I need to talk to Sapphire about in private."

Jade looked confused. "But why I can help?" Iona shook her head.

"I am sorry Aunt Jade, but this is very important, and can only be for the ears of the one who will walk the bridge, please give me just a short time alone, I promise it will not be for long, wait in the outer chamber for me to call you." Jade looked disappointed but she understood.

"More secrets and hidden riddles, guess I should have known better, after all you are her daughter." She turned and winked at Sapphire, and then made her way across the wide room towards the door. Iona took Sapphire gently by the arm and led her over to the seats, she sat down and Saff sat beside her, Iona smiled a gentle warm smile.

"I feel your apprehension please ease your heart, for although you are fearful of the power of the bridge, you must know that you opened it once before and can do so again, even though you have never walked it, have the faith in you that I do, as this night I can see clearer than any in my life before." Sapphire gave a deep sigh.

"The thought of travelling to a place that has held Jett captive frightens me, what if I cannot return here?" Iona smiled.

"If you succeed Sapphire, here will no longer be important." She frowned unsure of what Iona meant and Iona gave a nod. "Can you not see? Albanlin helped construct the bridge, he is the power and creator of the Whitelines, he has seen everything and has prepared for this moment, he must have told Merlin, or at least set him on the path to the discovery of the bridge. Merlin was the guardian of all in the realm of Albanlin, and I think Sapphire centre of your circle, that tonight you will set off to do a little more than recover Jett."

It took a few moments for Sapphire to truly understand and she gasped. "Now I understand." She turned to Iona with an amazed look on her face. "No one can know this, it is too dangerous, and no one must leave the castle, we must all be gathered when it happens, you must not let anyone leave no matter what happens." Iona gave a smile and gently wrapped her arms around Sapphire.

"I am queen, and for now my word is rule, but remember this my sweet teacher, even Jett must not know." Sapphire went to speak, but Iona squeezed her a little harder. "I know Sapphire, but we must play things out as they were written, for the fate of everything is now dependant on discretion. Oh poor Aunt Jade, she hates all these secrets, but suddenly this feels so big, I think only you and I can have full knowledge of this, a slip now will cost us everything, and the dream will be lost forever." Iona released her and looked her deep in the eyes. "Summon your strength and rest a while, go and rest in your room and I will call you when the time arrives, I will assemble the others shortly."

Sapphire rested, with the help of Jade who was soon called back into the room, Iona prepared, and then let the rest of the woodland and Fae leaders' troupe into the room. They quietly seated themselves in the seats that had been placed close to the edge of the Table of Iona, Queen of the Fae on earth. Jade acted as Iona's assistant, and took the sword from Rowan and placed it on the table opposite the Sword of Knowledge.

Iona carefully watched the sky through the glass ceiling, waiting for the time when the moon and stars would be perfectly aligned, and spoke to the group as she waved her hands across the table bringing it to life.

"Gentlemen and Ladies, for those of you unaccustomed to the tables of power this may seem a little strange, but as we wait for the right moment to open the bridge, which may be any time in the next day, I will fill you all in on what took place many years ago. For many of you have heard the tales told, but few of you have witnessed what really took place, I will warn that for some of you, this will be unpleasant."

Her wrist twisted, and a cloud rose up above the table and shimmered with a silvery essence, pictures grew out of the cloud for everyone to see. "Firstly, we shall look to the capture of the Lord Hearne, for at the moment of striking hard at the hooded man, the Dark One had also planned something for her little assistant, who she had veiled in secrecy and sent out of the realm of Avalon shortly before the confrontation with my mother the Lady of the Woods."

The pictures cleared, and Ursula could be seen deep within Loxley Woods, not far from Hearne's Rock, she screamed and wailed as she shouted to Hearne to save her, and when he finally appeared, she cowered on the grass at his feet. Ursula begged the lord of the woodland to save her from the Dark One, and begged forgiveness for her part in all the wrong doings that had been done to the woodland world, her tears streamed down her face as the old man bent low and lifted her face to his, he wiped the tears from her eyes and comforted her.

The pictures froze above the table as everyone stared captivated by the scene, Iona walked slowly round the table looking at the pictures as she addressed them. "You see a child of Fae descent, corrupted by Morgan le Fey." There were sudden gasps around the room, and Iona nodded as the watchers looked back to her. "Ursula of the boat people, cast out into the world alone to fend for herself with a gift from her mother, for it was she who was born of this Isle and gave her daughter the gift of sight."

The pictures began again as Ursula wept in the green lords arms, and Iona continued her commentary. "The Fae are known for their ability to hide their true feelings, it served us all well after the death of Gwendolyn White Circle. The Fae scattered to the four winds and adapted to life in the world of man, Ursula was born of the line of Ariel a powerful seer to this realm, and her gifts of sight are very strong. Not all of her life has been corruption, for once she was a gentle girl who was in love, living her life amongst the boat traders in the south, it was the prejudice of men that slaughtered her family and only love, which drove her onto the streets and right into the path of her dark mistress. The cunning of Morgan le Fey should never be underestimated, as you see her choice of diversion was very effective. The Hooded Man stood at the threshold of death, and as she struck with her spells to prevent Runestone from aiding him, her little assistant struck a fatal blow to our lord."

Everyone watched as suddenly Hearne stood up and looked to the south; Ursula snatched a pendant from her neck of a long black claw, and stuck it deep into the leg of Hearne. "Freeze."

The picture floated above the table of the long white fingers clutching at the claw that was embedded into the leg of Hearne. "That is no ordinary weapon, for it was made from a shard taken from the Star of the Merle, it was fragmented from the star when it struck the Sword of Truth in Avalon. It is my belief that the meeting of a pure power with pure evil, caused damage to both weapons, the result being the thin shard collected later by Morgan le Fey."

It was unthinkable as gasps of shock echoed round the room, and the picture floated in the air as they stared with startled eyes at it. Iona smiled at Jade who had seen these pictures before, and continued to walk around her guests. "What happened next I am unsure of, but as you watch the Lord Hearne becomes engulfed in black smoke, watch the floor below his feet?" Iona clicked her fingers and Ursula jumped backward away from the old man who looked in great distress, smoke belched out of the floor and swirled round him as a black seven pointed star burned itself into the grass and with the blink of an eye, he dropped through the star and disappeared completely.

"Your enemy uses more than combat to achieve her goals, no one saw the events of that day coming, not even my mother who understood her tactics more than most. It is easy to dismiss her as a mortal, as many of the Ruling Council did in the past, but it is the mortal side of her that is the most dangerous, for her greed and deviousness are her greatest achievements."

The pictures changed and Robbie stood on top on the cliff at the edge of Citadel Mount, he shook hands with Fagan and lifted his bag onto his shoulder, as Rune walked up and gave Fagan a huge hug. Robbie walked down the steps cut out of the rocky floor, and into the cave toward the white shimmering wall of stone and disappeared. Amethyst hugged Jade, and Fish embraced Rowan, Steph stood at the side of Rune and smiled as Fagan talked to her, everyone seemed happy and relaxed as they said their goodbyes.

Robbie reappeared in the crumbled doorway of what looked like an old ruined part of the abbey; he looked happy as he walked out with confidence. Judith screamed as she fought on the floor, but it was too late as Robbie was snatched by four Cutters and wrestled to the ground. The cold moment of Lance, as he thrust the sword into Robbie made most of them jump as they watched with horror. The moment of burning the pupils of Judy's eyes was cold and cruel, and all of them recoiled as they saw the pain it inflicted on the young girl, who was also Lance's younger sister, some of the viewers who were all battle hardy, turned and looked away as they shuddered.

Tears rolled down Jade's face and Rowan hung his head, Halbert watched in disbelief unable to comprehend the scene unravelling before him, as the picture widened to show the Specialists hanging from the trees cut and slashed, the picture snapped back to Rune as her head shot round to the wall of rock, her eyes flashed violet as she screamed and let go of Fagan, everyone twisted in shock as Rune ran down the steps towards the wall, she hit it hard and bounced off it in a bright flash, the doorway had sealed and she could not get through.

The pictures changed as Lance slid the Sword of Destiny out of Robbie's scabbard and placed it in his. On a cloth was Courage and Justice with the sceptre, he rolled them up and then tied them to the saddle of his horse, he looked back at the horse that bore the unconscious body of Will and at the doorway nervously, as he shouted out his orders, and pulled himself up on to his mount. Whipping the horse hard, he set off at high speed, pulling the spare laden horse, and leaving the bodies of the Specialists and their leader hanging. The doorway exploded in blue light and Sapphire came rushing through, but it was too late to save him, he was gone, the picture faded as several of the group wept, Iona walked slowly back to her empty seat and stood behind it.

"You have all seen the act of cowardice used by Lance Knox. Morgan le Fey used her knowledge of the realm to set her trap, it was known to my father that the Curtain of Light was heavily guarded, but no one knew of the secret doorway of Merlin, or at least that is what they all believed. As you can see, she has delved into everyone's secrets in her lust for the power to rule, in the coming days do not presume you are safe, and it is for that reason everyone will remain in this tower until the Sword of Truth is returned to us."

Iona rested her hand on Rowan's shoulder as she spoke, like many in the room he had only ever heard the various stories told, seeing the pictures had brought back everything, and he felt the anger and pain mix with his heartbreak. Iona gave his shoulder a squeeze as he looked to the floor. "The truth has been revealed this night to all of you, and as you can see, we sit here as the moment comes closer to the edge of all of our interwoven destiny's, unlike our enemy, we are not blinded by our achievements as we sit here listening to their pounding guns outside, but they are, as they have learned nothing from us. Yet tonight we have learned a great deal from them, and as my father taught those around him, complacency will always defeat them."

Rowan lifted his head and his eyes were red as he looked at Rafe who was speaking. "They have two hundred thousand men and cannons to aid them, no offence but what does it matter if they are complacent or not? We are not strong enough to match them if the protection of the Fae fails." Iona smiled.

"Five swords are stronger than a thousand armies my good General, were you not forty Specialists against ten times what sits at my door?" Rafe gave a nod.

"We were, and we failed... we lost our lord who we loved, and inch by inch without hope we lost everything else."

"But Rafe, don't you see it? That is the whole point, we were a sword short." Everyone turned to look at Rowan, who had been looking thoroughly downhearted, and yet suddenly, there was a sparkle in his slate grey eyes that gave them all a little hope. "Without Jett and her sword, the bond was broken, if she had been with us, it may have been a very different story. She was flaky at times but never a slouch, she out of all of us never let down her guard, she could sense a trap long before we got to it. No, if she had been with us, I know she would have alerted us." Iona gave a broad smile.

"Lord Rowan has much wisdom, for he is right, the bond of the swords was a huge protection, for they protected their mistress and the man who bore it. There was no coincidence in the fact that my father received the Sword of Truth first, and then passed it to Jett as he took up Destiny. All the swords fought to guide their masters to the aid of Destiny, and when they fought side by side they were never defeated."

The door opened and a group of young men walked in with trays of drinks, Iona turned to the gathering. "We shall break as we prepare, for we have a long day ahead and one more guest to arrive before we move to open the way for Jett's return." Chairs slid back and the talk began instantly, as everyone mingled and discussed what they had seen, Iona bent down and kissed Rowan on the cheek, as Jade watched and smiled.

Dawn was starting to draw a line of white on the horizon over the thick trees of Loxley, when Rune with Furry Face came along the old path at the side of her home. As she approached the side of the house and the start of her garden, she slowed her pace as she saw the line of white light edge the horizon, and glint off the still water of the Mere. This was her centre, the place she had rooted her life, and although she had stood here thousands of times alone, previously she had known that Robbie was just off somewhere attending to the village affairs of the woodland. Standing alone and staring down the long expanse of grass that led to the edge of the water, she knew he would never again walk out of the trees to meet her, it was hard and it hurt her so deeply, but she knew that she had to find the courage to live and the strength to fight.

Her hair was a bright fiery red as the sun rose up in the sky, and her eyes burned the brightest of blue as she stared out over the water, under her eyes small lines had drawn themselves, and Rune now looked as if she had aged. On her hand the sapphire ring gave a small glint, casting lines of blue into the trees, and she stirred from her thoughts and took a long deep breath. With one final moment alone in her woodland, she took a step forward, and walked round the white fence to the front of the house, where all through her garden the flowers lifted their heads and burst into bloom.

Rune slid open the large glass door and stepped into her home, Steph was asleep on the comfy chair, and the old figure of her great grandfather sat smiling at her from the long settee. She unfastened her long velvet cloak and hung it up on the rack next to the sage green cloak of Robbie's, and Hearne rose from his seat and walked slowly across the room towards her. "Come Daughter of Life, it is time to take back what has been stolen." He lifted his arm and carefully placed it in hers. "Your table is waiting to be awoken, cast off the veil and reveal yourself to the world again, and although I know of the pain you carry, hide it safe and cherish the love that binds it, for now is your time, you who have taken the rune stone of all into you. Fear not for this time your journey will be at my side, as will that of your mother."

Rune felt his arm on her shoulder and leaned onto it, taking comfort in the love he held for her, her voice was soft and thoughtful. "I am ready Grandfather, finally after all this time I understand my life and the circle I control." Hearne smiled.

"The lessons we learn are hard, but only now do you truly understand the gifts of life, for you have witnessed them all, and you have learned as you have given and lost them. Come and walk into the world again and start this world anew."

Steph opened her eyes and gave a slight yawn, seeing the old lord with Runestone she stood up and came round to her daughter. Rune smiled as Steph slid her arm around her and leaned against her, there was no need for words as both of them warmed each other with love. Rune linked her mother's arm. Hearne gave a small chuckle.

"It is time, you my precious flower, go to your table, and I think that your mother and myself will make for the kitchen, it will be a long day, and we shall require food of the wood to nourish us. When we have prepared our feast we shall join you, and then we shall gather and begin again."

CHAPTER SEVEN

THE FINAL GATHERING

As the day drew on it was clear that something was wrong. Morgan le Fey had felt the power surge, so had Raven Merle, and fearing the worst; the Dark One had made a speedy return to her castle deep inside the Hidden Realm, to find her assistant was encased in the glass box in a very deep sleep. Raven scoffed as she saw the assistant that she was not that keen on sleeping. "You should have left more protection, she is good at transcribing, but honestly do you really think she has the power to defend against the Violet Witch?"

The Dark One prowled round the box checking to see if there was any sign of weakness that Rune had used to escape. Her red malicious eyes looked through the glass at her young dark grandchild. "You doubt her abilities, let me tell you Raven, she has grown in immense power over the years, you see her as your lesser, but beware, as she has a very lethal bite when she uses it."

The pale face of Raven smirked as her dark eyes glinted through the glass. "Still, she was not up to it was she? Had I stayed maybe things would have been different." The Dark One walked round to her table to consult her books.

"You feel you are more worthy of the Flower Girl? Be careful my little Raven a fall of arrogance stings deeply." She turned from the glass box, her long dark hair whipping into the air with a snap.

"Well you should know, just how many times have you lost to her now?" The Dark One stiffened as she lifted a coloured powder in a small vial.

"Your ignorance of the Flower Girl is your weakness Raven, do not underestimate her talents, for we have sparred together many times, and you may find your lack of respect may be your undoing." Raven spun round to face her grandmother, her voice was calm, although it contained more than an air of offence.

"You lecture me on underestimating her, and yet your box is empty." The eyes of the Dark One flickered a deep dark red.

"Do not make snap judgements because you lack the gifts, you have no idea of her true powers, and should tread carefully when finding fault in the work of others." Raven stared defiantly at her grandmother, her voice rose a little, and her tone changed to more of an accusing one.

"I am not the one who lost her, I would have made sure there was greater protections, this will change everything at a point when we were about to strike the final blow. Have you any idea of the damage you have done by leaving her here in the hands of an amateur?"

The Dark One lifted a thin white hand with a long black fingernail and pointed it at Raven Merle, her eyes glowed with a dark sinister light, and Raven lifted her hands to her throat as her airway restricted. She gave a gasp for breath and gritted her teeth as her defiant eyes stared back at her grandmother, but she refused to yield as the Dark One lifted her hand, and Raven floated up off the floor her eyes widening and her face starting to redden. The Dark One sneered at her, her voice cold and obviously angered. "You forget your place little Raven, don't you ever judge me, for I have spent years in my craft and could easily swat you like an annoying fly. Your powers are strong, and it is true you have learned much for your short years, but never think you will gain the better of those who have studied longer and deeper, you have a long way to go before you will be a match for me, or the Flower Girl, do you understand?"

She flicked her finger, and Raven shot back through the air to the chair by the fire, where she fell into it gasping for air, and the spell ended. She filled her lungs with oxygen, as the Dark One scowled up the room at her. "Get your breath back and you can help me, there are things here you need to learn, fix your tone and we shall work together with no problems, come and see the cleverness of the Flower Girl, should you ever meet her this will serve as good understanding."

Raven breathed deeply as she rubbed her neck, a look of hatred in her eyes. The Dark One moved round the glass box muttering to herself, she looked up and gave a slight smile as she saw Raven move slowly down the room, a look of injured pride on her face, she lifted her head above the glass and looked over at her granddaughter.

"When we have freed my assistant, we shall prepare and go to the lines outside our little fairies camp, if your brother truly is dead, then we must help Victor regain the initiative, I am sure your will find it a very pleasant experience."

Rune walked down the stone steps and into the cool room below the house that housed her large stone table. The lights flickered and brightened the moment she entered and she gave a small smile as she felt the presence of her table within her. For over thirty years it had been dormant in Loxley, and the surface had faded to that of pure white, but deep within her it had been there as her companion connected to the rune stone and helping protect her. Her fingers touched the cool surface and violet flashes jumped up from the table, as she stroked it whilst she walked to her seat. She sat down and lifted her hands above the table, and a bright violet twenty pointed star rose through the whiteness with a large silver runic R in its centre.

Rune wasted no time as her hands quickly swept back and forth across the surface, and as her eyes began to shimmer with violet, she closed them and focused her mind.

"Hear me my daughter."

In the large fortress in Scotland, all the members of the gathering milled around talking of what they had seen. Chairs moved into small groups as they ate and drank, unaware of the Queen of the Fae, who remained close to her table and stood quite still with her eyes closed. Jade was talking when she felt a presence grow inside her, and she looked across the room to Iona stood by her table, her mind focused, and her eyes closed tight. The two small tears that fell and splashed on the table were enough to let Jade know that a mother was talking in private to her daughter, a daughter she had lost at just one month of age with her imprisonment. Jade gave a smile as she turned back to Rowan who she noticed was also watching Iona, she lifted her hand to his arm. "She is fine, leave her and all will be revealed in time, this moment is important."

Rowan looked down to her with a shrewd look on his face, and Jade gave a slightly embarrassed smile. "What is going on Jade Opal?" She knew that lying was not something she could do easily in front of him, but she winked and gave him a big grin.

"It's girlie stuff." He did not completely buy it as he looked at her trying to act innocent, something she had never truly been able to master, he looked back at Iona who had her head down looking into the images on the surface, and he gave a slight nod as he looked down at Jade.

"Why do I feel you are not being as honest as you could be?" She gave him another big smile and reached up and kissed him, he smiled back at her. "OK I will leave her alone with this so called girlie stuff, but somehow I am not sure I trust you at the moment."

Rune wiped her eyes as she talked to her daughter, on the table the pictures appeared and she could also see all of her family and friends, her table had connected with Iona's and the pictures of what had befallen appeared at the side of her daughter in Scotland. Rune watched feeling the pain of those who had suffered, especially Judith who was not just blinded, but also broken hearted at the loss of Robbie and also William.

Iona explained what had happened and what they intended to do, as she spoke through Rune's mind, her table leapt into action tracking everything that Iona told her, and she sat alone in her room below the house, the truth of everything was slowly revealed and Rune began to understand what was needed.

It was not long before Steph and the Green Lord came down the steps with food, which was something of silent amusement for Steph. The house was built for Rune and Robbie, and although Robbie had grown to be stocky like his father, Hearne was a considerable size larger. The large old man had to stoop, and almost go down on his knees to get his head under the doorway at the top of the steps. It was a task that was hard enough, but he was also trying to hold level a tray filled with a large jug and three tall glasses of clear pink liquid, and eventually as he made it intact, Steph who could not help but giggle suggested he sat while she returned for the rest of the food. The old man smiled at Rune.

"You know what is planned and have looked into your table for the answers?" He watched the images swirling on the surface of the table. His bright dark eyes watched her carefully, as he saw the ability, she had learned over the years left to sleep. "This will not be easy Daughter of Life, but we are gathered here as protection to the blue star. You understand that at first there may be no memory of these moments, but over time for you and your daughter and the blue star, it will slowly return? Even I will be blind to any additional events, and may never truly recount them."

Rune lifted her head and her blue eyes shone brightly from her pale white face. "I understand what may happen, but if we are to save the world you made, what other option do any of us have grandfather? I have seen in the table and I know the risks, but I am life gathered with the creator and the guardian, all of us must work together to ensure that we aid Sapphire in her destiny." He gave a gentle nod at her and she understood. "The doors will not close, Opal has assured it."

He gave a gentle smile. "My daughter has always been able to use her skills to outwit even me; she worked it out long before any of us did." He stared at Rune for a moment trying to work out what was in her mind. "You will not be able to stop it happening Runestone, the time it will take to fully understand will be too long. I know of the pain you feel, but we must focus on the task at hand, Sapphire is now our most important concern, for if she fails, all is lost."

Rune stared at him, although he was not sure if she truly was looking at him, it felt more like she was looking through him lost in her thoughts, her voice was soft and quiet. "I know." She looked down at the table and began to watch the meeting in Scotland, as the sound of Steph came back down the steps. Hearne thought for a moment as he watched the events of Sapphire and Opal in the glade of the Hidden Realm shortly before the Dark One sent her Darkmares to seal her in.

"I wonder?" He rose slowly from the table. "I must leave you for a moment." Steph looked at him surprised.

"But I thought we all had to stay together?" The old man of the woodland gave her a smile.

"I will not be long, fear not, I will return before the tea you brewed is cooled."

She watched as he turned and crouched down to walk up the steps, and as his footsteps disappeared, she turned back to Rune who was waving her hands, and pulling pictures up on to the surface of her table.

Outside Hearne moved swiftly into the trees, his long strides paced deep within the woodland in minutes, where he slowed and checked that all around was clear. With a deep voice he called into the woodland. "Come small child of the slumber pictures, for I have need of you."

The ferns gave a slight rustle, and two nervous bright eyes peered out from behind the serrated fronds. Hearne gave a wide smile and lifted his hand to gesture to the small child like creature; he lowered himself down closer to the floor. "Come, you have no fear of me, I am your protector and have urgent need of you." The timid little Sandling came out from behind the fern; he gave a very regal bow and his eyes blinked rapidly. Hearne gave a deep chuckle. "Is that so, I have to admit she is indeed my daughter, but you must not fear me simply for being her father, there are some who would say I am too soft." He chuckled as the little blue haired creature came closer to him. "Tell me my little guide to the blue star; what does your mistress call you?"

The small boy like creature gave a large blink and Hearne nodded. He slipped his hand into his pocket and took out a bright blue shimmering dragonfly. "Cal, this creature carries messages for many, especially those who have the gifts of sight, and need to act with great speed." It crawled onto his hand and gave a small flash of white light, and Cal blinked and stepped back. The dragonfly crystallised and Cal watched as it turned to sapphire and sparkled giving off splashes of blue all around them in the sunlight. Hearne held it out to Cal. "Take this to your mistress when you meet, she will recognise it and know what must be done."

Cal understood and took it; he placed it gently in his pocket and gave another bow. Hearne rose to his feet and bowed back to the small creature. Cal turned, and at great speed ran back into the deep fern. He gave a satisfied nod to himself and turned back on the path. "I have done all I can, may it be enough, for things will turn and the outcome will be determined by those who see further than any of us."

Releasing Ursula from her box had taken several hours. When she was finally dragged screaming in terror out of the box onto the floor, the Dark One understood the depths and skill Runestone had in her armoury of powers. Ursula trembled on the floor in front of her mistress, her mind filled with the vision of bright blue eyes that looked into her soul and terrified her. Raven scoffed as she walked back to the table to prepare to leave and her grandmother calmed her assistant back down.

Packing jars and items into her cloth bag, she looked at her grandmother. "Are we going yet?" The impatience of the Dark One showed as her red eyes lifted and stared at Raven. Raven just stood there looking bored. "What? I only asked."

Ursula was taken to her table and Tom was called and instructed to watch over her, and then the Dark One collected her own things, and together with Raven, they left to visit Victor and Nadia on the front lines outside the large stone fortress built and protected by Iona.

The reaction to the death of Lance Knox by Victor was not as many would have expected. On witnessing the scene of his adopted dead father's body surrounded by violet flowers, one might have thought he would show some sort of grief, but that was not to be. His main concern was for his mother, and after several minutes of looking at his father's body, which bore a white frightened grotesque face, he simply left the room and went upstairs to care for his mother. He ensured that the body was covered and hidden, before carrying her downstairs and straight out to a waiting car, where he placed her with her maids into the car and ordered the driver to head home. He assured his mother that he would be there as soon as possible, as he had to take care of his father. Weeping with a lace covered cloth to her face she waved as the car pulled away, and Victor turned to the two guards. "Get that mess cleaned up and tell the carpenter I need a casket of quality; I will be in the operations room when you have finished." With that he left and went about his duty.

To everyone it did seem very cold indeed, after all most of them had thought he was the warmest member of the family, especially compared to his father Lance. It looked like a strange scenario, but this was after all no ordinary family, and Victor was very astute and realised the moment he saw his father's body that he had a very big pair of shoes to fill, especially if he was to take command of all the war and replace his father and inherit everything.

Victor knew that it would not be long before Raven Merle arrived, and he was certain she would be looking to gain all, and he was on the edge of finally breaking down the defences of the fortress and taking all of the Fae and its lands for his own. It had meant to be the jewel in his father's crown, and he had no intention after all the hard work he had put into the fight in handing it over to his aunt. The large cannons were almost complete, and he gave the order to every smaller calibre cannon they had to pound the walls relentlessly, time for Victor was running out, and he had to crack the defence of the Fae before Raven arrived.

It had been a long day of watching images, talking in groups and waiting for the right moment. Inside the fortress as the final gathering prepared for Sapphire, the increased bombardment of their defences became very apparent. Dust fell from the ceiling as the floor vibrated, and Iona who was now stood at her table swiping her hands across its cool surface was starting to look very nervous. Rowan was on edge as he looked at the dust falling with each new thundering explosion outside, he talked quietly with Rafe and Halbert Thorn, as Yvee and Frayne listened. Jade felt his apprehension and walked quietly over to the group, where Rowan was talking of preparing his mobile attack units. Jade carefully took his wrist and pulled him to one side.

"You cannot leave here; Iona has forbidden it Rowan." He looked at her bright green eyes as she watched him carefully, he knew she was going to pull rank on him, but he felt torn in his loyalties.

"What?" He gave a long sigh. "What else should I do, wait here and let the roof fall in on all of us?"

"That will not happen Rowan, you know as well as I do that Iona will not let any of us be harmed, but if you go running off into the mountains, your chances of returning are zero. You worry more about me than Iona, don't think I will not do whatever I can to prevent you leaving, because I will, and you know what I mean when I say you will get a little more than big wifey bother Rowan." She smiled sweetly at him and he gave a frustrated sigh.

"This is not fair Jade, people's lives depend on me, I must do whatever I can to spare as many lives as possible."

"Good, I am happy to see we both agree, so sit back down and wait, because by being here and helping you will spare more lives than running off into the hills." Rowan scowled as Jade turned to see Rafe and Halbert watching her, she gave them a hard stare from under her long white fringe, Rafe turned to Halbert.

"Told you, come on it looks like we are here for the duration, sit down and don't piss her off, I have seen what she can do with that look, there are many Cutters who have not made it past her determination. I say we give them a chance and then if the walls fall, we make a run for it and gather the troops to defend the place."

Halbert who knew his aunts temper well decided to agree with Rafe, Frayne gave a nod as he looked back at his mother and agreed with them, Yvee tittered. Jade gave a happy smile and walked back over to the table where Rowan was now reseated waiting for the moment to begin.

As the afternoon faded into the evening, Hearne returned and Steph was brought up to date on what was happening, she too watched through Rune's table and saw all that was shown to the gathered group inside Iona's chamber. Rune finally stood up from her seat and lifted the rolled cloth off the floor. "We need to prepare the time is almost upon us."

Rune unrolled the fabric and took out the Swords of Courage and Justice; she walked round her table and placed them in their correct positions. She returned to her seat and lifted up the bright violet sceptre that they had recovered in Avalon, and had been claimed by the Dark One, and placed it into the centre of the table where it glowed on the deep violet star. Hearne smiled and nodded his head as he watched Rune work understanding, that she had learned more than he realised connected to her table. Rune sat back and took a deep breath; she was nervous and it showed slightly. Steph watched not exactly sure of what Rune was doing, but understanding the significance of it. "So, what do we do now sweetheart?"

"All we can do is wait, the time is coming and Iona will make her move when the moon is in the right quarter."

"But it is still light, how will she know?"

"Today is July 19th, it's exactly thirty years to the moment, from her table she can see the moon above her, when the moment arrives, we shall act to open the bridge." Rune looked at Hearne. "Is Cal prepared?"

The old man gave a chuckle and it echoed like a small brook passing through a cave. "Yes, he is ready; you amaze me at how observant you can be at times my sweet and fragrant flower." Rune gave a small smile; it was her first for some time.

"I am sorry grandfather, but it is now my task to see everything." Hearne sat back in the small seat and rested his hands on the edge of the table, small flashes of white and violet jumped out from the tips of his fingers and into the smooth surface.

"I think your moment is about to come, take the sword and get ready." Rune lifted the Sword of Destiny and stood up at the side of her table, on the floor below her a circle of shimmering violet appeared and she took a long deep breath and then said loud and clearly. "Hear me, for I am Runestone Sapphire, Daughter of Life returned unto you."

Iona called the gathering to order, and they all began to slowly return to their seats as they continued their conversations. They seated themselves but talked idly to each other in low tones, as outside the fortress shook, as the guns pounded down on them. Iona's table gave a mighty blast of violet light, which lit up the whole room, and Rune's voice boomed into the air.

Every member of the room stopped dead, and turned not quite believing what they saw or heard, as the violet figure of Rune rose up through the surface of Iona's table clutching the Sword of Destiny close to her chest. Jade's eyes filled with tears as Rowan's jaw dropped, he rose slowly to his feet as he watched her appear, he saw the sword and looked up noting the sad look on her face, and his eyes filled with tears of joy, pain and love for the woman who had meant so much to him as she stood at the side of his friend and brother. The rest of the gathering watched speechless as Rune looked at Rowan and smiled.

"Hello my old friend and kin, I am pleased to see you here, and happy you have made it so far. I am in your debt my dearest brother for all you have done to honour his name and care for his family." Rowan gave a gasp as his tears rolled down his face.

"He was my mentor and my teacher, how could I not continue the work of such a man of the highest honour, I loved him as I do you and the children you bore, I would have given my life freely to continue his, had I known of the perils he faced."

"Listen to me Rowan of Loxley, for I feel the pain that twists inside you, I feel the blame you carry around but you must let it go, for there is no hand here that has blame for the death of my dearest husband. The one responsible lies dead at the end of the valley, Lance Knox has faced me and paid the price of his dark deeds." There were gasps all around as the others all looked at Rune in shock, Rune gave a solemn nod as she looked round the gathered members, and she stopped at Halbert and smiled.

"How like him you have become, he would be so proud to see you as you stand here with your uncle defending his realm and supporting your sister. The mantle of Lord of Loxley is heavy, I know of the pressures and the weight your father carried, and you have done well My Son in his absence, rest your heart for soon we shall walk in green lands again and I will once again hold you in my arms."

Rune turned back to Iona as Halbert stood lost for words, fighting down the wave of emotions sweeping through him. She lifted destiny and passed it across to her daughter. "This is the mistress that they all serve; it is your task with Sapphire to unite them again." Iona lifted the sword from her mother's hands and slid it onto the table, so that the tips of the two swords already on it touched the blade, Rune turned back to the gathering who watched transfixed.

"Today I have retrieved two more of the five swords, it is now your task and duty to bring back the fifth and unite them with their mistress, for only when the five swords are united can we defeat the army of Knox. Good luck my loyal and faithful servants of the Green Lord, know that he sits at my side in Loxley with my mother Guardian to the Whitelines, we shall do all we can to aid you." Rune slowly began to sink into the table as Jade reached up and gently pulled Rowan's arm, he flopped into his seat lost for words as she smiled, and as Rune sunk back into the table, the room broke into a hum of conversations.

Iona walked slowly round and hugged her brother for several long minutes, and then she turned back to the table and clapped her hands. "It is time." The noise died away as they watched the two remaining swords rise up through the table and take their place. Up out of the centre of the table rose the bright violet sceptre of the king, and Iona gave a reassuring nod. "We have the four and their mistress, plus the sceptre to power our cause. Call for Lady Sapphire for now is her time to open her table and walk onto the bridge built for and used by Sequana."

Down the corridor, Sapphire sat alone in her small room finishing the bowl of hot stew. She had slept for most of the day, and feeling a little more refreshed she had eaten as she prepared for her long awaited task, which had been set as her destiny on the day of her birth. Sat at the small table set next to her bed, she could not help but notice the flashes of orange and violet as the shells of the dark army landed on the far side of the wall. Each flash stirred the butterflies in her stomach, and she understood that she could not fail in her task, as it would bring total destruction to everything she had known.

The wall again lit up with a bright flash, and she blinked as she reached for the cup of strong herbal tea, movement caught her eye and she suddenly felt a great warmth rise inside her. Sapphire turned and her eyes filled with tears, as the violet slender figure of Runestone stood smiling at her. "Hello sister of my table, I wanted to see you while you were still alone."

Sapphire stood up and Rune walked smiling into her arms and embraced her, Sapphire was so overwhelmed she could hardly talk. "Oh Rune... I have missed you so much, not a moment has passed that you were not in my thoughts; I have desperately wanted to see you and tell you how sorry I am for not being fast enough to save him. How will you ever forgive me?" The deep pain inside her surfaced as Rune squeezed her hard holding her as tightly as she could, as Sapphire released her deep painful bitter sobs of anguish.

"Saff, why do you blame yourself? Oh my poor sweet sister you were never to blame, how could you think such things, no one could have known that she had learned so much of our ways, you must not carry such a burden." Sapphire wept and Rune held her as she quietly talked to her.

"You have worked so hard and under such strain for all of us, caught as I was in her lair, I knew you would find me and come to my aid, you have shouldered too much for too long, and that is why I come here tonight, for I feel your fear and I want you to know that you will not be alone in the task, from my table I will be with you throughout it all."

Sapphire gave a big sniffle as she slid back from Rune's hold, Rune smiled as she wiped away the tears from her cheeks. "I am your centre, and together we shall finish the work he started, and turn around the fate of the realm he loved so dearly, for tonight my sweet sister, if we can achieve our goal, the tables will turn and all of the pain will be erased forever. Come now dry your eyes and we shall talk for a moment; the time will soon arrive for you to go to my daughter."

As the darkness moved closer in the evening sky, and the guns fired volley after volley at the unseen wall of Iona's defences, high up at the far end of the valley came a blood curdling scream. Morgan le Fey stood high up on the wooden platform and her rage thundered down the valley. Her face was white and twisted, and her eyes burned with deep red malice and hatred. At her side her youngest granddaughter and sister to Lance joined forces with her as the men below quaked with fear and fumbled as they loaded the cannons. On their own they were greatly feared for their cold evil, but together they had become a force of terror that went beyond the imagination of any of the soldiers. Explosions rocketed from the platform as they screamed in rage, and balls of red fire shot down the valley, impacting on the shield of Iona, creating massive explosions of bright light, and shaking the very earth on which the massive fortress had been built.

Gripped with fear, some of the soldiers of the Dragon and Raven hid or threw themselves to the floor, for the wrath that emitted from the two dark sorceress's was like nothing they had ever witnessed, as more fire and light erupted out of them and flew down the valley towards the tall stone fortress protected by the queen of Fae.

Up on the high walls of the fortress, the guards of the Fae held the wall to steady themselves, as the shield flashed with every colour, and the ground below them shook violently. Clinging as they did to the wall, not a word was spoken, but in the mind of every one of them, they knew the time was coming and soon the defences would fail, and the Violet Isle would face its darkest moment. If they could not hold back the sweeping tide of black clad soldiers, the last of the green realm would fall.

CHAPTER EIGHT

SHROUDED IN THE MIST

Not knowing what had happened to Una was something that concerned Iona, and it had weighed heavily on the mind of Sapphire for a long time. Sapphire's visit to Fagan had answered some of her questions, but even so, no one actually knew where she had gone after leaving Woody asleep in the cottage. Rune knew that if she was to fully understand the whole picture, then she must find out what had happened and why her grandfather had set Una the task and not that of her mother Stephanie, who was after all set to become the new guardian of the Whitelines. Even with the immense power of her table, the task of finding Una proved to be a very difficult one, as she pried into a realm that held many of the secrets of the Ruling Council.

The few days that had followed the departure of Fagan, for Una had been a mixture of fear and excitement. She had been very surprised as she rode slowly across the Whispering Dunes with Woody, as she had never expected to have found another who shared so many of her experiences or interests. Once he had managed to get over his nervousness, he begun to grow slowly in confidence, and feeling more at ease, Woody had opened up and shown the true depths to who he really was. The day long ride through the tall swaying grasses under the bright sunny sky had been very hot, but one of the most pleasant Una had experienced in quite a long time.

Deep down inside he was a kind and very gentle soul, but he was also surprisingly funny and was far more intelligent than Una had ever thought, his knowledge of folklore and plants was possibly one of the most informed she had ever known. After their arrival at the old cottage on the edge of the vast Shrouded Lake, for the following two days Una found herself becoming more and more captivated by him. Woody understood the difficulties that Una had faced coming out of the age of sleep into a world that was nothing like the one she had known. He completely understood the loneliness she had felt, as he too had grown up for a great deal of his life on the sides of the mountains tending his flock, with only his mother for company. He listened intently and answered her with well thought out answers and the more time she spent with him, the more she found his company appealing to her.

The night the mists came Una knew that she would soon have to leave, something in the air left her sensing the powers of the land, and she became nervous and a little afraid. In a moment of self doubt as she sat with Woody talking after their meal, he took her hand and squeezed it, telling her he would not leave her alone. The power she felt inside him, and the concern he showed in his sincere regard for her overwhelmed her, and she leant forward and kissed him. The surprise on his face was obvious, but the surprise of her own feelings was the biggest shock of all, not understanding how, Una felt a strong surge grow within her, and she knew that she was falling in love with him.

Waking the following morning on July 22nd held tightly in his arms made it much harder for her, as she felt the calling within her telling her it was time to leave. After dressing she walked out of the door and saw the black hooded figure waiting for her at the end of the jetty. Una walked slowly sensing the power of the visitor before her, she could feel nothing evil or dark, but the hidden tatty figure still filled her with fear. Her eyes flickered violet as she approached him. "Are you the guide sent by my grandfather?"

Her voice seemed to seep into the thick white mist that flowed across the water to the strange figure that awaited her, who gave her no response. Una slowed her pace unsure of what to do, she knew Woody was still sleeping and in the mist her voice felt dulled, and she was not sure he would hear if she called him. The hood twitched slightly and the voice below was dull and yet powerful. "Have you the staff?" Una gave a nod.

"It is safe within the cottage with my companion." The figure gave a gentle chuckle.

"You have no need to fear me Una of the White Circle, I am not your guide but I have an interest in ensuring your safe passage on the Shrouded Lake. This is a realm of great magic, and there are things within the mists that can lead the untrained astray. Go to your companion and give him my assurance that you will return safely, then take the staff you hold so tightly in your palm and it will guide us to the other side."

It startled her to realise that this strange dark robed figure was aware of the small staff concealed within her palm, her step faltered slightly as she stopped, and then looked back over her shoulder to the small cottage set back on the edge of the trees. The mists behind the figure swept back revealing the long white boat and he turned and stepped down into it. "You have but a few moments Una White Circle, take them and use them wisely, for you face a mighty task and will be some time before your return."

Her hesitation ended, and she turned and ran back up the jetty to the thin earthen path that led back to the cottage. Woody was still curled up fast asleep when she entered, and for a moment she stood and simply smiled as she saw the look of contented peace on his face. Not wanting to wake him, she took a sheet of paper off the cabinet, and scribbled a quick note thanking him for all he had done. For a moment she paused in thought and gave a glance back as he turned in his sleep, then with a nod of her head she turned and added a little more to the note promising him she would not desert him and would return, she gave a slightly embarrassed smile as she placed a small kiss after her name, and then quickly folded it and rested it on the desk.

Seeing the old book, she lifted it up and read again the passage scribbled inside the cover, which she knew was in her mother's hand. Una was starting to understand that her mother had left the book deliberately, so that there was a record of what she had done, and feeling a little nervous she lifted her bag and slipped the book inside, knowing that if she did not return, then Woody would take her things back to the others.

Her heart was beating a little faster as she turned in the doorway, and took one more last look at the quiet sleeping form of Woody, she felt torn and nervous, but this was a task set by her grandfather, and she knew that it must be important. Feeling the anticipation rise, Una left the cottage and took a deep breath as she walked down the jetty to the long white bobbing boat, where the hooded figure stood at the stern waiting. He gently waved his arm in a gesture for her to board and sit on the blue padded seat towards the front. "It will take some time to cross, make yourself comfortable and I would say try to relax and clear your mind, for you are about to see things no mortals from these realms have ever encountered."

Una stepped down into the boat still feeling unsure, she was not keen to sit with her back to this strange tattered and hooded figure, she looked back at him as she lowered herself into the seat. "Do you have a name? It appears you know mine; it would only seem polite for you to at least allow me the pleasure of knowing yours." He gave a slight nod and she thought he gave a small chuckle.

"Your mother referred to myself as Old Friend." Una sat back in the soft seat, her hand squeezing the small tear shaped gem hidden in the centre of her palm, as the boat rocked and then slid silently away from the jetty, and into the ever thickening mists.

"You and my mother knew each other then?" His voice seemed to echo slightly as the mist swirled in all around them, and Una was uncertain as to how he could navigate, as she could not even see the surface of the water it was so thick.

"I had many encounters and conversations with Gwendolyn White Circle, I did indeed call her friend, and in the time that we knew each other, we both gave each other good advice. You remind me greatly of her, as I have watched you grow from the small quiet child you were into the woman of talent that you have become. I will say I do miss her; she was indeed a powerful and intriguing woman."

Una noticed the softness in his voice as he spoke of her mother, it was obvious that he had been very fond of her, and yet knowing she carried her mother's power of perception she could feel no sense or presence radiate from him. "You are not of Fae, I would know." He gave a small giggle.

"As I said, you are very like her, and yes, I am not of Fae, but origins need not concern you for now, I need you to simply relax and try to clear your mind, from this point on it is your senses that will guide you onto the path of your destiny. Be at peace, drift on the lake as one with all that surrounds you." His voice carried a dreamy tone, and although she tried to resist, Una closed her eyes and felt her body lighten as she relaxed.

Rune's eyes faded back to normal as the violet flickered in her pupils, her face was pale and the flashes appeared brighter than normal, as she looked up at her mother and the old lord of the woodland as the pictures faded on the table. "So now both of you have seen everything, Una was taken into the mists of the Shrouded Lake as she began her task set by my grandfather." Steph looked puzzled.

"But that was thirty years ago, where is she now? Rune none of us have been able to contact her in all of the time she has been gone." The old lord gave a nod.

"None of you can, it is not called the Shrouded Lake for nothing. From the moment her feet left the dunes, it would have been impossible for anyone to see or feel her. That lake is a very special place created by three of us, it is the only part of all the realms where the White Lord gave a contribution, it is a place where time can do anything it wishes, and a place where you can work unseen, I find it is no coincidence that Fagan's mother decided to build a home there, it was a place that even the powerful Rhiannon would not have been able to look into. I must confess that if I had intended to build a bridge, then that would be the place I would build it."

"But why even build one? What purpose did it serve to Sequana, I mean come on let's face it, this bridge has done nothing to aid this realm." Steph looked at the old man sat at the large table of stone, and her confusion and frustration showed on her face. She could see that even now at this moment of desperation faced by the Green Realm, Hearne was still reluctant to give up all of his secrets. It was Rune who answered as she watched her grandfather.

"Until you take the staff as destined, the secrets of the Whitelines cannot be yours Mother. The time to reveal that will come, but for now it is to remain hidden, is that not so Grandfather?" Steph gave a long gasp of frustration and sat back in her seat.

"This is ridiculous all these secrets are the reason the world is in the hands of Knox, if everyone had just been a little more open, then just maybe things would have been different, it is like bloody government all over again and that's why the world of modern man failed. Everyone is so dammed bothered about protecting their own corner, and what is actually good for the masses is thrown right out the window." Hearne stretched his long bark like arm across the table, and took hold of Steph's; his eyes carried an air of sadness as they appealed to her.

"I am sorry my granddaughter, but you must understand that in some things I am bound by the oaths I swore. We set a path long ago that was based on what we saw in the future with our limited sight, and we have done all we can to aid the lives of men using the knowledge we gained. There are some things that were deemed too dangerous and powerful to be trusted to the lines of men, and they are hidden and protected, entrusted to only a few, and until your time comes, I cannot say more." He gently gave her hand a soft squeeze. "Even I have to answer to the White Lord."

"Fat lot of good that is for poor Una lost on some lake when we could really use the powers she holds of protection about now." Steph gave a long sigh and felt hopeless.

"Una is not alone." Both Hearne and Steph turned to look at Rune, who had her palms flat on the surface of the table and her eyes flickered with violet light. "I cannot see or sense Una in the mists, but I feel the White Lord is all around her."

Una woke with a start and jumped in her seat. It was dark and the boat bobbed slowly as the water lapped all around it, for a moment she was unsure of where she was. She had not meant to sleep, but from the moment she had settled back in the boat, she had felt an overwhelming feeling of calmness, and had slid into the soft padded seat and let her mind drift. She sat up as her mind cleared, and tried to see in the thick darkness just where exactly she was. All was quiet except for the dull sound of the water as she strained her eyes to try and see if her guide was still in the boat with her. "Hello... Are you still there?"

There was no response, and she felt a chill tingle as it ran down her spine, visibility was minimal and she could hardly see her wrists let alone anything else, the fear began to rise within her as she moved forward slightly and took hold of the side of the boat to steady herself, as it bobbed gently up and down. "Hello... Hello is there anyone there?"

The panic began to slip into her as she shivered in the seat of the boat, it was cold and the goose bumps rose quickly on her arms. She pulled at her cloak in the darkness and wrapped it tightly round her. No response came, only the lapping of the water against the edge of the boat, she tried her hardest to strain her eyes in the thick dark, hoping there would be some point somewhere that she could make out to give her a little hope. She twisted in her seat and slipped her hand across it to support herself, it touched something warm and she felt her hand naturally curl around it. Without understanding why, she gripped it hard and lifted it up, there was a burst of bright light, and the white mists that surrounded her snapped into view as she looked at the long old carven staff of her grandfather's, as the uppermost end burned with the brightest flame of pure white, she had ever seen.

The mist seemed to roll back as she moved the staff as if it was pushing it away, and Una could see that the boat was tied up at the side of a long stone ledge. It was the first of many steps that rose up into the darkness above her, but glad to see solid land; she quickly stood up and swayed as the boat rocked. "Where the hell am I now?"

Una stepped out of the boat, and took a step forward, she lifted the staff to light her way, more steps appeared and she began to walk slowly up them, carefully watching the path ahead. Either side of her the rocks were rough and glistened with specks like diamonds, the droplets of water from the heavy dampness of the thick mist sparkled. She picked up her pace staring forward as the mists pushed back with her approach, trying to define where the steps led, but they appeared to move ever upward in front of her, only revealing the ten before her. The sound of her soft shoes patting the damp stone was dull as if everything within the mist was insulated; it was almost as if her ears were partially covered.

Feeling tense and uncertain, she knew that she had no choice but to continue, and as much as she felt the nervousness of her situation, and being isolated away from Woody and the warmth of the sun, Una knew that there was no going back, even though everything about this place gave her the creeps, she had little choice but to follow the steps and see what her grandfather had planned for her. She gritted her teeth and tried to move as quickly as she could on the steep wet slightly slippery steps, not even aware that she was counting them in the back of her mind.

In the back of her mind the numbers rose. "440...441...442...443." She stopped breathing hard. There in front, she could see the last steps up, and then what looked like a long expanse of flat stone cut directly from the side of the rock face. She was uncertain, but in an odd way it looked very familiar to her. Una turned and looked back, but the steps below were hidden in the soft folds of the heavy white mist that swirled behind her, disturbed by the soft breeze of her own movement through it. "Oh thank Hearne for that... What is this place anyway?"

She slowly circled round holding the staff forward and as high as she could to try and see as much of it as possible, there was no way of working it out and she knew that moving forward was her only choice. Her stomach gave a loud whine and she smiled. "Don't suppose there is much chance of a friendly fire and hot stew up here, oh well no point standing around Una, come on girl, upwards and onwards."

She quickly took the last seven steps and walked onto the wide ledge of stone, and just ten strides in she began to understand where she was, as the high rock wall appeared onto which the light of her grandfather's staff illuminated the large bright golden doorway that marked the entrance to a sacred tomb.

Una stopped as the memory from her distant past flooded into her mind, where as a young teenager, she had been part of the party that had joined Rhiannon lying to rest her daughter Eleanor after she had been killed by the Dark One. The pictures of that sorrowful day swam through her mind at the sadness of the loss of one who was so fair and loved by all in the realm of Avalon. The thud of the heavy gold plated door echoed from the past into her mind, as she stood holding up the light, and staring at the intricate markings of the runes that protected her resting remains.

Una turned unsure of whether she should enter, and suddenly became aware as she looked back behind her that the mists had cleared. Looking back to the steps she could see they were still hidden, but she had risen above it, as it was now only waist high, and behind her for as far as she could see was the thick fluffy floor of cloud that shrouded her world below. The rest of the sky was a deep inky black, lit with the sparkles of millions of bright shining stars, and the huge close sphere of the white glowing moon. She felt it catch her breath, as she realised now where she was, and that she had been here before. Una had climbed to the highest peak in the Forest of Time, and she now stood at the top of what everyone knew to be the most sacred mountain of the Fae, which they all referred to as The White Steps.

From her previous visit as a young woman, she knew there was little above the tomb carved into the top of the mountain, as it housed the high beacon, which had been lit during the funeral of Eleanor. Standing looking in awe at the huge moon, she knew that what she was meant to do must be within the tomb, her only problem was that she was uncertain to how the tomb door would open, after all it was very sacred and kept well protected by Rhiannon herself.

Una turned and looked to the door, which stood twelve feet high, and eight feet wide, covered in gold plate it was not going to be easy to push open. "Don't suppose there is a key lying around?" She lifted the staff high and there came a resounding boom deep within the mountain top, with no sound at all, the huge door swung open sending even more goose bumps up her spine. "Ok that's freaky."

Una took a deep breath and slowly walked towards the doorway, out of the mist and so high up suddenly her shoes seemed really loud as they flopped on the stone floor, and they echoed back at her from inside the vast room beyond the door. For a moment she slowed lifting herself so as to tip toe and make less noise as she approached the door, and then she thought for a moment and gave a giggle. "What the hell am I doing? I am supposed to be here doing this, hell I have the staff of Merlin, what the hell is up with you Una, come on girl get a grip.... Great now I am talking to myself, hell Harry would have a field day if he was here."

Una gave a long deep breath, and then as quickly as she could, she marched into the open doorway and entered the tomb. Five steps inside, the huge door swung shut and as it hit the frame it gave a large chiming boom, and she jumped and screamed out in shock. Her heart was racing, and it took a few moments to calm herself under the bright white light of the staff before she could move. Having been here before she knew what to expect, and there in front of her was the clear crystal tomb that held the body of the young looking daughter of Rhiannon.

Even though it had been an age ago, through the heavy polished crystal, Una could see the delicate body preserved in all her beauty, lay on a bed of white silk as if sleeping. It stirred the memory deep within her, and she felt the anguish stir in her stomach with her sadness, as she approached closer to see the detail of her soft pale face and long golden hair. She had been a young woman when she had known Eleanor, and she had loved her as much as everyone, for she had been so filled with life and love that no one could possibly believe anyone would wish to harm her. Una felt her throat tighten as once again she looked down at her friend, seeing her there preserved as Una had known her, and remembering all the laughter they had enjoyed, and the many conversation they had shared. It brought back the pain, and her eyes filled with tears with the huge waved of emotion that swept over her. She placed her hand on the clear crystal and two tears dripped down onto it. "Oh Eleanor, I have missed you so much my friend."

"Such deep sentiment, and after so long, you honour your friend greatly." Una gave jump, squealed, and dropped her staff, and the lights went out throwing the whole room into a blanket of blackness.

Iona looked up from her table at the high walls, where the lights flashed brightly through the windows, with the deep heavy thundering of the masses of explosions going off outside. Everyone looked nervously round as the floor shook, and it was obvious that Victor was now firing everything he had at the fortress to try and finally breakdown the shield. Raven and her grandmother sensed the weakness in the shield, and filled with the rage of seeing Lance dead, they fired endless spells at the walls of the fortress, and for those sat round the large table bearing the golden tree set on a violet background, it was obvious that the queen of Fae was feeling the pressure, she looked down at the group and then across to Sapphire. "It is time and not a moment too soon."

Sapphire gave a nod and stepped forward as she took a long deep breath, she then placed her left hand onto the surface of Iona's table, and closing her eyes she focused on the bridge as Rune had told her too. Everyone in the room was silent and holding their breath, none of them knew quite what to expect, after all, this as far as anyone else knew had never been done outside of the Forest of Time, and no one had ever been present to actually state what would happen.

The floor shook with another huge volley of explosions, and many of them gripped their chairs to steady themselves. Sapphire was still with her eyes closed, she looked pale and ill, and her face was worn with an age of using all of her powers. Jade watched concerned for her, and hoping that this would be her final task as she was not entirely sure that Sapphire could handle much more.

Rowan watched Iona, like her mother, he knew that she would show the signs of connection first. His slate grey eyes fixed on her as she looked up for a moment almost aware of him, and his eyes met the slightly flickering violet of hers. He could see instantly it was taking everything she had to hold the defences and open the window for Sapphire, and as hard as she was fighting to hold on, Rowan could see she was afraid. Without thinking he quietly rose from his seat, and Jade looked up at him, she watched as she saw he was watching Iona with a fixed gaze unaware of anything else in the room. Nobody seemed to notice as he quietly stepped past Jade to the side of Iona, and leaning into her slightly he whispered. "Let the shield down, open the window, all hope is with Sapphire not us."

He gently slipped his hand on to hers on the table as she lifted her head and stared into his deep slate grey eyes. The violet swirled around them as he had seen in her mother's so many times, and he smiled and gave a gentle nod. Jade watched understanding the moment, and seeing the love Rowan held for the girl he had raised as his daughter, tears welled in Iona's eyes as she fought hard to hold everything together, but Rowan gently gave her a nod and smiled. "Open the window and return the sword, it is what your father would tell you to do."

The tears ran down Iona's cheek and she blinked. "I love you Uncle." His voice was soft and caring.

"I love you too my daughter."

The table gave a jolt, and thick white swirled into it, Rowan held her hand as her eyes filled with intense violet, and the whole room shook as a power from the start of time thundered into the table of Iona.

A gust of wind exploded into the room, everyone recoiled in their seats, as it blasted up out of the table, and funnelled into the tower, blowing out the huge glass windows above, and was sent funnelling into the star filled sky. The gathered members all shrunk down in their chairs holding on for dear life, as the power surged around the room and grew into a large white pulsating orb. Iona screamed out as the force blasted towards the orb and it turned a dark midnight black.

"NOBODY MOVE, SAPPHIRE NOW IS THE TIME; GO BECAUSE I CANNOT HOLD IT OPEN MUCH LONGER."

There was a flash of blue, and Jade who was sat with her eyes screwed up against the power of the wind blasting past her face, tried to see where Sapphire was, but she was gone and no longer holding the table. Everyone around her was fighting to stay seated as some of their chairs began to slide on the smooth stone floor. Rowan was holding on to Iona, who was lost in a bright cloud of intense purple light. Jade felt the earth move as a massive explosion went off outside the castle, the whole room tilted and pitched, and her chair slid slightly towards the huge black hole that had appeared to cut through everything and was now just a huge gaping void, in front of which Sapphire stood with her hair streaming past her face and flapping into the void. Holding her yellow bow and with her cloak flapping in front of her, she took one glance back and her eyes met with Jade's, she smiled as Iona screamed through the noise. "NOW!" And Sapphire turned and stepped into the void as everything in the room lifted into the air, and was dragged towards it.

The void instantly snapped shut and everyone on their seats crashed into the floor in a huge pile against the wall. Rowan's voice echoed round the room. "She has gone, put the shield back now."

"What the bloody hell are you doing sneaking about in the dark? You scared the living hell out of me." The tall black hooded figure offered a hand as he held the glowing staff up so Una could see, she snatched his hand and he pulled her up, where she stood panting and getting her breath back as the wave of sudden fear washed slowly away inside her leaving just her heart racing.

"Sorry...I just assumed you knew I was here."

"Why would I? I woke up alone in the boat and there was no sign of you, I assumed you had done your bit and left." She brushed the dust off her cloak, more as a way of deflecting her annoyance at being startled; she looked back up the figure who handed her the staff.

"Your path lies down those steps, and along the passage where you will walk into the valley. Follow the path until its end and your guide will meet you there, for my task here is now ended." For a reason she could not explain she felt surprised.

"You are leaving? Why is it you will not be my guide, after all you have come this far." The dark hooded figure stepped back.

"This is your task not mine; I have other things to attend to, and so I will say good luck Una of the White Circle, use well the gifts from your mother and you will pass back this way soon." He turned and walked towards the large door, which sensed his approach and swung open, as it did the light of the moon flooded in silhouetting him and making his robes look much darker.

"What if I ask, you to stay with me?" He turned in the doorway.

"Do not ask I have honoured my promise to your mother, and now I am required elsewhere, walk straight and true and use your mind to navigate with the staff."

Una watched as he stepped back and the large heavy door swung shut, it gave a large boom as it met with the frame, and she felt the shiver run down her spine, for a moment she had hoped she would have company, but as with all things connected to her grandfather, she knew that this was her task and it could not be shared with any other. She gave a long sigh and turned in the direction of the stairs, and the passage that would lead her through the top of the mountain and out on the other side. "Oh well no point hanging around, although you would have thought he would have brought along something to eat, especially considering I missed breakfast."

She lifted the staff and began heading down the steps carved out of the rock towards the tunnel, which looked very long and dark. "Might have known, why is it they never arrange these things out in a flowery meadow? Tunnels and passages in the dark, really they have no imagination at all."

CHAPTER NINE

THE BRIDGE OF INTENTION

The window snapped shut and Sapphire stood in total darkness, at her feet stood the small figure of Cal, who smiled as he looked at her and blinked a large blink. She crouched down to come face to face, feeling reassured that he was there. Inside her stomach was twisting with apprehension, and the thought of a task she was not entirely sure she would be able to do. "I am glad you are here, the thought of being here alone terrifies me." He looked around and everything was totally dark, and yet she could see Cal as clear as day. "OK this is weird."

The small Sandling took hold of her hand, and although very small, it felt warm in hers, and she felt a little courage flow into her. She gave him another large smile. "Here we go again, we have done some running around together in our time Cal...So...Have you any idea of what I do now, there doesn't seem to be anything at all to follow or guide us?"

Cal dug around in his pocket and pulled out the bright blue dragonfly that Hearne had given to him; he held it up and blinked several times. Sapphire understood and took the small jewel off him; she stood back up and looked down at him as she held out her palm with the blue dragonfly on it. "Ok so what now?"

Cal squeezed her hand and then blinked again and gave her a big smile, he slid round to her side and gave her hand another squeeze, and Sapphire closed her eyes and thought hard. "Hear me Grandfather of the Whiteline."

With her eyes closed she did not see the dragonfly as it glowed brightly in the darkness, Cal gave a tug at her hand, and she opened her eyes to see the dragonfly come to life and flap its wings and lift off from her hand. As it flew away in front of her, it left a fine golden thread which Sapphire grabbed as she looked down at Cal. "OK so far so good, what now?" He blinked. "Wait...what for?"

Suddenly the fine thread went taught, and with an almighty yank of her arm, Sapphire shot into the air, dragged along by the dragonfly at high speed. Cal who was as equally surprised blinked rapidly, and Sapphire gave a nod as she shut her eyes wishing now she had not eaten so much earlier. "I know.... Believe me I am not enjoying this either, just don't let go of me Cal."

The two of them shot through the darkness at an alarmingly high speed.

Sapphire held the thread as tightly as she could, terrified she would lose it and get lost in the darkness. Cal slid his free arm into her belt and squeezed as close as he could to her, and with her arm pulled close round him still holding on to his tiny hand, the two of them hurtled through space with stomach churning speed, and no idea of where they were going or where they would end up.

Holding Cal tight, Sapphire could not open her eyes, the momentum and motion were unbearable and she fought hard as her stomach retched and reeled, she moaned more to herself as she thought Cal must be feeling equally as retched. "OH Hearne this is horrible, I think if this goes on for much longer, I am going to be sick."

At the end of the passage Una stepped out into what she could only describe as a deep ravine. It was still very misty, but she could just make out the top of the high walls of pale grey stone. The pathway through it was ten feet wide and littered with large boulders and small stones, in which flowers and plants, of which a few she had never seen before grew out in a riot of blooms. The trees that lined the walls growing out of the cracks, were bent and twisted with thick gnarled trunks, and as she wandered along the fine path that wove its way round boulders, she felt herself enjoying the scene of rugged beauty.

The view towards the end of the ravine was obscured, and it was hard to try and make out how long it was, or where it would lead her. The silence was absolute, apart from the soft pat of her shoes on the stone dusty floor, and she found it a little unnerving. "Why no birds? There are flowers and trees; you think there would be something to nest here."

It was curious, and as she continued along the silent path, she noticed other things that did not seem to be right. The flowers were colourful and beautiful, and yet she could see no signs of pollen or anything an insect could devour, and there were no insects at all, never in her life had she not heard that familiar buzz of activity around so many flowering plants.

She came to a point where a huge boulder blocked out most of the ravine, and pressing tightly up against the rough wall, she barely made it as she squeezed past the boulder, and came huffing and puffing out of the other side. Gasping for breath she almost stopped breathing as she looked at the ravine and felt the gratitude of what confronted her. The Ravine was slightly narrower, and still littered with large boulders, but unlike the ravine behind her, the flowers were much sparser, and the areas in between them were filled with vines and sprawling trees adorned with every kind of fruit. "Oh thank Hearne, I am starving."

Quickly she hurried to the wall, where large succulent bunches of thick black grapes hung in abundance, she pulled it off, and slipped the fat juicy fruit into her mouth. The moment it touched her tongue she felt delight, as it squashed and exploded with juice on her parched tongue, and she chewed taking every possible pleasure from the moment.

"Oh that is good...I am so hungry and thirsty." She pulled a fat red orange off the tree at her side and without peeling it she bit a large round hole in it, and then sucked out the sweet juice quenching her thirst and feeling the sweet tang of the orange as it tingled her taste buds back to life. Una gathered up the fruit and filled her pockets, and then sat on a smaller boulder as she hungrily ate, it was like paradise, and she was spoilt for choice, as she looked at the range available. There were fat red apples, dates, plums, peaches and pears, and the floor was littered with bilberry and strawberries, that crept up to the walls lined with every type of grape she had ever seen. Her stomach felt like she had not eaten in years, and she sat happily and contentedly eating her fill.

Things felt clearer with a fuller stomach, and Una looked up the ravine to see if there was any sign yet of where it was leading her, she felt the feeling of dread slip over her as the thick mists seemed to be gathering in front, and in the already very silent ravine, she did not fancy walking almost blind as well. The white mist rolled down towards her, and she slipped off the rock and carefully began to walk along the path whilst she could still see it. It was not long before she was surrounded and could not see further than a few feet in front, where the dark shapes of the large boulders loomed out of the mist like grotesque threatening figures. Her ears strained for any sounds, but as on her arrival, everything seemed muffled and distant. Carefully she walked forward her arm slightly out stretched, as if feeling her way through the thick white blanket that engulfed her. "Oh I don't like this." She lifted the staff up higher, but even with the bright white flame burning above her; it was as if the mist absorbed the light coming out of it.

The sound of her soft shoes padding along on the floor gave a muffled echo off the walls, and it unnerved her as it sounded like others walking above her. Una felt the chill of dread as she moved slowly on and then suddenly, she stopped feeling startled, and froze as she strained to listen. "Was that whispering?"

Lost in a haze of bright violet, Iona fought with her powers to regain control of the shield. The truth was she was feeling exhausted as the opening of the portal for Sapphire had taken a massive amount of her strength, and now she fought with all her determination and failing strength, to try and repair the shield which was being bombarded with spells and massive bombs.

At the front of the fortress was chaos, as alarm bells rang out and men poured in from all over to fill the breached holes in the walls. Bodies lay strewn and bloodied, tossed from the walls by the massive explosions, covered and half buried in large pieces of masonry. Up the valley the Dark One screamed with delight as Raven Merle hurtled yet more fire balls down the valley at the smoking fortress, while the large guns that were now fully in operation, pounded the fortress, booming every second in a constant rain of shells.

Iona was almost bent right over her table as she summoned every part of her into the defence of her realm, Jade and Rowan were by her side as she fought, whilst the others collected themselves off the floor and lifted their chairs from the tangled mess, as the floor pitched and shook under the heavy pounding of the guns. Iona gasped as she fought. "I am losing it."

She fought with her mind, and closed her eyes as tears streamed into them, and she tried to fight down the panic that was growing inside her. Rowan felt helpless doing his best to encourage her, but she could barely hear him as she fought to pull the power of the Fae together. Jade bit her lip feeling helpless and unsure what to do, as Rowan looked to her for guidance, but she shook her head back at him.

"Rowan, I don't know what to do, she is holding on to Sapphire and it is draining her." He understood and it felt like a no win situation, she could not let Sapphire go adrift, but if she didn't the fortress would be destroyed with all of them in it. Jade gave a scream and Rowan looked to where her eyes were fixed in fear, the table had shaken and a fine crack had appeared on its surface. Panic flooded into Rowan, he had no idea of the powers of the circle and how they worked, the line gave a chink and ran another three inches and parted a little. He looked at Jade feeling her panic and desperation, and then moved round to her side.

"Rowan it's breaking what can we do?" He swallowed hard as he watched the crack run another inch.

"If it breaks, we lose everything including Sapphire." Without knowing why, he slammed up against the edge of the table and the split in the centre shrank. He felt a wave of hope and grabbed Jade by the sleeve and dragged her to the edge where he leaned against the table even harder. "Jade push... Help hold it together until we know Sapphire has made it."

Rowan looked across the room to the others, his eyes met with the bright blue of Halbert's and he yelled to him. "HELP YOUR SISTER, HOLD THE TABLE!" He instantly understood and began dragging the others together, and pushing them up to the edges of the large round table, Rowan gave a huge sigh and shouted at them. "LEAN AGAINST THE TABLE AND HELP HOLD IT OR WE ARE ALL FINISHED!"

They all understood and pushed with all their strength, their eyes fixed on the crack in the centre of the table, as the crack joined back and they held it together. Iona was lost in the brilliance of the violet light and Rowan could hear her breathing increasing as she fought to hold on. Fear coursed through him and he understood that she could not hold on much longer, in a final act of panic and desperation, as Jade forced her powers into holding the table, with her eyes now burning in a bright dazzling green, he slammed his hand down onto the cool table and screamed with all his might.

"RUNESTONE FOR THE LOVE OF HEARNE HELP HER, SHE IS YOUR DAUGHTER!" Rowan felt like electric had fired up his arm, and he yelled as he lifted into the air and shot backwards, crashing into the wall. Jade screamed as she saw him fly backwards, Rune's voice bellowed from somewhere inside the deep violet light.

"I AM WITH HER, DO NOT INTERFERE!" Jade turned away from the table to see if Rowan was all right, and the floor gave a massive lurch upward. The centre of the table fractured and the room filled with bright light. There was an ear splitting explosion, filled with the screams and yells of the others, light exploded upwards in a ball of purple fire, and then everything suddenly went dark.

Sapphire screamed as she was flung upside down and then twisted out of control. She clung to the fine thread in panic, as she was whipped and swung in every direction, her arm tightened on the small little Sandling, and she felt her insides twist and turn, the feeling of nausea filled her mouth and nostrils, and she clenched her eyes closed even tighter and tried to hold back the vomit rising to her throat, as her mind reeled out of control and she desperately fought to hold on. "Don't let me go Grandfather, oh please do not let go."

Her feet snapped up past her face and she somersaulted twisting violently round, her arms flung out her side, and she felt the tiny sweaty hand of the little Sandling slip. "No Cal." She opened her eyes and almost vomited as she looked to the small figure hanging on for dear life. Streaks of silver were hurtling past her, and her eyes lost focus as they streamed past her face. Pulling with all her might as she clenched her teeth, she dragged the little figure, which under the pressure of their travel made him feel like he weighed tonnes, back towards her. Panic shot through her as she finally got him back close to her and she locked her arm round him, clinging on for all she was worth. "You will not leave me Cal; I will not let you go."

Something slammed into her back and she screamed in pain, as her back burned as if every bone in her body had been broken. Her eyes danced with silver specks as she lay gasping and shaking with fear, but the momentum had stopped, and although it took several long moments to understand, it suddenly hit her, she had arrived, and without thinking she let go of Cal and rolled on to her side and was violently sick.

High up the valley on the wooden platform above the troops and cannons of the black army, Morgan le Fey stiffened and her arm slipped sideways towards her granddaughter. "Wait...something is wrong." Raven, who was for the first time in a very long time really enjoying herself, turned laughing towards her grandmother having just hurtled a ball of bright orange fire down the valley. She noticed the strange look on the pale white lined face and stopped laughing.

"What is it?" Morgan le Fey's head twitched from side to side as if she was sensing something that frightened her, she turned back to the fortress as a plume of violet exploded out of the tallest tower of the fortress, not quite understanding what was happening, although her grandmother seemed to be very aware.

"Leave now.... GO!" She flung Raven Merle backwards off the platform as her red eyes fixed on the bottom of the valley. There was a second flash of brilliant white, and then she saw it. A wave of white light flowed out from the front of the fortress, and everything in its path disintegrated and disappeared as it moved along the bottom of the valley, terror struck her heart as she saw everything being swallowed, as it picked up speed and headed towards them.

As if it was her greatest fear, she screamed with all her might and grabbed Raven Merle, as she jumped off the platform and a thick black cloud exploded in front of her. With a snap of her fingers, she was air borne, dragging her young granddaughter up with her and lifting as high as she could above the valley. Down below the soldiers saw the wave of light coming their way destroying everything in its path, and they turned screaming, dropping their weapons as they ran back to the head of the pass. The wave swept like water over everything taking the cannons, soldiers and Victor with it, and behind it there was nothing but thick empty black darkness.

Una twisted as she strained to hear the voices. "Hello... Who is that?" She moved forward a few feet listening intently, and as daft as she felt, she was sure she recognised it. It came again but it sounded louder. "You are married? How could you treat me this way? I loved you and I am having your child." Goosebumps ran up her arms, as her own voice echoed in her ears from her past, and the thoughts of the moment long ago seeped back into her mind. "Who is that...Why are you doing this? That is private and between just Kane and myself... You have no right to do this...Show yourself."

"Don't be a fool, you were never meant to conceive a child, I am married, how could you ever think we could be together, it was a moment of madness and never meant to last." Una felt the hurt rising inside her, as she hurried further forward to try and find out what was happening. "Kane is that you, why are you doing this, is it not bad enough that you hurt me before?" Her footsteps echoed as the voice grew louder as if she was running back towards her past, and tears filled her eyes at the thought that anyone could be so cruel. "Please stop this, that is my private life and you should not be sharing it with the rest of the world. Please I beg you don't do this to me."

"My God grow up child, this is not some tale of fancy, you have had your fun and you most certainly got your fair share of trinkets, I have a wife and my lands to administer. What did you honestly think I could leave her, a woman of land for you?" Una ran blindly down the path in the swirling mist, as her tears streamed and she felt her heart breaking again. "Oh Kane, please stop this, you have hurt me enough in this life."

She sobbed as she ran at high speed not seeing the rocks but skilfully dodging them. "Why are you doing this, will you never leave me and let me find happiness?" She twisted under a tree, and leapt over a group of small stones, as her feet echoed all around her in the thick fog, bouncing off the walls back at her. The voice changed and her heart tore into two.

"Mother... Mother where are you I need you?" Una screamed at the top of her voice as she ran. "Mac...Oh Mac where are you I am coming?" Her heart pounded in her ears with her wails of heartbreak, her tears clouded her vision, as they streaked down her cheeks, and she continued to run blindly into the thick mist up the ravine. Other voices joined in as Eleanor called out to her, and then her mother shouted to her and she had no idea what was happening, or even if they were real or just memories floating to the surface in her loneliness, lost to the world in the blanket of fog. "Una...Una run... Run to me Una my child, come to me and do not stop."

Una wailed louder as she yearned for her mother, who she missed so terribly and had given the life of her child to save. The voices in the mist shouted and yelled, and she could not bear to relive the pain of her past. "Oh Una my darling what have you done? Oh my sweet child no, no you should never have given the life that was meant to be your happiness, OH Una my darling why did you have to do that?" In her mind she saw the face of distress on her mother, and she wailed out in the mists. "Mother I am so sorry, but I had too... Can you not see I had to? How could I ever refuse you the life you needed to protect all of us, I had too, it was the only way, why can you not forgive me, I did it for the love we all hold for you, please you must forgive me."

Una fell to her knees and buried her face in her hands as she wept, never in her life of toil had she felt so broken hearted. "All I ever wanted was to save you; can you not see how much we loved you?" Her shoulders shook as she sobbed into her hands feeling every bit of the suffering and the pain she had endured, locked inside her for her entire life, and it felt like a curse that completely overwhelmed her to the point of her own destruction.

"Una...Una my child, hold up the staff and come to me. Una please you must not let this destroy you, come to me child, I am here waiting for you." Una lifted her head as her tears dripped onto the floor, through the haze of her tears and the mist, she could just make out a shadowy outline of a woman, she swallowed hard as she tried to force back the sobs. "Mother is that really you or just some nightmare to torment me further?"

"Una I am here, I cannot walk where you walk, come to me, I am here and I am waiting, hurry child." Una slowly rose to her feet uncertain as to what the truth really was, she could see the faint outline of the figure, but was this just another terrible dream? Was something else going to jump out at her, or taunt her into breakdown?

She lifted her father's staff and it burst back into flame; she had not even been aware that it had gone out. Nervously she began to walk staring at the pale figure in front of her, part of her living in hope, and part of her expecting some evil trick. The staff burned brighter as she watched the figure grow in size as she got closer, and then almost like slipping a curtain to one side, the mist vanished as she stepped out of it, and there was her mother with tear filled eyes wearing a wonderful smile, who snatched her into a loving embrace and held her tightly. "Oh my precious child, I knew you of all of them could do it, Oh Una my darling I have missed you so much."

Una felt like a small child in the arms of her mother, as she heard her soft voice and felt her warm embrace. She slipped her arms around her and pulled her close, just enjoying the moment and hoping it would last forever, as Gwendolyn whispered her words of love to her. "Your father will be so proud of you, there are few who pass through the Valley of Time, and cross the bridge of intention and not be driven into insanity. He was always so sure you were stronger than the others, and I do believe he was right. Now come precious daughter for there is much to do if we are to have a victory, Sapphire should be with your father soon, and truth is almost in place ready to return, take my hand and we shall wait for the stone that was written to turn back the pages, and bring about the reunion of the five swords."

CHAPTER TEN

ABRUPT DEPARTURES

The whole camp was in high spirits, and fires burned with cooking pots as happy faces sat covered in the blood and the dirt of battle, to talk with pride of their victory. Set back from the fires at the base of the rocks Jett sat alone not feeling particularly merry. Her sleeve was torn and she had the marks and scratches of a tough fight, and even though these strange happy people had welcomed her on the day of her arrival, and she had grown within their ranks proving she was without doubt a warrior of talents that amazed all she fought with, somehow after the long fight she did not feel too much like rejoicing.

The simple truth was she had remained within the group as payment for the welcome they had given her, she had arrived in a strange land amongst people who spoke a language she did not understand, and even though she had done her best to use sign language, and had actually picked up a few of their words, none of this had the ring of satisfaction that she had felt fighting side by side with her friends and family at home. She was a Specialist and felt a great loyalty to them, and as the strange group rejoiced across the wide camp, she had realised how much she loved that close circle that surrounded the Hooded Man.

Her dark eyes stared lost in thought from below her long black straight cut fringe, and the dancing flames of the large fire cast shadows that frolicked across her cheeks, as she thought of home, and fingered the butterfly shaped pendant round her neck through her unbuttoned black tunic. Pictures of Rafe laughing and joking crossed her thoughts, and for a moment she swallowed hard trying to hold back the wealth of loss she felt, she had missed him so much, and all she really wanted was to pull him close and hold him in her arms forever. She gave a long sad sigh as she remembered her life, and saw Robbie, and Rune's eyes, Jade laughing and Blades flying through the air like a cat, Bear collided with a huge mound of a man and laughed. Rune's eyes watched her, Maddy fired besides Crystal and flames and ice erupted everywhere, as Rune's eyes glared at her. She blinked not sure but was someone calling her? Her body stiffened as she slowly came out of her dream squeezing the pendant harder than she had realised, she shook her head for a moment as she tried to concentrate, and as she closed her eyes she suddenly felt a very familiar feeling, one she had not sensed since she had fallen at the bridge in Avalon, and found herself in the strange land of Maybeyan.

With almost reflex movement she was up on her feet with her eyes closed, as the image returned, it was, she could not believe it, it was faint and she could hardly hear the voice, but there was no doubt in her mind, those were Rune's eyes.

"Rune... Rune I am here can you feel me, Rune can you hear me?"

Even in her thoughts she sounded desperate, but there was no doubt at all, Rune was there and trying her hardest to connect with her, the joy surged up inside her as she leant on the large rock concentrating with all her might to try and keep the two bright blue eyes surrounded with lilac in her mind. She was sure that Rune could see her too, but she was just too faint to really understand what Rune was trying to tell her. With one last final effort she pushed at her mind to try and hold the connection, but she was tired and exhausted from a day of hard fighting, and she collapsed to her knees with a gasp at the base of the rock, and the connection was broken. "No... I don't want to be left here, Rune come back I need you to find me and take me home." She felt the tears in her eyes and pushed her face into the cold stone with a moan, as the hope that had flooded her body for that one long moment now ebbed away in despair.

Curled up and hidden behind the large stone, under her tattered and torn green cloak bearing the crest of a red lion, no one saw her as she released the distress and frustration, and as the night slowly drew on, she lifted herself back up, and walked slowly further away from the group and sat against the foot of a large tree, watching the others through the trees as they ate and drank and made merry, and again her thoughts drifted back to the group and her feeling of loneliness grew again.

For some time, she sat alone staring into space, her eyes slightly blurred from her stare, but as her mind came back to the present moment, she found herself blinking as she watched across the camp, and the strange figure that was walking amongst them completely unnoticed. Jett leaned forward and rubbed her eyes just to make sure, but it was not an illusion, there in the front of the entire group was a tallish figure robed in all black with a large hood pulled up over their face. Jett leaned back on the tree and slid upwards trying to stay in the shadows, as her hand slid slowly along her belt and gripped hold of the hilt of her sword.

The figure stopped as if sensing the air, and she felt her hand flex on the cool hilt, and she prepared to pull out the glowing blade of the Sword of Truth. Slowly the figure turned to face her, and she knew in an instant that she was its target. A feeling of cool calmness washed over her, as her eyes fixed on the figure as it began to walk in her direction. The figure walked almost as though on a leisurely walk, such was the confidence of the strides, and it bothered Jett a little as she naturally assumed that whatever it was that was coming her way meant trouble.

They came straight up the path and in through the parting in the trees directly in front of her, and thinking that this was to be the moment they would attack, rather than wait for the challenge, Jett pulled out the glowing blade and took her stance. The figure just simply walked straight up to her, and she raised the sword for the strike, the robe parted and an arm shot out five times faster than Jett, and sent Truth flying through the air. "Put that away for goodness sake; have you any idea how valuable it is?"

Jett stumbled for words as she looked at her sword shining brightly, planted firmly in the grass. "One would have thought Jett Amber that here you would be a little more welcoming of family." Her bottom lip dropped with shock as the figure raised his arm and cast back his long black hood.

"GRANDFATHER!" Jett launched herself into the air, and into his open arms and burst into tears. He gave a smile and pulled her close as she mumbled something quite inaudible into his chest.

"There now, come on, there is no need to cry, it has taken some time I can tell you, but I am here and you have nothing more to fear. Your family has missed you and they are somewhat eager to have you returned to them, I would also add that we have little time and if you wish to make your goodbyes, I would suggest that now may be a good time." He released her and she looked up at him with a bright smiling face as she wiped her eyes. "There we are, now that is the face I remember."

"Jember?" Jett gave a sniffle and smiled as she turned to face the very well dressed man in a suit, and wearing what could only be described as a very jaunty looking hat. Merlin turned with a smile.

"Ah, Jariden, just the man, I am afraid to say that I will be returning your prize fighter back home, we all knew this time would come, although I must confess it came somewhat slower than we expected, but never mind, Jett... Oh no hang on... Jember will be leaving with myself shortly, I believe any farewells would be welcome now." Jett looked up at her grandfather not understanding a single word of what he said, the fact he could speak their language fluently surprised her, but she was not entirely sure why, after all he was Merlin.

Jariden gave a nod and took a small step forward, he spoke, but he was so fast she could barely pick out the words that he was saying. He looked saddened, and Merlin smiled. "Oh how nice, such a great compliment."

Jett was about to ask what he had said, when Jariden put his hand in his pocket and lifted out a small wooden box and offered it to her, she was surprised and felt a little embarrassed, going away gifts was not something she had anticipated.

She nervously took it and went to open it, but he coughed and stepped forward touching her hand as if to not open it yet, she understood and smiled. Then without any warning at all he pulled her suddenly into a tight hug, Jett softened a little, understanding he had done so much to help her and care for her; she brought her arms round and gave a mighty squeeze. His use of her language was little, but he spoke slowly and softly as he embraced her.

"You have helped many here, we grateful and you will never forgotten, take care good friend." His words carried great weight, and she felt the pangs of separation build within her, for a moment she found it hard to speak, and she gave a gulp to push down the sudden emotion she felt.

"Thanks for everything; I could not have made it through without you. You have been a good friend Jariden stay safe. Say goodbye to everyone for me, I am not sure I could." It was all she could muster as they parted, and he smiled and she knew he understood, Merlin patted his shoulder and Jett turned and wiped her eyes whilst she lifted up her sword and dropped it into her scabbard. She lifted the patchwork bag she had bought at the market containing her things and turned back to the two men.

Merlin was shaking his hand and talking fast, and when he had finished Jett gave a small wave and with her grandfather at her side, she walked into the trees away from the camp, several yards away she turned and looked back, and he was standing watching her, she gave a smile and waved, and he lifted his arm in salute. Her throat and insides felt tight, somehow leaving felt very difficult, and she had not understood the bond that she had formed with them all. They too had become friends in her year alone in this strange place, and now saying goodbye was painful. Merlin looked down and smiled.

"Good friends always live in your heart Jett, it matters not that we are leaving, for the connection you have made here is strong, and it will never break, no matter how long you leave it until your return." She gave a long sad sigh.

"I know... It's so strange to be leaving... I really thought that I would find Ruby here, and although I didn't, I did find some very nice people. They will be very upset I did not say goodbye, but to be honest I am not sure I could have done. As much as I have grown fond of everyone I do not belong here, my place is at home with Rafe and the others." Merlin gave a smile as he reached out his arm and placed it on her shoulder.

"Life is a journey, with the wandering of paths and faces, you will meet many more as you travel, and with hope you will touch the lives of all you meet. Then when you leave, you will have the honour of being remembered for the things you have done, and you will honour them in the same manner. It is all we can do as we travel through life, and when your time comes, all those you have touched will remember you for it... Now home... Oh yes, I do believe it's this way, Sapphire poor girl will be getting nervous."

"Saff is here?"

"She is, although I have not actually met her yet, she arrived a short time ago at a spot I had prepared, and as we speak, I believe she is being watched over by a friend of mine. I was off on my search for you, but we have been communicating with our thoughts, and she will be guiding you to Una, as Sapphire has had somewhat of a busy day.”

“Cool it will be nice seeing them again.”

“It will indeed, right if I remember well, it will be down here near the lakeside.”

Gwendolyn took Una by the hand, and walked her round the rough rock wall of the high cliff, where there was a set of steps carved out of the stone. “The time is almost upon us... Come and take your place, and while we have the time we shall talk.” The carven steps rose steeply up the side of the high rock, and as Una walked up them, they wove round the side of the rock face revealing a massive drop that fell away into darkness, almost as if it was the very edge of the world, and she shuddered and moved closer to the wall, feeling a little uneasy, as there were no hand rails to prevent her falling.

“What is this place mother?” Gwendolyn was already walking at quite a brisk pace up in front of her.

“This is the very edge of the first realm, and what you are about to see is the point from where Hearne in the first days stood and watched the work he had created. Here he spoke with the White Lord, and between them they managed the kingdom of all realms for as you will soon see, there are far more realms than any have ever imagined.” Una looked up at the large wall above her as the steps wound their way slowly upward, taking them ever higher.

“This feels like the top of the world.” Gwendolyn gave a small titter and looked back smiling.

“I suppose my darling it is, for there are no other points I know of in this world that are higher, we will soon be at the summit, and you will see for yourself.”

Una was breathing heavily when she finally reached the top, and as she turned and looked out from the top of what was a huge drop, she gasped in awe. With her mother at her side, she stood so high up that everything below her faded into the darkness. The sky above her was filled with bright multi coloured shimmering clouds, which hid the planet like realms of many different forms of worlds and life. They spread for as far as her eyes could see in every direction, it was breath taking and she gasped with her amazement as her mother rested a hand on her shoulder.

“These are all of the other realms, and as you can see, there are more than any have ever realised. Your high lord Hearne and Eve were very creative in their time, and every one you see contains life in as many forms as you could possibly imagine.”

“Wow... How many are there?” Gwendolyn gave a laugh.

“I have no idea to be honest, there are so many and all so very complex, that even I have struggled to remember all of them. It is my task now as watcher of the lines to learn them all and ensure there is harmony across all of them, and to ensure their safety and survival.” Una turned away from the view to her mother as she stood looking out across the void.

"Is this the task you have chosen instead of moving into the other realm to rest, is this why none of us can contact you since you left?" There was a tone of sadness in Una's voice, and Gwendolyn turned and lifted a hand to her daughter's face.

"I am at peace and happy, but I do miss you all so much. Una my darling, a time will come when you too will have the choice to sit in the great house and rest, or be reborn into another life, and only then will you fully understand, but this for myself is an undertaking I chose, as in doing this I remain Gwendolyn the White Circle, and I am not reborn with the loss of the knowledge of those I love, for to move into another life and forget you and my other precious children was not a thing I could easily do. Even though we can no longer be together, I can stand here and watch over all of you." She slipped her hand into Una's. "Come we must prepare; I feel the time is coming."

"What exactly have I to do, because I really do not understand why father chose me for this task?" Gwendolyn walked Una across the flat top of the high mountain, to a large golden circle set within the surface of the floor. Around its edges set deep within the stone floor were carved many runes that Una could not read. The centre of the circle was a dusty red in colour, unlike the pale grey of the rest of the floor, inlaid in gold in its centre was a large rune that Una knew very well, for she had seen it many times on the surface of Rune's table. Gwendolyn noticed that Una was starting to understand the significance of what she was seeing, and as Una looked up at her, she smiled and nodded her head.

"Yes, my darling... here is the centre of all things and the passage of time. This is the centre of all circles, it is the Runestone. It is the most powerful physical object in this kingdom, and this is set deep within the core of the one we follow and love, Runestone Sapphire." Una was lost for words.

"But why am I here, surely this task should be for her, do they expect me to wield this?" Gwendolyn smiled.

"No my child, Rune will tap into this by connecting her essence to her table, for she is the only one with the power to wield it, your task is to use the power of your own core, and provide the power of protection to those who will walk from another realm set further away than these. It is no coincidence that you are born of the White Circle, for the White Circle is the symbol of knowledge and purity, of which you have an equal measure. You hold the gift of the power to protect, and never has that gift been needed more than at this time."

"Yes Mother... But... But Rune has the same gift, and in her it is far stronger than mine."

"It is, but she cannot do this task, for it was decided long ago that only one from the line of Fae could witness this event, and regardless of what Rune has achieved, she remains a descendent of the Green Circle, not white. Do you remember the poem your father taught you about circles and lines?"

"Of course I do, he made me say it at least a thousand times."

"Then stand in the centre of the runestone and recite it." Una looked a little puzzled, but she followed her mother's instruction, and felt a little silly having to say a poem from her childhood. She took a deep breath as she thought of the words; it was after all a very long time since she had said it.

"Time breaks all circles, stretch it out across all time." Gwendolyn chipped in.

"That is me, my circle is broken and I have passed on, leaving my gifts of the Whitelines to all of you." Una gave a nod, thinking it made some sort of sense, and then continued.

"Lay it down in the void, a broken circle, or a line."

"Louder Una, say it as loud as you can so all the worlds will hear it."

"Return to the blind, cross the boundary make it shine!"

"Yes.... Louder my angel let the White Lord himself hear you summon his powers."

"Build a bridge of intention; take the circle to the line!" Gwendolyn looked up to the sky.

"Hear me guardian of the Whitelines and know me as Wife, and this is your Daughter as we call to you." Gwendolyn leaned back and lifted her hands into the air, and as she drew her arms across the sky, the many other realms, which were glistening clouds of every colour, parted in the air and swept aside clearing a path. Una looked, and far off in the distance there appeared to be the tiniest blue flickering star.

"Behold my daughter, one of the twinned stars, across a span greater than any can travel from here, are a cluster of realms not created by our Lord of Green Realms, for they are the design of Erathome and Tideguyde. Long after this realm was created Tideguyde left to find Erathome, and when she joined him, she discovered he had started the creation of many other realms of his own, and it is the reason she never returned. Sequana discovered she had inherited some of the pure power of Tideguyde, for in the creation of the Fae of the moon some traces of the moon queen were left over, and it created a connection between them. Sequana with the help of the White Lord came here and created a bridge to make a passage that would connect to other realms, you used it to come from the Valley of Time to this place, it is known as the Bridge of Intention, or to most others as The Bridge of Sequana."

Una looked out across the darkness to the faint blue spec in disbelief. "So it is all true? For as long as I can remember people have talked of the bridge, but it has always been a myth. Tideguyde really did it? She found him and created another series of realms, it's like a whole other universe compared to ours, but why has it been so hidden?"

"It was hidden because that was the wish of Erathome, it appears he was jealous of the work of Hearne and Eve, and so he left to create something of his own, although it appears that Sequana found both of them, and after a great length of time, she was able to convince them to allow a passage from one universe to another, as long as it was governed with great responsibility, hence here I stand on watch to ensure that the bridge is not exploited.”

“But who will I be protecting, surely if the bridge can be used, it must protect those who use it.” Gwendolyn gave a nod.

“It does, but there is one who did not take the bridge to get over there, and the rules of the bridge demand that only those who pass along it, can return by the same means. The Sword of Truth was cast across the void by mistake, and in doing so it has caused great damage to the realms, as it is a very powerful object that belongs on this side of the void. While it resides over there, the remaining swords will be out of balance and it will work to the disadvantage of those who carry them, you must protect the sword so it can return, and the balance between both separate universe’s be restored. Sapphire will guide the sword to the other end, it will then travel back to here under your protection, it is why your father’s staff has been loaned to you, for he used the bridge to leave this realm, and he has given his return journey to Jett, and alas he will never be able to come back to this side again. His power will find the staff; it contains a great deal of the power of the Whitelines and will greatly enhance your abilities to connect to him so far away.”

Una felt the surprise grow inside her. “Jett is all the way across there, no wonder we could not trace her.” Gwendolyn looked worried.

“We must get her back soon, because although she feels no different, the power that sword contains may place her in great danger. The time is coming so we must prepare, for I sense Sapphire and she is close to meeting with Jett, come Una, the time is almost here and we must be ready at a moment’s notice.”

Jett stopped on the grass and stared at Sapphire. “Wow Saff what the hell happened to you? No offence girl, but you look older than Jess.” Sapphire smiled as she walked forward and hugged her.

“I worried about you a lot; see the grey hair you have caused me. It’s a long story and we do not really have the time; I will tell you later.” Merlin gave a soft chuckle as he watched the two embrace.

“Although there is one more task which I do feel requires some attention before parting.” Jett turned back with a large grin on her face.

“What do we need to do?” Merlin turned and pointed to the trees, which grew fifty times taller and wider than anything Jett had seen in Loxley.

“We have some goodbyes before we leave.” From behind one of the wide trees a small figure appeared and Merlin gave a regal bow, Sapphire and Jett noted it and did likewise. “I would like you to meet Tula, she holds the balance of power here, and has for many thousands of years, and as guests to her realm, I believe thanks and pleasantries should be observed. Tula has followed your progress here Jett, and she has given you a great deal of protection, you must speak with her and thank her for the care the people of this realm have shown to you."

It made sense to Jett, and she turned and walked slowly across to the slender figure, who had now climbed onto a branch several feet from the floor and sat swinging her legs playfully watching Jett approach her. Tula was very slender and almost twig like in her stature, her hair was as white as snow with brownish black tips, that seemed to create an appearance of being almost like birch bark, as the stripes created even patches around the long flow that draped off her shoulders and down past the branch she sat on.

As Jett came closer, she gave a happy little giggle and smiled, her eyes were as bright as polished turquoise, and they contained a great deal of wisdom and the spirit of life. Jett came to a halt a few feet in front of her and gave her a short bow; Tula giggled and spoke with a voice that was gentle and filled with joy. "I am pleased to finally meet you in person Jember of Maybeyan, and Jett Amber of your own world, I have watched much of your time here with a keen interest, for you are unlike any that have passed this way in the past."

Tula had a familiar air to her, which reminded Jett very much of Rune and her sister. From the bits she had picked up from Jariden over her time, she understood that Tula was known as a forest spirit of great power, and standing there before her feeling the warmth radiate from within her, Jett could understand why Jariden spoke of her with such warmth and affection. "I am pleased to finally meet you, I have heard many things about you, and I am glad of the chance to meet and offer you my thanks, for I am aware that it was you who asked the others to take care of me."

Tula gave a nod, it was clear that Jett had learned more and understood more of the language than she had let on, and she gave a playful giggle, as she delicately slipped off the branch, and dropped her feet to the floor. The gentle disturbance of the forest spirit created a slight breeze, and from behind her a host of dragonflies of every colour buzzed into the air and flew about her head, before seeking out more fine twigs and branches to settle on in the warmth of the sunlight. Tula came forward, her eyes fixed on Jett as she took in every detail of her appearance. "You look battle worn and weary, I have heard of your valour in aid of the people loyal to Princess Aurora. We are very grateful and offer you our heartfelt thanks, for all you have done to aid their fight, but I cannot lie to you when I tell you, that I will breathe easier knowing you have returned to your own world."

Jett felt the jolt of surprise hit her as the comment stung. "Was I not a welcome visitor?" Tula gave a soft smile.

"You misunderstand me, I meant no offence and you were very welcome, but I fear you carry a jewel of great power, and since its arrival it has shifted the balance against our favour. Knowing it has returned will bring a more even level to both this and your own world." Jett looked down at the hilt of her sword, she did not understand how a sword that fights for the truth could change the balance of any world, in her mind it could only do good as it fought to uncover the truth, and combat the likes and deceit of others. Tula watched understanding her feelings.

"This is a sword of power, a power from another world, I understand it is a sword meant to reveal truth, and in your world that is exactly what it will do. In this world it will work as it should for some time, but eventually because it is not of this place, it will work against itself and undo much of what it has done. I understood this from the moment of your arrival, as I have felt its intentions matched with yours, but believe me my friend, the day is not far away now when its power will tip the scales, and then all you have achieved will unravel, it is a good thing that you take it from this place now and preserve all of your deeds as the hero you have become to many." Jett could see what was meant and she shook her head.

"I had no idea, although I did not know that I would end up here." Tula lifted her hand to the hilt of Jett's sword.

"The sword was wounded quite badly; I believe the blade has a similar appearance to the one who wields it?" She gave a giggle as she pulled it gently, and even though Jett knew she was of no threat, she still felt apprehensive and her hand instinctively went to grip the hilt. Tula gave a slight giggle. "Have no fear, I am no threat to you, I sense the value you place in keeping this sword at its finest, I feel it only right to reward this sword for all it has accomplished by adding the final touch to its healing."

Slowly Jett drew her hand away from the hilt, and Tula gently lifted the sword out of its scabbard. Rainbows danced across her face as she smiled, seeing the intricate designs of all the leaves of the trees engraved into the blade. Jett looked at the long black scorch that marked over a third of the blades edge, she had tried several times using every type of cleaning method, and yet it was unchanged from the moment it had impacted on the Star of the Merle. "It was touched by pure evil; I have tried everything but nothing seems to remove it."

Tula gave a gentle chuckle, her bright blue eyes danced with impish delight as she turned the sword over in her hands. "It needs a great deal of love and a touch from the natural world that created it, I think a little of this may be just the tonic it needs."

Tula gazed lovingly at the blade, and whispering words of kindness, she slowly rubbed the edge of the blade with the tips of her long thin fingers. All around her a faint bluish green aura appeared, and shone down on the blade as she spoke very calmly and quietly to the sword, Jett gasped in awe as she saw that the thick black smear began to glow with the same kind of light, and then faded away and returned to the bright shining metal it had once been. Jett gave an audible gasp of amazement.

"I cannot believe you have done it, honestly I thought it would last forever." Tula smiled and handed the sword back.

"Love and the power of the land can do many things, it can repair everything and bring things together, even when the distance is further than any could imagine. You hold a great deal of love within you Jett Amber, whether you fully understand its true power I am not sure, but I will say that what I have seen stored within you gives me great joy, and I truly do understand why you were brought here instead of being cast into the void where the darkness truly intended you to go."

Jett's dark eyes stared for a moment unsure of what Tula truly meant. Tula just smiled and handed her the Sword of Truth back. "The time approaches Jett Amber, you will soon have to depart this world and return to your own, our time here is almost over, and although I am very aware that you may have many questions about your time here, I would say that the time to answer all has passed, we have just a short time left, is there anything else I can help you with to repay the debt we all feel we owe you?"

Jett slipped the sword back and thought for a moment, below her cool exterior her mind raced and heart pounded, for there had been one question she had wanted answered since her arrival, but she was not sure if it was right to ask. Tula sensed the building pressure and smiled at her. "You may ask me without fear."

Jett shuffled her feet as she thought of how she could phrase it and get the most direct answer, it was impossible to hold herself back and she suddenly blurted out. "I felt my sister as I came here, did she bring me here? Is she here?"

Tula lifted an arm and touched her shoulder softly. "I see the hole within you caused by your unresolved questions about your sister, and I would say let go of it and free yourself from the pain you hold so deep down inside. Does it really matter that your sister has passed on to another place and way of being? Jett you must accept that her destiny was to part from your side and move on to bigger things, she had to leave your side so that you could become the person that your destiny has preordained for you to become." Tears welled in Jett's eyes.

"I just need to know she is safe and not alone, I never had the chance to say goodbye and tell her how much I really loved her. I don't think you can understand the bond we shared for years alone. I promised her that I would never let her be alone again, and now I am frightened that I have let her down and she is somewhere else alone and afraid." Tula slipped her arms around her and pulled her close, as Jett wept onto her shoulder.

"You cannot carry this burden my valiant warrior, you must let it out, and let go of all the pain you feel." Tula turned her head and quietly whispered to her.

"Your sister travelled across the Bridge of Intention with a trusted guide, and you are right in your instincts because they are very strong. She did reach this land, Jett your sister was reborn into another being, and although there may be some similar attributes in the person she became, she is no longer the frightened half blind girl that you knew. The rules of the worlds we both live within prevent her from revealing herself, this you know is the law of all worlds, and she chose to take on the role she now holds, and does it with happiness and great companionship. Trust me when I tell you with all my heart that she is happy and content, and will never feel the pain of being alone here within the realm of Maybeyan. Go home in peace, for although she has moved into another phase of her life, she will always have the love you gave her, for as I have already told you Jett, the power of the love we hold never truly fades away. She knew throughout her whole life how deeply you loved her, for that was with her in her final moment, and it eased her passage from one world to another, trust me in this for I know it to be true."

Tula gave her a soft kiss on her head, and released her from her arms. "Time has passed, you must return to your guides for the moment to return is upon you. Dry your eyes and leave here with a full and happy heart my dear friend." Jett gave a huge sniffle and wiped her red eyes.

"I am sorry I never meant to cry like this."

"Never apologise for feeling a pure emotion, go with the blessings of this land and with peace in your heart Jett Amber."

"Thanks Tula."

"It's my honour." Jett gave a weak smile and turned to walk away; Tula lifted a hand and wiped the tear that had stroked down her own cheek, as she watched Jett walk back across the grass. Jett stopped and looked back at her for a moment.

"Did I meet her?" Tula smiled.

"Yes, you did, it was brief, but you met and spoke." Jett smiled and gave a nod.

"Then I achieved what I came here to do." Tula gave a happy nod.

"Yes, you did, against all the odds and the rules of both our councils you did indeed do it, go home and be happy for you have accomplished something no one else has ever done." Jett smiled enjoying the thought.

"My sister expected nothing less."

"I believe you are right." Jett gave a happy chuckle, and turned back to Sapphire and Merlin who waited patiently for her to return. Tula watched until they were all together and then as they all spoke, she quietly slipped unnoticed back into the green of the trees and waited a moment longer out of sight. "Goodbye sister, I love you too, and I will be with you in the sword you carry forever more." She quietly whispered to herself.

Steph felt a little panic as she watched all the different pictures on Rune's table. The fortress seemed to have disappeared with all of the soldiers into a thick blackness, and Sapphire looked blurred and hardly visible. Below the feet of Una stood alone in the circle at the top of the highest peak of the First Realm, the dull red circle marked with the large rune had begun to glow and pulsate. Steph looked to her daughter, but Rune was no longer visible in the brightness of violet light that burned brightly all around her, the panic and fear were building inside her as she swallowed at the dryness in her throat and spoke in alarm. "What is going on? Why is it black at Iona, what has happened to them all? And why is Sapphire so blurred, I can hardly understand a word she is saying?"

She felt the long smooth fingers of her grandfather as he reached across the table and took her hand. "Be brave my dear Granddaughter, for tonight you are witnessing the true and full power of your daughter, for she is life and the stone all has been written on, and as the centre of all circles, tonight she is righting the wrongs of the past."

Steph felt a cold tingle run down her spine. "Wrongs of the past, what do you mean?"

"Watch and be strong, for there will be a moment when you will require all of the strength you possess." Her neck snapped round to look back at the bright light that was her daughter, and as she turned to see her, the old lord gripped her hand tighter, and Steph felt the scream rise in her throat as the light around Rune intensified and exploded out of her swallowing the whole room.

Gwendolyn screamed from her place on the edge of the rock wall. "Now Una...Focus everything you have on your father!" Una screwed up her eyes and she felt the long staff, which she held tight in the centre of the circle vibrate. Her thoughts focused, and she gave every part of her mind to the love and pictures of the man that had been there for her all her life. Gwendolyn saw the flash of white light, and then watched as a long line of the purest white streamed out of the top of the staff, and like a rope lashing through the air, it shot out across the top of the cliff, and hurtled up into the sky above, like a long uncoiling rope.

Una shook as she held on as tightly as she could to the staff, and across the vast void of darkness Merlin stood with his eyes closed above Sapphire, as she sat on the ground within a large circle of white, edged in violet with a large blue five pointed star in its centre. Jett watched fascinated as light streamed out from under the closed eyes of Sapphire, and bounced across her cheeks, the clouds rolled into the sky above her, cutting off the sun and casting the whole of the lake and the woodland around her into darkness. Jett gripped the hilt of her sword and the patched cloth bag, as she waited for the sign that her grandfather had told her to make her move on, and she felt excited and nervous at the thought of returning back home across the space to Rafe and the others.

Sapphire leaned back and opened her eyes; Jett jumped back in surprise as a burst of deep blue light erupted out of her, and shot straight up into the sky. "Whoa girl you've really been practicing." She looked up and saw where the light penetrated the clouds cutting a wide clear hole straight through into the empty blackness beyond them. Merlin spoke in a loud voice.

"Focus Sapphire, I feel it is coming." Jett watched amazed, as high above her she saw a streak of white light shoot across the sky like a shooting star. "You missed it!" Merlin roared, as Jett watched the light bend and head back towards the tall column of blue shooting higher as Sapphire pushed her mind to its limits.

Gwendolyn screamed across the rock as she saw the blue line thousands of miles away bend and twist as it tried to snare the light emitting from the staff of Merlin. "Una concentrate, you missed it and we have so little time, for the love of Hearne think of your father and all that he means to you."

Una shook even more violently as she tried to focus on her father, as her legs and feet shook on the floor, which was growing hotter beneath her thin cloth shoes. She took a long deep breath, and then with everything she could muster she screamed inside her head.

"FATHER HEAR ME PLEASE!!!"

"YOU GOT IT!" Jett screamed, as she jumped in the air and saw the white light hit the blue, and spiral round it as it came falling in a rapidly descending swirl round Sapphire's blue light. The excitement exploded inside her as she suddenly felt the rough hand snatch her, pulling her sideways and her grandfather's rough voice echoed in her ears.

"Stop fooling around and pay attention, we have but a few seconds to do this." He shook her as he spoke roughly, and the smile fell from her face as she saw the hard serious stare in his eyes. "Jett this has never been done before so pay attention, grip your sword and no matter what happens do not let go of it. Hold onto it with your life." She barely had time to say the words.

"What do you mean it's never been done before?" When the white light came flashing down, Merlin pushed his fingers on to her eyes to close them, he pressed hard into them, and Jett saw an explosion of white light inside her head, and with a tremendous jerk she was dragged backwards.

"I love you Jett Amber, hold onto the sword." His voice trailed away as she felt herself suddenly shoot violently upwards and backwards. Her head swam, and her stomach twisted and pulsated violently, and she felt the vomit rush up into her throat. It was so fast she had barely the time to swallow or breathe, and fear filled her, as she understood the peril, she was probably in.

Her whole body shook like she was being pummelled, and she tried as hard as she could to grip on and hold the sword with all her might, but it felt impossible to move any part of her arms. Fear swept through her and she wanted to open her eyes, but was too terrified to chance it and see what was actually happening to her, and her head continued to swirl with bright spots from the intenseness of the white light.

She lost all track of the moment and time, it may have been only a few seconds or it could have been hours, she no longer knew as fear engulfed her, all she could do was concentrate on her arm and try to understand what was happening to make sure that her arms were not moving. It was like a long bad dream, and she no longer knew if she was conscious or blacked out, for a moment she felt like she had lost all control, as if this was her last moments of life, and a deep strong calmness washed through her and she felt like she might have relaxed, but such was the fear that she tried to make herself rigid again, and jerked violently so she did not lose the sword.

Somewhere deep within her terror a faint voice seemed to speak to her, at first it was hardly audible, but as she tried to focus on it, the voice grew stronger. "Jett... Jett... Jett for the love of Hearne you have to let go you are killing me."

It took a few moments for her to fully recognise and understand what was being said. "Oh Jett please you are safe now... let go or you will crush me."

Jett and Una lay on the floor, Jett had her arms squeezed rigid around Una, and she was slowly suffocating the life out of her. Gwendolyn pulled on Jett's arms with all her might, but it was to no avail as Jett clamped on tight, filled with the terror of letting go of her sword. Gwendolyn slipped and fell backwards out of the circle as Jett's eyes snapped open in terror, and looked right into the bright deep violet eyes of Una. Una spoke through gritted teeth in obvious pain and feeling her last breath running out of her.

"Jett sweetheart it's fine you are safe... please Jett open your arms or you will kill me." Una tried to draw in one last gasping breath, as Jett realised what was happening, and suddenly unclamped her arms and jumped back away from Una. Una rolled over and gave a long drawn gasp as she sucked the air back into her lungs. Jett sat bolt upright on the floor shaking violently as she quickly looked round and realised, she was no longer in Maybeyan. Her breathing was rapid as her heart pounded, and her eyes focused on Gwendolyn and she knelt down in front of her and smiled.

"It's alright Jett, you are back where you belong and you are safe." She could not speak as her whole body shook, and she just gave a nod to acknowledge she understood. Gwendolyn smiled and moved towards Una, who coughed and retched as she regained the vital air to her body. Jett just looked round in a trance as she waited for the fear to abate and her body to return to normal

Una sat up and tried to compose herself, as she took another deep long breath and regulated her breathing, she looked at the shocked white face of Jett and smiled. "Welcome home, we have missed you."

CHAPTER ELEVEN

SECOND TIME AROUND

Merlin looked at the tired worn eyes of Sapphire as he cupped her face with his hand in love. "You have done so much, and I see the strain it has put on you, are you sure you want to do this?" She gave a weak smile.

"I have spent thirty years planning and preparing, Rune will be with me for a little while, so I will be fine." He could not help but feel worried, she looked utterly spent and he could already see that more of her hair had turned white with the strain of sending Jett back.

"You have your grandmother's spirit, but it is not worth killing yourself Sapphire."

"I would rather I died than them, this is the only way to save them, and so I must try." He understood, and he also knew of the difficult choices that everyone had made in their attempts to free the world from the tyranny of the Knox line. He gave a gentle nod and then pulled her close and hugged her with great love.

"There are no guarantees this will work, but I will watch over you for as long as I can and protect you from here. Just do the best that you can, and no one could ever ask more of you." He released her from his embrace and smiled at her. "You know what to do?"

Sapphire gave a smile. "I am ready." She slipped her hand into her pocket and pulled out the blue dragonfly, Merlin lifted the bag and her bow, and helped slide them on to her shoulder, he took three paces backwards, and behind Sapphire, a bright blue orb of pulsating light opened up in the air. The small figure of Cal stepped out of the light, and took Sapphire's hand in his and gave a big blink with its large eyes; Sapphire took a long deep breath. Merlin gave her a reassuring nod.

"Remember Child, I love you. Focus on the moment you want, and when you arrive release the dragonfly and let the Whitelines take their course, you will not have much time so move as fast as you can, you must time everything down to the last split second. Good luck and may the power of all of us protect you."

With the small figure of Cal holding tightly onto her hand, Sapphire turned to the bright blue orb and hesitated as she took another deep breath. "I love you too Grandfather, stay safe and thank you for everything."

"Go with speed and all of my love." Sapphire looked down at the small figure gripping her hand tightly.

"You ready for this?" He gave a bright smile that warmed her heart and then blinked, and without another word, Sapphire took a long step and walked right into the bright light. There was a burst of bright blue and then it was gone, and all that Merlin could do was close his eyes and help hold her safe for as long as she was within his range. He felt her hurtling through the Whitelines of time, and hoped and prayed to the powers of the council to see her safely to her destination.

There was a burst of bright light and Sapphire came running out of the orb, dragging the small figure behind her. She gasped for breath as she ran up the long stone steps towards the edge of the canyon. She jumped the last three still holding on tight to the small Sandling, and then with a slide of her soft white scratched boots, she skidded up to the wall and peered round.

The battle was raging under the heavy dark clouds of Avalon, and she knew the time was close. As she stared through the dim light, masses of men in black raged along the top of the wide expanse of rock towards the group in green cloaks, surrounded by the swarming masses of the Fae soldiers dressed in blue, and she gave a deep sigh of relief.

She fumbled in her pocket and looked down at the slightly ruffled Cal. "We made it; we are here just in time." There was a flash in front to her right, and she saw Rune and Jade walk out from her archway on the top of the tall Rest of Arthur. "Wait for it Saff." She breathed quietly to herself, she knew the moment precisely as she had watched it a thousand times in her table, and she counted down the moments as Rune and Jade fired their arrows in support of their husbands and the Specialists. An overwhelming tiredness seemed to creep through her entire body as she waited, the bridge had drained her of a lot more of her energy, and for a moment she rested as she counted down the seconds in her mind.

"Just a little longer... five... four... three... two." She lifted the dragonfly into the air, and threw it straight up with all her might, sending it high above the white stone of the Citadel Mount. "ONE!"

There was a massive burst of light, and the earth gave a tremendous jolt, Sapphire fell backwards as her eyes watched Jade get tossed back away from the stumbling Rune, and in the distance, almost as if watching in slow motion, Sapphire saw the sudden blackness as the Dark One burst into the air, as Robbie and the group were thrown down onto the floor, and bricks and stone rained out of the sky.

Her back hit the stone and she gasped in pain. As she scrambled to get back up, a second burst of even brighter white light exploded into the air blinding her, as the dragonfly released the Whitelines. Scrambling up on her knees, and gasping in pain, she could only hope that her plan had worked, from this moment on she knew what would happen, and had to carefully follow the plan if she was to be any help to them at all. Sapphire closed her eyes to synchronise her thoughts to the actual events.

Rune sat up as Jade clambered back over the edge of the rock on to the top of it. "Rune what the hell happened?" Rune was on her feet, as her eyes blazed with violet, Jade saw the urgency in her face and quickly scrambled to her feet, her head was bleeding and she wiped the blood from her face, as she crossed to the side of her sister. Jade connected to Rune and gave a gasp of horror as she saw the Dark One slightly raised in the air on a black cloud holding Robbie by the throat with one hand.

Morgan le Fey gave a sinister smile as she watched Robbie's face starting to turn blue. "Give me your witch and I will drop you and let you live."

He fought as his lungs felt like they were ready to explode, he wanted to scream 'Never' as loud as he could into her cold white face, but there was no way any sound could pass his air tight throat. She lifted her black hand, and through his straining tear filled bulging eyes, he saw the Star of the Merle and he knew that it would soon be over; he closed his eyes and concentrated with all his might.

"I love you Rune."

"No fight her, I am here."

Rune turned looking at the floor, she saw the bow, and bent down and snatched it up. Rune went for her quiver, but it was empty. "Jade quickly I need an arrow, find one." There was panic in her voice as one of Rune's tears hit the floor and a small violet sprung out of the stone. Jade twisted searching the floor as she panicked.

"There all gone Rune, we used them." Jade's eyes covered the whole surface of the Rest in the darkness, but the quivers were empty. "Rune I can't find any." She started to cry as her heart pounded, and she ran to the edge of the wall and looked down to see if any had rolled off the top and fallen below. "Rune please you must do something." Her tears were streaming from her eyes as she looked to her sister in desperation. "Save him don't let him die." Rune was blurred in Jade's vision as the terror took hold of her.

The panic was surging through Rune, as she turned back her eyes exploding with violet light and deep down inside her a voice and pictures from some past moment entered into her mind.

Eve pulled an arrow that was woven between the laces of Rune's empty quiver out and looked at its split shaft, and tattered white feather. "This place has a forge, it does appear you need more arrows, and some repairs to your equipment." Rune gave a smile and gently took the arrow from Eve's hand.

"This arrow will never be fired; I carry it with me always as a memory of my first time hunting with Robbie. It was damaged and unusable, but I kept it as a keep sake." Eve smiled.

"The last arrow of your woodland realm and one it appears that carries much of the love that binds you both together. Keep it safe, for if the love it holds is as deep as the love I see in your heart, then it carries the hopes and dreams of all the realms."

The moment hit her in a burst of clarity, and she twisted grabbing the quiver tied to her waist. Her hands shook violently as she pulled at the laces on the only arrow she had left, an arrow made of love in Loxley. She tugged at the laces as she felt the force on her heart of Robbie's last attempts to live, and her heart screamed out with her voice. "JADE HELP ME, I AM LOSING HIM!"

Jade flew across the top of the rest, and with the glint of steel, her hand grabbed the arrow and her dagger sliced through all the laces pulling it free, Rune snatched it from her, and twisted back to face the mount, the arrow came up on the string, and Rune closed one eye as she sighted the bow.

The arrow was straight and clean, without a marking down its long smooth clean shaft, the touch of Eve and mother of life, had given life back to the love that Rune held for Robbie. Rune took a deep breath as she saw the star in Morgan le Fey's hand give off a slight glint. "For the love we hold, and the love of all this realm is to us, may you be straight and sure and give life to those who fight for it."

The string of the bow gave a twang, and on the opposite side of Morgan le Fey, a loud snarling roar echoed off the stones as Furry Face jumped up on to the rock level with her. His second roar was fierce and loud as he exposed his long sharp gleaming white teeth.

Just for a second the Dark One turned and saw the tiger, she recoiled back in fear and surprise, and out of the darkness to her opposite side violet glinted. The arrow hit the star and exploded with violet light. The Dark One screamed in pain, as her body was torn from the star, and she let go of Robbie and he crashed gasping and choking to the floor. Furry Face pounced at the Dark One with a massive roar of hatred, and she slipped backwards and fell from her cloud and smashed screaming into the hard floor.

Violet light exploded everywhere, and Rune came out of the light in a raging temper. "YOU EVER TOUCH HIM AGAIN AND I WILL RIP OUT YOUR HEART BITCH!"

She grabbed le Fey by the scruff of the neck, and dragged the startled witch up on her feet and with a reaction quicker than a striking cobra, her fist swung with all its might into her face with a resounding crunch. The Dark One screamed in pain as she hurtled backwards flapping and flailing, her feet slipping on the rubble, there was a blast of bright green light, and Morgan le Fey was lifted into the air and tossed screaming and ranting over the edge of the cliff.

Everyone sat in the rubble covered in dust and stunned as they saw Rune and Jade side by side raging in anger, it was an awesome spectacle and very scary. Robbie gasped as Rune turned and dropped to him, she pulled him into her arms and held him tight; Jade gave a smile at the group. "Hey guys, how's it going?"

On her knees out of sight and feeling the energy flow out of her, Sapphire watched as Rune dropped to Robbie and lifted him into her arms. Sapphire breathed a deep heavy sigh as she struggled to stand, and leant for a moment on the wall to steady herself. "We are nearly there Cal." The small figure gripped her hand, the concern for his mistress was obvious on his face, he could see how much it had taken out of her, but knowing her as much as he did, he knew there was no way she could stop now, as she had set in place the motion, and had to work fast to ensure the plan worked.

Sapphire worked quickly preparing from the bag that Merlin had given her, she slid out five stinger arrows and then shouldering her bag, she took her bow from Cal and began to walk slowly down the stone steps towards the cave she knew concealed the entrance to the passage known as Merlin's Gate.

Out of sight, concealed within the cave she waited as she focused her strength, and concentrated her mind to focus down the tunnel and into the newly added extension of it, put in place by the Dark One. She felt the overwhelming tiredness as she pushed her mind to search out the life force of Lance, knowing that the Dark One would be using the veil to hide herself. It took longer than she wanted, but she was becoming weaker by the moment as she closed her eyes and then focused.

Her mind wandered and strayed, as it searched down the path and out of the end of the tunnel, and into the clearing where Lance and his group waited and prepared as the Dark One prowled unseen by Sapphire and her son questioned her plan.

Morgan le Fey turned her cheek and eye visibly swollen, and snapped at the soldiers. "Move those weapons; I want all of this space clear when they come." Her cold white face turned to Lance as the last of her patience dwindled. "Yes, it will work; I have planned this for years!" Her words snapped out and she realised, and tried to alter her tone. "It has taken a long time Lance, but believe me, this is fool proof, even our little flower girl will not see it coming, they think they have won, and in their stupidity, they will walk right into the trap." Lance gave a nod, his blue eyes as cold as her red.

"I hope so, we have too much at stake, and with that bumbling old monk fouling things up at Lincoln we really need to take the power back and use it with brutal force." Morgan le Fey walked over to the side of the archway where she examined her work.

"It is fine, they will walk freely into the passage, and when they step out at the top of the Tor, they will not even feel the change where my tunnel starts. Two strides will bring them ten miles to you, and in the blink of an eye they will be yours." She ran her hand across the stonework admiring her work. "It is almost time get your men ready, I shall return to Avalon momentarily and wait under the veil." The Dark One bent down and lifted a white robe off the floor. "Fools, they put such hope in their stupidity."

With her eyes still closed, Cal lit the fuse and Sapphire lifted the bow, the fuse fizzed away as Sapphire allowed the fuse to burn down shortening the time. When she guessed the moment to be right, she released the arrow, and it shot at the wall in front of her, and disappeared into the long hidden tunnel created by Merlin.

The soldier at the other end who was cleaning the area in front of the stone arch as Lance and his mother talked behind him, looked up as the archway flashed. The arrow hit him hard and embedded itself in his thigh, he gave a scream in pain and then it ignited as a second arrow came through the archway.

Back in the cave at the other end Cal watched his mistress as the tunnel boomed a deafening roar, and she fired yet another arrow into the tunnel, it was her fourth, and he understood she had put less tension on the bow string, Sapphire was ensuring the arrow fell short of the end and blew away all of the inside of the tunnel closing it forever. Part of the plan was to make sure that neither the Dark One or Rune, could reopen the tunnel, and in doing so she would ensure that Robbie and the group remained in Avalon until Amethyst had gained her full powers and could open the exits.

The last explosion was closer to the entrance, and it was a little more powerful than she expected. The blast came through the wall and blew her backwards into the opposite wall; she landed heavily, smashing against the rough stone, and yelping in pain as she slid to the floor, and chunks of stone rained onto her. Cal was on hand quickly as he saw the scratches on her face and the deep cut across her cheek. Sapphire waved his hand from her face, she was weak and so tired, but they did not have the time. "Avalon is sealed, I cannot leave Cal, only a dream spirit has the ability to leave this realm now, time is running out help me."

Cal felt the weariness inside her, and his wide bright eyes filled with tears as she closed her eyes and lay back for just a moments rest. "Oh Cal I am so tired." He could see the strain that all of this had added to her, her hair was almost snow white, and her face had more lines under her dark eyes, as she looked like she had aged another ten years. Allowing her a few precious moments to gather her strength, he took her by the hand and squeezing his eyes tightly shut he focused all of his being on Sapphire, there was a loud pop and the sound of singing birds and the scent of damp leaves floated into Sapphire's thoughts.

Cal gently nudged her to open her eyes, and with a reluctant sigh she opened them and looked up. High above her the tall trunks broke into masses of fine twigs covered in leaves, as the sun broke through them streaming bright beams of light down on to her face. It felt like the most beautiful thing she had ever seen, as the true wonder of the green world bathed her face. She did not want to move, and just wanted to lie there warm and snug in the deep fern, watching the birds and smelling the scents of the world she loved, but she felt the sharp tug at her arm, and knew this was her final task, as Cal spurred her on one last time.

Deep in the forest of Loxley a young girl cloaked in a heavy black robe fell to her knees and wailed out into the air with pain. "Lord of the woodland save me.... Hear me My Lord, for I have run away and she will kill me, save me lord and let me repent and undo the pain I have caused." She buried her head in the grass and cried with deep bitter pain and terror, wailing with her fear.

From a few feet away, a kindly old voice spoke. "Ursula of Fae, you have wronged many in my house, why should I now take you into my care?"

Ursula looked up as her tears flowed down her face. "Save me Lord of the Green Realm, I have deserted her, and wish only to undo the pain I have caused, please I beg you show me mercy or we all shall die." She lowered her head, and shook with fear, and the old lord felt the turmoil and fear within her.

"Come lost child of Fae, I will protect you from the darkness, and she will not find you where I shall take you. Do not fear and take my hand." Hearne stepped forward and his robes rustled like the leaves blowing in the autumn wood, he leaned down to the small huddled shaking figure, as she slowly lifted her tear filled face. Hearne smiled and stretched out his hand.

Ursula reached up, there was a yell from the far left, and the silver glint of an arrow whistled between Hearne and Ursula. Hearne stepped back shocked and Ursula screamed in pain, as her blood splattered into the air, the head of the old man whipped round in a rage. "WHAT IS THIS TREACHERY?" And he stopped as he saw the tired, aged, dirty, tatty figure in blue leaning against the tree trunk, hardly able to stand as she held up her bow with another arrow fitted and glinting in the sunlight.

"Step back My Lord, this is a trap, she carries a deadly weapon."

He looked back at the figure of Ursula sat cradling her blood soaked hand as she wailed in pain and stepped back from her. On the floor to her right, the plants had turned black, and a small cloud of vapour rose up where the claw shaped splinter of the Star of the Merle had landed. Still holding her arrow firm on the string Sapphire staggered forward, the small figure of Cal leaning into her leg to prevent her from falling down. The blood ran down her cheek and stained her blue top, and dripped on to her white boots, as exhausted and weary as she felt, she breathed a long sigh of relief to see her woodland lord safe and out of reach of the young deadly assassin.

"My Lord Hearne you are safe." Her legs buckled, and she dropped to her knees as her bow and arrow fell to the floor, Hearne moved swiftly catching her in his powerful arms, as he dropped to his knees and gathered her to him. Ursula seized her moment, and sprang up from the floor, and ran screaming into the woodland to escape, as the old lord looked down at the old worn face of Sapphire in his arms.

"Oh my dearest child of sight, what have you done?" Sapphire gave a weak smile hardly conscious as her eyes filled with tears.

"I have done it... I saved you... All of you." She closed her eyes with a smile still on her face, as the old lord looked to the small Sandling for more information. Cal gave a bow and reached up his hand and closed his eyes, the moment that Hearne's hand connected, the whole story of Sapphire blasted into him as the pictures of everything flowed into his mind, and he saw the past as it had happened, and how she had used the Bridge of Sequana to travel back through time to this point and change everything. As he grew in understanding he knew what he must do.

"Come my little friend, we still have much to do, gather her things and follow me, she has given all of her life force and we cannot tarry here, we must act fast." Hearne gathered the limp Sapphire into his arms, and standing up he turned and walked quickly off into the woodland in the direction of Hearne's Rock. Cal lifted her bag and bow and ran behind doing his best to keep up with the long powerful strides of his lord.

Rune looked at Robbie and Fagan. "There is nothing I can do, it has been completely destroyed, there is no way of opening it up again, we will have to wait until Amethyst gains her full powers and the realm becomes unsealed. If you don't mind Fagan, we will put on you for a little while longer."

Fagan gave a mighty sniff, and smiled a broad smile as he looked round at all the gathered Specialists. "Well, I must say, I am as tickled as a daffodil. To be of the truth I will say I felt as wilted as a buttercup in the hot sun, when I thought of ye all leaving. Tis fine by me, and I says let's make it one to part on with barley beer and sesame bread." Jade gave a happy giggle, and the others all smiled at the thought of another night and a chance to celebrate with Fagan. Rune slipped her arm round Robbie who smiled his throat still burning with the pain of the grip of the Dark

One.

Rowan lifted his bag off the floor. "To Fagan's it is then." Rune gave a smile and waved her arm across the air in front of them, and one by one they trooped though her window into the open glade in front of Fagan's long wooden house, and the place that for the last week had become very much like home.

Sapphire lay on the moss lined bed deep within the white cave on Hearne's Rock, as the old lord did what he could for her to make her comfy; he looked to the small Sandling. "The Lady Opal has prepared you say, but she is now trapped behind the ring of power put there by Morgan?"

Cal gave a mighty blink and pulled from his pocket a glass like orb, and the old lord smiled, as he understood fully what Opal had done. "She always was far too clever for her own good, but I think now my little friend, we can all be glad that she has used her wisdom to bend the rules once again." Hearne examined the orb carefully. "You say the other one is contained within her circle?" Cal gave a nod and blinked, and Hearne gave a soft smile. "This is a good thing; now all we must do is gather the core of who she is."

Hearne rolled the glass orb on his palm and it began to spin, Cal stepped back and watched as he saw Sapphire take a long breath, it was her final one, and as she breathed out, her body began to shimmer. The old lord whispered to her quietly and she let her final breath escape her lips, and as she did so, a long faint stream of blue light flowed out with her breath and into the spinning orb. It mixed inside as a dream would when being created by the Sandling's. Cal marvelled at the skill Opal had used to create such a thing. The old lord stood and looked at the ball as it spun to a stop in his hand. "She is gone." And Cal looked at the old worn face of his white haired mistress, who appeared very much to look like she was resting and at peace. Hearne waved his hand, and Cal watched as slowly Sapphire's body collapsed and turned to dust, and the old lord turned to him and smiled.

"You will have to wait for nightfall, I will call out to the Lady of Life and she will meet you and aid you, go now to the realm and wait until she arrives, for she will help to release Opal, and then you can hand her this." He bent down and handed the orb filled with the blue swirling mist to the small Sandling, Cal smiled and gave a large blink as he took it from the lord of the woodland and slipped it safely into his pocket. Hearne gave a smile. "Protect that with your life, it is a very valuable asset to my line, and one all of us should be in awe of, for Sapphire used up ten lives to protect all of us and we should honour her sacrifice."

There was a loud pop inside the cave, and the old lord gave a long sigh and walked slowly through the entrance of the cave and out onto the wide shelf of limestone high above the woodland of Loxley. The figure dressed in a long tattered black cloak turned as he walked forward.

"Did I not tell you to have more faith? Your line is stronger than ever now, the Redstone is very powerful and it feeds into all of the circles, just look at the work of our sighted one, has she not inspired you with the courage she has found buried deep within herself? Sapphire of the stones has proved her worth beyond question, even though you doubted her abilities, I am proud of her, and with luck Opal will be free by dawn and we can turn this all around."

"We have travelled a long way My Brother to arrive at where we already were, there is still much to do and a bitter battle to fight."

Albanlin gave a soft chuckle under his hood. "Somehow, I do not feel the concern I once did, Morgan has her match now, and the power that grows between all of them is more than I could ever have expected, truth will return and reunite with them, and Avalon will have a new queen, and the Redstone is based in the centre of everything, this is all better than I expected. You worry too much, you always have."

Hearne gave a long sigh, and his face carried the sadness in his heart. "We once thought as they will now, and yet in our arrogance we lost sight of the very things we ask the new ones to treasure, and we have paid a bitter, bitter price for it. What you call worry; I call wisdom, for much I have learned in these days of trial and pain. I am sorry Brother, but for me the joy of this Earth sank when she took the stone into a place I can never enter, and I will mourn the reason that everything I created lived, with the loss of her."

"She chose her path, out of the love for everything you did with her, do not dishonour her by not rejoicing in the gifts she gave to all your creations, for it was Eve alone that saw the true potential for this world, and it is your charge now to make it so." Hearne lifted his weary eyes to Albanlin.

"It will be so, and even though little Runestone is her likeness in every way, I still know the price given by my wife to save everything, and I will honour her sacrifice in the land of making all my days." Albanlin turned sharply.

"Surely you are not considering leaving this place?"

"She is gone... My time to return draws near, for I have done all I can here and soon a time will arrive when only the spirit of the stag will walk these trees to comfort the hunter. This place has always been marked with the sign of the wolf, and it will be the keen eyes and skills of craft in the green leaves that protect this place, the stag will remain, but only to reassure the wolf, the process has begun and there is no turning back."

CHAPTER TWELVE

NEW LIFE

As the group settled into their late afternoon celebration inside the long wooden cabin that was home to Fagan, outside on the wide expanse of grass the monks who had been saved by the hooded man bent to their knees and prayed. Fagan had offered them shelter and food inside the large barn, even though they had all seen the woodland fighters as enemies, they ensured that their prayers contained thanks and a blessing for Robbie and the Specialists.

Rune stood for a moment on the edge of the trees and watched fascinated by what she saw as a strange ritual, and then clutching the white star shaped container in her hand, deep within her pocket, she turned into the trees and opened her violet window. Stepping out on to the white top of the Isle of Tears, she felt a shudder run down her spine, and shivered as she saw the faint transparent figure of Eve stood in the centre of the large star. Rune took a step forward feeling the chill of the moment mix with her inner pain, for she knew that this would be the last time she ever saw her Great Grandmother, Eve came slowly forward.

"You have done well, this realm will be ruled in safety for another thousand years by the queen that takes her seat as we speak, the line of the Fae of the Moon will be forever grateful to you and your companions, although as we speak there is still great need and other tasks of importance to settle before you can look forward and the duty of this and all of the other realms." Rune was unsure of what Eve meant and her face showed it, Eve gave a smile, although it was hard to distinguish it in the bright sunlight that reflected off her transparent face.

"Do you not feel the strange sensation of knowing something here has befallen before?" It was odd that she mentioned it, because Rune had felt a little strange, almost as though she had done this before.

"Do you know of something that I should be aware of?" Eve moved a little closer.

"Use your senses, for you are the Lady of Life now, and nothing can be hidden from you easily, seek out the centre of all the circles, and look to your family hidden in other realms for aid, for much has happened and you must seek out the truth, for it is now your task as the centre of everything Runestone Life."

"Is my Grandmother in danger?"

"Have no fear she is safe within her circle of protection, but she has need of you, finish here what you have started and then visit the circle of my stone and look deep, all the answers will await you there before travelling on to my daughters aid."

Just the mention of finishing what she started brought a pain to the inside of her chest, and she looked down as a wave of anguish ran through her. Rune opened her hand and revealed the white star shaped container. "When I place this in that hole, you will be destroyed forever won't you?" The tears welled in her eyes as the faint figure came closer.

"This has always been my destiny Runestone Life, for I have handed the torch of life to you to carry, do not be sad, my life has been fulfilled, and I have known love so deep and so powerful, it will take me into the cosmos and beyond."

Rune shook as she felt the grief building inside her. "But why do you have to die, why can you not stay as a spirit to others as you have me? It makes no sense for you to end here and now, I will always need you close." She gave a long bitter sob as her heart broke, and Eve surrounded her with her love for she no longer had the form to take her into her arms and hold her.

"Our time is coming to an end as is the natural way, it is the time for you and your Hooded Man to go forth and rebuild everything to your view of the world, just as I did many thousands of years ago. Dry your tears My Lady of Life, for inside you I will always live in the gifts I bestowed on you. Now place the stone in the seal and leave, I shall take it where it will never be found again, happy in the knowledge you will always be safe because of this. Go with love to your children and hold them for me, for there is the key to your future."

Rune wiped her eyes and gave a big sniffle. "Goodbye Great Grandmother, thank you for all you have done to help me, I love you and always will." She knelt down and took one last look up where she could just make out the outline of Eve, she smiled down at her and gave a nod, Rune placed the white star shaped container over the hole, and let it slip into place, and as the cold white stone gave a small click, Eve faded from view and the sky above filled with thick rolling grey clouds. Rune stood up straight and watched as the light flashed out from the sky and the deep heavy rumble of thunder growled into the warmth of the day. She lifted the hood of her thick violet cloak, as the first heavy drops of water splattered onto the white stone at her feet, and just for a moment she felt as if Eve had whispered into her ear.

"Behold the rain of life, to wash away the filth and renew this land and reinforce your power of Life."

By the time she reached the wooden rail that ran down the stone steps to the small wooden jetty at the base of the high edge of the Isle, the rain was pounding

down and drumming on her hood. Rune took hold of the rail and looked out
across the wide empty mud filled crater that had been the huge Lake of Passing
on her arrival into the realm, and as she watched across the wide lake, she could
see the water running with speed off the rocks and dropping splashing into long
streams that wove through the soft mud, building in size to flowing torrents
that would become the great pools that would merge and refill the lake again,
life was flowing back into Avalon, as from here, it would soak through the soil
and reinvigorate the dry parched roots of the trees and plants. She gave a smile
knowing Avalon would once again bloom and grow into a new realm of green life.

Turning back for one final look through the heavy rain at the smooth star of
white, Rune lifted her hand and as she signalled farewell to the final resting place
of Eve, her window of violet opened, and she stepped through into the large green
circle within the tall stones of Avalon. From the moment her boot touched the
grass, she felt a strong familiar feeling, almost as if her table was there at hand,
Rune's bright blue saddened eyes swept the floor, and fixed in on a small white
flower. She smiled seeing the white daisy that represented her grandmother, and
took the few paces forward, bringing her into the centre of the tall circle of stones.
Kneeling down she carefully lifted the leaves that grew thick around the base of the
plant, and the glint of silver caught her eye. Slowly she drew out the talisman on
which was the elaborately crafted runic R.

She felt the surprise as she looked at it lay flat in the palm of her right hand,
as her left instinctively went to her neck to check hers was still there, and yet she
knew before she touched the many chains that this was hers, she just had no idea
of how it had got there, because she never took it off. Standing back up in the
pouring rain she wiped it carefully on the inside of her cloak, and then gave it a
squeeze.

She gasped as her mind flooded with images, and staggered slightly forward
afraid she was going to fall. Her eyes closed as the colours of a million images
flashed into her mind, showing her the pictures of all that had been and feeling the
power of her own feelings, she slipped gasping to her knees almost thinking she
was going to faint as she fell forward on to her hands.

Rune drew in long breaths, as the pictures slowed and she began to understand
what she was witnessing, it was hard to understand whether this was real or some
surreal nightmare as she gasped in horror, and felt the heavy soul wrenching pain
of watching Robbie die hung from a tree. On her hands and knees in the middle
of the circle of stones, as the rain pounded down from the sky soaking her long
violet cloak, Rune wailed, her tears mixing with the rain as she relived the memory
of the time before Sapphire opened the bridge, everything came back to her in
graphic clarity, as it raced through her heart and mind, and she sobbed bitter tears
into the damp earth, covering it in a thick carpeted layer of violet flowers.

She was not certain as to how long she had been there, but when her mind came back to normality it was already dark, but the rain was still pounding and she was soaked through to her skin and was shivering violently. It took her a few moments to understand everything, and make a rather shaky attempt at getting back to her feet. For a moment she stood and stared out between the large stones lit by the low bright moon above them, the talisman still clasped tightly in her right hand, her bright sapphire blue eyes shone out from her pale face plastered with her wet fire coloured hair. She blinked and lifted her left hand to wipe her hair from her mouth, and then she lifted her right hand holding the chain and let the talisman drop free of her grasp, it spun glinting in the moonlight as she opened the clasp and slipped the chain inside her hood and fastened it round the back of her damp neck. The air flashed with bright violet for an instant, and she was gone leaving the ancient stones of the circle to witness the last of the pounding rain storm, as the waters flowed throughout the realm under the watch of a new moon that signalled the coming of new life and a new era of the queen of Avalon's rule.

The long grass that stood high above her head parted, and Rune saw the path that wound through the trees towards the circle of trees that she knew was home to her grandmother. Cal stood quietly waiting and gave a long regal bow to her as she stepped out and onto the path. "Hello my small friend, do not be downhearted for I am here to help your mistress." He gave a wide excited blink, and Rune offered her hand to him, he took it and they started out along the path.

Rune felt very calm, something that she found odd, considering this was not a realm she relished much, as on her previous visits she had felt a great apprehension, but she now felt different, almost as if there was something within her that reassured her of her safety. She could certainly sense the concern inside Cal, as he held tightly to her hand, and yet the feeling of boldness grew inside her and mixed with the annoyance that yet again the Dark One had tried to capture and imprison one of her family.

As they came round the trunk of a mighty beech like tree, and the wall of dense green trees came into view, Rune felt the anger grow as she saw the long line of silently waiting sentries of the Darkmare guard. Her anger grew rapidly, as they all turned in unison and raised their arms to lift their masks, and reveal some grotesque image intent on instilling her with fear, Rune's eyes flashed with an angry violet. "Don't even think about it, there is nothing in those empty heads that can frighten me." Her arm came up swiftly, and a blaze of violet light flashed like a sabre across the woodland. "Get out of my way; I will deal with your mistress later." Wretched wails rang into the air as the Darkmares lifted off the floor, and were flung like rags across the leaf covered earth, scattering and rolling in pain like old pots and pans.

A wall of fire erupted out of the earth and Rune felt her patience being tried again by Morgan le Fey, her finger snapped loudly as yet more Darkmares lifted into the air screaming and the flames exploded as Rune walked straight past and into the trees.

Opal sat very still with her eyes closed on her log in the centre of her circle, her hood was over part of her very pale face, and Rune bent forward a little to see if her grandmother was alright. Opal did not move but remained as still as a statue, Rune came a little closer speaking in a hushed tone. "Grandmother... Grandmother... it's me... Rune!" Her eyes snapped open quickly and Rune gave a slight squeal and jumped back. "Grandmother... Hearne help me you scared me." Opal gave a little chuckle as she looked around and slipped her legs forward and stretched them.

"Rune my child.... Oh dear my legs are stiff." She gave a smile. "How long has it been, I don't think my legs have ever ached so?" Rune blinked unsure of what her grandmother meant.

"How do you mean, how long?" Opal lifted her arms and stretched up in the air.

"Oh dear, I must say I feel like it's been longer than any other time."

"Do you mean how long has it been since Sapphire left you, because if you do, it's been over thirty years, there is no way you could have been asleep for all that time."

"Thirty years, really?" She stood up and swayed a little. "Well that explains the aches and pains, good grief I have never meditated for such a long time, I wondered why my stomach was feeling so empty, I think a good stew is in order." Rune was lost for words and gasped in amazement.

"No way... you are having me on?" Opal smiled.

"Rune my child you are soaked to the skin, come and sit by the fire and we shall eat and have a good warm cup of tea." Rune just stared at her not quite sure if her grandmother was joking, or had really been sat there for thirty years. In an instant the familiar fire with the old black pot hung above it, sat in front of her as Opal guided her down to the old log and released the clasp on her cloak. "There we go, if you lay it out here it will be dry in no time." She turned to the now rapidly bubbling pot and lifted the wooden spoon to stir it. "Hmmm I feel I have quite an appetite."

Opal tapped the spoon on the side of the black pot. "Just a few more minutes I think." She dropped the spoon back into the pot, and then walked round the end of the thick fallen log and came up behind Rune, where she took Rune's long red hair in her hands and began to comb it out using her fingers. Rune gave a sigh and closed her eyes as Opal pulled down on the long red hair freeing up all her knots and dropping it straight down Rune's back. "Oh and for the record, I was not asleep, I never sleep, like you in that glass box I was resting my eyes and my body, my mind never sleeps and watches everything, as does yours."

Rune smiled, feeling the warmth that was growing inside her as her boots steamed dry in front of the fire. "Sorry Grandmother, I should have known that you would have been watching over all of us, thanks for guiding Saff, I just wish she could have had more support and not used up all her life force. It was a large price to pay, and so sad that she gave up everything."

"What?" Opal dropped her dry hair and walked back round to the pot. "What on earth are you talking about, she gave up nothing?" Rune opened her eyes.

"But she did all of that and then died in Hearne's arms."

"Fiddlesticks... I might not know everything about the secret powers of the Fae, but I saw enough of Gwendolyn's tricks to pick up a few pointers." Opal looked positively put out, and Rune straightened in her seat.

"But I saw her die in Hearne's cave, how could she live, she had aged well beyond her years?"

"Really Runestone, sometimes I worry about you... You saw Sapphire fade away, and as you know that is a completely different thing to death... What you actually saw was her essence pass into the sphere of dreams and the visual embodiment of Sapphire disappeared, how could you think I would let her go off filled with worry and self doubt? No, I just took a leaf out of Gwendolyn's book and let her think that she was wholesome when she ran from here to save all of you. Sapphire is perfectly fine and preserved in her young self here where she has been safe and protected." Rune looked round surprised.

"She is... Where?"

"There." Opal pointed of to the left, where moments ago Rune had looked and seen nothing, and there on a mound of soft leaves was Sapphire fast asleep in a bed of silk. Rune rose slowly feeling the happiness grow inside her, Opal gave a satisfied smirk.

"As I told you, there was not much in my time at Avalon that I missed, do not forget Runestone Sapphire, I grew up in that woodland you have come to love so much, like your sister I had quite a strong side for adventure. Little happened around the Forest of Time and Avalon that I did not notice. Gwendolyn may have thought all her secrets were safe, but you would be surprised what a child of life can accomplish under the leaves. That forest was more than just a playground, it's where I received my full education, and even though the Fae were secretive during Rhiannon's time, Gwendolyn was much too excited at times to pay full attention to her surroundings. I may not have known how to find and open the bridge, but I knew a great deal about how to use it and stay safe, and when I suspected that Gwen had passed her secrets to Sapphire... Well let's just say I used a secret or two of my own to keep her safe."

Rune felt the joy explode out of her, and pulled her grandmother into a big hug. "You are a marvel, thank you for watching over her." Opal gave a loving smile.

"It was guesswork much of the time, but once I realised that Gwen had seen further into these days than the rest of us, I guessed that she gave Sapphire the gifts knowing you would be taken and unable to help everyone. I thought it safer to risk a phantom rather than her human/Fae self... We are very lucky Runestone that it paid off, there was more than a few moments when I was unsure, I did try to contact Gwen, but old white fussy pants prevented me, he said it was against the rules, like that has ever been an issue before." Rune was more than impressed and gave a smile seeing something very Jade like awaken in her grandmother.

"Maybe Lord Albanlin realised you had taken the right steps; I am sure he would not have let you if he had thought you were wrong." Opal raised her eyebrows.

"He can be a pest with his lines and rules for everything; sometimes the natural path is one of chaos and is the right route to take. You wait until you meet him, you will see, he has everything written down and orderly, and oh if you bend the rules a little, you would think it was the end of the world the way he bangs on, believe me child, if you ever have dealings with him stand your ground and stick to what your instincts tell you, it was the way of my mother and it should be yours." Rune gave her one more squeeze and then stepped back and turned towards Sapphire.

"When will she wake?"

"Not yet, we have a few things to do before we bring her back."

"Like what?"

"She must be restored as she was, but with full knowledge of her past, Sapphire learned much in those years and I do not think they should be wasted, after all she has a queen to train."

"So she too will know everything, is that wise? I would think keeping quiet would be more prudent, after all we have erased that part of everyone's past." Opal lifted her hand to Rune's shoulder.

"I think she has earned the right to keep the knowledge she gained, let's be honest she will take her seat as the centre of the Circle of Sight, what she has lived through will give her the authority and experience to lead them all to bigger and better things, that can only work to the better for all of us." Rune gave a nod.

"I trust your judgement Grandmother, Ok so what do we do now?"

"Nothing... I believe her small companion has earned this moment." Opal turned and smiled to the small silent figure that stood watching his mistress sleeping. "Cal you have what she needs, let the dream become her reality."

The small Sandling gave a low bow to Opal, and then silently walked over to the side of Sapphire. He slipped the precious sphere of blue swirling light out from inside his pocket, and lifted it up and placed it carefully in the centre of her forehead. Rune watched with fascination as he lowered himself back onto the floor and to her surprise he began to sing, Rune turned to Opal and quietly whispered.

"I thought Sandling's could not speak?" Opal smiled as the most beautiful music seemed to flow out of Cal.

"We all speak in one fashion or another Runestone, but I must admit I do love the sound of a dream being awoken, I think it is the sound of pure love."

The music lifted into the air surrounding everything, and Rune felt her heart relax and fill with love, it was so soft and gentle a song, and yet it touched her deeply and her eyes filled with tears of wonder and happiness. The sphere on Sapphire's head seemed to pulsate in rhythm with the music and Rune watched as it began to stretch along the length of Sapphire's sleeping body. Soon the whole sphere was hovering above her as Cal lifted his head back and sang with passion and love. The Sphere lowered slowly and Sapphire slipped inside it with ease as the blue swirling light bathed her entire body, Cal lowered his tone as his song slowed, and Rune watched entranced as Sapphire gave a slight jolt and then took a long deep breath. The light that swirled all around her was suddenly sucked inside her mouth, and she relaxed and sank into the softness of the silken sheets, Cal's song came to an end and he bowed to Sapphire, and then pulling a long silver pin from inside his lapel, he lifted it up and stabbed at the clear bubble around her. The was a gentle pop and he turned to Opal and Rune and smiled with a huge blink, Rune felt a little sad that the song he sung had ended, but she smiled and wiped her eyes.

"That my small friend was very beautiful, you sing with great wonder, and I feel privileged that you let me hear you." He gave another bow, as behind him the gentle moans of Sapphire caught their attention, she sat upright rubbing her eyes and blinking as she looked round at the familiar surroundings and then spotted the smiling face of Rune. Cal moved back as with a look of joy, Sapphire swung her legs out of the bed, stood up and wobbled as the feeling of weakness unsteadied her footing, and Rune swept forward and caught her in her arms. "Whoa Saff steady on, you have been out for a while." Sapphire burst into tears as Rune lowered her slowly into a sitting hug back on the bed. "Hey no tears, you did fine and everyone is safe."

Sapphire buried her face into Rune's chest and sobbed, as Opal gave a gentle nod. "We live to fight another day my children, but I think a little food, drink and talk before we make any other decisions."

Bringing Jett back across the void had been exhausting, even with the help of Merlin's staff, Una had swooned and felt very weak, so with the aid of Jett, Gwendolyn helped her daughter down the long stair cut out from the rock, and brought her safely to the end of the Valley of Time. The mist still swirled in and out of the canyon as the light faded, and Gwendolyn suggested they spend the night there before travelling back in the morning, Una lay down on a bed prepared by her mother, and Jett lit a fire to cook the food Gwendolyn had prepared for them, Gwendolyn then hugged her daughter and embraced Jett welcoming her back and then left to return to her duty on the watch,

It was well past dark when Una felt strong enough to sit and eat, and wrapped in a blanket close by the fire, Una sat with Jett and spoke as they ate. Jett told of her arrival in a country known as Maybeyan, it was similar to theirs, only there were parts where the trees grew taller than that of the Forest of Time, and everyone spoke in a different dialect which she found difficult to learn. Jett told of her strange arrival, and being caught by the group who had become such good friends in her time there, they fought to free and defend the Princess Aurora from the evil overlord Valdez.

At first she had been very frightened to be alone and out of contact from Rune and the others, and the group who discovered her had been very suspicious, thinking she may be a spy, but as with all things she used her sword to great advantage and won the allegiance of the group, going on to help them fight to victory. It was a long a graphic tale told with enthusiasm, and Una smiled and nodded as she ate her food and felt her strength finally returning. Jett finished her tale talking of the woodland spirit Tula and how sweet she was, and gave a happy smile as she rested back on her bag and rolled up cloak. "So that's me, what have you guys been up to in the last year?"

Una paused with the spoon at her lips. "Did you not hear anything my mother said to you?" Jett gave a bold smile and shrugged her shoulders.

"Not really, I was too excited at being back... Why what did she say?" Una gave a giggle.

"You never change, do you? Off you flash to a world not even in our ring of realms, and you have a wild time and return here without a care in the world. Jett my mother told you that although for you it has been just under a year away, here it's only been nine days. Well at least it had been when I left, things got so weird on the way up here I lost track a bit." Jett thought for a moment as Una slipped the spoon inside her mouth and began to chew, Jett lifted her eyes to meet Una's violet.

"How exactly is that possible?" Una swallowed and gave a slight giggle.

"Now that is the question you should have asked my mother. To be honest Jett it's all a little odd to me too, but that is the lines of Fae for you, as with all things Fae they guard their powers closely, and even though I am of Fae, only enough to allow my aid is given... Think about it Jett How did Iona before she was born help Robbie in the Hidden Realm? How could she appear in the realm as a small child just days after she was born, or appear in Carnac to Treen and Sapphire as a grown woman? The lines of the Fae know many things, but I doubt you or I will ever truly have the answers to our questions." Una put down her bowl and took a drink from the flask; she could see the confusion in Jett's eyes. "I would let it go to be honest, what is important is that we get back as quick as we can, when I left, Robbie was planning to attack the Dark One, and somehow I think he will need your blade by his side again."

Jett settled back in deep thought, in the darkness with the glow of the fire her eyes felt heavy, and yet somehow she felt sleep was a long way off. Una sensing her unease began to fill in the gaps of what had happened on the edge of the Mirrored Waters, and the fight between Rune and the Dark One. She told her of Fagan and the cabin, and laughed as she recounted Smoke's version of the Marsh Hound and Jade's not telling him it was dog meat he had fed to Steph. Both of them giggled quietly in the darkness until Jett felt tired and lay back, her mind now deeply set on the one thing she had missed the most. "I can't wait to get back and feel Rafe's arms around me again, I missed him more than I ever thought I could... although please don't tell him Una, I mean... Well, you know how big headed he can get?"

Una nodded in the darkness, "Yeah it's fine, I won't breathe a word, I was just thinking of Wilson." Jett sat up.

"Who the hell is Wilson?" Una suddenly felt flustered, she was thinking and had voiced her thoughts. It had completely slipped her mind that she had not actually told anyone yet, she sat up and looked at the enquiring eyes of Jett across the firelight, her cheeks felt warm and she felt a little more than flustered, as she tried to hide the large beaming smile that had crossed her face like it had when she was young.

"Wilson... you know... Wilson Allwood...the guy from the outlaws... You know Jett, Woody." Jett gave a gasp followed by a loud laugh.

"Woody... seriously Una, you tagged and bagged him.... Bloody hell I thought his cherry would rot and fall from the bloody tree before he used it."

"Jett!!" Jett gave another loud guffaw of a laugh.

"Wow Una, you naughty dirty girl, you snuck up and nailed the wood man." Una felt her face burning, and her voice rose a little higher than normal.

"It's... It's not like that at all Jett; we have a lot in common... He is a kind, gentle, deeply thoughtful man; we really found a great deal we have in common. It ... it was mutual affection." Jett squealed with laughter as Una's face burned almost as purple as Rune's eyes.

"I bet you have, I bet you both had some seriously big itch in common and enjoyed a little bit of mutual scratching." Jett flopped back on her cloak holding her tummy as Una gasped with embarrassment.

"Jett Amber for the love of Hearne, those things are supposed to be private." Jett wheezed as she gasped for air laughing, she crawled back up on to her cloak and took long repeated breaths as she waved her hand in the air at Una.

"Una... Honestly... Your face..." She gasped another long breath. "So tell me... Do they call him Woody for any other reasons?" Una's jaw dropped as Jett lost all control and fell backward rolling off her cloak, and kicking the half filled mug of tea on the fire. Her laughter was aided by the look of abject shock and terror on the bright purple face of Una. She rolled on the ground laughing hysterically unable to look back at Una's scandalised face, as it just made her laugh even more.

It was a good ten minutes later when she crawled up on to her cloak fighting the repeated giggles inside her belly. "I am sorry Una, but you looked so funny, the last time I saw anyone go so red it was when Ruby and me caught Louisa in the cleaning room with the captain of the guard, I think it's very nice and actually pretty cool, I know we mess with his head and stuff, but he is actually a pretty good woodsman when he is not tripping over."

Una smiled acknowledging Jett's approval, she understood how his nervousness got in the way of things at times, but she actually found it quite endearing. "He is very kind and a very honest man, after Kane and his lies, I think I can handle some decency."

Jett smiled. "You deserve happiness, and so does Woody, I got to admit I cannot wait to see him, does he walk a little less limp now you have drained the bag as it was?"

"Jett, for the love of Hearne will you stop it?" Jett winked with an evil smile.

"He does then, he has got a bit more upright since eh?" Una gave a snigger and laughed as she saw the defiant cheeky look in Jett's eyes.

"He has a bit." Una and Jett laughed and chuckled in the darkness, their happy voices bouncing down the long canyon of the Valley of Time, as far away across the huge span of the forest a flash of bright purple brought Rune through the trees and across the grass towards the long wooden house that housed the Specialists. Robbie coughed stood by the door and then gave a smile as he saw her come through the trees, she saw him waiting and hurried her pace, as a bright loving smile lit across her face. She swept up the steps and across the wooden floor and he pulled her into his arms, his voice was weak and quiet and somewhat strained. "Hey Gorgeous, you are wet, but isn't this rain wonderful?"

She sunk into his arms and moved to kiss him. "Hi beautiful... forget the rain and take me to bed, I missed you and want to make love to you now."

CHAPTER THIRTEEN

RENEWED FUTURES

As the moon rose to its peak, across the forest and throughout all of Avalon, the rain poured down. Inside the long wooden house built by Fagan, a few sat round the table quietly talking with Rowan and Jade, Rune lay awake curled around Robbie as he slept, and she watched him from his chest, no one would ever know of the fate that turned around and restored her love to her. It all still felt like some crazy dream, but spending the evening deep in conversation with Saff, she had felt the fear rise up inside her, and the pain she had felt at his graveside had returned making it real again. She did not like keeping secrets, but together Opal and Sapphire had sworn a pact with her to keep the real truth from ever being known, all that mattered was that those they all loved were once again safe.

Robbie had been clear that as soon as the realm was unsealed, he wanted to leave and head home, but things had changed, and Rune understood the relevance of the swords more than ever, without Jett and the Sword of Truth, they had been weakened, and it was only the foresight of Gwendolyn that had saved everything. Things had to change, and even though Robbie had to lead by example, Rune knew there would be no way she would ever allow him more than a few paces ahead again, she had been sloppy and wrapped up in her own things, and that moments lapse had almost cost them the whole fight.

Reflection was in the air, Rowan too was talking quietly with Big John, Skip and Bear whilst Steph and Smokes sat quietly by the fire listening, they had planned an assault on very little information, and even though Rowan had been there at the side of Robbie, he was not altogether happy at the huge risk they had taken, and the discussion took the line of making sure they found out as much as possible before going in blind again. Deep down under the trees of the Hidden Realm, Sapphire sat in thought as she adjusted to being back where she started, Opal kept her company and talked through much of the things that had happened, but in Sapphire's mind the pictures of those she loved and cared for hanging from trees was still very vivid, Opal could see that Sapphire was starting to formulate her own plans for the future.

Opal handed her a mug of tea, made from one of the plants from the forest, Sapphire who was lost in thought, snapped out of it and took the cup, her gaze fell on the tiny figure rolled up in a blanket by the fire. Opal gave a soft smile understanding the bond that had formed between them both. "Sandling's are the most loyal of all companions child, because they become attached to your spirit, it will not matter what danger or task you face, for young Cal here will remain by your side always." Sapphire lifted her eyes and gave a sigh; Opal gently nodded her head as if she understood the process that Sapphire was going through. "You will never be alone whilst Cal is paired to you."

Saff understood the piercing blue stare of Opal, there had been so many times when she had thought that Opal could see right into her deepest inner self, she gave a small smile. "Rune helped me turn the clock back, but even so, I have still had countless years to think of these times. I think if I am truly honest, I would say I was glad not to be in Avalon and be away from the others, jumping through windows to help the Sage, and then bouncing back to Rafe and the Outlaws. When it all went wrong for them, I found myself alone and was forced to think of what I needed to do to find the answers... Maybe it is selfish, but in my time alone I have found peace and strength." Opal smiled.

"I think you may call that wisdom, you are very lucky Sapphire, for you have seen one way life can be, and you have been given the chance to go another way, and avoid all that was pain to you; I see the sprouts of hope growing." Sapphire sat quietly for a moment.

"I don't want to return, I was caught in that trap before, and I want to be free of it."

"Which trap was that?" Opal knew full well what Sapphire had referred to, but she thought it would be best for it to come from Sapphire's lips. Saff looked up and met the wise old gaze of Opal.

"I was happy in the circle of Callanish, and then mother told me of the Hooded Man and his fight, and I think I let myself get carried away with wild romantic notions and fantasies. From the moment we left and we met up with Keith in the woodland at Settle, I got caught in a trap and I have felt torn ever since. I fell in love with the idea of a folk hero, one I had never met. When I met Keith, I became so confused as to if I loved him for who he was, or just because he was the symbol of something I thought I loved, and from that moment, I have been lost and mixed up inside myself."

"And being free to find your own way and be guided by the gifts you carry felt better?" Sapphire gave a nod.

"It did... I cannot deny that at times I was panicked and unsure, but that in itself felt liberating. I think these past years I have been exactly what I had always thought I would be as a centre, and to be honest now we are all back here again, I really do not want to give it up and go back to being caught again in a trap I made to begin with." Opal gave a nod of understanding, and looked her straight in the eyes.

"Then you must continue on the path you have been on for all these years alone, for it is that path that you have searched and found your true identity on."

"If only it was that simple, Keith will not understand, and I am not that sure Robbie will either, I mean at the end of the day a war is coming that will be hard fought, both of them will want me in the group." Opal leaned forward and took Sapphire by the hand.

"Listen carefully child, for like you, I too have had many years alone to think, I do think that Robbie will require your services, but Rune understands that your place is in her circles and the group has changed, for you are charged with the task of looking at the road ahead to ensure the safety of all of them, I feel that is a service that will continue will it not?" Sapphire gave a nod.

"Of course it will, I will always faithfully serve my circle."

"Well then, in that case, I feel Robbie will have no problems, in regard to Keith, yes I agree to leave him will hurt, but I also feel that to stay will also hurt him equally. Sapphire in time your spirit will fight to be free, and in doing so things between you both may deteriorate, simply because of how you feel now you may grow to resent Keith. I would say fly now while he has the time to recover and find another life, for if you stay and then things go ill, he will have less time in the future to recover and rebuild his life." It made a great deal of sense to her and she knew that Opal was indeed right.

"I just wish I did not have to hurt him; he is a good man and he deserves better than this."

"There are lessons to be learned in all aspects of life, and no doubt through this he too will gain wisdom. I would however also say this to you, do not burn your bridges Sapphire, for as you have seen in recent days, they also provide a good way back. I think you should go and set up your circle and be at one with yourself, and then when you feel able, make sure you are happy with the path you have chosen, for if you are not, it is never too late to change. Be certain before you sacrifice everything, and keep in touch with Runestone, for if you wear the veil as you have, even she will not find you in times of need."

"I will never lose touch with Rune; she is my centre."

"I am pleased to hear it, now tell me what will you do next?"

"I think I need to return to the Sage just to make sure he is getting well, and then I will return to Loxley and talk to my mum."

"I take it after that you will return to your stones at Callanish?"

"I think that is best, some time alone to absorb everything that's happened and find my feet again will do me good."

"I think Sapphire, you have made a good decision, it is important now more than ever that we all have someone who can watch from the edges, the power of the Fae is growing, but it will be sometime before another to match the power of Gwendolyn will rule. It will be your place now to learn all you can of Fae, for a time will come when the new queen requires your knowledge, and you must be ready to share it with her. Dawn is not far away now, so I would suggest a little sleep like our small friend here, and then when you leave tomorrow, you will be refreshed and ready for anything.... Goodnight Child, there are things I must attend to, so I will see you before you leave."

Opal patted her shoulder as she stood up, and lifting her white hood, she walked across the wide circle of grass and into the trees. Sapphire felt a great relief as she slipped off her seat and rolled out her blankets on the floor, the thought of sleep again actually felt very inviting.

High above the realm of Avalon, in the darkness below the largest moon seen in over a thousand years, Amethyst, daughter of the Fae prince Rayne, and Gwinne of the Green Circle, stood alone in the rain, wrapped in a hood and cloak of pale sky blue. Below her hood, her deep violet eyes watched as the water drained from the rocks to fill up the lake, and begin the process of renewing the realm. Deep down below her, in the deepest dungeons of the mount, her Marshals herded the last of the scratching and biting Houlen into the holding cages, alongside the last remaining feral Marsh Hounds, with the cut and bloodied soldiers of Mason Knox. All in all she held over five thousand prisoners, and the rest were scattered within the realm or left for dead where they had fallen.

Amethyst felt strange, she had lived out the past week in fear, afraid that she would never walk free or breathe the night air again. The victory over the Dark One had felt good, but she knew deep down it had not been hers; Robbie had called to him her army and led them into battle, the victory belonged to him and his small loyal band of fighters. The news that she was with child had brought a great deal of happiness and joy to the castle, James had been in great spirits ever since, but her joy had been lessened as her mind was preoccupied with the ring.

Over the last few hours as the moon passed overhead, and was now moving towards the edge of the forest and dawn approached, she felt her heart ease. The ring had begun to glow with a strange silvery light, and hope was rising in her chest in the knowledge that soon it would shine like the moon, and she with her loved ones would finally be safe. Even now below her cloak she carried her sword, as she knew right up until the dawn flashed over the horizon in the east, the Dark One could return and she would be powerless to prevent it. So for now, she stood and watched for the sun, her hand occasionally slipping from beneath the wet cloak as she checked on her ring.

Behind her came the slap of wet feet on the cold white stone of the top of the mount, and Altman hurried along holding his blue cloak up to shield him from the heavy downpour, he slid slightly as he halted at her side and gave an unstable bow, his voice raised above the thundering on the mount top. "My Lady, will you not take shelter below? This is hardly the weather to be outside."

Her voice was soft beneath her thick hood. "All my life water has been my comfort and happiness, I will wait until the first light of the sun, tonight I take the air of freedom, and tomorrow I will breathe easier knowing the realm is back under the control of a line of Fae. I am fine, and even though the realm is not mine to rule yet, I will never the less watch over it in its weakest hours."

"But My Lady you will be soaked to the bone."

"I have lived my life in water, a little rain will not damage what the seas and lakes of the world have not, no I am happy to watch this land take in the life that the rain brings, and start the process of renewal that we all will finish in the coming days."

"Well, if you insist Lady Vivian." He shrugged back under the cloak as a stream of water that had built up on the top, drained off in front of his face. "Is there anything that I can do to be of assistance?

"Yes... Altman I wish it to be known by all, that I cannot and will not use a name that was not given me by my mother and father. I will not take the title of Vivian, even though it was the name used by my grandmother, my name is Amethyst Diamond of Moon, and that is how I wish to be addressed. I have given it great thought, and I mean to start as I intend to rule, and that will begin by being true unto myself. I have also thought that the name would be more suited to that of my daughter, and so she shall be Vivian of Avalon is that clear?" Altman gave a bow beneath his wet cloak and also smiled.

"If that is your wish Lady Amethyst, then I shall ensure that it is so, is there anything else?"

"No, I think that will be fine to begin with."

"Yes My Lady, I shall return below, but should you require anything at all, there are forty guards watching over you." Amethyst gave a nod.

"Thank you, I will send word should I require it."

As Altman turned, Amethyst turned to meet him, her bright violet eyes shone from inside the hood. "Altman wait."

"Yes Lady Amethyst."

"Thank you, Altman, you have been very kind and helpful this past week, I want you to know how much James and myself have appreciated all you have done." He gave a broad smile.

"It is my honour to serve you My Lady, and I hope you know that I am true and loyal to both you and your husband, and if I may be a little bold, it has been fun and very enjoyable. I am sure that the coming years will reward all of us with great happiness." He gave another bow and stepped back, then turned and ran as fast as he could across the surface of the Mount towards the crude shelter that had been erected above the entrance to the steps down below. Amethyst looked to the forest under which she knew Robbie and the group including her sister now slept, and more to herself she whispered quietly.

"Thank you, Robbie, I have no idea how, but a day will come when I repay the favour, and come to your aid as you did mine."

Rune woke shortly before dawn with a start, she sat up and rubbed her eyes, the vivid images of her dream were still in her thoughts as she took a deep breath and breathed in the cool night air. Wiping the sweat from her brow, she turned and gave a sigh of relief as she saw Robbie's pale skinned back as he lay face down with his face in the pillow, his long brown hair was splayed across his back and onto the sheets. She sat for a moment as the light of the moon, which was brighter than normal, flooded in through the window and bathed the room in a soft pale blue glow.

On the small wooden dresser she saw the quiver of arrows with new laces, and woven in between them was a scorched arrow with tatty burned feathers and a black tip. For Rune it was the most potent symbol of her life, and it had been a vital weapon against the Dark One. Sat in bed looking at it, brought to mind every moment from her past, where Robbie had been the very source and focus of her life. It reminded her of how she had just for a second taken her mind off him, and it had been almost fatal, deep in her heart she vowed it would never happen again.

She swung her hot legs off the bed, and the floor felt cool on the soles of her feet. Standing by the window she looked out on the wide open grassy area that was bathed in moonlight. Rowan walked slowly along the edge of the trees, sheltering from the worst of the rain with Jade on his arm, and Rune smiled to herself, as she watched him talking as Jade clung to him and giggled quietly. She could not hear the words, but somehow she knew that Rowan was talking about their child, and Jade listened with a look of love and total adoration, as her quiet man talked of how they would raise their children in the woodland.

Dawn was not far away, and Rune knew that soon the realm would pass into the rule of Amethyst; she turned to the chair at the side of the bed and lifted her green pants off the back. As she slipped them on and stood to fasten them, she felt the warmth of Robbie's hands as they slipped round her waist, his voice was soft and still very strained. "Rune it's still dark, come back to bed." She sat down and he slid up behind her and rested his head on her shoulder, his skin felt soft and warm as he brushed up to her face, his hair softly stoking her neck and breasts as it fell down in front of her, she was tempted, but she wanted to be up when the dawn broke.

"Amethyst will soon come to power, and even though I cannot be by her side as I am not of Fae, I would like to watch from the Lookout just to be sure all passes well." He kissed her neck and she closed her eyes, feeling the goose bumps lift on her arms. "Oh Robbie please, I have to do this."

He gave a giggle and slid backward away from her across the bed. "Well, if you have to get up and watch, I will join you; just let me grab a coffee on route."

A little over ten minutes later they came out through the old wooden door, Robbie was a little dismayed to find their supply of coffee had run out, and Fagan had provided him with a hot steaming mug of herbal tea, which he had assured Robbie would speed up the healing of his throat. Rune giggled as she saw his face screw up as he sipped it. "Oh Hearne, this is not right, this stuff just does not have the kick I need first thing in the morning." Rune slipped her arm round him and smiled under her thick green hood.

"That's what happens when you get too spoiled; don't forget how lucky you are to have a mother who can grow the good stuff, most of the woodland world has to make theirs from dandelions." Robbie sipped his drink and scowled.

"Even that is better than this stuff; it tastes like earth and has a funny aftertaste. You know I have been thinking, you can open windows anywhere, can't you?"

"Hmm!" She gave him a just what are you thinking sort of look, he smiled.

"Well you know we could pop over to Brazil and see if there is anyone still alive over there still growing it, I mean if there isn't, it's indigenous to the region, so there must be loads of beans just hanging about ready to be picked." Rune gave a laugh.

"You never cease to amaze me."

"Yeah, but think about it Rune, we could use it as a holiday for all of us." She shook her head and smiled.

"I will have to think about it, I mean after all these powers are supposed to be used for the power of good." He smirked.

"I would imagine not having to drink this stuff would be good for everyone, it's disgusting."

"You know Robbie you can be quite grumpy in the mornings."

"No, I am not; I just get grumpy when there is no coffee left. If you think I'm bad, you should see my mum when the coffees gone, hell she could rival any of Mason's Cutters."

Robbie stepped down onto the grass, and they turned and began to head past the barn and onto the path that led them up past the cliff, and round the heated pools to the dirt track that climbed up to the summit of the Lookout. Far away across the wide plain of Avalon, Amethyst kept watch through the final hour of the night, the shimmer of her ring slowly intensifying as the night wore on.

By the time Robbie and Rune had reached the top of the high rock to view the scene across Avalon, Jade and Rowan had seen them through the trees and had hurriedly joined them. Rune stood on the edge, her senses feeling the growing apprehension in Amethyst, she understood the moment where the power flooded into the body, and her experience at first had been one of terror as she felt the overwhelming force of nature pass into her. Robbie stood quietly at her shoulder, the rain appeared to be easing off, but even in the dim light he could see the lake was still only half full, and the rest of the realm was brown and dried, or patched in an acrid burned black.

"Can all this really be restored Rune?" Jade turned to look up at him, she too had thought the same thing, Rune stood still her bright blue eyes gazing out from under her hood, her voice reflective and soft.

"It is never too late to turn the tide, even in the dying moments of everything, the power of life can gain its strength, it is the reason we fight, and even though we have lost some of the battles, we will win this war because we will fight until the last moment. Life is not easily vanquished, especially here in a realm built from the love of all things."

The moon rested on the edge of the western horizon, as the first light crept up over the hill to the east. Amethyst turned understanding the moment was close, as she turned and began to walk slowly towards the ruins of the old Citadel, the first light of the day raced across the sky and struck the fading moon, for a moment it looked like the moon had bobbed back up for a second, and the sky turned a deep fiery red, as a single beam of blue light shot back from the moon and collided into the rising sun.

Amethyst gasped as if something burning hot had hit her in the centre of her back, and with a terrifying scream of pain, the ring on her finger exploded in the brightest shimmering blue. Rune flinched feeling the moment of pain and terror within her, as from the high rock a massive ball of blinding white light exploded in the distance. Like the ripples on a pond the wave of blinding light swept out over Avalon, blotting everything from sight, Robbie pulled at the front of his hood to shield his eyes from the light, and both Rowan and Jade turned their heads to avoid being blinded. Rune never moved, her eyes shone with violet light, as she connected with Amethyst to ensure she was safe.

On top of the Citadel Mount, guards fell to the floor shielding their faces as the light engulfed everything. Fish who had been prepared by Altman stood at the top of the steps, his face was lowered, and he tried to shield his eyes with his hand as he yelled with all his might into the blinding light for Amethyst. Nothing could be seen or heard of the future queen, she was lost inside the light and out of reach of any, the floor began to shake and tremble and Fish found it hard to keep his balance. He lent on a large rock, and then let go fast as he realised the huge boulder was slowly sliding across the floor back in the direction of the old ruined building. Altman seized his hand roughly and pulled him to the side. "My Lord you cannot do anything, Avalon is in control and starting the process of repair.

Please My Lord you must move from here, the stone is returning and you will be hurt."

Fish could not see anything, he felt the hand and heard the voice, but it was barely audible as the moving rocks rumbled past him. The arm tugged, and he staggered as the floor gave another violent lurch, and he had no idea of what direction he was being pulled in.

"This is insane." He yelled into nowhere, hoping that Altman who he still could not see would hear him, the servant just pulled at him harder, and with the floor shaking and then lurching, he slowly staggered and stumbled in the direction of the servants arm.

Back at the Lookout above the Forest of Time, Robbie crouched as the light intensified. He screwed up his eyes and could just make out the dark silhouette of Rune stood just in front of him; squinting past her he could see lightening bouncing through the white light in vivid blue, and it reminded him a little of the night at Robbie's Mere, when Opal had left and Rune had replaced her, although in his mind, this did seem to be lasting a lot longer than back then. He glanced to his side to see Jade sat with her back to Avalon and the light; he could just make out her face as she smiled below her hood.

"It's a bit dramatic don't you think? I mean when I got my powers Rhiannon just dropped my marbles in my hand and in they went, none of this screaming and wailing and blinding light stuff." She leaned forward so her hood almost touched with his, blocking out a great deal of the light. "You would think considering they have hidden away all these years they would tone it down just a little, wouldn't you?" Robbie gave a giggle.

"I must admit it would be nice to see a little of the ceremony."

"I know, but it's all the secret stuff, I don't know why they hide it, to be honest Robbie they are Fae, I mean it's not like any of us can copy it, it's a whole other level of powers."

"Well can't they sort of turn into little flying people or something like specs? Wouldn't you like to do that, you know fly?" Jade gave a giggle.

"How do you know I can't?" Robbie felt a thrill run down his spine.

"Wow Jade can you?" She burst out laughing.

"Don't be silly, I am Green Circle not Fairy. Really Robbie you have one for a daughter, you should try and at least learn a little more about the difference between us and them." He gave a nod.

"Yeah obviously... although to be honest at times I find it all just a little bit complex and confusing." She gave another giggle.

"Yeah, Rowan does too, he just takes it all in his stride, I suppose it's the same for you being with Rune, I mean wow, now she has some really scary stuff going on doesn't she?" Robbie frowned.

"What do you mean scary?" Jade gave a huge deep laugh.

"It's just too easy, you and Rowan are no fun, you just believe everything we tell you." He gave a sigh of relief, just for a moment Jade had worried him, he was happier knowing she was just joking, although there had been a few times when some of her gifts had proven to be very scary, and he wondered if Jade really had been joking with him.

The white light suddenly turned an intense blue, and from nowhere there was a gigantic explosion that rocked the whole of the floor, Robbie flung out his arm, such was the force in the ground that he fell sprawling sideways, and felt Jade land heavily on top of him. She gave a squeal of surprise and then started laughing, and he pulled at his hood which was over most of his face, dust swirled round in front of his eyes as they focused. Rowan was flat on his back and Jade lay across Robbie's legs giggling. "That was wild." She was covered in dust and sat back shaking her head, casting thousands of small particles into the air, and it was then that Robbie noticed the sky.

The light had gone and the sky above was a deep dark blue, thousands of white trails seemed to flow across it like meteors, as they streaked down to the ground in Avalon. Jade rolled off his legs to Rowan, and Robbie got back to his feet, Rune was still stood watching out across the large vale of Avalon, and he moved to her side.

"Isn't it beautiful Robbie? The Fae of the Moon have a new queen to this realm, and they are returning after a thousand years of waiting, soon Avalon will ring to the sound of craftsmanship and the joy of a new life." She turned and slid her arms inside his cloak, and he looked upon her pale face and her dazzling blue eyes. "We are done here, you have aided the lines of Fae and will be forever honoured, it will soon be time to go home." He was not sure why he asked, maybe it was something in the way she had said it.

"Soon... Don't you mean now?" She gave a soft smile.

"Be patient, we have another meeting and then will be the time to head back to the Mere, I am waiting for the signal and as soon as I get it, you will know." Rune turned to Rowan and gave him a broad smile as she saw the wonder in his face. "It is a sight to behold is it not?" He blinked and then looked at her.

"I have seen many things of wonder, yet this seems to stir me deeply." Rune patted his arm.

"I have to return, but this should continue for several more minutes, stay and enjoy it, for it may be many thousands of years before the chance arises to witness such a spectacle again."

It lasted for another forty minutes, and Rowan sat with Jade and took in the wonder. It had not been missed back at the long house of Fagan either, for he had roused the whole house, and dragged them outside as he danced a merry jig of joy with Harry, knowing that his race had returned and he had a new queen to serve.

Even the saved monks had noticed and had gathered out in front of the barn, where they had viewed the sky with suspicion. In their minds anything that made the erratic giant figure of Fagan and the Specialists so happy, could not be good for them and the mission to be built by Brother Argus. It was clear that there was a division within the gathered monks, for they had spent most of the night debating, and a great many of them had talked of the Hooded Man and how it had been he who sent his men into the Cutters to save them from slaughter. Although not all of them were so easily swayed, and a large group scowled at the Specialists, referring to them as Pagan heathens and the enemy. One in particular had been very vocal in the discussions of the Hooded Man, he was an old monk of about seventy years, and he made it quite clear he would have nothing to do with the coven of witches ruled by the Violet Witch herself.

Brother Benedict gave a vicious scowl at the green clad figure of Rune as she came down the path laughing and talking with Robbie. As Rune approached, he pointed to the sky and shouted on the top of his voice. "WHAT IS THIS TRICKERY OF WITCHCRAFT?" Robbie tensed, but Rune simply placed her hand on his arm as it went for his sword, and smiled at the gathered group of monks.

"It is the same trickery and witchcraft that pulled your ungrateful terrified self from the blades of the Cutters, if you do not like it Brother, you will not have much longer to wait before you can leave, the new queen has allowed all of you safe passage out of Avalon."

"I walk with the one and only true God, I do not ask the permission of any whore queen set up by a witch, I walk where I please and do not ask her approval." A Large hand gripped him hard by the throat, and lifted him off the floor; Fagan turned the old monk round to face his wild angry eyes set under his thick bushy eyebrows.

"Ye walk with who ye like, but in her land, ye does as she says, and when she says, otherwise ye can stay here and I will find a good tree to bury ye under where ye can rot and feed it for eternity." Rune lifted her hand to Fagan.

"Please Master Keeper, I gave my word none would be harmed and have safe passage from here." Fagan scowled at the old frightened looking monk.

"This one stays." Rune shook her head.

"This is my forest Master Keeper, and I bade them all welcome in safety, please do not let me be proven to be unworthy of my word." He dropped the old monk with a thud.

"What... Never... Ye is life and the kindest most elegant flower to grace these tired old trees, never in my long life would I let such a thing be said of ye, but none shall tread these paths with such disrespect for ye grace and kindness while I stand up on these flat feet. I would roll em in the brambles and feed em to the blackthorn, grumpy bunch of buggers them, they would put em to some slow pain and more I tell ye." Rune smiled at the shock on his old lined face.

"I am honoured by you Master Keeper, and happy to know such a man of high honour tends my forest." Fagan gave a stout nod.

"I gave her my word I would protect and serve ye always, I loved her as I do all of ye, so I won't have such words spoken under these leaves, and I don't give so much as a buttercup who he walks with, in here it's my watch." Rune was very touched at his loyalty considering the short space of time that she had known him, but he was very sincere and she understood his love of Eve, who had been his greatest companion in the woodland. Fagan gave a long last stare at the monk who had remained on the floor where he fell.

"Good... Right... Just ye lot think on... Right, it's tea then, I will brew a fresh pot." He turned and walked at great speed back to the house, Rune turned to the old monk as Robbie eyed him suspiciously.

"Gather your things and prepare, for as soon as I get the signal, you will be taken safely to the gate you all entered at, once you are through it, you will be free to roam where you please as long as you never try to return to the realm of Avalon. Your monastery is destroyed and the Citadel has been rebuilt and is the domain of the Queen of Fae. But before you leave think of this, your lives all belong to my husband, for under woodsman law he spared them, be careful to whom you align yourself in the future, for he will not be merciful a second time. Go with the grace of whomever you serve as your god, but be less quick to judge in the future."

Several of the gathered monks nodded in agreement, a few of them put their heads down, Brother Benedict just looked with eyes filled with hatred at Rune and Robbie, it was obvious he was never going to forgive them for saving his life.

CHAPTER FOURTEEN

RUMOUR AND REGROUPING

With no news of Robbie, apart from a few hurried words from Rune, and a rough briefing from Sapphire, gossip was starting to wander around the stockade, and out into the wider world. Most of what Rune had told to Jess and John had remained confidential, the news that Robbie was finding it hard and had been wounded alarmed Jess, and she refused to even entertain any thought of losing him, and threw herself into the construction of her new greenhouses. John Lox was worried, he had expected them back sooner, and after fifteen days with very little word, even he had begun to think the worst.

The Cheese Shop was rife with gossip, as Agatha Patterdale played up for sympathy telling everyone how brave her granddaughter Melissa was, by going along into such terrible danger with Jasper. Anne Kirk seldom lost her temper, but her patience was starting to wear very thin with Agatha, and after she had spent the best part of her morning leaning on her gate telling everyone she was sure that Robbie had faced an awful death, and how the Specialists were depleted to just a handful, her Melissa was doing her best to patch them up, but it was a horrible and dangerous time for all of them. Alice tried to stop Anne but there was no more holding her back, as she strode out of the Bakers Shop, and across the yard to the low wall.

"You stop this, do you hear me Agatha Patterdale? I won't hear no more of your gossip and wicked untruths. How can you stand there telling the world our boy is dying or possibly dead, with his two poor children waiting at home for their parents, and that poor girl Alice worried out of her mind already?"

Agatha folded her arms looking smug as the small group gathered at her gate looked on. "Untruths? I will have you know that it is common knowledge that they are all in trouble and losing the fight, and if you don't believe me, you just go and ask John Lox, he will tell you I am right. I have it on good authority from those working in the hall that things have gone against us, Carlisle is struggling to hold them back on the northern moor, and in the south there are constant attacks all along the guarded borders, you go and ask any of them and see who is right Anne Kirk? It was John Lox himself, told you that the boy would only be gone for five or six days, well it's been over two weeks now and he is not back yet, and rumour has it, it won't be any time soon. Old Mr Simmons walks round looking worn out and exhausted; just the look on his face should tell you how bad it is, and even the vicar has done a flit." Alice Kirk gave a gasp.

"Oh Agatha Patterdale you should be ashamed of yourself, Father Warren has gone away on an errand for Lord Loxley, I know that because Sissy Barber does his cleaning, and he gave her a key the day before he left. He sent a personal note right to this shop cancelling his bread until further notice." Agatha frowned knowing she had missed that little snippet of information, but she was resolute that she was right.

"It doesn't change things one bit, everyone knows he is a bit flaky, he can't decide what faith he is with his services for the Earth and then the Christians. I heard he even helped out the Buddhists and that small group of Jews with a service. If you ask me he has spent too much time locked away in his church and has gone off the boil as it were, it would not surprise me in the least, if he hasn't flitted for good. Lord Loxley is still well over a week late, you tell me what's happened then, if things were going as swimmingly as you say Anne Kirk where is he? Lying in a hole somewhere, if you want my opinion?"

"And that is all it bloody well is Agatha, and I will thank you to mind your own business when it comes to the welfare of my son." The group turned round to see a very stern and angry looking Jess, Anne lifted her hands to her mouth, as the others all parted and moved expecting trouble, as Agatha looked down at the floor, and then lifted her head and looked right in the eyes of Jess.

"I am only saying what others are thinking and whispering. After all, it's not just your boy lost is it? There are a lot of folks round here who want to know where their kin are since they skipped off with your son, it's not like them at the hall are telling us anything."

Jess looked hurt, but her anger was just simmering below the surface as she tried her hardest not to explode, she thought for a second, the hazel of her eyes igniting as she tried to remain composed. "The relatives of every fighter here are given constant updates when we get them, everyone of them knows as much as we do."

"Aye and that's the point isn't it? You lot know nought because he is lost to you."

"MY SON IS NOT DEAD OR LOST!" Jess shook from head to foot as she tried to control herself. "You listen to me all of you, you keep your mouths shut and stop spreading rumours that can harm the fight we have. My son is out there with some very brave people risking his life to protect all of yours, so if you have a doubt or a query, you bloody well come and talk to me for the facts, not this over indulged old maid who has nothing better to do than gossip and make bad cheese."

Jess turned and walked back up the street away from the shops towards the hawthorn lined lane and the farm, her eyes filled with tears and she sniffed as

Agatha shrieked with outrage, and the Kirk sisters could do little but scurry into their shop and giggle.

The tears flowed as Jess ran up the lane away from the town, Beth was stood at the farm gate when Jess came running towards her in floods of tears, and Beth caught her in her arms. "Oh Jessie Love what on earth has happened?" She wrapped her big arms round her and pulled her close in a tight loving embrace. Jess wept unable to talk, as Beth guided her slowly round the house to the kitchen door. "Oh Jessie Love... Come on and tell me everything, we will have a nice cup of tea and that will make you feel better, come on now love don't cry."

When Jess finally told Beth what had happened, Beth was absolutely furious, Jess did everything she could and finally calmed her down, and begged her not to go down to the shop or tell John. Although it made Beth's blood boil, she kept her word, which was until the following day when Beth accidentally bumped into Agatha on the market.

Within seconds and in front a good many witnesses, Beth had her up against the pot stall, held firmly by the scruff of her neck. Beth was red with rage, and as it appeared equally as terrifying as her husband. "You listen to me you vicious old harpy; you keep that forked tongue of yours well and truly behind your teeth in future. If I hear any more rumours about our Robbie or see you upsetting our Jessie again, you will have more than bad cheese to worry about, because I will come looking for you, and I will give you your first honest day's work of your life, you will be hanging in the wheat fields scaring off the crows."

Needless to say, the gossip that day was rife, but it was less about Robbie, and more about his aunt who had indeed cemented her reputation amongst the women to match that of her husband. There was more than one smiling face that day on the market.

There was no denying that over two weeks with no news from the Hooded Man, it did increase the rumour that Mason was winning the war. Around the cathedral in Lincoln things were starting to get a little heated as supporters of Brother Argus arrived daily, and demanded that the bishop announce who the new council would be, and to make a statement in support of Mason Knox. Bowman Jersey felt increasingly worried about the welfare of Father Warren, especially after his life had been threatened, and with the secret knowledge that he had joined the new council of the church, Jersey made the suggestion in his letter to Loxley that some protection of woodsmen should be moved nearer the cathedral.

Mason on the other hand was feeling positively delighted when he returned to York. The rebellion in London had been completely wiped out, Scotland was going reasonably well, and his industries were relatively unaffected, and although there were skirmishes above the moors at York, his army were holding back Ian of Carlisle and preventing them breaking through to aid Loxley. He had problems in Devon with Caerleon starting to push forward, but with all of Cornwall free, he was able to use the harbours to ship out men and supplies to the aid of all the rest of Britain.

Across the Channel in France, Baron De La Roche was gathering together another army to the south of Morbihan, and should he need more soldiers they were equipped and ready to ship into the action. From Birmingham south, his largest city of stone was preparing to arm up and set off to war, already a great deal of his scouting groups had met and fought with the woodland soldiers, and the woodland realm was now in retreat moving further north to surround Loxley.

He gave a happy and contented smile as he sat with Dana and Mark Richard Dale for his lunch and discussed the campaign, the time for him to strike and strike hard was coming, and the thought of it positively excited him, his dream of ruling once and for all was almost a reality.

In the south of England just over the rise from the shoreline, where the waves pounded onto the beach of small stones and white sand, Louisa stood and watched the faint shape of one of Mason's ships pass on the horizon. The gulls screamed and shouted, as they were lifted and dropped on the fast breeze, and her long blonde hair lifted and danced round the edges of her raised hood. Behind her in the sands, Ox grilled five plump gulls over the fire for his breakfast, whilst Dove and Rigger slept curled deep inside their blankets. Silas was still at the Lockup with Martin, as they checked out what guards were on duty, and tried to cut through the locks and open some of the massive steel containers.

The Sage was sat off to the left on the highest part of the dunes, out of sight and lost in thought. Ben was on the beach picking up driftwood for the fire with Marcus, and here on the sand, Louisa felt like she was a million miles away from anything sad or bad. Her only reminder of the fight behind her was the dirt on her clothes and the lingering smell of smoke, all of them looked a little the worst for wear, and had parts of their clothes singed or burned from where they had fought through the flames and shelling to rescue others, she closed her eyes and just breathed in the cool sea air, and it felt almost like being back home in Newport.

She did not notice the flash of blue behind her as Sapphire arrived back; it was the pat on her shoulder that brought her to her senses. "Hey are you dreaming?" She opened her eyes and smiled.

"Saff you made it back, how are you?" Sapphire gave her a hug.

"I am OK, it's been sort of weird but busy, you know what it's like?"

Louisa gave a nod. "Yeah, tell me about it, so... what's new and where do we go from here, is there any news from Robbie?"

"It's why I am here, I spoke to Rune last night and things have gone well in Avalon, the new queen is seated and Robbie will be heading back to Loxley shortly. Rune wants me to take you and Ox with his men back for a while; I think

Robbie wants to work out where he stands before he plans anything else." Louisa gave a shrug.

"It's not been too much fun in London; I would imagine that will set things back."

"Yeah, well it's up to him to look at it and try to find another way round, for now it looks like you may get some time off."

"Oh that would be nice; I think I could sleep for a month."

Sapphire gave a smile. "Ok I need to talk to the Sage and then I will be back, we will have to collect Rafe on route, that should be pleasant, I would imagine he is a bit cross with me, but hell he has made it a passion of his. So where is our wounded leader?" Louisa lifted her thumb.

"He was over there a while ago, said something about needing to think." Sapphire gave a look over towards the dunes.

"Ok I will find him and have a chat, then we will be off." She turned shouldering her long yellow bow, and trudged through the soft sand in the direction of the high dunes. Louisa sat down on the soft sand covered grass, and just rested her eyes again. "Sleep... Oh and in a bed, yeah I could do that."

The Sage was sat in thought, his mind filled with the moments he spoke to his father, and how his father had shown so little regard for a son who he saw as a barrier to his plans. He had always thought that he would be able to sit with him and find some sort of reasoning to a way of ending this without the death of Robbie or his father, but as much as it pained him, he realised that Mason was in too deep and in love with the power he held, and there was no way of going back.

Sapphire walked up the side of the steep hill covered with the clumps of the long brown grass that danced and shook with the wind, her long blue cloaked flapped round her with her hair, as the breeze coming in off the sea lifted it and tossed it round her face. Her eyes sparkled with a new sort of life, and the Sage noticed how she appeared to have more of a purpose in her strides. He gave her a smile as she came towards him, her white boots sliding softly in the sand. "You look happy; I see the formation of your circle has brought you a sense of purpose."

She looked down at his sling and smiled. "I do feel better today, not sure why, but I do. How is the arm, it looks likes Louisa has taken very good care of it?" He glanced at it.

"Yeah, I think she regrets it, and would rather I had bled to death."

"She knows then?"

"Hmm... I am not sure she sees me as the leader of goodness I was to her now, but I felt it was right to explain why I tried to convince my father to stop." Sapphire turned at his side and looked out across the dull blue waves that crashed up on to the beach, scattering new stones to the mass. She stroked back her hair glad to feel the breeze on her face.

"It was not the smartest thing you have ever done, but I think in time she will understand why you tried. I guess I am still puzzling it out, did you honestly think you had a chance to convince him to stop?"

"If I had and we were negotiating peace now, it would have been worth it, but I think it's clear he has been swallowed by the dreams of his corruption, let's face it, if his son has no sway with him, then no one will."

"No offence Billy but he threw you into Loxley as a small child to spy, I know it's not what you want to hear, but let's be honest here. If he would do that just to gain an advantage, there was no way you were ever going to have a chance, and now you are probably higher on his wanted list than Robbie. It was foolish to show your hand too early, you do realise that your grandmother now knows you're alive, and she will at some point come looking for you?" She looked down at him sat on the sand, but he continued to stare out across the sea.

"I am not worried about her; we have clashed many times over things."

"Yeah, then you were classed as family, I think you should think a little bit deeper; this is no longer a squabble in the family, you are now outside and an enemy. No offence Billy, but you have the gift of sight, but you do not have any of her powers, and she will not hesitate to use them on you."

"The connection between us is broken, she will not find me easily, I mean let's face it, I walk past her house most nights and she has no idea I am there, no I will carry on and if she appears then I will deal with it when it happens."

"It's up to you, but just be careful, you have done a lot of good for the fight, don't throw it away now." He gave a laugh.

"Yeah, London was a swimming success."

"Losing Brian has hurt, he was an odd sort of fellow, but he did have a lot of contacts. Although we managed to get a lot of wounded men out and move them to New Avon, in time they will heal, and we saved a lot of fit men, just give them a week or two to rest up and they will be a big help in the north. All is not lost just yet, which just remains for me to ask what exactly you intend to do, and why on earth did you bring everyone here?" He stood up and gave her a big smile.

"That is the big question Sapphire... Why indeed come to this deserted little oasis?" She frowned at him, not quite understanding why he suddenly looked so happy. The Sage gave a wink. "This is my father's piggy bank, it is a secret he has shared with few, I am not even sure Lance knows of this place. Over there my friend, stored in those neat little boxes is the total sum of just about everything the Cutters plundered from the old world, there is gold and art and all manner of valuables, but they are not what I am after, I want the really good stuff."

"Like what, gold is pretty much the most desired commodity of everything?" He slowly shook his head.

"Not if you are a Woodsman." She wasn't completely sure what he meant.

"We make pretty much everything we need, what has Mason got that is so valuable to us?"

"He has tinned food for starters, millions of plundered tins preserved for an age that will not rot or perish. He has thousands of bales of fabric, stacks of gunpowder, solar panels, generators, shoes, nails, tools, and not to mention a mountain of scrap metal that he gathered and brought here. Sapphire this place is known as Area Eight, it is one of about thirty places my father planned in the very early days. This is his supply store to everything he has in mind, and the contents of those thousands of containers over there are why he has such confidence he will win this fight. Saff, locked up safe and secret here is the means to rebuild any kind of world you desire. I intend to siphon some of it off for everyone in the Woodland. Just think of what we could do with it all in our fight against him, I mean let's face it, there is a massive shortage of explosives, Robbie will not be able to blow things up for much longer, not unless we top up his supplies." Sapphire gave a gasp as she understood what he was intending to do.

"Yeah, but hang on a minute, a job this big will take thousands of men, and we just don't have them, and not to mention how the hell can you do all of this with soldiers all over the place? You know I am sure your men are good, but you will need to steal it, then transport it, and all in secret, are you sure you have thought about this properly?" He gave a shrug.

"Well yeah, I will need a little help, I had hoped to bring in some of the London forces, and I was going to send out scouts for boats."

"Boats! What the hell will you need boats for?" He looked a little irritated.

"To ship it out and take it round the coast, I figured if we all dress up and fly the dragon colours we should have easy passage, think about it, it's the one thing my father would never expect, he thinks he is the master of the sea. We nick it and ship it from the beach, he has been doing it for years, so why don't we?" Sapphire could see he had a point.

"It's still a massive undertaking Billy and what if you all get caught?"

"If it helps us win it will be worth it, and with the right man in charge I think it's more than possible." She gave a slight chuckle.

"I take it you think you are the right man?" He gave her a broad smile.

"Well, if the jobs vacant, I am not exactly doing much at the minute." She gave a giggle and patted his good shoulder.

"Leave it with me and I will let Rune know, scout out the area and find out what you can, selling this to Robbie might not be easy, but if anyone can it's Rune."

"He still does not know I am here then?" Saff smiled.

"Rune has kept to her word, he knows he has a green friend working very hard for him, but no Billy, he has no idea it is you. For now, it is enough he knows he has a strong loyal supporter." Billy gave a nod, but she could see the disappointment through his masked eyes. "He will one day know everything; Rune will tell him how much you have done to help him." He gave a sigh.

"Yeah, I suppose so." She smiled and pulled him close for a hug.

"Get that arm mended and learn all you can, oh and by the way, lose the beard, the way it's growing up on your mask makes you look like a white sheep dog, the stubble looked better." She laughed as she turned. "I am off for a while on other things, so Rune will be in touch, but no doubt our paths will cross in the forest at night, say hi to your little companion from me, I think Cal really likes her."

The Sage stood at the top of the dune and watched as Sapphire slowly disappeared from view, and his mind turned back to Loxley, and his eyes carried the usual sadness that many were used to seeing. For some time he just watched until he saw the blue flash in the sand far off and knew that Sapphire had left. His arm ached and he rubbed it slowly, and then set off back to the camp to wait for the arrival of Martin and Markus, his plans now had to be voiced to the others, and between them they would have to find a way to make it work.

For most of the night, in the wide expanse of empty land between the walls of York and the start of the trees, there were sounds that many within the ranks of the Woodsmen were not familiar with. Just before dawn a rider who had ridden through the four miles of woodland to the heart of the operation, and the large headquarters built high up in the canopy of the trees arrived and requested Rayne to come to the front line. For Rayne there were few surprises, as he had sat and watched Mason build his stone cities all over the country, and so as the sun rose above the horizon, he stood with General Haughton and looked out on what had been a wide barren land running up to the walls of York, with nothing but grass wild flowers and small sapling trees.

In the first light of day, it was clear that Mason had been busy using his earth movers during the night, and they had dug out a huge trench that ran one hundred yards parallel to the walls of York. Rayne lowered his scope and smiled at the General. "We are lucky, this tells us it will be a little longer before he intends to march out in a full assault." The General was not entirely sure why.

"It will... What makes you think that, and why exactly is this lucky?" General Haughton stared at the large black metal machines that were currently moving back, as large flat vehicles carrying what looked like the sides of houses moved forward." Rayne pointed to the long row of machines heading towards the ditch.

"We are lucky because he is building this himself, in the past his mother has played a part and his stone walls have gone up almost overnight. The very fact he is doing this himself means his mother is busy elsewhere, so firstly we won't have to deal with her just yet. Secondly if he is building this himself that tells us he is looking to build something a little more lasting, which could mean he intends to use York as his northern outpost. That General is very good news because it will take him longer to build his walls so he has a nice secure castle for want of a better word, to fire his cannons off."

"Cannons, well why go to the bother of building, surely he will just roll them out and start firing, which is pretty much what we all expected?" Rayne shook his head.

"Not Scarlet, she said he would do this, you see at the moment he has to cover a lot of ground in order to reach deep into the forest, she predicted he would build some sort of battlement to place his long range guns on. He knows that here on the edges we have our men scattered in small groups amongst the thinner trees, no Mason needs to find a way to hurl his explosives over our heads to where we have much more men. He knows in the deep woodland with lots of cover, one of our men becomes equal to fifty of his, because we have the skills to move unseen and fire on him where least expected. He will hit us from the air before sending his men to face us, but what we will do is run closer so his bombs go over our heads, and then when his men come out, we will attack with force and then retreat as he recalibrates his cannons to fire closer. This is all good news for us, Scarlet was bang on the nail at predicting his officers, according to her documents he has brought in a guy called Dale from down south; he likes to use as many cannons as possible before sending in his men. This is good news we are running to schedule; I will be leaving shortly to visit my daughter and Treen will be taking back over, she will be very happy to see this."

Once Rayne had returned to the headquarters, General Haughton watched as the large trucks carrying the huge flat house like walls moved into position. Shortly after large cranes moved out across the gap and lifted the huge panels into place, and as they did, he began to understand that Mason was putting in place the sides of a giant wall to be poured from cement. It would be a fast and quick way of setting up his fortress, as trucks loaded with steel frames moved slowly in rhythm, and smaller cranes lifted off huge pre made meshes to drop between the double lines of panels over the trenches. The arrival later that day of huge cylindrical containers made him shudder, as he realised that through the night they would begin to pump into the frames, and within a few days when the frames were removed, a huge stone castle would be just over one hundred feet in front of them, and Mason and his soldiers would be a hell of a lot closer to the trees.

CHAPTER FIFTEEN

PARTING OF THE WAYS

It had been a long wet frustrating day for Robbie, although for the rest of the Specialists it had been very busy. Preparations to move out and head home brought about a mass of activity, as the group all packed up their things and straightened up the house for their departure. Blades and Gaynor were given the privilege of picking some of the herbs from Fagan's vast garden, which he knew were not available anywhere else. Blades had already bagged a great many of the special white flowers, which not only had healing properties, but had enhanced her cooking to a point that no one had made a single complaint about it. Treen and Jaz were stronger and back to normal, although they both still ached where they had been scratched by the Houlen, Fagan gave them both a pot of a thick sticky foul smelling orange ointment to use to ease the pain and aches, and Fagan assured them within the week they would never feel another twinge again.

Bear gathered together all of the arrows that Jade had made, they were in his opinion some of the best he had ever fired, and considering Fagan's views at first about making weapons, he thought it would be rude not to use all of them. Gaynor was thrilled when Fagan gave her a roll of the fabric he had woven, instructing her to make both William and herself decent cloaks for the crowning ceremony, Rune eyed it enviously as she studied the quality of the weave, and had to admit that Fagan was indeed very skilled on a loom. John and Todd sorted through the various sets of armour that Fagan had offered them, and with his permission they carefully wrapped it up to return to Loxley for others to use, and Robbie paced around impatiently checking each and every item to return with them, while he drunk the special tea Fagan had given him, and found much to his distaste that his voice was still hoarse but recovering, and his neck was feeling less sore.

All in all, as the sun hovered above the west and the day began to draw to a close, most of the work and packing was done ready for the return. Robbie stood on the steps as the long line of monks prepared to leave and he addressed them. "I am pleased to see each and every one of you alive, and whether or not you believe it, I am not an enemy of your church as has been stated previously." He lifted a small black book up in his hand, which Rune recognised as the book given him by Sister

Mary, it was obvious many of the assembled monks recognised it.

"This was given me by a sister to your faith, and someone who was very dear to me. I have over the months read a great deal of this book, and I find within the pages some great wisdom." This really made an impact and several of the monks looked at each other in disbelief, as Robbie gave a nod of recognition to them. "I will not deny there are many things I share in common with this book, for in the faith of my father I was taught similar beliefs, but it is in that common understanding that I find it hard to understand why it is you would venture into this realm and build a monastery to the glory of Argus, a man known to be the servant of Mason Knox."

Rune gave a small smile as she saw the look on the faces of many of the monks, and it was clear to her that a great many had no idea that Mason was backing their leader Brother Argus. Robbie stepped down from the steps and walked toward many of them still holding the small black bible in his hand for them to see.

"You will be taken safely from this land, where you may return to wherever you please, and in return I ask only one thing of each you. I do not ask for your loyalty or your support, you may choose what in your heart you feel to be the right path, but I will tell all of you here and now that I did not come to this fight by choice, I came to this fight through need." His head gave a slight nod as he walked slowly, looking each of them in the eye.

"Yes... Need. A need to ensure that every man in this country will remain free, free to choose to work his own land, and build his own home to share with his family, in a place of safety where he could choose his own faith and worship wherever he felt, and know that throughout his days he would not have to answer to any for how he cared for his family or to whom he prayed. I am a lord of my own land, and so I already have the loyalty of those who are free and support me, I do not need the support of the church to help me win this war, and believe me Brothers of Christianity I will be victorious, and I will seat the new king, and help him make this a fair land without the use of your so called witchcraft, because regardless of what you have heard, there are no witches serving the lands of Loxley." He stopped and looked at Brother Benedict.

"I will not support those who enslave free men as workers as they did Megan who is stood over there in front of you. Megan is from the old city of Scarborough; she once lived on the edge of the woods with her family, her father worked hard in his fields to feed them and raise them to be decent. I will not steal the land of others as Mason did with her family, and bulldoze her home to build factories of stone. But I will defend them, I will as I have with Megan free them, and let them decide their own future and fate as free people, and I will not stop until I have torn down every wall of oppression and blown to hell every factory that uses slave labour, so as you leave I ask one thing of all of you."

He stopped square in the centre of them, where they all had a clear view of him, and he had their full attention as every one of them hung on his words and fixed their full concentration on him.

"Gentlemen, go back to your homes and honour the words in this book, teach your faith to all and encourage them to be free and treat each other with dignity and respect. Speak out against oppression and rally to the aid of those in most need, and most importantly of all, remove your support from the enslavers and murderers of the innocent and let me deal with them, for I can tell you now that for the treachery committed by Brother Argus against my family and the people of this land he will pay, and it will be by my hand that he pays, as will the Empire of Knox. Think of my words as you leave here with my blessing and go in peace, just remember if you choose to follow my enemy, then I too will have no choice but to face you again, and that occasion will not end as peacefully as this one."

Robbie turned in front of his silent audience and barked out his orders with authority. "Harry, Hawk, Bear and Blades, lead them down the woodland path safely to the carts and their escort out of here, and then return as quick as you can." Hawk walked up the grass to the front of the line, as the others with their bows on their shoulders helped to escort the monks in an orderly line towards the trees. Robbie came back up the steps to Rune's side; she smiled and slipped her arm round his waist.

"That was very eloquent; I really enjoyed listening, as did all of them." He watched as they began to walk slowly out of the open glade in the direction of the exit.

"If just half of them turn from Argus and try to help, it will make some difference. Somehow, I think I will see some of their faces against us again, I must admit Rune from the little I know of their beliefs, I do find it hard to understand why they follow Mason, they should be on our side, it's what their Christ taught them."

"We all interpret things differently Robbie, and some of them would rather follow than lead by example, there are many from our faith serving Mason willingly, which is against everything all of us here believe in, yet some chose to ignore the obvious, although they are free men, so at least have the choice." She kissed his cheek, and smiled, he gave a small grin.

"You are as always right." She gave a small giggle.

"Trust me, I know stuff." He gave a laugh and nodded at her as she laughed along with him and then leaned in and kissed his cheek again.

"Ok back to work, so where is Rowan and Jade?" Rune gave a giggle.

"This is a very big woodland, where do you think they are?" He gave a long sigh.

"That bloody sister of yours will wear him out; I just got him back on his feet and she I feel has wasted very little time getting him off them again." Rune gave a giggle, as did a few of the others. "Ok then, I shall proceed for the moment without my general, let me know when he staggers back into view."

As promised, the monks all were led to the road where carts waited to transport them. Long lines of blue clad soldiers from Avalon helped the older monks into the carts ensuring they were comfortable, and then escorted them down the long road, surrounded by burned out trees towards the bridge that crossed the mouth of the lake. Within two hours they were taken over the ford and onto the white road towards the Curtain of light, where they were unloaded and allowed to walk freely through the curtain, and back into the world they knew on the outer edge of Glastonbury, where more carts were waiting and an escort of Cutters to guide them. It was not long before the rough manner in which they were treated, made all of them think about the polite respectful way the Hooded Man had treated them. So their journey out of the area began, although they were not free to travel where they pleased, the guards were under strict instruction to take them to the north gate, and then follow the road to Wells and the cathedral where Brother Argus awaited them.

It was an hour later when Robbie came into the small room at the end of the long house to find Rune sat on the bed writing in her journal, she looked up as he walked in and smiled. "Has he shown up yet?" Robbie shook his head.

"No, there is no sign of him." Rune's eyes glowed violet for a moment and she smiled at him.

"They are on their way back now; they should be here in about twenty minutes." He sat down on the bed with a bump.

"Good I want to get back as quickly as possible, we have been away too long and I need to find out what has happened in detail, somehow I think Mason will be wasting no time and getting ready for a full scale attack, and I need to be there if he does." Rune lifted her hand and rubbed the back of his neck, and enjoyed the soft feeling as his hair stroked the back of her hand; he moaned and let his head relax forward. "Oh that feels good."

She thought for a moment before speaking. "Rob tomorrow I want to come back here alone. This realm has now come under my charge since Eve has left it. I want to discuss a few things with Fagan, and then go and see Amethyst, I also want to visit Eve's garden. I may be a few days will that be OK?" He gave out a long breath as he relaxed while she massaged him.

"Will you remain in touch with Jade?"

"Yes, I will maintain a contact at all times."

"I don't want you trapped here again on your own, I will worry about it." She understood the panic he had felt when she had disappeared on the bridge at the Mirrored Waters.

"That cannot happen again, Amethyst has her full power and the realm only responds to her command, the Dark One will not be able to enter here again,

Amethyst has already seen to that." He gave a gentle relaxed nod.

"OK then, I will miss you, but if it is important to your realm then you must do it."

It felt like a strange moment between them, Rune watched him knowing he had a lot of responsibility on his shoulders, and yet he had just acknowledged that she had a realm that was separate from his. She marvelled at how he could be so down to earth at times, and just be so accepting of the circumstances around him. She was surprised that he would recognise her position here in the forest without question, as he did his place as the Lord of Loxley. Since she had received her gift of the runestone, it had worried her that Robbie may see it as something different and separate from his world. She had worried it may even threaten him, but here he was just as always, relaxed and contented and more understanding than she had honestly ever had thought possible. She came out of her thoughts and he was looking at her. "What?" He smiled.

"I was really enjoying that, why did you stop?"

"What.... Oh sorry I got side tracked for a moment." He smiled as she began to rub the back of his neck again, and he leaned forward and relaxed.

It was well over an hour later when everyone gathered at the front of the house that for just a week had been their place of haven and safety. Fagan had been a wonderful host, who in his small way had enhanced the life of all of them with his strange wisdom and helpful advice. Maggs wept openly as she hugged him, as did Steph as the old man of the trees walked round saying his goodbyes. John and Bear both gave him a huge hug and he was deeply moved by their affection, Rowan took his hand and gripped it firmly. "Fagan, I regard you as a friend of great worth, it's been an honour to share your home with you. I thank you with all my heart for the care you placed on protecting my lord and his lady, I think with your good advice and wisdom, your new queen will rule for a long time."

Fagan gave a smile, but his eyes below his thick busy white eyebrows had lost a little of their sparkle, for even though he had spent so long alone, and his guests had disrupted his routine and his home, his heart ached to see them leave. He nodded at Rowan and took a moment to catch his breath as the wave of emotion passed over him. "I will miss ye all, it has been long since I sat with such company, and I have enjoyed it greatly. Tis my honour to call all ye friends, and may the paths all of ye walk grow green and weed free my friends."

He looked to Jade who had huge tears in her eyes, which ran down her cheeks as she gave a big sniffle. He swallowed the huge lump in his throat and his eyes sparkled. "Fare ye well my little green eyed wood nymph. Ye have left such a mark on my heart that it will soar for days knowing ye walked in my woodland as did ye grandmother, for I see much of the wild briar in your determination, and all of the love of poppies in your heart. I shall miss ye there is no denying, but hope that ye will return one day with more little nymphs to grace the floor of my trees." He moved to open his arms, and Jade leapt into them and gave a huge sob.

"I wish you could come with us; I hate leaving you all alone like this, who will care for you if you get poorly?" Fagan wiped the tear from his cheek as he looked down at the mass of blonde curls pressed into his shirt. He stroked back her long hair and she looked up with green tear filled eyes, Fagan slid down to his knees and came level with her face, his voice was soft quiet and loving, and he spoke as if what he said was only meant for Jade's ears.

"I will never be alone because I carry with me a heart that has been touched by the wonder and beauty of a green eyed wood nymph, whom I have great love for. I will talk to my trees just as I showed ye, and through them will come word of ye in the other world, for here is the centre of all things, and everything of the world ye live in is known here, so I will watch and learn of all ye do. My people have returned to Avalon, and with them the grandsons of my sister, they will take post as the new makers to the realm and will be frequent visitors. Do not fear my dearest of friends, for I too have aid when needed, ye go and live a life with ye children and be happy, and if ever ye needs me, I will be here hoping ye visit." He smiled as Jade wiped her eyes, and she gave him a big grin, he nodded softly.

"I love you Fagan, and I will come and visit, and we will bring the children, but please if you need me talk to the trees, and I promise I will hear them and come."

"Then we is good? Oh hang on, if memory serves me well, we is cool, but not smoking... And as happy as a star burst poppy, soon we will meet again on the road of green." He stood back up and gave everyone a big smile, Rowan took Jade's hand as they all lifted their bags, and Robbie came out of the door and down the steps followed by Rune.

"Fagan my friend there are no words to thank you for all you have done for us, this is not the last for I will return many times you have my word." Robbie took his hand and gave it a firm shake.

"Ye will do well Lord of the wooden town north, but never forget, it's the bindweed that gets them so be the biggest." He turned to Rune and smiled, and lifted his hand to cup her cheek. "Ye is her likeness in every way, stand a moment so I may gaze on her a while longer."

Rune stood just for a moment knowing the deep love he held for Eve, she knew how much the knowledge that Eve was gone forever had caused him pain, and she clasped his hand and gave it a gentle squeeze.

"I will be a frequent visitor to my realm my master of all the trees, we have many times of pumpkin juice and sesame bread before us. I will return within the next few days for the rest of our party, and there are things of which you can be of help to us all, and so I would speak with you on them. For now my treasured friend, keep safe until I return."

Rune pulled him into a warm hug and he smiled with happiness. The group prepared and Rune opened her violet window into Robbie's Mere, and feeling a little sadness, they all turned and walked through the light. Jade turned as she approached the window and looked back and waved, Fagan gave her a smile and lifted his large hand in salute, and she turned and went through and the window closed behind her.

All was quiet in front of the old cabin, and the old man gave a mighty sigh and turned to walk up the steps. "OI! YES YOU, ARE YOU EVER GOING TO UNTIE US?" Fagan gave a chuckle as he walked across to the barn, where just inside the door the two captive soldiers were still bound to the post.

"Well, well, all ye friends are dead or prisoners of the realm, I will cut ye free, but I suppose it is up to ye what happens now. Ye could run into the forest, but there again there are things in there men from the world ye live in have no name for, as they is just too frightening and horrible to name. Ye could go down that path where ye came from and surrender to the new queen, and beg she does not cut ye to bits in the market square for the evil ye has done to her realm. I will leave it to ye to decide, just leave my home, for if ye stays, ye will talk to the scythe, and I can assure ye it will be the shortest conversation ye ever has... Now go." Fagan cut the rope, and in a flash the two ragged prisoners ran for the path in the trees that would lead them back into Avalon, he gave a chuckle and pulled the door closed, then headed back into his much quieter house to make some tea.

Rune was barely through the window, when she dropped her bags and ran with all her speed through the gate and up the steps to the house. Louisa smiled and was about to say hello, when Rune dashed right past her, and headed for the stairs to the nursery. Robbie smiled as he swung open the gate followed by the rest of the group; he nodded as he came up the steps to the house. "Nice to see you again Commander, tell me how are the boys doing?" Louisa thumbed and pointed to the side of the house.

"They won't come in, they say they stink too much, Isolde ran me a bath, I hope that is alright?"

Robbie dropped his bag just inside the door. "No problems, I take it you are back until we have another task, if so make yourself at home, as you see everyone else does."

Most of the Specialists trouped into the house, Rowan and Jade took William, Gaynor and Judith to their house through the trees, and Steph and Smokes borrowed Rune's buggy to drive home. All of them looked dirty and tired, so Louisa headed to the kitchen to help Filomena who was busy preparing a meal.

Robbie leaned in on the doorframe and watched as Rune sat talking with both her children cradled on her lap, he smiled as she looked up, and he could see the happiness in her eyes. "Happy Now?" She gave him a nod and looked back down at the children. "I really stink Rune, so I am going to get changed and then we can spend the night just you me and the kids OK?"

"Yeah, I would like that, let's eat in our room and let everyone else relax down stairs." Rune looked back at the children and talked quietly to them as Robbie headed down the hallway to his room and clean clothes. It was so nice being home at last, even though he knew that would mean more problems to solve and men to organise, but that was tomorrow, tonight it was just going to be Rune and him.

Louisa and the Outlaws had arrived mid afternoon with Rafe and Sapphire, Rafe had gone to his house in the village to clean up, and Sapphire had gone to see her mother. They had walked from the gates back up the farm talking and sat on the bench in the orchard. Telling her mother she was leaving was not easy, but Melanie listened and in many ways she understood more than Sapphire realised. Finally, after many tears and hugs she opened her window and left. Melanie promised to talk to Keith and Jasper on her behalf, as she understood that this was difficult for Sapphire, as she did love Keith, but not enough to stay, which would be what he wanted her to do.

As the sun slipped down in the sky and all at Loxley rested, Sapphire stood above her father's grave in the centre of the large stone circle and watched the darkness fall, for her it felt like a veil slipping over her life, and alone again, she knew she had to focus and concentrate, for she was the one with the strongest gift of sight, and she had to prepare and face a very different future. Now she had seen how delicate the balance was held in, she knew she had to look into the future and make sure the balance never slipped away for the woodland realm again.

This was to be her time of learning as she prepared in earnest for the training of her circle, and for the training of a future queen of the Violet Isle. There could be no more distractions from now on, and her mind was set on practicing everything she had learned, for one day she knew as the centre of her own circle, the Dark One would come looking for her, and when she did, Sapphire knew she would need to be ready.

As with all things in Loxley, Robbie did not get the night he had planned. It was not long after he had finished his bath and prepared for his quiet night, when Melanie arrived to talk to Rune. Not much longer after Melanie's arrival, John and Beth arrived with Alice and Jessica Sapphire, closely followed by Jess, and all plans went out of the window, as a full on family and Specialists evening of fun started.

Having heard all about the new greenhouses from Jess, who was delighted Harry was back to help out, and John gave Robbie a full run down on what was happening at York, as well as all the gossip and Beth's confrontation of Agatha, it was well past midnight when he finally rolled back the covers and slipped into bed against Rune feeling mentally and physically exhausted. He closed his eyes and let his tired aching body relax into the mattress with a long sigh, there was movement beside him and he opened one eye, Rune giggled in the darkness as she slid over and sat on his waist. "Hey gorgeous." He smiled.

"Hey beautiful." Her eyes danced with delight.

"We are back at home in our bed." She leaned over and gave him a long slow passionate kiss, and he responded knowing sleep was now a much longer way off than he had planned; life at home was very quickly getting back to normal.

CHAPTER SIXTEEN

COMING TO TERMS

Dawn had arrived, although for Jett and Una it was hard to notice, as they sat on their high edged platform looking out at the black sky filled with small shining dots. The final goodbye between Una and her mother Gwendolyn was long and tearful, and Jett had walked into the long mist covered valley to give them both a little privacy. Through the mist she could just make out the shadowy figure of Una as she hugged her mother, and separated by the misty veil, she finally had a moment alone to think and examine her own feelings.

Jett leant up against the high stone cliff wall, and looked at the floor. Her mind raced and she felt a strong tug at her heart, there was excitement at the thought of returning home to Rune and Jade, and thinking of Rafe her heart beat fast, although deep down inside she also felt a pang of pain and sadness. Jariden and Rora had been such good friends and she had indeed grown very fond of them, even though she had tried so hard to avoid becoming too involved, she knew now her heart betrayed her, and she felt the tears welling just below her eyes, knowing she would never see the happy faces of her new companions again.

It had been almost a year for her, and yet Una had told her here, back in her own world, it had been just eleven days since she had fallen on the bridge in the crystal cave. All of it felt confusing as it swept through her mind, and mingled with her turbulent emotions. What felt like just a few moments was far longer than Jett realised, and she was suddenly aware of Una's voice as she looked up from her deep thoughts. Una smiled her eyes red around the edges. "Are you OK?" Jett gave a nod, and leaned off the wall, flicking her head to lift her long fringe from her dark eyes.

"Yeah fine, are you OK, you look upset?" Una gave a weak smile, and wiped the last tear from her cheek; she gave a snort and nodded.

"I will be fine now, I have had the chance of saying goodbye, I think mum will be fine now." Una turned and looked into the mist that led down the long valley back to the tomb of her oldest friend, and the lake beyond where she hoped Woody would be waiting, she took a deep breath. "Let's get on with this, coming here alone was not very pleasant, I am so glad you are with me on the return, this place gives me the creeps. Come on, let's go home."

Without any more words, both of them took a step forward, and moved into the thick white mist, Jett's mind still wandered, and Una tried hard to concentrate, hoping that the voices of her past would remain silent now that she had company on the long journey back. The sound of Jett's long golden spiked heels, clicked on the smooth hard floor and echoed off the walls, giving company to the sound of the soft padding along of Una's thin cloth shoes, and to Una it made the thick white mist that clouded their path, feel much less oppressive.

The new day gathered unto it many new hopes for Runestone, who rose early and hurried as she prepared for the day ahead of her. While Robbie slept, she ate a small breakfast, and then headed below the house to the dimly lit room that was home to her table of power. The huge table gave a pulse as she walked in, and she smiled seeing the deep violet twenty pointed star rise up out of the cool white stone, as her table came back to life to serve her. Hurriedly she sat down and began to pass her hands across its smooth surface, pictures formed and rose out of the table to show her what was happening within her realm.

Gwinne and Rayne were busy preparing high in the trees on the outskirts of York, as they readied for the trip that would take them with Rune to Avalon, to witness the crowning of their daughter and new queen. In the small cottage just down from Loxley Farm, Treen swung her thick cloak over her shoulder, and kissed Skip goodbye, and walked to the small gate where she mounted her horse on route to Rowan and Jade's place. Rowan was already prepared and sat in the garden of his house, as he waited for Treen, who he would accompany to York to take control of the woodland forces in the week's absence of Gwinne and Rayne. Rune gave a sweep of her hand, and watched as the pictures sunk back into her table, new one's rose out of the surface and she viewed life around the stockade of Loxley.

There seemed to be little change as down the main street, the Kirk sisters busied themselves at the bakery and Agatha Patterdale prepared her shop. Ruben Stein stood on the main street talking to Jonathan Appleton the cattle man, who had been on route to see Alf the butcher to arrange the weekly delivery for slaughter, and over the main gates, David Williams took the daily watch as the night commanders dropped down the ladders and headed for their barracks.

There was activity all around the walls, as John Lox had taken charge and had been busy in the last few weeks adding to the fortification of Loxley. Along the walls made of the deeply sunken trunks of tall pine trees, crews worked hard in the early light, as they began the long day of building new watch towers right the way around the five square miles of wall. The lookouts at the rear of Loxley had been strengthened and widened, and the carpenters were busy building new ones every two hundred feet, which were connected with eight foot wide walkways that ran along the top of the wall, to create a place for the swelling numbers of new bowmen that were being drafted from the local area to defend Loxley. Rune felt a shudder run down her spine, she knew that Robbie wanted to try and avoid an assault on the stockade, it had always been his hope to meet Mason's men under the trees where he knew he had the greatest advantage, but it was clear to see, if all went ill, Loxley was preparing for what could be a long siege and a bloody battle with the Knox Empire.

The light outside grew stronger as the sun rose high above the trees, and Rune knew the time was almost upon her, so with a final sweep of her hand, she opened up her window in York, and Gwinne and Rayne came through hand in hand, and walked onto the soft green grass of Robbie's Mere, to meet up with Rowan and Treen. The rattle of the cart announced the arrival of Crystal, who had spent the night at Steph's house, and slowly the party came up the steps and into the house, where Filomena and Isolde were waiting with the children, ready for their visit to see the Queen of Fae of the Moon crowned to rule the land of Avalon.

Robbie was in a deep sleep when Rune came back up to the bedroom, it had been a very late night and he had not got into bed until the early hours. Rune smiled as she sat on the edge of the bed and watched him sleep, his hair was tangled and splayed out across the pillow, his chin was rough with dark stubble, and his face was very pale considering the time they had spent outdoors in the Forest of Time.

She leaned over the bed and softly kissed him, he stirred and moved slowly on the pillow, she kissed him again, but longer, and he gave a whine as he slowly came out of his dream and into reality, his eyes opened to see the two large bright blue eyes staring at him from within the fiery ring of Rune's hair, bathed in the bright light from the window. He smiled and she moved back slightly, her long hair stroking across his shoulder. "Hey beautiful, I was dreaming about you." She moved in closer and kissed him again, this time he lifted his arm and held her softly as he kissed her back. "Hmm... What time is it?" She slid his arm from her waist and sat back up.

"Time for me to go, the others are waiting downstairs."

"What? Oh Rune I thought you were going to wake me earlier so we could have some time together." Rune gave a bright smile.

"I was, but you looked so peaceful, and I had a lot to do before leaving so soon, so I thought I would let you sleep in.... It was pretty late when you got to bed last night." She stood up as he slid up on the pillow. "Plus I knew if I woke you I would not have achieved a thing, I know you well don't forget, and as much as I would love to have spent the morning alone in bed with you, we have commitments Robbie." He looked disappointed, and she laughed at him. "Poor baby... I will only be a day, and then we can spend every morning alone if you want to, it's just today is very important to Amethyst, and I cannot let her down now can I?"

He grudgingly nodded his head, "I suppose so." Rune gave another giggle and leaned back over to kiss him. "You have a busy day too, so let's get as much done as we can, then when I get back, we will do something alone OK?"

"Yeah Ok." Rune stood up and crossed to the door. "Don't forget, Saff is out of action for the moment, so if you need to move around you will have to ask Jade. Just make sure she checks where her doors have opened first, she does have a habit of letting her mind wander, and she ends up somewhere else. If anything goes wrong get her to contact me and I shall come straight back, oh and don't forget Fuse will be here in an hour to give you all the updates... Ok I think that's everything, have fun and I will see you soon, watch out for Furry Face, there is meat in the store."

Robbie gave a nod and she was gone, he heard the group downstairs talking as he swung his legs out of bed, but by the time he had lifted his shirt off the chair, everything had gone quiet, and he knew Rune had taken them through the window into Avalon.

For the next hour he took his time around the house, and by the time Fuse arrived, he was dressed but feeling restless. Robbie had missed home, Avalon for him had not felt very easy at all, as most of the time he had felt overwhelmed and under pressure, being back at home had eased the pressure a little, but he wanted a break, and he knew that was not something that could happen, it was Fuse who suggested they discussed the state of events whilst walking in the woodland to the rear of the house, a suggestion that Robbie jumped at with enthusiasm.

From the moment they stepped under the canopy of the trees, Robbie felt his tension ease. It was a warm morning with the hint of showers in the air, and the woodland around him was lush and fresh. He breathed in the deep aroma of the damp earth, tainted with the lightest of scent from the wild garlic that had faded from flower, yet still left a subtle hint of odour around them. The leaves above him stirred slightly, and with every step forward he felt the vigour of life run into his soul, Fuse gave a smile seeing the almost instant change in him. "I take it Lord Loxley It's nice being home again?"

"Oh you have no idea how much I miss this... There is no other place on earth that feels and smells like this place."

Fuse understood, he too had begun to feel more and more at home in Loxley, in his mind it did have a certain character and charm that was impossible not to love. They followed the path and Fuse began to fill Robbie in on all of the happenings around the stockade, John had told Robbie about the new watchtowers and the ramparts for the new influx of woodsmen, but Fuse filled him in on the other things that affected life in Loxley. He expressed his concerns about the gossip and told Robbie of the meeting with Beth and Agatha and the danger it caused to morale, he talked of the new greenhouses Jess was building, and how that would bring other benefits to the food production. Fuse was in the centre of everything, and as such it was his thoughts and insights, that had the greatest impact on what Robbie learned about a community he was actually the lord of. Robbie listened respectfully and took note of everything, and by the time Fuse had finished, they were deep in the woodland in the large clearing Robbie often came to when he needed to think.

The clearing was wide open to the cloudy sky, yet beams of the sun broke through and streamed down illuminating the fallen stump, and some of the many wild chicory flowers that appeared to glow in an intense pastel blue. Robbie sat down with Fuse at his side, and slipped his water bottle out from the small bag, he took a large gulp of the pale pink liquid within that tasted slightly of Elderflower and had a rose like scent. He passed the bottle to Fuse who took it gratefully, and Robbie took good measure of him.

"How are you feeling Fuse?" Fuse took a long gulp of the liquid and smacked his lips feeling refreshed.

"I have no complaints My Lord... Like all men my age, I feel frustrated at the loss of youth, but I am satisfied with my life." Robbie gave a nod understanding the old man who had become one of his most trusted aides, and a very good friend.

"You look pale, maybe you should slow down a little and get out in the sunlight a little more, the days inside the hall are long and hard, I think my friend maybe you should slow the pace, you know, let Skip take the helm for a while and recharge a little." He could see how tired Fuse looked, and even though he knew this was not what Fuse would want, he knew how much he respected Robbie's opinion.

"I feel a great debt to you and the others... Please do not misunderstand me, I was happy in service to the old duke, and Brandon is as you know like a son to me, coming here and being a part of something that has helped so many others less fortunate than myself has been a great privilege. I hope you are not thinking of retiring me just yet My Lord, although I knew the time would come some day?" Robbie gave a smile.

"It is not that day yet, but like all of us, you too have worked very hard, and I think a time will come that will test all of us, but until that time, I think everyone will benefit from taking a little time out and resting up. Shorten your days and take some walks around the place, relax a little and chat to some of the people who live around the place, enjoy life a little while Skip is at the helm." Fuse gave a small smile, he appreciated the concern expressed by Robbie, and the thought of a little private time did hold great appeal.

"It would be nice to sit in the sun and read a good book, although a little fishing would be wonderful, I have not been able to fish for some time now, and it is something I do miss a great deal."

"Well, that's not a problem, we have fish in the Mere, although I am not very sure what they are, I think John has a few old rods lying about somewhere, and if not I know for a fact Harry has several... Well that settles it, a day fishing will be order of the day, just say when and I will arrange it." Feeling some relief at knowing Fuse would rest up, and thoroughly enjoying being deep in the woodland, Robbie turned to his most pressing matters. "Ok so what have you heard about Knox?"

Fuse straightened up and took a deep breath. "That's what concerns me most My Lord... To be honest considering the sheer numbers and the fierceness of the fight on the moor, I did expect him to pass straight through York, and attack here when were at our least prepared. He has not done that, and for that reason alone it bothers me a great deal, instead of facing us head on with superior numbers, he has decided to fortify York and wait, and call me old fashioned, but to me that is wrong." Robbie understood as it had crossed his mind several times.

"Yeah, I must admit I am not certain of his next move, I can only think that the discovery of William stayed his hand, and he turned his attention to Avalon. It did feel like we were expected, and to be honest I was really surprised to find so many from the church there, it's not at all what I expected."

"The Church is a battle ground we will need to prepare for My Lord. If the rumours are true and the reports, we have had from Jersey are accurate, then I fear there will be another fight there that we will have no choice but to step into." Robbie was a little surprised.

"Why will the church require our aid, most of it is opposed to Earth Faith, they would rather destroy us, why do we need to help them?" Fuse gave a small laugh.

"Stevens is a very smart fellow, he has always been slightly on the outside of the rest of the church, and now he is bishop and leader. I believe he will choose to believe the work of Leenard Rimmer, a historian of high reputation, something we must never forget. Yes, I do believe that our bishop will choose a new church council that will uphold the facts of Leenard and side against Mason, and if that happens, then the church will divide and take sides, and Mason still has enough power to control the weaker minded. The new bishop will need your help My Lord, and regardless of what has happened in the past, he is the legitimate Arch Bishop and head of the church, his approval of William as king will go a long way to supporting your cause, you will find other allies with John Stevens at your side. If the rumours coming to us are correct, I think there are already plans a foot to unseat him, I have heard a few things recently about a group of religious mercenaries called The Brethren, I think the time to send aid is very close."

"I have never heard of them, who are they?" Fuse considered the point for a moment.

"There was one who came through Monmouth many years back, he caused quite a stir in the old abbey, my lord the duke was asked for aid and helped remove him from the area, nasty and vicious he was, and he swore to get revenge and have the duke excommunicated." Fuse gave a chuckle. "The duke was a very generous man who had been quite a benefactor to the abbey so his soul was safe, but I remember it caused some very distasteful feelings for quite some time after. I had never heard of them, but my lord duke had, he informed me they were monks who had become soldiers and were used by the church for their more unsavoury tasks."

"What like the Knights Templar of old?"

"Hmm similar, although I would say much more brutal, the Templar were religious knights dedicated to the preservation of the church, these Brethren are more like religious hired muscle."

"Cutters with crucifix's, great." Fuse gave a large laugh.

"Exactly My Lord. I do think some men close to Lincoln would be a wise move."

"OK, I will sort it with Skip later, so what else is rumoured with Mason?" Robbie was starting to see that in just over two weeks a lot had happened, some he knew from Rune, but he wanted as full a picture as possible. Fuse appeared far more relaxed sat out in the sunlight and he stretched out his legs and gave a happy sigh.

"You must understand we only have rumours at the moment, I am trying to confirm everything, but recent events will take a little longer to confirm. Let's see now, London you pretty much know about thanks to Sapphire, but it's the midlands where my attention lies at the moment. There have been far more sightings of scouting parties than normal, but the word behind the walls are that Mason is preparing more soldiers. We know very little about his midland operation, apart from he produces a lot of his food stocks and clothing there. We recently got word from one of the traders who visited that he has a very large number of troops held up there, and they are preparing to move northward. I must admit Scarlet thought as much, but we could never confirm it, apparently life down there is far stricter than Scotland or the city at Scarborough." Robbie gave a nod.

"I always expected some sort of attack from the south, Rowan always thought it was Mason's plan to squeeze us in the middle and flank us from east and west."

"Rowan is a wise man, Scarlet always thought the same, and we do have plans if they do, but I must admit, I would like to try and get some concrete confirmation to find out just what he has in mind, I have units from Warwickshire looking into it."

"How are we looking in the north?" Robbie stood up and stretched his legs; he looked back at the grey haired old man, who he noticed watched him carefully as he spoke.

"You are very strong in the north... Grace has proven to be as strong and capable as her aunt; she has rousted out all of Mason's men from Aberdeen and has cleared the entire coast down to the walls of the large fortress on the Firth. Ian in Carlisle is very strong indeed, and all of the west coast is ours and heavily fortified, I very much doubt there will be an attack anywhere along that stretch of coast, Mason would find it far too costly." Robbie gave a nod as he thought through all he was hearing, Fuse stood up.

"You have done very well considering how long we have been in this My Lord, I would say considering how long Mason has been preparing, you have done extremely well indeed, you must be patient and have faith, things are slowly working your way." Robbie gave a long sigh as he stared into the trees, he knew not that far away was the large wall that protected the life he loved, and on the other side of it Mason was planning to attack it.

"I have the faith my friend, but faith alone will not clothe and feed us in a siege, he has been raping villages and towns, not to mention the derelict zones for years to equip his army, we have just the woodland and fields around us for our needs, and it feels like time is running out for us." Fuse nodded as he made his way back towards the path at the edge of the clearing.

"It's not much I know, but we still have enough to be going on with, hold your nerve until he shows his hand, until then we stock up and prepare, you will see. Whatever the outcome, Mason will meet his match here on the soil of Loxley."

"I hope so my friend, I really do." Together they walked back under the canopy and into the dappled light of the day, and Robbie talked of lighter things and the joy of being home.

The parade of the new queen around Avalon was a lavish affair, which began in the town of Avalonia. Amethyst dressed in a long golden robe, was seated on a long float carried by fifty of the strongest men of the Marshals of Avalon. At her side Fish who was dressed in pale blue robes trimmed with gold, held her hand and smiled as the thousands of onlookers waved and cheered. The procession left the town of Avalonia, and headed to the water's edge, where a long golden barge awaited the new queen. The long float was carefully lowered on to it, as the high ranking guests and dignitaries took their places on the long rows of gold and blue covered seats that ran either side of the float bearing the queen, and when all were seated, the barge slowly drifted off from the dock, and crept slowly along the bank side of the lake.

It took most of the morning for the barge to travel along the far side of the lake, past the fork shaped island and round the back of the Isle of Tears, before it came back into dock at the bottom end of the long Queen's Road, where carriages awaited the guests. Once everyone was seated, their carriages fell in behind the long float bearing the new queen, and it was carried up the snow white paved road, back through the town, and on to the steep incline that led up the mount towards the large white citadel and the crowning ceremony.

Rune with the children was the guest of honour, and travelled in an open golden carriage behind Amethyst, she was overwhelmed by the change in the place, it had been only a day, and yet the trees were lush and the buildings where gleaming white, and the wide open plains that had been blackened and burned, were thick and lush with tall swaying grasses. It was the power of the Fae of the Moon, for the moon had passed through its full phase, and in doing so, the full powers of their line had awoken and the realm had renewed. It was a paradise and exactly as Rune had expected to find it when she had first arrived, she was more than happy to see that as legends of the past had told, many of the trees bore large succulent red apples.

The one thing that surprised her most was the masses of people that now filled the realm. Thousands of them lined the route cheering as they passed, and she could only wonder where they all had appeared from, Isolde smiled at her, noting her thoughts.

"The people of both lines of the Fae went into hiding My Lady, but now the queen has returned, they felt the need to come home and rejoice. Long have they hidden in other realms waiting for the moment when their queen returned? Today is a day of great joy, for the true Fae way of life has returned home, as it will do one day when your daughter takes up her rightful place."

Rune understood, even though she was not of the Fae, it made sense, and she thought of Robbie in his beloved woodland at Loxley, and how important the Mere was to both of them. All she could do was wonder if this was what it would be like when Iona finally reached the age of eighteen, and she was paraded around the Violet Isle. She looked out on the fair faces of the men and women, and she realised how in this their natural home, how different they were from the people of her realm. Here on mass it was easy to see the pale colour of their skin, and the elegance of them all, they were indeed strikingly different from those living within the woodland realm. The road was lined ten deep, and Rune had to wonder just where all of them would live, she leaned over to Isolde. "There must be thousands of people here, how can the realm host homes for so many?" Isolde gave a smile.

"You see before you a small part of the realm of Avalon, for across behind the Citadel mount and across the marshes there are many villages and towns, this here which you have seen is just the centre, a capital almost of this realm, there are many miles of this realm few seldom explore, this place is home to far more than you see here."

The Citadel on top of the mount was a sight to behold, it was gleaming white exposed in the bright sunlight, and shone like silk, its walls almost as smooth as glass. The four tall thin towers at each corner rose into the air, and in the centre the high central rectangular tower rose even higher, capped with a dome of gleaming gold, she felt her breath catch in her throat as she saw it for the first time up close.

The procession halted at the base of twenty snow white smooth steps, that rose up to two enormous doors of gold, decorated with fine engravings of the moon and stars, in front of which were two large golden seats with pale blue velvet pads. Banners of long pale blue silks flapped in the soft breeze, and below them one hundred trumpeters lifted their long trumpets to their lips, and heralded the arrival of the queen.

Amethyst looked breath taking, as her father gently guided her onto the steps, followed by Fish, Crystal and Gwinne. The people of the realm flocked up the long white path and surrounded the Citadel cheering wildly. Rune followed Isolde and Filomena with the children, and was guided to the foot of the steps, where a long row of blue clad seats awaited her. She sat down looking up at Amethyst and Fish, as the finely dressed courtiers surrounded them and prepared for the crowning ceremony.

Just for a moment she looked round to where the edge of the cliff was, she was unsure why, maybe it was just the memory of knowing that was where Jade had blasted the Dark One over. There was a sea of happy smiling faces covering every inch of the top of the mount, she smiled feeling the happiness in the air, and then her heart gave a jolt as she noticed the only black clad figure in the thick crowd. The figure was hooded in a black tatty robe that covered their face, she knew instantly that they were watching her, the hood tipped forward in recognition, and the pace of her heart lessoned as she realised who it was in the crowd. Rune smiled and gave a courteous nod back, and the bang of a loud drum caught her attention, and she looked back to the mount, as the preparations were almost ready to begin. Rune turned back to the crowd and instantly noticed the figure had gone, all that was left was a sea of faces cheering the view of their new queen and her consort, as they prepared to take their seats and be crowned.

The crowds settled and there was total silence, and Rune turned back to view the Citadel. It felt almost eerie to be surrounded by so many people, and she was sure you would hear a pin drop it had gone so quiet. From the far right of the Citadel, a tall figure robed in blue appeared, he walked with great confidence holding onto a long golden staff, which he struck on the floor as he walked, marking each of his steps as he approached Amethyst. His voice was loud and clear, as he spoke in a language Rune had never heard before. It felt strange that she did not recognise it, she had after all a good grasp of all languages, it was one of her many gifts, and yet she understood nothing the man said at all. He came to the side of Amethyst and faced her, and in a deep bellowing voice he asked her something, but Rune had no idea at all of what it was. To her surprise Amethyst answered him in the same tongue; Rune leaned over to Isolde and whispered quietly to her.

"Do the Fae have their own language, because these words are unknown to me?"

Isolde gave a smile and nodded.

"Yes, My Lady, there are many secrets the Fae do not share, and their tongue is one of them." Rune nodded suddenly understanding that by not being of their line, they would never have shared it. Isolde slid in close and whispered.

"He is the great seer of the Fae, and he is charged with custody of the crown until such time as the new queen comes. He is asking her if she will serve to the benefit of all Fae of earth and moon, and execute her duty as required by the laws of the Fae, and she has accepted. He will now offer thanks and pray for her reign to be a long and prosperous one, at which point he will ask the people to accept her." Rune was fascinated as she listened to the language and watched the ceremony almost captivated by its ritual. Isolde stayed close to her as she quietly explained everything as it happened.

"He has asked the new queen to present the crystal knife, for it is seen as the key to the kingdom, Lady Amethyst will present it to everyone, at which point the crowns will be placed and a prayer offered. Lord Fagan will then ask the people to accept her as queen." Rune felt her lip drop.

"Lord Fagan?"

"Yes, My Lady, he is the son of the great seer Sequana, and the high seer of Avalon, they say he is a man of many gifts, although he is a hermit and hard to find when sought, apart from the queen, he is one of the most respected members of the realm."

Rune felt a smile cross her lips; how could she not have known? His ability to talk to the trees and understand everything going on in Avalon should have alerted her to his gifts. A small chuckle left her lips, as she thought of those moments alone watching the Mount with him at her side giving her advice, it suddenly dawned her that he was able to see things far more clearly than she had at the time, and in doing so he had helped push her in the right direction. Fagan was not a hermit because he had chosen to stay behind alone, he was in the forest because it was the one place, he would be hard to find, and therefore could live his life without being pestered all the time from those who wanted to know more about their own lives. It was also quite obvious that as the guardian of the crown, he could not leave Avalon just in case someone did find their way in and steal the most important jewels of the Fae.

Rune was snapped out of her thoughts with the sound of a deafening roar. The crowds cheered and yelled and waved their weapons in the air, and as Rune looked up, the tall blue clad figure she now knew to be Fagan, held a bright crown of sparkling jewels above the head of Amethyst. The crowd roared even louder, and he shouted something in Fae, and lowered the crown onto Amethyst's head. The crowd went wild and the trumpets blared out, and another man lowered a smaller crown onto the head of Fish.

The new queen sat at the top of the steps, as the Fae screamed and yelled with delight, all around her the sea of bodies jumped up and down, waving wildly drowning out any words or music being played by the trumpeters. The new queen was finally in place, and Rune felt the joy rise up in her heart. "We did it Robbie; we got her here safe and seated her."

The sky above exploded with fireworks or so they appeared, for these were unlike any Rune had seen before. Massive booms came out of brightly coloured flashes, and streaks and spirals of what looked like coloured smoke or dust burst out across the whole of the realm, Rune smiled as she saw Iona look up and give out a squeak, although the crowd was so loud, sat close to her she almost did not hear it. Amethyst and James stood up in front of their seats with happy smiling faces as Crystal and Gwinne hugged them both, Rune knew that they would shortly descend to the lower halls where another very secret and private ceremony would take place, and sadly that would only be conducted in front of the eyes of the Fae Ofmoon.

It was past midday by the time the ceremony finished, and Fagan lifted his large staff and banged heavily on the two golden doors. The boom seemed to echo, and reverberate right through the whole of the mount, and the two doors swung open to allow entry into the heart of the realm to the new Queen of the Fae of Moon.

After the private ceremony, the rest of the day would be conducted below in the large feasting hall, where a royal banquet for honoured guests would take place. Isolde took Rune by the arm, and led her up the steps where Rayne and Gwinne waited for her, and finally she would get her first chance to see the Citadel in its fully restored splendour, something she had heard a great deal about.

Robbie and Fuse had taken much longer than they had expected, but it was a nice day, and such was their talk as they caught up on each other that they had dawdled as they walked, and took the longer route back to the house. Raised voices could be heard as they came close to the edge of the trees, and Robbie stopped talking as his ears pricked up, and he tried to find out what was happening. As they stepped out of the trees to the left of the house, both of them could see a very red faced Hawk pointing at Rafe as he yelled. Louisa stood between them holding up her arms to keep them apart, Hawk's voice was filled with accusation and anger.

"I SAID PACK IT THE HELL IN GUY'S!"

"ASK HIM, GO ON YOU BLOODY WELL ASK HIM WHAT HAPPENED?" Louisa was trying her best to calm the situation as Rafe leaned angrily forward gritting his teeth, his fists clenched, restrained by Louisa's arm.

"ASK ME WHAT? YOU'RE FRIGGIN MAD, YOU KNOW THAT?"

Robbie came quickly forward. "What the hell is going on?" All three of them looked at him coming round the side of the fence, closely followed by Fuse; it was

Rafe who answered first pointing at Hawk.

"It's that bloody fool; he has gone and lost his friggin marbles that's what's going on."

"ME? You are the one that buggered off with her, and she was fine before she left, why don't you just admit it, you ain't kidding anyone with this bloody fake innocent act you know."

"Why you!" Rafe struggled to get past Louisa, and she forcefully pushed him back. "You got a frigging nerve, OK you want a piece of me, come on a try your luck."

Both of them surged forward, Robbie stepped forward, and snatched out and caught Rafe by the collar as his fist flew up, Louisa closed the gap between them, and pushed hard into the chest of the red faced Hawk, and struggled him backward away from Rafe. Both of them cursed at each other, as Robbie gave a second yank, and Rafe went sprawling backward onto the ground behind him.

"PACK IT IN NOW!" Robbie's voice was louder than theirs, and carried a huge amount of authority, his eyes glared as he looked from Hawk to Rafe. "You should be ashamed of yourselves, what the hell is going on?"

Both of them went to speak, but Robbie glared back at Rafe who was getting back up off the grass. "Not you, Hawk first." Rafe looked angry, and gave a faint growl. "Back Off Wolfie." Robbie's voice was stern and Rafe's growl suddenly went silent, Robbie turned back to Hawk.

"Right Commander, you pull yourself together, and in a manner befitting your lord, you tell me what the hell has got you so riled up." Hawk's face was still very red, and the anger was clear for all to see as he held his fists tightly clenched, but Robbie was equally as angry and he calmed down a little and lowered his tone.

"I want to know what happened between him and Saff, because we was fine before she went off with him, and when she got back she left me a message with her mum that it was over between us. I want to know what he did, because he is the only one who knows."

"Oh yeah why not tell him the rest, go on tell him you thought we were sleeping together, go on."

"WOLFIE, I SAID SHUT IT." Robbie looked back at Hawk. "You think Sapphire was messing around with Rafe?" Hawk gave a nod and stared defiantly at Rafe.

"Yeah, I do, it's the only thing that makes sense, we were fine before she left, we even talked of marriage."

Rafe shook his head. "This is bullshit, I don't need to stand here and listen to this shit." Robbie turned to look at Rafe.

"You stay put till I say you can leave; I will not have this behaviour between my men, you stand down Commander and wait until we get to the bottom of this." Louisa gave a long sigh, and Robbie looked at her. "Do you know anything about all this?" She shook her head.

"Saff was fine on the way back, I mean she had stuff on her mind, but she said nothing to me." Robbie gave a nod.

"OK you go inside with Fuse and I will get to the bottom of this." Louisa gave a nod and turned to Fuse who was watching carefully, both of them went inside and Robbie waited until the door was slid shut, he turned to Rafe as Hawk stared at both of them.

"Did anything happen with Saff while you were away?" Rafe looked even angrier and shook his head in disbelief.

"I cannot believe you of all people would ask me that."

"I am sorry Rafe, but it's my job to know everything and maintain the peace, I have to ask you and give you the chance to explain your side." Rafe gave a nod.

"I suppose so... I know I don't always fit, and maybe I am a little different in my approach, but Jett is the only gal for me, and both Saff and Keith are my friends." Rafe stared defiantly at Hawk as he spoke. "I might be a little unruly at times, but I don't shit on my mates, and he should bloody well know that, so just for the record, no I never laid a glove on her, and I never would... I honestly do not know what went on, she left me a few times to do stuff for Rune, I would say he should talk to her if Saff split, but I am telling you now, it wasn't anything to do with me." Rafe looked straight into Robbie's eyes. "And that is the truth My Lord." He was angry and also Robbie could see he was hurt. He turned back to Hawk.

"You heard what he said, and to be honest I think you already know he is not lying. Look Keith we are a team, and a very close one at that, I really do not know what is going on with Sapphire, but I do not believe she would go off with someone else like that. I think you should wait to talk to Rune, she will be back later this evening, talk to her and see what she can tell you."

Hawk gave a nod and looked down at the floor. "Yeah OK... Sorry... I will be back later to see Rune." He turned and marched off across the grass toward his horse, Rafe came up to Robbie's shoulder as Keith mounted his horse and without looking back, he kicked in his heels and rode off down the track.

Rafe shook his head. "Poor bugger, he is really cut up about it."

"Yeah, he is Rafe, which is why you should have handled yourself better, he is your friend and he is hurting like mad, you should have stowed that temper of yours and been a little more understanding, especially considering you have been missing Jett as much as he will Saff."

"Yeah, I am sorry, it's just the moment he blurted it out, he caught me off guard, he is a good mate and I never thought for a moment he could think I would do that, I just lost it for a moment." Robbie turned towards the white gate to the garden path.

"Think on in the future and keep that temper of yours under wraps, if you lose it again like that you will find those commanders bars will come off pretty quick, the last thing we need at the moment is an officer who cannot hold it together." Rafe looked stunned.

"What? You have got to be kidding me, may I remind you it was not all me." Robbie gave a nod and looked seriously back at Rafe; his voice was calm and quiet.

"He has a good reason for losing it; he is falling apart, what was your excuse? You are an officer, it's your duty to hold it together and calmly sort everything out, I've got to say Rafe considering the situation, I did expect better from you."

Rafe looked stunned. "Seriously, you have got to be friggin joking?" Robbie walked through the gate, and then he stopped and looked back at Rafe who was just staring at him.

"I wish I could say I was Rafe, but I am not. We have the fight of our lives coming and we all need to keep our cool, if I think for a moment you are not, then I mean it, I will pull you out of your command." He turned and walked back up the path and slid the long glass door open. Rafe stood motionless at a loss for words, and just stared at the empty path.

CHAPTER SEVENTEEN

SEEKING THE FACTS

"Are we there yet?"

Una stopped, and looked behind her into the white swirling mist, where the shadowy figure of Jett loomed out towards her. Jett gave an innocent look from under her long black fringe. "What... I was only asking?" Una shook her head in disbelief.

"Honestly Jett, you are worse than a teenage boy on a carriage trip, so for the hundredth time in two hours, no we are not. It's hard to put a time limit on things in here, all I can say, as I already have, is that I felt the distance from the tomb to the place where all the fresh fruit grew was the shortest, and considering we passed that place some time ago, I can only hope it will not be much longer."

Jett shrugged her shoulders and smiled. "OK then, off we go." She strolled past Una and walked on in front. Una gave a chuckle and shook her head again.

"Cheek of the devil Jett Amber, you know that?"

The click of Jett's heels echoed through the thick veil of mist in front of her. Una began to walk forward, like Jett she had thought the journey back would be shorter than it had been, and she tried hard to remember the first things she had seen when she had entered the high walled valley. In her mind she played back the moment of discovery and the large rough shaped boulders, which she had woven round, and then the walls lined with vines and fruit trees. It made no sense as she had walked passed them in what felt like hours ago; surely she thought to herself, that they should have arrived before now.

Somewhere in front hidden in the mist Jett's dull voice sounded out. "Hey I think I found a door." Una felt the lurch inside her chest and quickened her pace as she swept forward towards the sound of Jett's voice. Jett was looking up at the heavy lintel of carved stone above the doorway, Una did not recognise it, but if this was the door she had come through, her back would have been towards it as she walked under it. Jett turned to her with a look of hope on her face.

"Is this it then, is this where we go back to our world?" Una was not entirely certain.

"Oh Jett I hope so."

"You hope so, what, don't you recognise it?"

"To be honest Jett, I was heading that way, I didn't look back so I really am not sure, but hey, if it takes us undercover and out of this awful mist I am not complaining."

Una slid her hand into her pocket and took hold of the small staff, she held it square in the centre of her palm and lifted it out of her pocket and held her arm out in front of her. "Dad I need your help again."

Jett jumped with surprise as the long staff shot out of Una's hand, and she twisted it so the staff rose from the floor upward in front of her. Holding it high the staff ignited at the top and light flooded out pushing back some of the mist. Jett peered into the long dark tunnel. "Urgh! It looks much more creepy with light, I actually think I might have been more relaxed with the lights off."

"It's the only tunnel here, so it has to be the right one, come on if memory serves me, it's not as long as it looks, you know what they say about the light at the end of the tunnel."

Jett stepped slowly into the tunnel and her voice gave an eerie echo. "Yeah, I do, problem is the lights at the wrong end and it's above us, if there is anything lurking in here, it can pretty much see us, and we cannot see it." Una felt a cold tingle run down her spine.

"Oh shush, Jett, I am not happy about it either, so don't fill my head with your nonsense." Jett gave a chuckle.

"Tell you what Una, you came through here last time alone, hell anything could have leaped out at you, and no one would have heard you scream. You're braver than you look." With a few feet of light and no sight of the ending Una suddenly felt very panicked.

"Oh Jett, I do wish you would keep quiet, well that's it, I have made a decision."

"Oh yeah what's that then?"

"I am running, are you with me?" No sooner had she said it, Una gripped the staff as hard as she could, and started to run forward into the darkness. Seeing the light suddenly rush forward, Jett felt much more alone and took off at high speed to catch up with Una. Their feet echoed, bouncing all around the tunnel sounding like there were hundreds running behind them, Jett looked back but all she could see was thick darkness, and spurred on by her own thoughts, she pushed harder at Una's side as together they flew at high speed through the darkness.

It was just a few short minutes when out of the darkness the stone steps appeared, and without stopping Una and Jett hurtled on to them and up as fast as they could. Both of them arrived at the top of the steps gasping hard as they entered into the large room that was the tomb of Eleanor. Una fell to her knees panting as Jett collapsed on the floor and laid back gasping for air; it was a few long minutes before either of them could speak.

"It appears child of the White Circle, your mother was right."

Una screamed with all her might, she shot backwards on the floor as Jett sat bolt upright, and Una smashed into her, knocking her back into the floor at high speed.

"WHAT THE HELL IS WRONG WITH YOU?" The tall figure in a black tatty hooded cloak leant forward and offered his hand.

"Excuse me?"

Una looked up at him, her heart pounding as if it was about to explode in her chest. "Do you make it a habit of creeping up and scaring the life out of people? For the sake of Hearne, buy some heavier shoes or something to announce you are there; you scared the living daylights out of me." The robed figure helped her to her feet, where she swallowed deeply and held her hand to her chest; he offered a hand to Jett and pulled her onto her feet.

"Once again, my apologies." Una regulated her breathing.

"I am over a thousand years old; a woman of my age should not be startled like that." She drew a long breath as Jett saw the funny side and gave a giggle.

"Cool leap Una, I have never seen anyone move that fast, and I know Blades." Una tried her best to ignore her as she looked at the hooded figure.

"Is that it, my task is over I take it, and I can return to the life I knew?" The tip of the hood gave a nod.

"You have done more than you will ever understand, but yes child of the White Circle, your task is over. Through the door you will find fire, food and blankets, for it is late into the night, so rest there, and in the morning, you will find the boat is moored at the foot of the steps. The lake is misty but relax, and it will take you back to the start of your journey and the woodsman who waits for you. All you need do is hand me the staff, for that is now to move to the hand of another and that is a part I still have to play."

Una lifted the staff off the floor, and felt a little strange, she knew it had only been loaned to her, but knowing it was her father's made it hard to part with. "I knew this time would come, but my father has guided me and now I fear I have lost him forever."

The hooded figure lifted a hand and took the staff from Una. "Forever is a long time, and in the world, he spent an age protecting you will find many things done by his hand. I think you will find when you return there is much of him left in the world, seek out his work and you will have his companionship always."

The figure turned and crossed the large chamber, and as he approached the two huge doors swung open to reveal the bright silver light of the moon. Framed in the light he stopped and turned back for a second. "Once you both vacate the chamber, the doors will close, and there will be no way back inside, remember the lost before you leave and say what has to be said, for there will be no other time to do so in your future."

Jett was not very sure what that meant, but Una gave a soft smile of understanding, the High Lord had granted her another moment beside her oldest friend, and another chance to part with good memories.

"Great food, I am bloody starving." Jett headed straight for the doors where the fire glowed red in the night, and a long leg of lamb hung on a spit dripping fat into the flames. A small basket contained bread and cheese, and there was even a large jug of what smelled like ale. Jett sat down and slid out her knife; she cut a long slither of the succulent meat off and dropped it into a small wooden bowl. "Hey Una come on, this is just awesome." She hungrily tore at the bread and then devoured the meat.

It had been a long day of celebration, and Rune was feeling a little tired. Crystal was spending a few more days with her sister, and would be travelling back later with her mother and father, so Rune asked Filomena and Isolde to ready the children and meet her at the doors to the Citadel. Fagan had been absent from the large banquet; it appeared that as soon as the ceremony was over, he had returned to the forest. Feeling the need for air, Rune made her way out of the large hall and down the lavish marble staircase to the foyer, and out through the doors onto the steps.

The night air was cool as the sun hovered just above the horizon, casting sheets of vivid red across the sky; she took a long deep breath and enjoyed the cooling of her face. Slowly she descended the steps and looked at the long plain that led to the tomb of Arthur. To her left rising behind the Citadel, was the rise where the Specialists had made their last stand, it was empty and barren, unlike the last time she had seen it just a few days ago, when it was littered with smashed rocks, and the bodies of the countless dead. She felt the shiver run down her spine, as her eyes instinctively moved back to the long road past the Tomb of Arthur, to the high wall in the distance that was the start of the valley leading to Merlin's Gate. As the sun sank lower the white stone shone red, almost as if it was stained in the blood of those dear friends and Robbie. The memory of the moment flashed back through her thoughts, and she lifted her arms and hugged herself, almost to reassure herself it was over, and could never happen again.

"Empty your heart Little Redstone, that time has passed, and has been unwritten, do not dwell on the moments you erased." The voice was soft, quiet, and familiar, and Rune saw the reflection of the hooded figure behind her cast across the floor at her feet as a shadow. She did not move, but continued to stare forward, almost as if by doing so, she would prevent it ever happening again.

"Whether unwritten or not, they happened to me My Lord Albanlin, I alone carry the full truth of that day, and as long as I remember it, I will prevent it from happening again." Albanlin stepped up to her side and looked to the road, Rune noticed how much taller he was close up, the lip of his hood softly flapped in the breeze as he spoke.

"It could never happen again, it was but a moment of weakness while passing the baton, our blindness has always clouded this time and with it came our uncertainty. That time has passed with the passing of gifts, and a new age of dreams is upon us. The moment to rise has been snatched from Little Morgan, the gifts you and the blue star hold will ensure it."

"Your faith in us is ill founded, for we are more human than spirit, and in that we have made many mistakes." The black hood twitched, and Albanlin gave a small chuckle.

"It is for that very reason I have such strong faith Little Redstone, it is the wonderful quality of humanity that holds the greatest hopes for you and your friends, and the reason I held your grandfather's counsel above all others."

"You did?"

"Oh yes, your grandfather was made of human flesh, but he was given the power of spirit, and in doing so we bridged the gap between both kinds, he loved humans and humanity above all things, and he brought an understanding of which we had no perception. The line of Little Morgan was always dangerous, but she was brought from the womb of a Celtic queen, and in that he knew that she would pose the greatest threat to all of us."

"But how I do not understand why?"

"Your grandfather once told me, we should not fear her because she was made from the old lines of power from Saxony, he feared the side she inherited from a mortal queen of standing, for in that she gained the qualities of humanity and a strong instinct to survive. He never doubted that it would be her greatest strength, and he was right, even I the White Lord of Time learned from my student in the end. You have many of the same qualities if you look deep enough, and it is for that reason alone you will defeat her."

Rune felt a little startled, how could he even compare her to the Dark One? "I am sorry My Lord, but I am nothing like her, I think you must be mistaken." He nodded his head and gave a chuckle.

"I think if you look, you will find you have more in common with her than you would wish... Little Morgan carries a Saxon line of a great and ancient power, but she is also half human as you are. It is a good thing Little Redstone that your mother chose to marry a reckless man and not a prince of power from abroad."

"My Father is not reckless; he is kind and loving and good natured to all."

"Opal did not think so at first, she tried to convince your mother to marry three different princes of power from other lands, but your mother refused, and when she met your father, it was your grandfather who gave his whole hearted approval. In doing so you gained the qualities that will ensure the survival of everything in the fight against Little Morgan. Never underestimate that side of her, for it was the human side her that was seduced by the Merle, and therein will lie your greatest understanding of her. Think and act like a human trying to survive, and you will always find a way to stop her, trust that side of you like your grandfather did. His wisdom here will be missed, for he alone saw that as spirits of great power, we lacked many of the gifts man created with free will." Albanlin lifted his arm in front of Rune, and an old white hand that was almost transparent slipped out from the sleeve. "This belongs to your mother now, take it to her and complete all of the circles, I will go to her once it has passed, and guide her as I did her father."

Rune looked down and saw the small staff, which she recognised as the one that had been loaned to Una. Her heart skipped a beat when she saw it. "Is Una alright, why do you bring this to me, when it was placed in her care? Please tell me she has not passed from this realm forever."

"The child of White Circle is safe and well, she sits on the edge of this realm covered from all eyes, her time in that realm will soon be finished, and I can assure you she will return with her companion unharmed." Rune gave a gasp of relief and lifted the staff from the cool palm of the White Lord.

"Oh thank Hearne, I was starting to worry as I have not sensed her yet, I am so glad Jett made it across safely, none of us were sure at first."

"Have more faith Little Redstone. I will leave you now, as I have a pressing engagement with the new queen of this realm, before I depart. Remember look to your human side and you will find the right answers, your eyes are strengthened through the blue star, use it from now onward." Rune understood and nodded in appreciation.

"Thank you, My Lord for staying by my side, your aid was a great help to all of us." She looked up, but the figure had gone, she turned and looked back, but the whole of the top of the mount was empty. She smiled as the breeze whispered past her ears and lifted her hair.

"I will be with you always child of my line."

Rune stood for a little while, as she thought of the words of Albanlin, she felt a strange feeling inside her knowing there was a cord of similarity between her and her enemy. It was not something she liked, but she had to admit it did make a lot of sense, after all she had lived a large part of her life unaware of the power that had been locked inside her, she had for want of a better word, simply been a normal girl, with all of the insecurities that came with it, and that had defined who she was long before she received her gifts.

Behind her she heard voices in the darkening night, Amethyst and Fish had come looking for her, afraid she would leave without a goodbye. Rune turned and smiled, as they walked up to greet her, Amethyst opened her arms and then burst into tears, Rune pulled her close and hugged her.

"I am going to miss you so much Rune, you have risked everything for me, and I wish we did not have to be separated." Rune held her tight.

"I will never be far away, and you will remain a member of my table, and a sister to my heart, we will talk often, so come now dry your eyes, this is not goodbye." Amethyst gave a sniffle as Rune released her; she wiped her eyes and smiled.

"As much as this is the most amazing thing for me, I will miss all of you bitterly, being a Specialist has been the best time of my life, promise me that if Robbie needs me you will call out to me."

"You are the Queen of Avalon, your aid will be welcome always in the long fight ahead, be at peace for I am sure we will all have more parts to play together before all this is over." Amethyst gave a nod, and Rune turned to Fish.

"Who would have guessed when you jumped into our cart that you would end here at the side of my beautiful cousin? You have served Robbie with great loyalty and friendship, and for that James I will be forever grateful." He gave an embarrassed smile.

"I was honoured to fight at his side, he was a compass to me, and pointed me on the right path, I cannot deny I will miss all of them, they became my family after Tony died."

"They will be family always and that will strengthen the bond between Avalon and the Woodland Realm. Your life here I am sure will fulfil you beyond your wildest dreams, but should you need us, we will all be regular visitors, and never forget that you are still a man of Loxley, and will always be welcomed home with love and affection if you choose to visit." He smiled and Rune pulled him into a warm embrace. "Be happy here with my cousin and live your life to the full always... Until we meet again my dear friend."

When the glade at Robbie's Mere flashed with violet light in the darkness to mark the return of Runestone, Robbie was already sprawled on his bed surrounded by his notes, snoring loudly. With the help of Filomena and Isolde, Rune put the children to bed, and then made her way down to the room below the house where her table came to life as she entered. Rune softly swiped her hands across its surface, and the picture of her mother sat at home with Smokes came into view, Rune smiled as she saw the contented faces of them curled together on the long settee quietly talking to each other. Rune closed her eyes and concentrated for a moment.

"Hear me Mother, I need to see you, it is very important. Una will return with Jett tomorrow and we must prepare, meet me in the glade of the Mere as quickly as you can."

It was late, and most of Loxley was sleeping, as Steph and Smokes mounted their horse's to ride to Robbie's Mere. The lights still burned brightly in the hotel, where Big John and Rafe sang drunken songs of bravery with Jay, Harry and Maggs.

Alice was curled tight in her bed with Bear, and Maddy sat alone in her father's house reading some of his many notes in one of his journals. Keith was passed out in his chair at home, two empty glass bottles on the floor at his feet, and Melanie sat high on the walls of Loxley as David prepared to end his shift.

It was quiet as the stars came out through the darkness, and shone down in silent watch over all of them, and far away on the edge of a land she did not know, Jett sat at the top of the high steps alone and slipped a small wooden box out of her bag, behind her the camp fire burned bright, and Una came out through the large golden doors wiping her eyes, as the huge doors silently slid back and closed, sealing the tomb of Eleanor forever.

Holding the box in her hand nervously, she had no idea why Jariden had wanted to give her the parting gift, and she felt a tug at her heart as she wondered if it was maybe some token of his affection for her. Nervously she flicked the small catch with her fingernail, and the small hinged top came open. "What's that?"

At the sound of Una's voice, Jett gave a startled jump and closed the lid tight, she looked up at Una and gave a smile, but Una could see the affect it had on her, she sat down quietly at Jett's side and patted her knee. "Was he very special?" Jett's voice was quiet.

"Yeah, he got me through when I had lost all hope." She gave a cough and her voice got louder as she turned to look at Una. "It's not like you think, honestly we didn't do anything, we were just mates." Una smiled as she saw for the very first time the colour rise in Jett's cheeks, as she flushed with embarrassment, she leaned in and lifted her arm round Jett's back.

"He must have been quite a mate then?" Jett gave a nod and smiled.

"Yeah, he was, I think he wanted more, I just don't know for sure because he gave me this and it seemed pretty important to him."

"What is it?" Jett gave a long sigh.

"Dun no, I have not looked properly yet, I guess I am afraid to, because it makes me feel strange when I think about it." Una nodded understanding.

"You are in love with Rafe, and you feel that having another love you is wrong?"

"Yeah... well something like that, I mean what if he is in love with me, I have gone forever and I am here with Rafe, or I will be when I get home... I mean I want to be with Rafe he is like right for me, but thinking about Jariden I feel all sorts of strange things."

"Love is a confusing thing Jett, we cannot always tell what kind of love we have for another person, we feel all these strong emotions when we lose them, and it takes a little time to figure out what we are really feeling. I think this Jariden helped you at a time when you were very vulnerable, he was kind and helpful and that got you through it all, only you will ever know if what you feel is the strong bond for the love of a good and loyal friend, or if it meant more... only time will tell. One thing is true, he wanted you to have that, and it was very important to him to make sure he gave it you, so I would say accept it in the spirit it was given and look at it." Jett looked down at the small carven box in her hand.

"Yeah, you're right, I will see what it is and then think about its meaning after." Una gave her leg another pat.

"That seems to be the best option, go for it."

Jett opened the small box again, as Una watched from her side. In the centre of the box was a round object wrapped in a piece of white cloth, she lifted it out, placing the box carefully down, and undid the cloth, both of them were surprised to see what it contained. Jett looked down into her palm to see a reddish engraved locket. It was oval in shape and decorated with a small five pointed star, surrounded by polished stones. It felt very light in her hand, but she was not sure what it was made from. It was hard like metal, but the colour told her it wasn't, and she could only think that it was something to do with the land of Maybeyan, and was not of the Woodland Realm. Una stared at it with wonder, for although it was plain in its makeup, it was also very beautiful, her voice was soft. "Open it."

Jett looked at her, and saw the excited sparkle in Una's eyes; she gave a nod and swallowed hard, as her finger fumbled at the catch. With a soft click it opened, and Una gave a gasp of surprise. Jett felt the tears building under her eyes as she looked into the left hand side of the locket, and saw small pictures of the group that had been her friends as they walked down a long road, towards some sort of large grey building. They were happy and smiling and chatting away as they had when she had been with them. Jariden wore his usual hat that appeared to annoy everyone, and Rora looked happy and relaxed.

On the right hand side of the locket, again small pictures moved as she saw the pale slender figure of Tula walking through the trees, she looked serene and happy and it brought to Jett's mind a flood of memories and moments for her long time amongst all of them. Her tears dripped onto her pants, and Una gave her a squeeze on her left shoulder.

"I understand now Jett, he wanted you to know that they were all safe, and he has given you the means to look in on them whenever you need to. I think it is a very special and wonderful gift, and I can see from your reaction it means a great deal. It's a shame there is no sound, I would love to hear their voices, but I think that looking at them you probably can in your thoughts." Jett swallowed hard and looked up and gave a soft nod, it was a strange moment for Una, as she had never seen such emotion, or seen Jett lost for words. "You have a treasure there Jett, keep it with you always." She gave a cough to clear her throat.

"Yeah, I will." Una looked down at the pictures again.

"You know that girl does have a very familiar look, she is almost like Ruby." Jett glanced back at the locket and then looked back at Una.

"What, Tula?" Una pointed at the slender figure.

"Hmm... Look at her, her facial features are very similar, although she does have blue eyes unlike Ruby's, but yes, do you not think she walks similar to her?" Una got no response as Jett stared at the pictures watching the graceful and elegant figure walk through the trees. Una was not aware, for Jett's heart had just skipped several beats, and in her mind, she remembered the final moments of her meeting with the tree spirit of Maybeyan, where she had asked about her sister, Tula's voice echoed through her mind.

"You cannot carry this burden my valiant warrior, you must let it out, and let go of all the pain you feel." Tula turned her head and quietly whispered to her. "Your sister travelled across the Bridge of Intention with a trusted guide, and you are right in your instincts, because they are very strong. She did reach this land, Jett your sister was reborn into another being, and although there may be some similar attributes in the person she became, she is no longer the frightened half blind girl that you knew. The rules of the worlds we both live within prevent her from revealing herself, this you know is the law of all worlds, and she chose to take on the role she now holds and does it with happiness and great companionship. Trust me when I tell you with all my heart that she is happy and contented, and will never feel the pain of being alone here within the realm of Maybeyan. Go home in peace, for although she has moved into another phase of her life, she will always have the love you gave her, for as I have already told you Jett, the power of the love we hold never truly fades away. She knew throughout her whole life how deeply you loved her, for that was with her in her final moment, and it eased her passage from one world to another, trust me in this for I know it to be true."

Tula gave her a soft kiss on her head, and released her from her arms. "Time has passed, you must return to your guides for the moment to return is upon you. Dry your eyes and leave here with a full and happy heart my dear friend." Jett gave a huge sniffle and wiped her red eyes.

"I am sorry I never meant to cry like this."

"Never apologise for feeling a pure emotion, go with the blessings of this land and with peace in your heart Jett Amber."

"Thanks Tula."

"It's my honour." Jett gave a weak smile and turned to walk away; Tula lifted a hand and wiped the tear that had stroked down her own cheek as she watched Jett walk back across the grass. Jett stopped and looked back at her for a moment.

"Did I meet her?" Tula smiled.

"Yes you did, it was brief, but you met and spoke."

"Jett... Jett are you OK?" Una was staring at her as she suddenly came out of her thoughts. Suddenly everything made sense, how had she missed it and not recognised the spirit of her own sister? Jett stared for a moment into Una's bright violet eyes.

"It was her... I never realised.... It makes perfect sense; I can see it now." Una smiled.

"I am glad it all makes perfect sense to you, so will you please tell me what you are talking about." Jett shook her head and then pointed back to the locket. Her voice rose as she felt the excitement build up inside her.

"That's her, it's Ruby, Tula told me that Ruby had travelled there on the Bridge of Intention with a guide, she told me that even though she was there, she would not be able to remember her past life here, and that she could not tell me that she contained the spirit of Ruby, but she was." Jett suddenly became very animated as her happiness and excitement burst out of her, Una could do nothing but sit and smile as she saw the bright spark in Jett's black eyes, and Jett talked faster. "Tula was telling me that she was Ruby, she told me I had met Ruby and talked briefly, but she was talking about that moment in time, I hadn't talked to her, I was talking to her... Una it was Ruby I was right, she did need to say goodbye and she did miss me, which was why I heard her when I was sent there, Ruby reached out to me to let me know she was OK and I was not to worry about her."

Una could do nothing but smile, as a brightness glowed out of her with happiness, she was almost like a small excited child as she bounced on the spot, and all Una could do was to naturally pull her into her arms and give her the biggest hug she possibly could. It was if some demon deep inside of Jett had been slain, and suddenly Jett bounced back to her bright loud happy self and it felt infectious as Una laughed with joy as Jett threw her own arms round Una and hugged her equally as hard.

CHAPTER EIGHTEEN

THE STRANGER SIDES OF MAGIC

The glade was pitch dark when Steph and Smokes rode onto it through the trees, even the lights of the house, which normally burned brightly into the night, were out. Smokes slowed his horse as he scanned through the darkness to see his way. Steph noticed the faint glow of lilac, and knew it was Rune waiting for her; she slowed the horse to a halt, and then slid off the saddle to the ground. Smokes followed her lead, dismounting at her side, and keeping as close as he could to her, he noticed the faint lilac that emitted from Rune's eyes.

A few feet in front of Rune, and very much to his surprise, Steph stopped and gripped his hand. "Pete kneel."

"What?" Steph pulled on his hand, as she slowly descended towards the floor. "Oh I get it." Pete then went down on one knee, and looked up through the darkness. It was as silent as the grave as he heard Steph speak.

"I bid you greetings, My Lady of the Violetlines." It confused him for the moment as this was their daughter Runestone, but knowing of the many other strange rituals he had played along with in the past alongside Steph, he obliged and bowed his head.

"Greetings My Lady." Rune responded in kind.

"I bid you greetings Father, and Lady of the White Line." The violet light in her eyes intensified, lifting some of the darkness surrounding him, and he looked up at his daughter, not seeing a huge amount as the light flowed from her eyes.

"Is everything alright Princess? I mean, it's pretty late and your mum and me rushed here as quick as we could, there is no trouble is there?" Steph gripped his hand, and he turned to look at her bathed in the violet light from Rune.

"She is fine Pete, this is not about her, this time is for me." Steph let go of his hand and stood up, Pete was not sure what was happening, and he could not understand what she meant. He watched as Rune embraced her with a smile, and then as she moved back, she lifted Steph's hand and placed something small in her palm. Rune stepped back and walked toward her father, Pete watched his wife as the palm of her hand glowed with a faint white light, he looked to Rune as she arrived at his side.

"What is going on Princess?" Rune 's eyes were fixed on her mother, and he turned his head slowly to see her covered in the pale light that emitted from her palm, she smiled and he saw the love in her eyes.

"I love you Pete." There was something in the way she spoke that filled his heart, but he also felt an ice cold shiver run down his spine. It happened fast... Too fast for him to respond to, as Rune drew out her sword and pointed it towards her mother, she spoke loud and clearly at her.

"Take the staff and follow in your father's footsteps." The Sword of Knowledge ignited, and the flames shot out from the tip and engulfed Steph. Pete opened his mouth to scream as a blinding white light shot out from the darkness. The whole glade of Robbie's Mere lit up brighter than daylight, and Pete felt the searing heat scorch his face, as he fell backwards screaming out his wife's name.

He landed with a heavy thump and his head spun, as dazed and confused he scrambled around on the floor trying to right himself and go to his wife's aid. The blinding white light pulsed down from the sky, and screwing up his eyes, he tried his hardest to try and make out where Steph was. All he could see was the blurred shape of Rune's back as she faced the mass of white light; next to her a shadowy figure in a long hooded cloak spoke. "You have done well Little Redstone, I will take her now."

Pete tried to stand, but his legs and arms were shaking violently, it was as if all of the strength had been sucked out of his body. Kneeling on his hands and knees, all he could muster was a terror filled scream. "STEPHANIE!!" It died in his throat as the weakness engulfed him, and he fell flat on his face, and fell the cold grass brush his cheek.

All over Loxley those who were up watched as the bright white column of white pulsated down in Robbie's Mere. John staggered up the rough track from the village hall, and stared at the sky, convinced he was far too drunk, and was seeing things. Harry and Maggs who had been a few drunken paces in front, dived for cover under the Hawthorn hedge, where they held each other tight, and Harry yelled as loud as he could at John.

"Whoa! Aliens and uncosmic beings man. John dude run for it, they do all sorts of unfunky stuff to your vibes and magnetise your man bits, run dude before they mate you with robots."

Robbie leapt out of bed and fell on the floor, as the light almost burned out his eyes; he crawled to the door and slipped through it, pulling it closed behind him to shield himself from the light. His first instinct was to head downstairs, but he could see the light pulsating across the room below through the railing, and decided to stay put until it was lessened in power. "What the hell are you doing now Runestone?" He gasped as he leant back against the wall to shelter.

Outside on the grass, Pete cried in pain and fear into the earth, his body shook at the thought of his wife burned alive by the flames of Rune's sword, his mind whirled as the thought of his daughter who he loved so much, doing such a thing almost sent him into insanity, he buried his face into the grass and wept.

It was a few moments that felt like a lifetime, when Pete felt Rune pulling at him. "Daddy, Daddy come on it's OK" He rolled back fast and blinked hard, still feeling the terror inside him, and everything was dark again, except for the faint glow of violet from Rune's eyes. He sprung up off the floor as Rune reached out to him.

"DON'T TOUCH ME!" She jumped back in fear, as Pete whipped his head round, looking towards the spot where his wife had just been standing. "Why did you do it? Why Runestone, why did you have to kill her, she was your own mother?"

The lights came on in the house casting some light across the empty glade, Pete's eyes were wide open and wild as he turned and scanned the floor for her body, his eyes came back to Runestone who was standing just in front of him with tears in her eyes. His eyes met hers and locked onto them as more tears streamed down her cheeks, her voice quivered as she spoke.

"Is that what you think, how could you Daddy? She is my mum and I love her, like I do you, how could you think I would do such a thing?"

His head spun trying to make sense of what he had seen, and understanding none of it. "I watched you burn her, I saw it with my own eyes, I am sorry Princess, but I saw you turn her to dust, if you didn't where is she? Where is her body, there is nothing there?" He looked down at the sword still clenched tightly in her hand.

Robbie came running up to Rune's side, as she stared at her father in disbelief. "It's the flame of truth and knowledge; it cannot hurt her she is the guardian of the Whitelines."

"What? That makes no sense at all." His knees buckled, and he fell forward, Robbie jumped and caught him in his arms, and he hung limp as Robbie lifted him up and turned to Rune.

"Come on we need to get him inside; you can tell me what the hell is going on there." Robbie turned and walked up the grass towards the house carrying Pete, Rune who was still feeling the shock of her father's thoughts, turned slowly and followed him.

Everything had gone instantly black for Pete, and he spiralled into confusing wild dreams, he slowly became aware of Robbie's voice, which was raised and quite loud, as the black drew back, and he returned to the long settee in Rune's living room. His blurred eyes opened and focused on Rune stood looking pale and very upset, he could hear Robbie shouting, but could not see him as he was stood behind the settee as he addressed Rune.

"Hell, Rune you are supposed to be the stone on which all is written, how the hell could you not know?" Her eyes were filled with tears.

"I thought he knew honestly... Mum tells dad everything; I just thought she had told him."

"That's the bloody problem with your lot, you are all so damned busy doing your thing that you completely forget that we are just mere mortals, and we know bugger all about the powers or how they work. Poor sod, you must have scared him half to death, and trust me I know what the hell that is like, I watched Scarlet try to slice you in half. It's bloody irresponsible that's what it is." More tears ran down her face as it reddened.

"LOOK I AM SORRY OK!" Her eyes flashed with bright violet, and the vase behind her shattered into a million pieces. Pete sat up as Robbie stormed across the room towards the stairs.

"Yeah, bit too late for that though isn't it? What with Keith exploding on my commanders over Saff, and Rafe driving me nuts about where the hell Jett is, and now this, it seems to me that as head of your circle you need to get things in bloody order, because it is buggering up everyone around you, so fix it Runestone!" He thumped onto the stair, and disappeared as Rune noticed her father sat up watching her, she exploded in yet another shower of tears.

"Oh Daddy I am so sorry, I did not realise she had not told you, if I had known I would have prepared you, I am so sorry, please forgive me?" She fell on the floor in front of him, and he pulled her close, and hugged her as she wept.

"She is alive then?" Rune blubbered into his shoulder, as she squeezed him tighter than he had ever known.

"She is fine, she has replaced granddad and has gone with the White Lord for a few days, but she will be back and better than ever. Please forgive me Daddy?"

"It's OK Princess honestly. It did scare the hell out of me, but its fine, come on don't cry now." He stroked her back and held her tight as she wept, and could do nothing more than try to calm her down. "Robbie sounded mad." Rune gave a huge sniffle.

"He has a right to be, I should have made sure everyone knew about this beforehand, I think it scared him just as much. I am so sorry Daddy, I could never harm any of you, I hope you believe that?"

"I do Princess, come on it's done now, dry your eyes and tell me just what exactly happened to your mum."

Rune and her father talked for several hours, and Pete went to sleep in one of the spare rooms. When Rune went to bed, she found the room empty; Robbie had gone up to the office to work. She lay awake for most of the night thinking and missing him, but she had understood how angry he had been. It had been her father who had made her realise how much fear Robbie must have felt when he saw her take her gifts from Opal, and it chilled her to think of it.

He was indeed very right, she had not considered anyone else in the rights of passage of power, and she truly understood how terrifying it must have looked to those who witnessed it. He had never lost his temper or shouted at her like that before, and she felt terrible that it had provoked such a reaction in him, lying awake alone felt like a bitter punishment, but it was one she had to endure, as deep down inside she was afraid to face him in such a temper again, knowing it was based in his fear of losing her, or anyone of the many family members that surrounded them.

When Rune woke the following morning, much to her disappointment Robbie had already left for the Village Hall. She ate her breakfast alone on the balcony outside her bedroom, and spent the rest of the morning playing with the children. Robbie knew she had to leave again, and she had hoped he would return home in time, but as the clock slowly ticked, she realised she would have to leave without talking to him. With a heavy heart she opened her window, and stepped through into the Forest of Time, she was surprised to find it was raining again, and she lifted her hood and hurried along the track towards the open space, where the long wooden house of Fagan resided.

Fagan sat in his rocking chair by the fireplace, puffing on his pipe; he sensed her arrival, and smiled as he waited for the tap on the door. It was a few moments before he saw the shadow through the curtain and got up from his seat. "Come in my sweet."

The door opened and Rune dressed in her long violet cloak stood in the doorway dripping. He hurried across to her. "Oh my, what a day for dogs and cats, come in my sweet and give me ye cloak to dry by the fire." Rune gave a smile and swept the long cloak from her shoulders.

"It is nice to see you again Master Keeper, I was not sure you were here for a moment." Fagan gave a grin, his large eyebrows rising as he did so, and took the cloak from her.

"I can be seen when I needs to be, but ye knew that didn't ye?" Rune took her favourite seat at the table, as Fagan hung the dripping cloak close to the fireside to dry off.

"I believe Master Fagan, you are more than adept at secret keeping, which is indeed another reason for my visit, you left the ceremony a little too fast for me to talk with you yesterday."

"Oh that's pretty normal for me, I don't like crowded places much these days, I find folk ask too much of a man if ye gets me drift?"

"I do indeed, although I wish you had told me of your gifts from your mother, it answers a lot of questions now that I think about it." Fagan moved up the room to the stove, and lifted the boiling pot up to a large tea pot; he poured in the hot water, and moved the pot to the table to sit for a while as the tea brewed.

"Ye had no real need to know if I am honest, I used what I could to advise ye, and it all turned out for the better." Rune gave a nod as he gathered cups and saucers and placed them on the table. "I was glad to help ye as ye know, but if I am honest, I don't see it as a gift, it's more of a curse as it was to my mother. Folks get a whiff of it and they are at ye like bees on a marsh lily, no I think it's better left alone, then folks stay away."

Rune understood, and in many ways his advice had been right, although there was a part of her that just wished he had trusted her enough to confide in her.

"I realise I am not of Fae, I do understand you have obligations to the line of your people. You should have mentioned your position to us, it would not have made any difference to us, around Robbie all men are treated as equals, you should have informed him you were Lord Fagan of the Fae." Fagan poured the tea.

"Aye I like that about ye Robbie, he sees a man for what he is, there is no real status in a name if folks don't know what ye are worth as a man. It is just another name like Beech or Fagus, both of em are the same tree no matter what ye call em." Rune smiled; his simple logic reminded her very much of Robbie. Rune lifted her tea and they drank and talked for most of the afternoon, Fagan had to admit that it felt very quiet in the wood since they had all left, and even though their stay had been only short, he had grown very fond of them and the hustle and bustle of the group.

Slowly the conversation turned back to Avalon and the new queen, followed by Morgan le Fey. Fagan told her the story of how the Fae had found out that she had taken Merlin, and planned the war against the king that eventually led to his death. He had taken the lead in seeking her out, and had faced her briefly before she had run, and it was at this point Rune began to see the true power of who Fagan really was. Her bright blue eyes stared at him from across the table, and Fagan knew she was about to ask him a question that Merlin himself had once asked her.

"Morgan is Fae isn't she? There have always been rumours of some Fae being seduced by darker forces, her grandmother was Fae, which must mean some of the line runs in her veins, and you must have been able to see something in her. You must have seen something that frightened her, and that is the reason she never came back when Avalon was empty and attempt to kill you. I know I am right because it is the only thing that makes sense." Fagan gave a smile and nodded.

"Ye are as sharp as ye grandfather, he too asked me the same thing." Rune's eyes shone with the brightest of blue.

"You did not answer him, did you?" He shook his head.

"No, I did not." Rune had guessed right.

"You were afraid that after all he had gone through to escape from the Hidden Realm, if you gave him the answer he would go after her and try to kill her. I think that you did not think my grandfather was capable of facing her and defeating her, tell me am I right?”

Fagan gave a long breath and stared at the table for a moment. When he looked up, Rune could see the sadness in his eyes. “He was a good an true friend, but I hadn't the heart to tell him she was Fae, and knew things his line did not. Even back then she was powerful, but ye must understand that ye cannot simply walk up and kill her, there are things ye must do to prepare for it, and that is why she has remained safe all these years. Oh I have regretted that day, I wish I had said something and maybe everything would have been different, I just don't know.” Rune gave a nod and smiled slightly.

“You saw his death at her hand, and you thought if you said nothing, he would not track her down and try to face her? What you did not know was that what you saw is the very thing that happened just two weeks ago, and you thought she had killed him, when in fact she had failed as it was all part of his elaborate plan to disguise his passing the torch to his daughter, my mother.” Fagan looked surprised, but he leaned back in his chair and scratched his white hair behind his big ears.

“The thing is that when I see things, well they usually come right, it's just that this time I got the wrong idea of the pictures. I wanted him protected, he was Father Whiteline, and how could I let him risk it?” She understood and knew how deep a friendship they had, but it did not change the fact that Fagan knew something that could help them.

“If you had not seen the vision of his death, would you have revealed to him what it was you saw?” He thought for a moment and took a deep breath.

“Knowing him as I did, and knowing what a good man he was, I would have to say yes.” Rune sat back and smiled.

“You are a good man Fagan, and a worthy friend for anyone, but if I was to ask you now, would you tell me what you did not tell my grandfather?”

“I would not tell just anyone, but ye grandmother made me promise that if ye asked I would, and so I am asking ye honestly and truly, do ye really want me to tell ye?” Rune could feel the tension build between them, she knew Fagan had news that could defeat Morgan le Fey, but she could sense that it would not be something he would not give unless she urged him to. She thought carefully for a moment sensing she should tread lightly.

“Does what you saw provide a means to destroying her forever?” He gave a resounding nod.

“Oh, I should say it does.” He smiled.

“Then I must ask you Fagan of the Fae to share this knowledge in hope of avoiding a war where many will die, for the hour is upon us and we have much to lose.” He closed his eyes for a moment and leaned forward resting his thick dark arms onto the table. Fagan opened his eyes and Rune saw a very distinct twinkle in them.

"I read her thoughts and dreams, and I saw the Fae magic within her, and she has used a secret known only to the Fae that has been guarded since the lines first walked in harmony with everything." The excitement bubbled up inside Rune a little as she leaned in and kept her voice as quiet as Fagan's.

"Can this secret be shared with those not of Fae?" He shook his head but smiled a large smile.

"I cannot tell ye how to do it, but I can tell ye what it is. Ye see this magic was the difference in everything, it is why she could not be defeated by Rhiannon when she killed Eleanor, and sadly it is how she was able to take the mortal form away from Eve bless her."

"I have always wondered how she could achieve so much when she was just a mortal, knowing she is of Fae changes everything." Fagan gave a very solemn nod.

"Oh it does indeed, thinking she is mortal as others have is her second biggest secret."

"You saw that in her, and that must have really frightened her, because if you saw that, you must have seen her biggest secret, which is also her greatest weakness." Fagan took a deep breath.

"In a way it feels like lifting a great weight to share it, and so to her big secret. Little Dark Eyes bound her life to the Raven; it is a deep secret how the Fae can tie their life force to other things in hope of gaining greater power and longer life." Rune gave a small sigh.

"We know she did that, it has been common knowledge for some time, it's why she has survived for all these years." He gave her a cheeky wink.

"Aye, but did ye know that in order to do it, ye must keep the animal alive and protected?" The surprise hit Rune head on.

"The Raven she used is still alive?" He gave her a slow nod.

"It is indeed, it is as old as her and living as we speak." Rune felt a shiver run down her spine, as the importance of the facts hit her, she gave a gasp.

"Oh, Hearne I think I understand... wow Fagan it's no wonder she is afraid."

"Oh believe me, she would quiver like rush in bindweed if she knew ye were here talking about it, ye see if ye gets hold of that bird and kills it..."

"Her life force will start to drain and she will become almost mortal, as her Fae life span is almost over. I knew she had done her spell incorrectly, and she had noticed something different, I felt that when I fought her. Oh Hearne, it is why she wants the new king, the blood of a royal line will rejuvenate the bird and give her another thousand years to rule." Fagan slapped the table hard, and Rune almost jumped out of her seat with shock.

"Exactly, I could not have put it better me self, even if I had lived to be as old as the oaks on the deep valley path."

"You do realise that if we can kill her forever, then everything she has helped to build will fail."

"Aye, and her monsters will die, and her walls will crumble, the green lord will be safe, and we can all get on with things without her and her son pestering us like swamp moss fleas on a hot day." Rune gave the moment a little more thought.

"I don't suppose you know where she keeps this Raven do you?"

"Aye, it's in her grandmother's home town in Saxony, from what I gather it's not easy to get to, but I reckon it's got to be worth a little look see."

"Oh Fagan you have no idea what this can mean to all of us, this could really turn everything around for us and end this awful war. Oh, we could all live in peace and happiness, just the thought is so powerful I feel overwhelmed by it." He gave a big grin, and lifted the teapot with a wink.

"More tea then?"

Travelling down the steep steps to the base of the mountain where the boat was moored was much harder than Una had first expected. She had woken Jett just a little after dawn, and after eating the last of their fruit, they began the perilous journey. The mist as it had been before, had swept right up to just below the top step, so once they were six steps in, they were blind to what was below them. The steps were smooth and wet from the mist, which made them very slippery, especially for Jett who wore her usual high heeled boots.

After a few moments of panic, where Jett almost fell to her death, on what was a sheer drop, Una suggested removing her boots and walking barefoot. Jett was not that thrilled, as the stones were as cold as ice, but she felt much more secure and stable, and slowly they progressed over the whole morning down to the dockside and clambered into the small boat.

It was quite cramped but with some careful shuffling they found themselves a comfortable way of sitting, and the boat drifted away from the dock, and into the centre of the Shrouded Lake. As before, sat in the boat hidden within the thick swirling mists, and listening to the lapping of the water against the boat in the silence, Una and Jett lost all track of time, and both of them drifted off into a deep peaceful sleep.

Woody was blissfully unaware of the little boat bumping up against the jetty, as he slept in the deepest and happiest sleep of his lifetime. Una sat up in the boat with a jerk, she looked around and realised where she was, Jett was sat up, and leaning back in the boat with her mouth wide open sleeping. Una gave her a soft kick. "Jett wake up... Jett.... JETT!"

"Huh... What? Sod off Rafe I'm knackered."

"Jett for the love of Hearne will you wake up, we are here." She sat forward and smacked her lips, as if she had some sort of foul taste in mouth.

"Urgh! I think I swallowed a fly or something nasty." Una was already out of the boat and on the jetty tying the boat to the rail.

"Jett we are back, we made it, come on we have no time to dawdle." She turned seeing the old cottage and began to run as her spirits rose high. Jett yawned and looked round the small tree lined piece of ground that the cottage was built on.

"God what a dump." She lifted her bag off the seat and slung it over her shoulder, then stepped rather unsteadily out of the boat. Slinging her boots over her shoulder she slowly walked along the jetty as she rubbed the sleep out of her eyes. Una had made it off the jetty, and ran across the short green grass and in through the cottage door. Woody was lay in the bed fast asleep and she stopped for just a second and smiled as she saw him. Her temptation was too great, and she crossed the room as quickly as she could, and sat on the side of the bed, and slowly ran her hand across his naked shoulder.

"Wilson, wake up, I am back." Woody groaned as he stirred and rolled over, he opened his eyes and smiled. Una felt the tingle run through her and leaned over and kissed him. "Did you miss me?" He blinked as if not understanding.

"Have you been somewhere?" Una smiled.

"I went to get Jett, don't you remember?" He sat up a little more and stretched.

"I think I have slept late or something, last thing I remember we were...." He spotted the dark silhouette of Jett leaning in the doorframe, and began to go bright red. "Oh err yes... well you know... err last night."

"Nice tattoo there Woody, didn't figure you for an eagle sort of bloke." Woody swallowed hard as Jett stepped in, and suddenly aware he was naked from the sheet up, he nervously lifted the sheet to hide the spread eagle printed across his chest.

"I err... Oh dear.... It was Beavis; he got me drunk and did it." Jett nodded as she looked round the room.

"Quaint, you got a pot I can boil?" Una sat back on the bed and noticed the dresser where the letter she had written the morning she had left was still neatly folded. Woody pointed to the stove where a black and burned old kettle sat.

"You can boil that." He turned to Una. "What time is it?" Una was starting to get a strange feeling.

"Looking at the sun it's just a little past midday." She looked back at Woody with a serious look on her face. "Wilson what day is it?" He looked at her with a very strange look.

"It's Friday why?"

"Friday... That is not possible I must have been gone days." She jumped up off the bed, making Woody jump. "It's not possible I left just after dawn this morning, it's been days not hours." Jett sniggered.

"Welcome to my life, it's kinda freaky aint it?" Una looked at her.

"What the hell has happened, it makes no sense at all." Jett shrugged.

"I kinda figured Rune was behind it all, and she is kinda cool with her powers." She turned at the stove. "You want your tea with or without your pants Woody?

It looks like you got a bit of an animal in you man." Jett gave a laugh as she lifted them off the table, and threw them on the bed for him. He slid even further under the sheet, as his face burned a deep shade of purple.

Jett as ever appeared to be enjoying herself as she made the tea; Una was still trying to understand what had happened to them. The irony was it had been she who explained how a year to Jett in another realm had in fact only been weeks back here, she suddenly felt like the tables had turned on her also. Jett slouched down on a chair and sipped her tea as she watched both of them. "So now we have established its Friday, what do we do now?"

Una suddenly felt the urgency of the moment. "We get packed, Wilson saddle the horses, Jett can have one of the supply horses, we can leave the provisions here. Robbie was about to face the Dark One when we left, he may need our help, so let's get sorted as quickly as possible and get going. We will be out of contact with Rune until we are back in the trees on the other side of the dunes, I say we ride and ride as fast as we can."

"Cool I'm in." Jett looked at Woody sat in his bed with his pants hanging off the bedpost. "Come on then Woody, pack the beast back and get your pants on, you been laid once today, I ain't, and I got a feeling Rafe is in for a very long night." He swallowed hard, and slid his pants carefully under the sheet making sure he hid as much of himself as he could from Jett.

The ride across the dunes was hard going. The sun beat down on the hot soft sand filled with endless miles of long green and brown rush like weeds and tall grass. The horses slipped and slid in the sand, making pushing them hard very difficult indeed. The sun burned on their backs like a desert, and the horses gasped and panted as Woody urged them on, looking for the most sure footed way through the maze of high reeds. As the sun moved across the sky towards the evening, they were forced to take more and more breaks, until all of their water was used. Jett panted in the sweltering hea,t feeling totally miserable and wishing the day would soon end, when suddenly Woody shouted from up front and pointed ahead, where the thick mass of deep lush green marked the start of the woodland, and the end of their tortuous journey.

With a rising hope and a sense of joy building within them, all of them pushed their horses that little bit harder to hurry towards their journey's end. They came over the last large dune, and the horse's slipped and slid as they descended as fast as their poor burdened horse could take them. Within the hour they rode laughing and cheering under the canopy of the trees, and within a moment of doing so, Jett felt that very familiar feeling that she had missed so much, as her contact with Runestone made a new connection. The whole of the woodland in front of them exploded in violet light, and Rune came running through her window wearing the biggest smile Jett had ever seen.

She was barely off the horse when the tearful Rune dragged her into a tight embrace. "Oh Jett we did it, we finally got you home safe." Fighting to hold back her own tears Jett slid her arms around her and pulled her tight.

"Hey Girl, I never doubted you would." Woody sat up on his sweating horse wearing a huge smile; Una wiped her eyes and sniffled as she watched them both hold each other for an age and talk quietly to each other. Woody slid down off the horse and walked up to the side of Una, she turned with tears in her eyes.

"Thanks Wilson, for being there for me." He gave her a boyish sort of grin, and she dragged him close and kissed his startled looking face hard. It was a long slow passionate kiss, and Jett gave a titter.

"It's going to take some time to get used to seeing that every day I can tell you, but hell, go for it Woody you waited long enough." Rune smiled suddenly feeling very happy.

"Come on we will head to Fagan's and then home."

CHAPTER NINETEEN

HOME LIFE

The visit to Fagan lasted much longer than Rune had wished, but Fagan was in high spirits and had laid the table for a celebration meal. Jett who was the centre of attention loved it, but as the sky darkened, Rune stepped out into the fine drizzle and stood on the porch watching the rain run off the roof in a fine stream. It was not long before Una appeared sensing there was something not quite right with Rune. She walked up to her side and stared out across the vast expanse of lush green grass to the trees.

"You have appeared preoccupied all evening Runestone, is there something I can help you with?" Rune shook her head and gave a long sigh.

"I am OK, I just have a lot on my mind, it's not been the best of times recently, I guess I'm feeling the strain a little." Una gave a slight nod.

"You and Robbie have had a lot on your plate, how are things between you?" Rune gave a slight giggle.

"I guess I should know better than try and fool you, especially considering your gifts. We are fine, we had a bit of a row, and I suppose it has got to me a little, I need to get home and sort it out with him." Una lifted an arm up her back to her shoulder and gave it a squeeze.

"Talk to him, you already know there is nothing you two cannot talk through."

"Yeah, I know, I will as soon as I get back."

"Good, I will always be here for you Rune, you have only to ask, you know that?" Rune tilted her head on to Una's shoulder.

"I know, Thanks Una."

"So, you will be going straight back tonight... Hmm would you mind if I stayed here for a few days, I don't wish to cause more problems, but I would like to go back over to dad's house with Wilson and spend a few days there alone, I think it will do both of us good." Rune understood and she gave a soft smile.

"Don't wear him out; Robbie already thinks there is some plot to exhaust all the men in the Specialists." Una gave a chuckle.

"He is a nice guy Rune, a bit clumsy, but I really do like him, and we get on better than I ever imagined we would. I think a few days out here together will let us talk and find out more about us, I will let you know when we are ready to return."

"No problems Una enjoy yourself, all the Specialists are on easy duties at the moment until Robbie and Rowan decide what is next for us, so have a nice holiday." Una kissed the side of Rune's head.

"What about you? Maybe some time off would do both of you good." Rune gave a long sigh.

"Yeah... I fear that is something we will not have the luxury off until all this is over, Robbie has too much on his plate, and I have other matters of urgency to look into."

"Matters of urgency, everything is alright, isn't it?"

"It will be Una, but I have a few things that will make a big difference to everything to seek out, if what I have learned tonight is right, I will have to pull in the talents of all of us before this is over. Thank Hearne we have Jett back, we will have great need of an extra sword." Una felt a chill and gave a shiver, she had never seen Rune so serious or thoughtful, and just for a moment, Rune had reminded her of her own mother.

It was a little over an hour later when Rune thanked Fagan for his hospitality, and opened a window for her and Jett. Una and Woody hugged them, and then mounted their horses to ride to the old house of Merlin. Rune looked at Jett and smiled. "Where to?"

Jett looked a little surprised. "How do you mean?" Rune shrugged.

"They have all missed you; do you want to head for the Mere, or the hotel? I would imagine Jade and Blades especially will want to see you?" Jett suddenly looked a little nervous.

"Do you think they would mind if I left it until the morning, to be honest I am pretty tired, but I would like to be alone tonight with Wolfie." Rune snapped her fingers and her window pulsated.

"Go on, this will put you right on the doorstep." Jett gave a beaming smile and hugged her.

"Cheers Rune." She lifted her bag and hurried through the window; Rune waited a moment as she heard Jett hammer loudly on the door of number six.

"Jonathan Rafe, this is the sex marshal, and I have orders for none payment of tax, open the door and pay up wolf man."

Rune gave a giggle as she heard something smash in the background, and then the thumping of boots on the stairs, there was a tremendous squeal from Jett and then Rafe's voice in tears. Rune smiled and clicked her fingers, and the window gave off another pulse of violet, she turned to Fagan who stood smiling, his white hair shining brightly in the last light of the day.

"Thank you again for all you have done, and thank you for sharing such important information, all of us will be forever in your debt." The old man gave a bright smile and stepped back to give a regal bow.

"It is and will always be my honour, My Lady of the Woodland Realm. Fare ye well, and may the flowers bloom in ye footprints always." Rune reached up and gave him a soft kiss on the side of his cheek; she saw the sudden look of surprise on his face as his thick bushy white eyebrows rose.

"Live well in my realm, my friend." She turned and walked through her window and came out near the water at the bottom of the glade. The window snapped closed behind her, and she turned to look at the house set back in front of the trees. Jade stood at the glass doors and waved when she saw her, Rune began to walk towards her as Jade ran down the path and through the gate. She ran excitedly down the grass wearing a broad smile.

"Is it true... She is back right... Cause I am sure I just felt her?" Rune gave a nod of her head.

"Yes Jade she is home again, I just left her with Rafe, she promised she will see you in the morning." Jade looked a little disappointed.

"Yeah the sex thing, I figured she would. OK so I will wait another night, so how was it with Fagan, I hope you gave him my love and told him I missed him?"

"I did, and he sends ye his deepest regards." Jade gave a giggle.

"Cool, I miss him; I wish he would move here." Rune walked slowly her mind half on Jade and half on the house. Talking with Fagan and then finding Jett and Una safe had taken up a lot of emotion, and it mingled with her deep unsettled feeling and upset over her argument with Robbie. She kept her eyes fixed on the house, as it got closer.

"Is Robbie back yet?"

"No not yet, I am glad you are back though, with Rowan in York I was getting really bored." Jade stopped as she noticed two tears roll down Rune's cheeks. "Hey Sis are you OK?" Rune stopped and turned to Jade.

"I had a huge row with Robbie, and he has not spoken to me since, I think I have really hurt him Jade, and I do not know what to do." The tears streamed and Jade grabbed her tight.

"Wow Rune this is not like you, come on how bad can it be? I mean, you guys are like the role model for all of us; he is probably just working late. You know he has been away for a while, he will have a lot of catching up to do." Jade slowly led the weeping Rune up to the house. "Tell me all about it and let's see if we can get this sorted."

It was quite late when Robbie arrived home feeling exhausted, he slid the door closed quietly and turned around to see Jade standing in the kitchen doorway. "Jade, what are you doing here?" She stared at him in a menacing way from under her long fringe.

"I am waiting for you, because my sister is upstairs breaking her heart." Robbie suddenly felt a cold shiver run down his back; Jade's tone was very serious; he glanced up at the ceiling knowing just above Rune was on the bed. "Have you any idea of the fear and terror my sister suffers whenever we go into a fight? Do you even know of the huge weight she carries on her shoulders, as she uses all of her energy to keep us alive? So she made a mistake, it's not like you haven't made hundreds fighting this bloody awful war."

Robbie went to speak but Jade snapped even louder at him. "You ain't so perfect see, now you listen to me Robert Loxley, you get up them stairs and you go talk to your wife... Do not make me come up there and show you my knives." She lifted a hand and pointed to the ceiling. "Get up there and fix it." He felt the impact, and knew it was best not to piss Jade off; he kept his voice as meek and mild as possible.

"I was going to... I have not eaten all day; don't suppose I could grab something to take up?" Jade placed her hands firmly back on her hips; her jacket slightly opened revealing her knife belt.

"Not happening Robbie, you go sort things out with Rune first, then you eat. You got that?" Her green eyes burned with fire under her fringe, he gave a nod.

"Yeah Ok I am going." He moved slowly across the room to the stairs, as Jade's eyes followed him, he stood on the first step then ran up the rest. Jade gave a giggle as she turned back into the kitchen where Louisa stood holding a cup and trying not to smile. Jade flicked her hair back and sat on the chair by the table.

"See he is a pussy cat if you have the right weapons."

Robbie had never meant it to go so far with Rune, but the demands placed on him and her had just got in the way. When he entered the room, she was asleep, although he could tell by how puffy her eyes looked that she had cried herself to sleep, something he deeply regretted. Regardless of Jade's threat, it felt wrong to wake her, so he quietly undressed and slid into bed beside her. He snuggled close smelling the jasmine and honeysuckle scent of her hair, and put his powerful arm around and held her close. He closed his eyes and drifted, feeling relaxed as the light of the moon lit up the room with a pale blue light. Rune was still snuggled within his embrace, and although her eyes were closed, she let a small smile cross her lips.

The sun had not been up very long, when loud screams erupted downstairs, Robbie sat bolt upright in bed still half asleep as the noise levels ratcheted up. Rune sat up at his side and grabbed his arm, as he went to jump out of bed, she pulled him back. "Don't panic it's not Mason, it's something far worse."

He blinked not quite understanding, his head still filled with sleep. "Huh?" She smiled at him as he blinked trying to focus properly.

"Jett's back and Jade has waited all night to see her." He gave a long groan and flopped back into the pillow.

"There goes the peace; I knew it was too good to be true." Rune rolled over on top of him and sat on his waist watching him.

"What?" She gave a giggle.

"You're awake."

"Hell most of Loxley must be with Jett back in town, I take it Rafe will be happy but very tired this morning, when did she arrive?" Rune laughed.

"What are you not excited to have her home? I brought her back with me last night, there is a lot to tell, but I think I will leave that until after breakfast." He gave a yawn and stretched out his arms.

"OK, when is breakfast?"

"Oh I don't know, it's about two hours off."

"Really that long?" Rune started to giggle and leaned forward and kissed him. He gave her a smile and pulled her closer.

Breakfast was in bed alone, and with all that Rune had to tell, it was a somewhat longer than expected affair. Obviously, Rune heavily edited a great deal of the story out, which would remain between just her and Sapphire. Most of it felt so farfetched, it was hard for Robbie to fully contemplate, and the final story that everyone else would be informed of, was that Jett had been thrown much further than anyone had realised, which was why it had taken so long to find and recover her.

By the time Robbie got downstairs, things had calmed down, and Jett sat in the kitchen as Robbie came in. It felt almost as if she had never been away, she sat on the stool wearing her usual black jacket and tight pants, with her long black boots with golden spiked heels, and the golden hilted Sword of Truth attached to her belt. He stood for a second and smiled, as she peered at him from below her raven black fringe. She slipped off the stool, and then as quick as a flash, she lunged at him and threw her arms around him. It took him a little by surprise, and he lifted his arms and pulled her into a tight hug. "Hey girl, it's really good to have you back home."

Jett just squeezed him even harder, and as he looked down at her pale face planted into his chest, he saw the tear run down her cheek. "I've missed you and I am so glad we got you home safe, are you OK, it must have been really tough on you?" She gave a slight sniffle and nodded her head, lost for words, which was a first for Jett.

He held her tight for several long minutes and slowly she released her grip, and looked at the floor as she took out a hankie and wiped her eyes. "Didn't mean to do this... Sorry Robbie."

"Cry all you like, no one will know, but I mean it, we have been very worried, and I am so glad to have you home to the family again." She gave a sheepish smile, and nodded a thank you. "Come on I need coffee, sit with me outside and tell me all about it."

Sapphire had been back at Callanish for two days, for most of the first she had slept feeling a deep sense of mental and physical exhaustion. The following day she rose early feeling a lot stronger, and within an hour of rising, she lifted the trap door to the old food cellar in her kitchen, and dropped into the large basement and began to clean. For the rest of her day, she worked hard storing her food supplies at one end, to free up the rest into a large open space. For most of the evening she mixed and painted lime emulsion onto all of the walls and left them to dry overnight. As Robbie stood in the kitchen with Jett talking, Sapphire was once again hard at work; she had just finished nailing a thick woven reed mat over the trap door in her kitchen to hide it, and had rolled up the corner to reveal the small brass ring sunken into the floor. It was not fool proof, but here in the wilds of one of the far islands of Scotland, she thought it would hide her room well enough if any stranger came by. Proud of her work she pulled on the ring, and the door lifted up revealing the small flight of steps down into the cellar.

Dropping the door slowly down behind her, she descended into the room that would become her private place to view her table. With bright white walls it looked so much better, and when the candles were lit in a wide circle round the whole room, Sapphire knew she had created the right atmosphere to conduct her art. The main feature of the room would be her table, which was in comparison to Rune's quite small, at only seven feet across. Her biggest problem was that because it came out of her pendant, it usually formed on the floor. Sapphire needed a stand or raised surface to sit the table on, and from what little she had in the house, she knew there was nothing remotely suitable. She sat down on one of the slightly wobbly old chairs and thought for a moment. "Hmm that is a problem, I mean it's not like I can pop out and buy one." Her thoughtful tone sounded deep as it echoed slightly off the walls. "Well the house is made of old stones and mortar, so I suppose I had better roll up my sleeves and get on with it."

Rune sat at her table and watched with a smile as she saw the difficulty Sapphire was in, she swept her hand across the table, and closed her eyes.

"Hear me Sapphire, for I have a gift to aid you."

"Rune, I am sorry I was going to talk to you later, I have been busy preparing."

"So I can see, here let me help."

Rune touched the surface of her table, and in Sapphire's cellar the slabs on the floor glowed with a faint light of violet. Sapphire watched as a seven-foot wide circle of stones fused into one large round slab. It twisted on the floor, then rose up out of it, and was supported by a huge rock boulder, which formed a table of stone, ready for her own table of sight to rest on, Sapphire gave a giggle.

"Being green circle has many advantages over the white; I have not the skills to manipulate nature. Thanks Rune you have saved me a few days of carting rocks up from the beach."

"I am your centre Sapphire, and I am always here for you, tell me how are you doing alone?"

"I am OK, I do miss Keith, but I think I have made the right decision, I want to use my table to gain more knowledge and skills, I think I need time alone to do that."

"You show great wisdom, but do not struggle alone, if you need me, I am always here. Use your table to cast the veil over you, you are isolated and alone there, protect yourself well."

"I will Rune, do not worry about me, honestly I am fine."

"Learn as much as you can, for I will have need of you soon on a special errand."

"Special errand?"

"Yes, news of great importance has reached me, I need a little time to work things out, but when the time is right, I will need your skills. I will visit our green friend in the south soon, he is wasted for the task of cat burglar, I intend to move him on to other tasks."

"Other tasks? You are not going to send him to Canterbury are you?"

"His path lies in pulling together those who support us and are scattered. Fear not Sapphire, for his fate like all of ours has changed, but watch over him for me and go to his aid if needs be."

"Alright Rune, I shall watch his movements, and I will be here when you need me."

"OK Saff, we will talk soon, stay safe."

Sapphire felt like she had really achieved something as she slipped her pendant off its chain and pressed it hard in her hand, the liquid ran from the pendant and expanded out, covering the whole surface of the round stone slab in white. She slipped the pendant back on the chain, which fastened back round her neck, and then with a smile she placed her hands palm down on the cool white surface and spoke quietly.

"I am Sapphire of Callanish, and Seer of the White Circle, awaken in my service."

From the centre of the table blue appeared and streamed across the table like ink in water. It flowed out forming the spikes of a five-pointed star in bright sapphire blue, and then the table gave a pulse of blue, and Sapphire's eyes filled with blue light.

She felt it tingle through her as the table connected to her with a sense of great exhilaration, and giggled almost giddy with the sensation it gave her. Looking down at the star she gave her first command. "Show me the knowledge of my line."

The table sprung into life, and much to her surprise, sensing her insecurity of her gifts, deep inside her mind, the table spoke to her in her own voice. It was the greatest feeling she had ever known, as slowly taking each step at a time; the table talked her through the whole process. It was the starting point of Sapphire's journey to knowledge, and refining her skills, here alone in her secret room, she now faced the task of learning everything she would need to watch over all of them and train a future queen of the Fae.

The following three days were busy as more reports came into Fuse at the Village Hall, Robbie was briefed with each new arrival, and his days became long as he worked until late each day. Having Jett back lifted the spirits of all the Specialists, who apart for a few were given light duties around the Stockade. Robbie thought it was better if they were seen after the many rumours circulated by Agatha and a few others.

Robbie had always thought the best way to defeat the Dark One was to take the small glass bubble she wore round her neck. From the moment he had seen it on her while defending his family on Iona, he had been convinced that it contained the bubble that held Mason's dream of power, as it looked very much like one of the bubbles he had seen at the well with Opal. To suddenly find out that somewhere in the world was a secret location with a very old living raven, it threw all his theories into chaos. For most of the time he sat in his office at the Village Hall trying to figure out his next move, he had missed Rowan, so for the time being he had waited, trying to work out his plans to stop Mason, and get William on the throne, in hope that when Rowan returned, together they would find an answer.

It had felt like a long and frustrating day for the Sage as he walked slowly along the water's edge, the sun was sinking after what had been a cloudy yet humid day, and behind his mask, his face was hot and sticky. His arm was healing, but it still gave him pain if he lifted anything heavy, and so he had spent several days having to sit back and watch, as Silas took charge with Markus, exploring the vast city of stacked steel containers, and picking the locks to reveal their inner prizes. The only good thing about the last few days, had been the discovery of several containers filled with tinned food, and as his stomach groaned, he knew he had not eaten this well since his days back in Loxley.

The sea lapped up the beach, sweeping quietly in to the base of his boots, as he walked slowly along its edge, the millions of stones and pebbles crunching softly with each step. His mind was lost in the thoughts of his frustration and restlessness, and he did not notice the figure that silently walked up to his side.

"Hello Billy, you appear weighed down, are you OK?" He gave a startled jump and Rune smiled. "I thought as much, my grandfather used to say he was off in a brown study. I never really did understand that, but lost in thought you reminded me of him."

The Sage thought for just a second. "Reminded?" He met the gaze of Rune full on. "He is alright, isn't he? I mean nothing bad has happened, has it?" For a moment his heart had skipped a beat, regardless of what had happened, he had always liked Leenard who had treated him with great respect and kindness. Rune gave a sad smile.

"He has left this realm for another, and he will not be returning. Nothing bad has happened to him, but I miss him deeply." The Sage gave a sigh.

"I am sorry he has gone; he was the fairest man I have ever known, and good to me always, he will be missed by everyone in the end." Rune frowned.

"In the end, how do you mean, have you seen something of the future." The Sage smiled.

"I see all sorts of things, but nothing too specific, to be honest Rune I have seen strange stuff recently and I have no idea what it all means." Rune understood he had the gift of sight, and she wondered if he had seen something of recent events, but could not work out what he had been witness to, and she changed the subject quickly.

"Billy I have come here to see you as there are a few things that I think you may be able to help me with." He gave a nod.

"Yeah anything, as long as I don't have to use both arms, I am fine." He lifted his stiff wounded arm, Rune noticed his wince, there was still a lot of pain in his shoulder, and she smiled remembering another time when he had been cut on the same arm.

"It appears to be a habit with you; sadly, I do not have any of Alice's cream to ease the pain with me." He gave a giggle as the Marshal on the old market came to mind.

"Yeah smoother days, it seems like so long ago since that day and the cart ride, fun times eh?" She could see the twinkle pass through his eyes as he remembered being with the Specialists, and then the cloud of sadness that followed. "So you said you needed my help?"

"Yes I do, firstly I need to know anything you might know about your grandma's grandmother?" He blinked surprised.

"Old Maud is dead, she died years ago. Why do you want to know?" Rune shook her head.

"It's not about Maud really, and more about where she came from. I know you were only with your father for a short time, but did he ever mention her?" The Sage frowned below his mask.

"Well not a huge amount, I mean I hated my grandmother and she hated me so we spoke little of her roots. Although... Dad always referred to her as the Old Saxon Witch, I know she died before he was born, but he heard a lot of tales about her from Hesketh, he didn't like her either. I do remember something about Grandmother's father refused to be called Anglo; he hated it and would only be referred to as Saxon. Dad told me he would go into a wild rage and kill anyone who besmirched his homeland and his family name."

"I don't suppose your dad ever mentioned where that homeland was did he?" The Sage thought for a moment. "To be honest it's hard to remember everything he told me, I do recall something about it being high up in the mountains, but to be honest they always referred to it as Saxony, but most of the country was called that in those times from what I can gather. Is it very important?" Rune gave a nod.

"It could be, I am not sure at the moment, but that does help a little."

"Good... You said a few things, what else can I do to help?" Rune smiled.

"You have done well coming here, but let's be honest being a burglar is not really your forte is it? I want you to leave here and head down the coast to the eastern borders, we believe there are a lot of scattered people living in the wild who are loyal to Robbie, I want you to find them and bring them together, we need to encircle Canterbury and protect it from your father, if I am right the woodlands are growing fast and he is finding it difficult to contain them. Billy there is a rich land filled with trees and a few people, I need a man trained in Loxley to seek them out and show them how to live there and aid Robbie."

His mind filled with thoughts of life under the trees again, he understood straight away what was needed, and he had to smile, for of all the things that Rune could ask of him, he knew this would suit him the best. "Woodland I can do and do well, but what about here there is a massive amount still to do?" She gave a nod of understanding.

"You are a man of Loxley, you are wasted on a beach, take Martin and the boy and leave the others to finish here, this task is more suited to Silas and Markus, I will get Sapphire to bring others here to help. Get under the trees where you belong, and help us pull together a woodland army to fight from the south, Sapphire will aid you as will I." He did like the idea and he nodded his approval.

"Yeah... That sounds like a plan to me, I can do that Rune." He gave a broad smile.

"Good, I have made arrangements for Phillip at Caerleon to work with the French fishermen we saved from Morbihan; they will ship out anything Silas can find us to use. I know you are on good terms with Wilbur, so I will arrange for him to pick you up and take you by sea to the east coast, remember you must clear Canterbury of all your father's men."

"Yeah no prob's, well, I will see what can be done." She came a little closer and lifted her hand to his wounded arm.

"Not saying this will do much; healing is more of a Jade thing these days." Her eyes went an intense violet, and the Sage felt the sudden heat where her hand was rested upon him. The heat radiated through his arm and shoulder, and he felt a strong sense of calmness flow into him, he closed his eyes for a moment, as the peace flowed all through him. Rune gave a giggle and he opened his eyes, she had taken several paces back and was watching him.

"I take it that's better?"

"Huh?" He shook himself out of what had felt like a restful daze, and lifted his arm. The Sage gave a nod and smiled as he felt the strength building in his arm, which although not completely healed, felt a hundred times less painful. "Yeah that's great; there is no end to your new tricks Rune."

"I must leave now Billy, remember Wilbur will take you, Martin and the boy, and all you have to do is focus on finding as many as possible and showing them the ways of the woodland. I will see you again soon." She turned towards the steep grass covered dunes and waved her hand, her violet window opened immediately.

"Rune...?" She turned.

"What is it?"

"I am not sure this will help, but I just remembered. Hesketh said something about how gran's dad loved to sit on the high wall and shoot at the peasants, kind of a sick guy if you ask me, but I think he called them Bohemians. Not sure that helps but you never know, he did know a lot about gran's younger days, I might be wrong but I am sure he was her lover once, kinda gross I know." It made some sense to her.

"It does help yes... Although the thought of her being anyone's lover is not a thought I wanted to have in my head." She gave a chuckle and waved as she stepped into her window of violet light, it snapped closed behind her leaving the Sage alone with the sounds of the waves. It was much later than he realised, as he looked round he had walked quite some distance with Rune. Flexing his arm with a smile, he turned on the shale and gravel, and began to walk slowly back to the camp, where he would tell the men of the new plans, somehow he felt it was news that would be greeted with great enthusiasm from Silas, finally he had a command of his own, and the Sage knew that would mean a great deal to him.

CHAPTER TWENTY

MOVING FORWARD

A whole seven days had passed since Rowan had gone to York, when two things happened. Firstly Steph arrived back with Rayne and Gwinne, and then a few hours later Rowan and Treen were returned from the outskirts of York. This had all happened the night before, and Robbie who had waited a week, felt the frustration inside him, as Rune explained that Jade had spent very little time alone with Rowan since their return from Avalon, and so Robbie had to wait to see Rowan until the following day.

It had been a long night of uneasy sleep, and during the morning he paced up and down waiting for Rowan, while Steph arrived and spent all morning talking to Rune. There was nothing unusual about that, except Robbie was convinced she looked younger, she also wore a pendant he had seen before, both Leenard and the Dark One had worn them, and he began to wonder if the strange circular white bead round her neck was indeed her connection to the Whitelines.

When Rowan finally arrived, Robbie wasted no time grabbing drinks, and heading up to his office to talk quietly, and after three long hours of looking at reports, both of them were starting to understand the way in which Mason would attack.

Rowan was convinced that the tall new walls that had been built to expand out the outer limits of York were a cover. He was sure that Mason intended to use them to distract them away from his real plans, and Robbie was now starting to understand what Rowan was thinking.

"You think he will use the height of the walls to use his cannons, surely he will send out a full frontal attack, I mean look at it, he has covered the dead ground and his walls are a matter of feet away from the trees. He could open his gates and pour thousands into the woodland, it would not matter how many traps we have, with superior numbers Rowan he could swamp all our defences and ride over them as he did on the moors." Rowan gave a nod.

"I know Robbie, it looks like the most likely plan because he used it to reasonable success on the moors, but that is my point exactly, it's because he understands now how we fight that he won't take that approach, not to mention the number of casualties he took, even outnumbered, he is still no match for trained woodsmen in that terrain." Robbie gave a sigh and sat back in his seat, he stared into the grey eyes of his most trusted friend.

"So, if that is not what he plans, what would you do in his place?" Rowan pointed to the map on the table covered with small red dots.

"Look Robbie, he has been testing our resistance all along the lines above Birmingham, if you ask me, he is looking for a route through. He knows Loxley is strong and when he finally gets here, he will need a lot of strength to attack, which is why using York makes no sense; he will have the fight of his life the moment he leaves the protection of the walls..."

"So by the time he gets through the woodland to Loxley he will be massively depleted and his troops will be exhausted after a very long hard fight?" Rowan smiled seeing Robbie was starting to understand.

"Robbie he must arrive fresh if he has any chance at all of getting the upper hand, and don't forget our young king to be." Robbie frowned.

"How do you mean, as long as he is in Loxley, he is safe?"

"He is, but you are not thinking like Mason. Look, Mason we know is a man of impatience, he does not like waiting for anything, and he will think of you as the same, simply because he will expect you to do as he would, so he will expect you to make a move to crown Will and take his thunder away from him." Robbie gave a nod of agreement.

"Well we do, let's be honest if we can crown him and get the country to support him it will weaken Mason a great deal." Rowan slid his finger across the map.

"Yes, we have not planned to do it yet, but he does not know that. Look Canterbury is ruined, Westminster is destroyed and crumbled, that leaves York or Lincoln as the largest Cathedrals that exist in or around areas he controls, which can only mean one thing." Robbie spotted it instantly.

"The Arch Bishop is at Lincoln and is allied to us, or at least he suspects so much, so we can only use Lincoln for a crowning ceremony if we intend to follow the old traditions of monarchy." Rowan sat back with a confident air.

"He has to take Lincoln, which can only be done by attacking our southern borders and I may add he has ships, so he will attempt to land in the east, I mean let's be honest, it is where we have the thinnest cover as it is so open and wild there, it's the only thing that makes the most sense." Robbie looked at the map, and saw the many red dots and instantly saw the threat.

"He will have a lot of wide open space to cover, but with his numbers that will make him hard to hit because he will be spread so wide, yes I see it now, it's the only thing that makes perfect sense, he has to get to Lincoln before we do to ensure York is left for his crowning. I cannot believe I did not see it, Fuse has been reporting strikes all over the south recently, so much so we have begun to move everyone from New Avon and the surrounding area and pull them back north."

"Let's not forget, if you are going to come at Loxley, the main gate is still the best way, he could set up camp on the hill opposite with a grand view, and storm the valley, wood can only take so much when you are pounding it with cannons. He wants to make an example of you Robbie, he is arrogant enough to want to walk in through the front gate and announce the place is his. Scarlet always said he would want to use the front door, and to be honest Robbie, I think she was right."

"Yeah, me too, she was the best at tactics, I think we need to look to Lincoln." Rowan lifted his empty cup and gave a sigh; it was empty so he placed it back on the desk.

"I think you need to do a little more than look Robbie, I think we should go and talk to the bishop, Father Warren has been there for some time, I think it's time to see where he intends to put his allegiance, I think once we know, then we will have a better idea of how to plan." Robbie gave a nod as he stood up and lifted his empty cup.

"I think you are right; I will talk to Rune. Come on I need a drink, let's find out what everyone is up to." Together they relaxed a little and made their way down the stairs to the first floor in search of everyone else, and by the sounds of the noise, the kitchen was the place to be, where laughter and talk lifted noisily behind the closed door.

It was a rowdy morning on the Mere, having Jett back brought with it some contagion, and soon there was laughter and chatter from every part of the house. A meeting had been called for late afternoon, and it was decided that it would take the form of a meal, and future plans would be discussed over the food, so with the jokes and a sense of fun, everyone gathered to muck in and help prepare for the dinner time meeting. Furniture was slid back to the walls of the spacious living room and the long tables were set up, and covered with deep green velvet cloths. Shortly after six in the evening all of the Specialist, and a few other members of the Lox household sat together and began their lavish meal.

Robbie sat at the head of the table with Rune to his left and Steph to his right, down either side the others sat and scooped the hot food onto their plates, at the far end sat his mother with John and young William, all happily talking away. Jett sat with Jade and Blades and was as loud as ever as she fooled around with Harry sat across the table from her, she suddenly noticed the empty chair and looked round. "Hey... Hang on a minute where is Hawk?"

Everyone looked up and it was Big John who gave a sheepish answer, after exchanging looks with Melanie. "Err... He took ill; he will be off his feet for a few days." John looked up the table towards Robbie, who gave a slight nod of recognition; it was obvious Rafe had said nothing to Jett.

"Well what has he got?" She turned to look at Alice sat a few seats away. "Have you had a look at him, you know just to make sure it's not something serious?" Alice looked very on the spot.

"Well no... I mean not yet, he..." It was Rune who stepped in.

"Sapphire has been called to the White Circle Jett, her task means that she will not be in Loxley as often as we would like, so as a result she has decided to break all ties with Loxley." It took a few moments for Jett to fully understand the comment.

"What? You mean she dumped him? Hell, I thought those two were more solid than Hearne's Rock." Robbie changed the subject.

"Keith will join us later, for now we need to focus on our next move." There was agreement round the table, but it was Blades took the lead.

"What have you got in mind Robbie?" Every face in the room fixed on him as he lifted his glass, and for the first time that day there was total silence. He placed down the glass and thought carefully about his words.

"I have been talking, that is with Rowan, Fuse and Runestone, and I think it is time we made our first move towards placing William on the throne. The way I see it we have to ensure that we have at least half of the church on our side, especially the Arch Bishop."

"No offence Robbie, but have you forgotten Canterbury?" Jett looked a little surprised; she looked round the table at all the others now looking at her. "Well let's face it guys, they all wanted Knox on the throne, it's not like they tried to stop him is it? Why do we need them on our side, I mean we are a lot better off without them?" Fuse smiled and gave a little nod of his head.

"In many ways I do believe you are right, but you have to consider the legality of such things Jett. We need to sit a king who for the want of better words, I would say the people support, for without the blessing of the nation, it will appear like we deposed one dictator for another." Steph took up the response.

"I have no wish to be involved with any member of the church, and to a degree I am with Jett, but Fuse has a point, the church did convince a lot of people that Mason was the right man to rule, maybe if we win over some of them, they could go a long way to getting more support for William." Rune rested her fork at the side of her plate.

"I have spoken with Bishop Stevens; he is a supporter of my grandfather and will inspect his documents fairly. He has a heart for truth, we have no fear in dealing with him, although I am cautious as to the rest of the church, we have already had a taste of Brother Argus, and since that time he has spoken out strongly against us. I think Robbie is right, we should pay a visit to the bishop and see what influence he has, and if it is possible, we should offer our aid to his cause." Jett shook her head.

"I think it's madness; Mason has been buying the church for years."

"But we still need a Cathedral Jett if we are going to crown William in public, York is out of the question now, Lincoln is the only place we have that will serve the purpose and is on ground occupied by woodland forces."

It was rare that Gaynor spoke, and as she realised everyone was looking at her, her cheeks began to redden. "He is my brother, and the true heir to the throne, we must do this right and allow everyone the chance to show their support, he will be king over all the land, not just the woodland areas." Jess gave a warm smile and slid her hand across the table to take Gaynor's in hers.

"It will be done right, for I see a sister who will ensure it. You speak well on his behalf and we shall abide by your wishes in this matter." Robbie clapped his hands together drawing the attention back to him.

"Then this is settled, we will make plans for Lincoln and pay this bishop a visit, I want all of you prepared with full arms by noon tomorrow here at the Mere. Ok now that is done let us enjoy the rest of this meal and our time together." He lifted his fork and began to eat again, murmurs lifted as everyone continued with their meal and held small conversations. Jett was obviously not happy, but Robbie knew her well enough to know, that out of all them, she would be the most dependable if it came to a fight.

As David and Melanie enjoyed the comforts and companionship of Robbie's Mere, Keith was gripped tightly by the arm as he leant up against the fence on the footpath down from the shooting range. Henry, the burly sergeant who watched the gate gave a sigh. "Bloody hell Keith, this is no state for a Specialist to be seen in, come on get yourself home and out of sight."

"Sod off Henry, who cares what they think." He pushed his head against the fence and wretched violently, emptying the contents of his night's drinking out onto the path. Henry gave a wince not enjoying the view.

"Christ lad, this is no state to find yourself in, come on I will help get you home."

Keith pulled his arm hard and dragged it out of the grip of Henry, rolling back onto the fence and trying to half pull and half hold himself up. "I SAID SOD OFF!" His face was red and plastered with his matted vomit filled hair, and yet his eyes burned with a deep and raging anger, Henry shook his head slowly.

"Don't do this lad, I am telling you straight, go home and no one needs to know of this, come on now it's not worth the trouble." He made to move towards Keith, but Keith reacted swinging his arm wildly with a clenched fist.

"I SAID SOD OFF, NOW LEAVE ME THE FRIG ALONE." Henry stepped back easily avoiding the drunken swing.

"OK we do it your way." In a flash Henry sidestepped, and then lunged at Keith, before Keith even knew what had happened, he found Henry behind him and his arm dragged up his back, as the firm grip of the old sergeant pinned it into place and restrained him. There was a soft blue flash behind them, and a woman's voice spoke.

"It's alright Henry, there is no need to take him to the lockup, I will deal with him." Henry turned to the dark blue clad cloaked figure and gave a soft smile.

"Ok Miss Sapphire, if you think you will be ok, I will turn a blind eye." The cloak moved as she came forward and Henry released his grip allowing Keith to slip to his knees.

"Thank you, Henry, I will be fine I promise." He gave a nod and then helped lift Keith to his feet with Sapphire.

"You behave now you hear me Keith? Go with Miss Sapphire and don't go giving her any trouble now."

Sapphire pulled Keith's arm over her shoulder and began to walk towards the stone road at the end of the path, Henry walked quietly behind keeping a watch, but Keith made no sound at all. At the end of the path next to the barracks, Sapphire thanked Henry, and then walked on down the road towards David's cottage, which up until recently had also been her home, Keith staggered quietly at her side, his head lolling around as if he was unable to control it.

By the time they had walked the mile home, and Sapphire had got Keith sat in a chair, and had boiled a pan and made two large steaming coffee's, Keith was starting to sober up and become a little more talkative. Sapphire sat in the chair opposite as he held his cup with both hands and stared into the steaming brown liquid; he looked a real mess and stank as if he had not washed in many days. His clothes were filthy and his hair that was usually so soft and silky was matted and dull with bits of leaf and vomit stuck in the tangled knots. Sapphire felt horrible inside and blamed herself, but she knew that her decision to leave was the right thing for the sake of everyone. Yet deep inside she felt the pangs of pain as her heart broke, her voice was soft and caring. "Why are you doing this to yourself Keith? You have worked so hard to get where you are, why throw it all away?"

Keith stirred as if coming out of his trance, and he looked up at her from his dirty face with blood shot eyes, he gave a laugh and shook his head.

"Yeah, fine one you are to talk about throwing things away, I could ask you the same question."

"I am not talking about us, I meant Loxley and the Specialists, and you think I don't feel the same as you do, is that it?"

"Oh yeah right, I can see you just falling apart about it." He gave a sarcastic snigger and took a sip of his drink.

"I am not falling down in filth drunk as a skunk, but I feel equally as lost and alone without you, but as I explained, this is how it has to be."

Keith suddenly jumped up and threw his cup at the fireplace. It smashed on the stone, the liquid spraying everywhere and the flames in the fire hissed loudly. "BUT YOU DIDN'T EXPLAIN, DID YOU?" He plunged his hand inside his jacket and pulled out a piece of stained screwed up paper, and waved it at her. "I got a friggin letter, that's it after all we had done and meant to each other, you just gave your mother a letter and then poof... off you went without a goodbye or anything.”

For a moment he had startled Sapphire and she too had stood up, she understood his pain, and even his anger, but she knew that he would never have let her walk away on her own. Sapphire could see the depth of the pain in him as the emotion of that moment when she had left flooded into her, she tried her hardest to hold back her own tears, as she saw two clear tears roll on to his cheeks. “I told you the best I could, if I had done it to your face, you would never have let me leave, and as much as this hurts Keith, I cannot stay here anymore.”

“But why... why the hell is it always the same with your bloody family? Why can you not just tell us all what the hell is going on so we have a chance to decide for ourselves? If it’s so bloody important I will come with you, let me be with you at your side to protect you as I have done.” He took a step towards her, the tone of his voice calming from anger to an almost begging tone, Sapphire could feel the pull of her own heart, but she knew it could not be so, and felt the regret growing inside her as she wished she had not left her table and travelled here, she shook her head.

“You cannot come where I have to go, there are paths ahead no mortal can walk upon, I am sorry Keith, I know you do not fully understand this, but it has to be this way.” He stopped as she looked away avoiding his gaze.

“UNDERSTAND.... OF COURSE I DO NOT UNDERSTAND, AND YOU HAVE NOT BLOODY EXPLAINED IT EITHER!” His anger raged up again and Sapphire knew that she had made a big mistake in coming.

“I cannot explain it Keith, there are things within the Fae that I cannot tell you, it is not permitted, I am sorry, please believe me I am so sorry. I should not have come here, I must leave.” She stooped to pick up her bow, and he lunged forward and tried to grab her. He was still very unsteady, and she only just managed to deflect his arm and jump back out of the way, he crashed to the floor in a pile, as she took another step back away from him and closer to the door.

“Forgive me... In time you will understand this was right for you, I no longer have the chance of the life we planned together, you must find another more worthy of you who will be able to give you that life.” The tears flooded into her eyes as he scrambled on the floor to get back up, Sapphire turned at the door. “I am so sorry Keith; I never wanted to hurt you.” She burst into tears, grabbed at the lock and the door flew open.

Keith scrambled up to his feet and tried to make it out of the door as he called to her, but as he reached the door hearing her sobs, there was a bright flash of blue light, and as he fell out on to the doorstep, the street was dark and empty. He sat on the doorstep with his back to the frame and looked into the darkness. “Don’t leave yet Saff, stay... I love you.”

The door to her room burst open in bright blue light, and she flung herself across the small bed and wailed out her grief into the pillow. Hundreds of miles away on the small deserted Isle of Callanish, Sapphire cried until she fell into an exhausted sleep. Back in Loxley, Keith sat on the doorstep alone in the dark, in a deep drunken sleep, where in his dreams his heart continued to break, and in the early hours when Mel and David arrived back from the Mere that is where they found him.

Robbie sat long after the guests had left and watched the scene on Rune's table with her. "Poor bugger, is there really nothing they can do to stay together Rune?" She gave a soft sigh.

"As much as this seems hard Rob, Saff has made the right choice; her life has changed more than anyone will ever truly know. She is the Seer of Fae now, and one day it will be her job to instruct Hal and Iona in the ways of Fae. I know none of this makes sense to you, but where she will go on her journey to discover the secrets of the Fae, Keith can never travel, it is better he gives up his life with her now, so he has time to build the life of his dream with another. Hopefully in time he will understand that." Rune gave her hand a wave across the table and the pictures faded away, she gave a smile at the look of sadness on Robbie's face, and leaned over to his shoulder and put her head on it. "This is the better way Rob; you must not worry about them so much."

He gave a long sigh and lifted his arm round her. "I hope so, Keith is gutted, it will take a long time for him to heal."

"Yes it will, but he will heal, and he will grow stronger because of it, and then when the time is right, believe me Rob, he has happiness in his future, even if it does not appear such now."

"I hope so Rune, he is a good bloke, well they both are... Good that is. We will miss Saff with her windows; she has played a very useful role so far."

"She will be with us often, and don't forget she can open a window for us from her table, so fear not, she will be there to help when we need it. Remember Rob, from now on Saff will be our eyes, and she will be able to see much farther than we have in the past."

"From tomorrow we will need it; somehow I think things will start to move at a much faster pace as of now."

"Maybe, we shall see?"

CHAPTER TWENTY ONE

PREPARATIONS OF DEFENCE

The following morning was busy, it had been hard getting out of bed, Rune especially wanted to lie in and snuggle up with Robbie, but preparations had to be made. After a slow start both of them had risen and had breakfast with the few that had remained at the Mere the previous night, and then as the day wore on towards mid-day everyone got busy preparing their weapons and ensuring they had everything packed in their bags.

In Robbie's mind he wanted this to be a fast operation, but he knew that convincing the Bishop that he was in danger could take much longer than he wished, but with events changing daily he felt the pressure of knowing he could spare a very limited time to the protection of Lincoln.

The house was a mess, with open bags and weapons everywhere, as the Specialists arrived and checked everything they had. The chairs and tables were littered with equipment, and there was a happy hum in the air as the group laughed and joked with each other as they sorted through their equipment. Having Jett back made a noticeable difference, Robbie especially noticed how the group who had been much calmer and quieter for some time now, appeared much louder and laughed more.

It was late afternoon when the group gathered, along with a full battalion of woodsmen, and travelled through the window opened by Rune to the woodland just south of what remained of Lincoln. Robbie felt a strong sense of ease as his feet hit the woodland floor, and he watched as the men spread out wide around him and melted into the cover. The air was damp, and there was a rich scent of the earth as he crouched beside Rune and Rowan to get his bearings. Rune pointed the way. "We need to head through those trees until we reach the clearing where we can get a proper view of the cathedral."

Robbie gave a nod and signalled Jade, who crawled over towards him. "Pebbles, take Blades and Fox and scout up front, I want to know if anything is around that may be trouble. We had reports of limited skirmishes so be on your guard, if there is anything creeping around here, I want to be the first to know who and how many." She gave a smile.

"Will do." She crawled off and gathered Blades and Fox, and as quick as lightening they disappeared into the trees up front. Robbie looked round at the long line of woodsmen behind him, he turned back to Rowan.

"You take the lead with John and Jett. Put Treen, Harry and Rafe to the right, and send Jay, Smokes and Bear left keep them wide of the pack, I do not want any scouts spotting us, we need to stay out of sight at all times. Everyone else can stay close to the centre with the rest of the woodsmen behind us." Rowan gave a nod.

"You want to keep the Specialist up front, use what you trust, I get that." Robbie patted his shoulder.

"We have a lot of new recruits mixed in with this lot, I want experience to guide us until I know how these guys behind have been trained." Rune smiled, she understood that Robbie wanted no mistakes, and with a unit half filled with new young faces, Robbie used the best he had to mark the trail and lead the group safely.

Camp was struck on the outer edge of Lincoln, after two hours of carefully moving forward. Robbie sat on the outer edge of the camp with the Specialists as he waited for a report from Jade, who had not been seen since she had left. The sun was fading when she slipped back into camp to give her report.

"You are not going to like this Robbie, but we have more than just a little company, Mason has a pretty big force set up in one of the towns three miles east of here. The good news is there are small groups of locals camped all the way down the road, it seems that this happens every second Friday, as the church hands out free food, so as for lighting a fire, we are safe there is a good mix of our people and some run away city dwellers mixed in there. I would say Mason plans on making sure your bishop does exactly as he is told, and if he doesn't, then let's just say he has the means to make sure he complies on standby ready for action." Blades gave a nod of agreement as Jade spoke. Rowan looked a little puzzled.

"But we hold this line, it's within the zone." Jade shook her head.

"Well we know that, but I don't think Mason does, because he has at least five hundred men down that road." Skip agreed with her.

"It's no big surprise Rowan, we have suspected it for some time now, you see round here is so sparsely populated it's hard to monitor every border. We are only about five miles north of the divide, and we know Mason has been pushing into the no man zone for some time now. Remember my friends the coast is not that far away, and he is the one with all the ships, he could land an army here and the first we would know is when they marched up the road." Robbie gave an agreeable nod.

"It's why we must convince the bishop that his new council of the church should move further north where we can protect them. This land is too open to police, we must make him understand his position."

"And if he won't move?" Bear's question was not an option Robbie wanted to consider.

"Then Bear, I fear for all of us, for that is not an option anyone in this land can afford." Bear gave a chuckle, as Robbie turned towards the others. "OK all these people along the road may help us, they will provide good cover, and it also means we can cook, it's going to be a long night, and my priority is to talk with the bishop and find out where we stand."

Setting up camp did not take long, and soon Robbie found himself sitting on an old log surrounded by ferns enjoying being back in the trees. Rowan and Jade had gone off to have a look round the small tented camps of people who had travelled to the cathedral for the service, and Rowan was also interested in knowing as much as he could about what others had seen further down the road. In his mind if there was danger around, he wanted to know every detail, Blades and Todd had been given the task of scouting the road and the size of any enemy encamped nearby.

Rune gave a smile as she approached Robbie with an old battered tin cup that steamed with the rich scent of freshly ground coffee, he took the cup as she slid down at his side, and he could see she was visibly very happy. "It's nice being back in the woods again, it feels a little like old times don't you think?" She gave a giggle.

"It's hardly different Robbie; we have spent almost most of the last year in one woodland or another. I suppose being back in camp under the trees is a place we feel most at ease, it's surprising really when you think about it." He gave a slight frown and she turned smiling towards him.

"Surprising? I don't see how."

"Well you know? I never thought when we met we would be spending so much time away from Loxley under the open skies. It's daft really, but I just figured we would walk in the fields and up the lanes, and hang around the farm, like everyone else does. When you think of everything that has happened, well who would have thought it?"

"Like what? Marriage, children, and ridding the world of a dark evil sorceress, and also her brutal stone loving son? I planned more, but we have not had time to fit it in yet." She gave a chuckle and snuggled up to his shoulder.

"You know what I mean, us?" He slid his arm up her back and pulled her closer.

"Yeah, I do, life has certainly been surprising that's for sure, there is a part of me that wishes none of this ever happened, but it's too late to go back Rune, we are here and if we beat Mason, then I suppose things will slow and we will get more time alone together." Rune slid slightly forward and gave him an odd sort of look. "What?" He was not sure what had occurred to her. Her bright blue eyes gazed at him for a second, and then her face straightened to one of a serious nature.

"You said if." He gave a slight shrug.

"And?"

"Robbie you never say if, you always say when we beat Mason." He was not completely sure why this mattered to her.

"If, when... They are just words, why does it matter so much?" She slid back from him and turned slipping her leg over the side of the tree so she could face his side, he turned slightly still puzzled as to why this of all things mattered so much, in his mind it was just words.

"Robbie they are not just words, they are intentions... How you phrase things indicates what you feel deep down inside, and that shows how you intend to act, you have never used if, and always thought and acted like we would win this fight, so why have you suddenly changed?"

It was hard to find the right words, being alone whilst Rowan had been away had given him a lot of time to sit and think; just looking at the constant stream of information flowing into Loxley showed him how much Mason had prepared, and how much more they would have to do to win this fight. Mason did have the upper hand; it was a fact, no matter how you tried to use a positive slant. He gave a long sigh and looked up into her bright blue shining eyes, he could see the concern and the love she held for him, but he also knew he had to be realistic. He turned on the old tree and slid his leg over so that he faced her and took her hands in his.

"Rune, he has taken York and has most of this country behind his walls working hard to ensure that whatever we throw at him, he can rebuff it. His ships move freely round the coast with troops and supplies ready to land anywhere and flood that place with thousands of his well equipped military, he rules most of this land. Ok we all know he rules using fear and terror, but none the less he rules, and it's the fear he creates that are a huge part of that, no matter which way you look at it, the odds are stacked heavily in his favour, we have the smallest chance of being victorious, and I am trying my hardest to make that happen, but let's be realistic, the odds are higher we will not win this war."

"Robbie that may be so, but I think you are not giving yourself and the woodland world enough credit, you have so much more than you realise, you cannot look on the dark side of things, you are the light everyone is drawn to." He gave another weary sigh and put his head down.

"I have done everything I have been asked to do and more, and yet I feel we are no closer than we were when we left Loxley with just a faint idea of how to get to Kirklees." He looked up and she could see the tiredness in his eyes. "Look at Avalon, it was a trap and we walked in without a care in the world, and it cost us Alley, it should have cost more, we are so lucky we did not all get killed, Mason and his mother knew long in advance we would have to go there and they prepared and were waiting. I've got to say Rune, for the first time since we began all this, back there in Avalon I really thought all of us were going to die... and even after we did all of that, what has actually changed? I will tell you what has changed.... Nothing, Mason is still in control because of his fear and brutality."

Rune slowly shook her head as she watched him.

"Robbie I am sorry but you are wrong, everything has changed. Ok so he took York, it was never our plan to keep it, and so what if he does have his factories all over the place, we don't need any, everything we need grows around us, so we just take what we need and use it, that's the point isn't it?"

He lifted his head to look at her and she gently took his face in her hands, as she stared deeply into his eyes. "I thought this was about fighting for a dream, you know the dream of that simple living boy, who wanted a life that was free to live as he chose, surrounded by the people he loved and not forced into a slaves way of living? Robbie you cannot ever give up on that dream, look at me, because I am here sat in the wilds and free as a bird as your wife. I am here my love, I am the dream you held close to your heart."

She took his hands and slid them over to her chest and pushed them hard against it, and so powerful was the pounding within her he could feel it. "Robbie, I believe in you and so do all of us, I took up my bow and lifted my hood and stood at your side, for you are the one who taught us that we stand up and fight for those who cannot fight for themselves. You have to look around you and remember why all of us are here at your side, you cannot forget for a single moment what it is we are doing here, because this is and will always be about the dream you held that inspired us, and all of those free in this land to look for something that was fair and just, and not the tyranny of a greedy evil sadistic old man."

"But Rune it does not matter, he is winning and I just don't know if we can stop him. If the church votes to join him, they will convert thousands from the open lands to support him, and our task will just get harder, don't you see that? Most of them hate us, they will take his side just because we follow a different faith, he has bought half the church, and the rest cower afraid to face him, tell me just how the hell do we beat that?"

She smiled at him. "Believe in me, believe in our children and the home we have, and the life we live free in this world, for we are here with you always. Take that faith and show it to all who oppose you, and protect it with every ounce of your being Robert of Loxley, for that is your goal to help everyone attain what you have already acquired, and trust me when I tell you, that the tides will turn and destiny shall reward you. The one thing we know is that there is nothing more powerful than the magic love binds between two people, and that is the one thing we know you have an endless supply of, and Mason has none."

There was something in the way she spoke, and the way her dusky freckles seemed to stand out from her pale white face, as her eyes sparkled with the brightest sapphire blue and the force of life. Deep down inside he felt a stirring, and it was as if Rune alone was able to reach deep within in and touch the core of who he was. She made sense and he knew it, but the doubt that had been building in him since the cave at Avalon was a huge hurdle to climb, and even then, looking into the eyes of the one person whom he loved more than life itself, it was difficult to fully overcome them. He thought for a moment as she watched, and then went to speak, but she simply smiled and lifted her finger to his lips before the words could come out.

"Don't tell me, just think about all the good we have done, and what our home truly means, only then will you find the right words to ease the doubts you feel."

There was something almost Steph like, or was it Leenard like? He really was not sure. For the first time since he had known her, he saw her parental line clearly demonstrated in her, and although she was younger than he was, it felt like her wisdom had started to exceed his own, was this because of becoming a parent herself? He was not sure, but as she rose and walked back into the camp, all he could do was watch, feeling that there was indeed a big change in her, and to him it felt like something extraordinary, and very powerful.

Wilbur's stores at Captains Cove had taken years to build up, but the time had finally arrived to open them up and use them to their best. The influx of people into what had once been a small seaside resort, had dramatically changed the whole place, and for the first time since the years before the Red Death, it was filled with the sounds of life. Grateful for their haven of safety, the people of Morbihan had wasted no time and set about rebuilding the place, and soon the community found it had a new centre to call home.

Boats were anchored and work began, Captain Calton Val-Andre had wasted little time refitting his trawler out, but it no longer resembled the tatty rust covered fishing vessel of the high sea. It was now painted entirely black, and had a long sharp battering ram made from a steel girder sticking out of the front. On deck on each side of the cabin, two ex-military artillery cannons had been bolted to the deck, and the holds below decks had been cleared of net and fishing containers, the captain had other ideas in mind, and his hold was now specifically designed for taking supplies off a vessel to transport back to Captain's Cove.

As Wilbur watched the refitted and renamed fishing trawler the "Avenger" just off the coast, he could feel that somehow these French refugees that had arrived filled with doubt and fear, had found a new single purpose in life, and he thought it might prove to be a huge surprise for Mason. Madeleine's last words to him resounded in his mind. "I know my people well, and Mason has made a very big mistake, not only will he find taking the land harder, he may soon find he will have a rival for the waves, we are people who work the water, and we know it better than he ever will."

Watching Captain Val-Andre, pull on the cord and release the black flag on the Avenger's mast, confirmed to him that Maddy was indeed right. The pirate flag unfurled and flapped open in the wind, and the engines of the Avenger gunned loudly, as other boats all along the coast started their engines, and waited in line to join their new leader and Captain of the fleet, the fishermen of Morbihan were finally ready for a war, and this would be a war fought on their terms.

Rune took Robbie by the hand, and they walked with Rowan and Jade towards the steep hill of rubble and earth that joined the road and led up to the old entrance road of the Cathedral. Robbie stopped in the failing light, and looked along the road leading away from Lincoln, where he saw the hundreds of small campfires situated between tents and makeshift shelters. Rune watched carefully as he viewed the situation.

"They are hungry Robbie, they have used what little they have, and now they sit and wait for the church to feed them."

He turned slightly and she caught his gaze and the lack of understanding in his eyes. "But I don't understand why Rune, some of these people are woodsmen, why do they not hunt and take what they need from the land?"

"The hand of Mason Knox is longer than you think, even here he can reach from inside his walls to harm the people, yet the woodland south of here is a fertile hunting ground, yet no woodsmen walk there." Robbie turned to Jade.

"Why do they not enter there?" It was Rowan who gave a response.

"From what we can gather the Cutters are still very active here, even though this is protected land, it is well known to those who dwell here that Loxley guards watch the cathedral, but beyond that the land is too wild to keep secure, and that has become the domain of Cutter raids."

"Then we must do something, how can we let all these people suffer?" The answer was not one Robbie wanted to hear, and both Rune and Rowan knew that the lines of the woodsmen were stretched and even in some places withdrawing, Jade however had no problems speaking.

"You don't have a choice Robbie; we have all hated seeing this, but what can you do really? Let's face it we are pulling back to prepare the lines, we need every available man, and we have moved as many as is possible further north, but the facts are Robbie that we have no spare land to give these people unless we start pushing Mason back."

"Then we have to find a way to start pushing back, I cannot allow people in these numbers to go without food. As soon as I get back to Loxley I will talk to Fuse, and I will find some way of stopping this." Rune gave his arm a squeeze.

"I think first we need to talk to the bishop, then we can look at helping these people, don't you?" He gave a nod.

"Yeah, first things first, ok let's get on with it."

They all moved back off the path and into the trees, and Rune opened her window. "Jade keep your eyes open and let me know if anything happens, we should not be too long."

"Will do Rune." With that Robbie and Rune stepped through the window and it snapped closed behind them, leaving Rowan and Jade alone at the foot of the steep hill to watch.

Every night, Bishop John Stevens, took one hour before he retired, to walk in the enclosed garden within the walls of the large cathedral, it was his way of escaping the constant demands on him, and gave him some precious moments of peace to think. His refusal to have a guard was a constant cause of concern, but deep down inside, the bishop knew here in the cathedral was the only place he was safe from the rest of the world. His belief that his god was his protector was unshakable, and so he walked around the small area of soft clipped grass, and enjoyed the scents of the flowers, as he sat alone quietly contemplating on the small garden bench.

The night air was warm, yet damp, and the scent from the roses appeared far stronger in the air as the light failed and darkness crept across the grass. It had been some time, and he was lost in his thoughts, when the sound of soft footsteps brought him out of his thoughts and back to reality. At first he saw nothing as the darkness deepened, but as his eyes focused better, he noticed the movement within the darkness of one of the far corridors; it was evident that despite his requests, someone was approaching to disturb his private time.

The footsteps grew louder, and he gave a sigh and rose from his seat, and shortly the figure appeared at the far end of the lawn. As they stepped off the paved stone, and on to the grass, they were revealed in the now dim light, and he noted it was a small figure dressed in a long black hooded cloak.

The figure lifted their arms and dropped the hood, and much to the bishops surprise, he saw the pale white face of Dana Knox. She loosened her cloak revealing her attire of a black tailored jacket and long black pants, that fell to the well crafted boots that now were silent on the grass. Around her waist she wore a fine belt of leather, on which hung a small holstered pistol. Her voice was soft, yet held some sternness, as he lifted his eyes away from the pistol and upward past the sparkling gems round her neck to her cold dark eyes. "Forgive the intrusion at such a late hour Bishop, but I have travelled here on a matter of great importance, it was not my intent to disturb your peace, however I was delayed somewhat by the crowded roads."

Somehow being delayed by others did not appear as something the bishop could envisage, after all, no member of the Knox family travelled without an extensive force, it felt highly unlikely anyone could delay such a brutal guard. "Lady Knox, I am indeed surprised and honoured you would visit me in person, when your husband usually conveys his wishes via other means. Please, take a seat, and may I offer you some refreshment as way of compensation for your inconvenience?"

Dana gave a faint smile and waved her wrist dismissively. "I have little time, do not stand on formality on my account, I can assure you this is but a short stop over on other business."

The bishop waved a hand and showed her to the seat, she gave a nod and sat down, there appeared to be an expectation he would seat himself beside her, yet he remained where he was, and she looked up to address him as she slipped her hand inside her cloak and withdrew a golden cigarette case. John Stevens was unsure as to why Mason would send his wife.

"I cannot help but feel a personal visit from you Lady Knox must imply there is urgency or importance to your business here, tell me how can I or the church be of assistance to you or your husband?"

Dana opened the case and slid out a long brown cigarette, which she slipped into a silver holder, and then placed it in her lips. From another pocket she took out a solid gold lighter, she leaned down and lit her cigarette, and then sat back so she had full view of the bishop as she exhaled the smoke. She paused for a few moments as she watched the bishop, he was quite sure of her purpose, and inwardly agreed with himself as she spoke.

"I shall not toil with formality Stevens; I feel you are more than aware of the many rumours that circulate about the direction of your leadership of the church, and the new council. As you are probably aware York has fallen and London has squashed all opposition, and my husband is very busy, otherwise he might have made the trip, he too has heard many rumours, and I have come here tonight on his errand to ensure certain agreements still hold fast." She took another long pull on the cigarette; it was clear she had not finished and so John Stevens waited.

"As you are more than aware Stevens, rumour suggests you will make a move to make a stand in support of this bastard child that Loxley intends to put on the throne, I am quite sure your memory will serve you to remember that my husband removed all opposition from other faiths to this church, and has therefore fulfilled his side of an agreement made ten years ago."

She cut to the chase quicker than even he had expected, and he thought for a moment trying to choose his words very carefully. "Well, I must say Lady Knox you do not mince your words." Before he could go on she interrupted.

"Cut the crap Stevens, you're either a supporter or plotting against my husband, I am here to ensure you are aware of your obligations towards Mason, after all he has been the greatest benefactor of your precious church, without him none of you would have survived and had the luxury that you have all grown accustomed to. I am sure Brother Argus has made you more than aware of the consequences should you defy us?" Bishop Stevens gave a solemn nod.

"I can give you my whole assurance that Argus has been very vocal, and indeed his emissaries have been very busy indeed, although I would ask, you are aware are you not that the announcement as to who will serve on the Church Council is not to be made until tomorrow? I can give you my assurance Lady Knox that I will act in the very best interests of this church and the doctrine it follows. I am more than aware of the pressure that exists on both sides of this conflict's leadership, but I must add that I cannot make a decision that will be influenced by politics: it must be made on what is right for those who administer this church to the masses. As for agreements with previous members of this council... well I must say I was not a party to those talks so can only speculate on what was agreed or spoken between them and your husband. I can however say that I have spent a considerable time discussing and examining all aspects of the current situation, which have been taken into account in the choices I have made. I would also like to remind your husband that as previously debated with him and others, I have made it abundantly clear that a church should not be a pawn of the state, and it matters little to me who rules the state as we administer to the spiritual guidance of all. As the leader of the council, it is my job to ensure that the best interests of this church as a priority."

Dana stood up abruptly, she flicked her cigarette as she faced the elderly bishop, and her tone was much cooler and sharper. "Make sure you do Stevens, neither myself or my husband will tolerate being crossed, the best interests for your churches survival lie precariously on which direction you choose, stray off agreed paths and you may find your precious church in more difficulty than you can imagine." She pulled her cigarette from its holder and tossed it into the flower bed, then slipping her case and lighter back into the cloak, she pulled up her hood.

"We are watching and will be waiting to hear from you, choose wisely Stevens, otherwise the next visit you get in person will be from my husband, and he will be far less respectful than I have been." With a flap of her cloak, she stormed off across the lawn towards four heavily armed guards, who had appeared during her discussion with the bishop. The elderly bishop stood silently watching as she disappeared again into the darkness of the corridor, he took a deep breath and turned.

"I take it you heard most of that?" Runestone and Robbie stepped out from another corridor and into the light as the moon rose above them. Runestone gave a polite curtsy.

"I did My Lord, you are far more observant than I had first expected, I was unaware you had noticed our arrival. This is my husband Lord Loxley." Robbie slid down his hood still watching the place where Dana and her guard had disappeared.

"My lord Bishop... You attract a very high level of ambassador, and it does appear you may be in far more danger than even I have realised." He turned to the bishop who took his hand with both his own and shook it with enthusiasm.

"Lord Loxley, I am even more surprised to find you a visitor, but you are most welcome." He took Rune's hand. "I was under the impression both of you were very busy at Loxley, this is a most enjoyable surprise, please let me take you to my office where we can talk more freely and I can administer my full hospitality."

Robbie looked up at the sky filled with the rising moon and stars. "Here is fine, no man could ask for a better setting, as for our unexpected visit, we find it safer to appear in unexpected places. I am glad to finally meet, although for a moment I was a little concerned for your safety, Mason is not a man who takes well to being refused."

"I can assure you I am quite safe, Mason Knox makes many threats, I think tonight just proves how very uncertain he is over his position, do not trouble yourself on my account, I feel I have many more years ahead of me to serve." He gestured for them to be seated, Rune sat with a smile and he joined her at her side as Robbie walked round slightly gazing upon his surroundings. Rune rested her hands on her lap.

"I am please we can meet again, I am happy to find you in good health and applying such thought and concern towards all matters in this regard, although I would ask as my husband implies that you be extra vigilant, as you have seen with Father Warren, Mason will stop at nothing to get his own way." Robbie stopped and gave a reassuring nod.

"Never forget Mason has many irons to his fire, and whether or not you believe your faith protects you, he does have many of his own people mixed amongst you. I have no idea of whom you have chosen for your council to lead this church, and I would not request you tell me, but if you do not show him people he is familiar with in the ranks of the churches leadership, he will see that as a deliberate provocation. This church does not provide sanctuary as it did in the days of old; Mason's hand has already reached deeply within the church, and he will not care or worry about taking yours or any other life from those who oppose him."

It was a sobering thought for the bishop, he had heard many tales of those who had crossed Mason, and none of them had ended well, but his commitment was to the church. He understood Rune and Robbie's concerns, but he knew this was the place he wanted to be. "I cannot leave here... Not now, the work here is too important, I cannot sit back and watch others corrupt the meaning of all I have been taught, no this is my task and I shall endure it to whatever ends." Rune's voice was calm and quiet, and he could tell by the look in her eyes that she wished otherwise.

"I admire your courage and commitment, but please do not throw away what you have so easily, there may be a time when you will have to leave this place and its many tasks in the hands of others. You must promise, when that time draws close, you will let us come to your aid and protect you, for the path you are taking will divide the church, and the day for choosing sides is drawing ever closer. We have men stationed close by to come to your aid, use them when they are needed."

It was a hard thing for him to accept, but Rune was right, no matter how much he wanted to remain in the cathedral, he had chosen members of the council that would favour Loxley and their proposal to place a king of true blood on the throne. The last few days had if nothing else highlighted the growing divisions within the clergy, the time of making a choice of sides was closer than even he had realised. Robbie spoke quietly.

"Tell me My Lord, have you ever heard of a religious group known as The Brethren?" John Stevens felt the chill run down his spine, and it was hard to hide his surprise and fear at the mention of their name, Robbie gave a knowing nod. "They are here within the ranks of your people, we have it on good authority that they represent the views of Argus and are in his employ, let me bring my guard within your walls to ensure your protection during this time." John Stevens was shaken and reacted instinctively,

"He would not dare... He cannot... How could he, he is a man of the church?" Rune gave a sigh.

"The time to choose is here, and Argus has clearly made his choice, our information is that he intends to divide the church, and then seek out and remove everyone who sides with us. You know what these men are capable of, the rumours alone will create the fear to sway a great many against you into the ranks of Argus." She took the frail hands of the old bishop in hers; he felt the warmth run out of her and into him. "It is time to act and act swiftly, you must make the announcement and leave, take the council into safety and help prepare the new king, for if you fail to do so, Argus will take over, and Mason Knox will wear the crown within the month. Let us do what we do best, and tomorrow we shall protect everyone who stands for the right to be free against Mason."

It was a very difficult choice to make, and John Stevens shook his head slowly. "There can be no blood shed on this soil, I cannot allow the fight from outside to enter within these walls, it goes against everything I believe." Robbie gripped his shoulder to give reassurance to his words; Rune saw the solemn look on Robbie's face, as his dark eyes watched the old man carefully.

"The Brethren have entered here with that very purpose in mind, they will slay all who stand in the way of Argus, let me bring in my own men to protect all of you, and I give you my solemn word as the leader of the Woodland Peoples, we will do everything in our power to avoid the death of any on your sacred soil."

The sad grey eyes of the old bishop gave a small glint of hope. "I have your word? You will escort and protect us all without taking the life of any?" Robbie gripped him hard and gave a smile.

"No life will be taken by my men on church soil, you have my word. Hold your service and then go ahead with your meeting, I promise they will not be seen unless they are required, but should the need arrive, you leave with Runestone and let us deal with the Brethren."

"But not kill them? They are after all ordained men, I do not agree with their ways, but they are men of this faith and as much as I dislike them, I am responsible for each member of this church."

"I cannot give you a full oath they will live if they walk from this place, but whilst they are on the soil of this place, they shall not die by the hands of my men." He looked a little relieved.

"All my life I have dedicated to the service of my lord and his church, never in all my days did I think it would come to this, I must act and act quickly to hold this church and all it stands for together. I must go to those close to me and talk, this has cast new light on things and I will need their input. Thank you, my friends for your kind concern, please be guests for breakfast in the morning and let me discuss matters further with you." Rune smiled and squeezed his hand.

"We too have much to prepare, I think it best if we are kept hidden unless we are needed, have no fear we will be with you throughout the whole day, even if you do not see any of us, we have ways of appearing less obvious than others." He gave a warm smile and understood her fully.

"How I wish things could be different, and we could meet and talk in public as friends." Robbie patted his shoulder.

"One day maybe, but until such times we shall use stealth to ensure your full protection. Go and meet with those who may share your burden, we shall leave by our own route to remain unobserved."

Robbie and Rune watched as the bishop made his way back to his offices, and to summon Simon his aid to collect the council for him. Rune felt a little of his burden. "He is frightened and doing his best to remain strong, he has aged since we last met, the strain of his position has shown itself on the lines of his face, we must do all we can to help him."

Robbie slid his hand round her waist. "We will, do not fret, I have a few tricks up my sleeves as well." Moments later in the darkness of the garden there was a violet flash of light, and then darkness descended and all was still and quiet.

As the night fell, all the Specialists sat round the fire, within the woodland on the edge of what was now the remains of Lincoln City. Rune had left them to return to Loxley and brief John and Fuse, as well as take care of the children, her time trapped in Avalon was still vivid in her memory and she was not yet relaxed about being away for some time. Sapphire paid a visit knowing Rune was alone, and after the children had been safely put in bed, both of them sat on the small bench outside the kitchen door and talked quietly. Rune filled her in on the day's events, and Sapphire told Rune of her time with Hawk and the mess he was in.

"I don't know what to do, he will never understand what lies ahead of me, how can I take him with me, or just leave him here until I return? Rune I am not even sure I will return; we are both in uncharted territory, even with my visions I cannot be sure any of us will make it through, and he could be sat here forever waiting."

Rune gave her hand a small pat. "I know it feels bad Saff, but he will heal in time, if you want my advice, I would say I think you have done the right thing. I am not certain he will ever truly understand, to be honest I am not sure Robbie truly understands everything. You must remember that we are sort of a different kind of being who have very different priorities, we must be the ones who take the watch of everything, but the line of men will never quite understand what that entails."

Sapphire gave a deep sigh. "What are they up to tonight; I do miss not being part of the team?" Rune smiled.

"You will always be part of the team Saff; it's just that you will often have to look elsewhere to discover what is happening behind the scenes. Robbie will be briefing them tonight about how to blend in and stay out of sight until needed; we must protect the bishop from those that would kill him and all other supporters." Sapphire gave a nod.

"I don't really remember a huge amount about him, but I do remember him putting a blanket round me, and talking to me to help calm me, he felt like a decent man, unlike the rest of his friends."

"I would imagine friends isn't really the right word, I saw how disgusted he was at what they did, he is actually a very kind man, he is in a very difficult position, and I feel the conflict within him as he truly wants to do the right thing."

"You know Mason will kill him, don't you?" Rune frowned.

"Have you seen something I should know?" Sapphire shrugged.

"Nothing concrete, but Mason will not be pleased with him, you must tell Robbie that he should be protected."

"He will be, Robbie has already assured him that Loxley will do everything to defend and protect the bishop and his council." Rune stood up and walked slowly round the open area in front of the outdoor steamer, Sapphire sensed a slight change in her.

"What worries you Rune, I feel the change around you?" Rune gave a smile and turned round.

"I forget how your skills have built, you are right, I have other matters on my mind, and I may need your aid, but what I will ask of you no other must know about, especially Robbie."

"Is that wise Rune? I realise it's none of my business, but I would say that Robbie is probably the one person you could say anything too, tell me has this anything to do with what we did and the Dark One?" Rune smiled again.

"I think I know how Robbie feels being around me now, you feel things much faster than any of the others these days, but in a way yes Saff, it does concern the Dark One, and I really do need your eyes working with me." Sapphire flicked her long auburn hair back from her face.

"What do you need me to do?"

"I want you to use your gifts and move around and see what you can find out about Morgan le Fey's life in Saxony. I have done quite a bit, but things are so busy at the moment, I need you to focus all of your power and your table on learning as much as you can about her family line." Sapphire gave a shrug.

"Yeah, no problems, I have nothing but time on my hands, and I am learning a great deal from my table, so it will be a good exercise for me."

"Wear the veil, Morgan has not worked out what we did, but I am sure at some point she may fall upon it, and she could come looking for you Saff. Never forget how much she wanted your grandmothers' power, if she finds out it was a White Circle who opened the bridge and spoiled her plans, you will become the top of her list, so protect yourself."

Sapphire felt a shudder run down her spine, she had not made the connection with Gwendolyn and her own power, she had just thought she had inherited the one gift. Just thinking that she could be a target gave her butterflies in her stomach, even more so knowing that the lines of power increased with each passing. It made sense that if she had craved the power of Gwendolyn for her perverse purposes, then if she found out about Sapphire, she would relish the chance to obtain a stronger version. Rune gave her a smile.

"Fear not, we have time and hopefully before she realizes, we will have her."

CHAPTER TWENTY TWO

TAKING THE MIDDLE GROUND

Robbie sat in the centre of his camp with the rest of the Specialists gathered round the fire, and told them of the night's events and his discussion with Bishop Stevens. Rowan listened carefully, as he watched the reactions of the others; Robbie finished his briefing and looked round each of them to see if anyone wished to add a comment, Jett stirred as she fingered her butterfly pendent.

"I am sorry Robbie, but I think we are risking ourselves for men who don't care if we live or die. I don't trust the church; I still say first chance they get they will turn on us." He noted her comment and looked to the others; John gave a nod in Jett's direction.

"I gotta say Jett talks a lot of sense, look at the monks in Avalon, we saved their lives and half of em still hated us, I don't trust em either, but if you think it's right for everyone, I won't sit here, I will be there beside you." A few of the others gave a nod of agreement.

Treen threw a large branch on the fire. "It ezz not going to be the easy, this church has few women, we will find it eez hard to mingle, and if you want us to be the out of sight, we will ave to use less weapons, I am no fan of this way." Rowan agreed

"Treen has a good point, long bows won't be much use, everyone knows it's woodsmen who carry them, we will be down to knives and swords."

"Does this place have any high up places like Canterbury, if so, we use the women up top to cover us?" Jade looked round; it did make a lot of sense. "I mean if it kicks off it won't matter really will it, we can just pile in as normal."

"I would prefer it didn't Pebbles, I have given my word to the bishop no life will be taken inside the walls." Skip gave a long sigh.

"That's a pretty tall order Robert if these Brethren fellows are in there, they have a brutal reputation, I am not sure they will settle for a good talking too." Robbie shook his head.

"We do not have a choice, our aim is to stay out of sight, and only reveal ourselves if we are absolutely needed. It is my hope the bishop can deliver his speech and then we can whisk him off as quickly as possible, this is sacred ground, and we cannot risk some of you losing your powers."

"Then it ezz simple, I have a gift and so does Jett that need none weapons, Pebbles can strike without err being seen, so we go it with the men dressed as the monk, and everyone else does the guard on the outdoors." Rowan agreed.

"That does make the biggest sense Robbie; as long as they do not kill, they will be fine. I think this could work, and the good thing is Treen and Jett don't even have to reveal themselves to use their talents." Robbie gave a satisfied nod; Jett still looked unhappy and gave a sigh.

"Ok, the way I see it, Rune will be in there with us, so that is how we will play this. The front row of the meeting hall will be free for our people, so all we have to do is mingle during the service, and hopefully we will spot just who is up to no good and mark them before they go into the meeting. There will be a lot of other people there so we will need eyes everywhere, although Treen I want you at the doors to watch the road, I am still unsure about what they have hidden and you have proven your ability to think fast on your feet, if we need you inside, we will call. Get some sleep, as tomorrow we will need to be well rested and at our sharpest."

The group all gave a nod and started to get up from the seats round the fire, Robbie looked up. "Jett hang back for a minute, will you?" She looked back at him and then stepped back over the log she had been sat on, and dropped back down onto it. Robbie waited until the others had moved clear; Jett already knew what he was going to say.

"You are wasting your breath Robbie; I still don't think this is right for us. I have already been lectured off Rafe and Mother, but I think you are wrong." He gave a nod.

"I respect your feelings and your honesty, which is why I am putting you outside with the others; I won't force you to do something you don't want to be a part of." Jett's head snapped up and her eyes flickered blue for a moment, he could see the anger cross her face. She stood up and her voice was raised.

"I didn't say I wouldn't do it, don't you dare treat me like a child, never once have I not risen to the expectations of my place and done my share. I am the bloody future Queen of Caerleon and I might add one of the best fighters you have, don't you dare exclude me just because I hold a different opinion. I might not like these devious two faced turncoats, but I won't be in there for them, I will be in there protecting you and the rest of this team."

Robbie stood up to face her and raised his hands. "Ok I get it calm down, I never meant to offend you Jett, I watched you and just thought you were not happy with the situation." She scowled at him.

"I am not... But that does not mean I won't back up all of you." Robbie gave a nod.

"I am sorry Jett, ok; you will be inside with the rest of us." She turned.

"Too Right." And she walked off across the camp, Rowan watched leaning on the tree.

"That was brave, I am not sure she could match Destiny, but I am glad I didn't have to find out." Robbie gave a long sigh.

"Must admit I didn't think she would be so pissed off about it, still it's good to know she will be with us." Rowan walked over to the fire and looked back as he watched her drop onto her blankets, as Rafe moved over towards her.

"She has had a rough time, from what I gather she did a lot of fighting when she was lost, she has come back really edgy, I think getting back into her stride is taking a little readjustment."

"None the less, she will be the sharpest one in there tomorrow, I am a little relieved because you can bet your last bit, if someone in there has trouble in mind, Jett will sniff them out faster than any of us." Rowan agreed as he watched her pull the blankets over herself and turn her back to Rafe.

"I got first watch, I think you should get your head down and sleep, Rune will be here at dawn, I will make sure John wakes you when she gets here."

As Dawn arrived, Jade sat in the trees watching the road, as a long line of people trekked towards the cathedral. Rune arrived in camp, and slowly everyone began to rise and prepare for the day. Robbie sat with Rune as the group got ready, and smiled as he watched half the group pull on the thick and itchy monk's robes. Blades and Fox laughed at each other and Harry strode around scratching. Alice was dressed in old scruffy clothes so she could mix in with some of the poor, and the rest of the Specialists prepared their weapons as they waited with the company of woodsmen who Robbie intended to place outside as a signal to Mason that he too was watching the day's events, it took several hours before everyone was briefed and ready to go.

Jade wandered back into the camp dressed as what was probably the shortest monk they had ever seen. Rune gave a giggle as she stood beside her with a robe over her own woodsmen attire, she periodically scratched. "How the hell do these people live like this? It feels like a punishment wearing these things, I wouldn't mind, but I got my own clothes on underneath." Rune smiled as she scratched.

"It won't be for long, but I must admit, if it gets rough in there, I am ditching this as fast as I can." She gave another vigorous scratch on her arm. Robbie and Rowan appeared quite at ease with their robes much to the annoyance of the others, and soon the time came where they had to break apart and make their way to the Cathedral.

Treen in her General's cloak, led the long rows of woodsmen with the rest of the Specialists onto the road, and made her way up to the Cathedral through the archway to the large heavy doors, where she positioned the woodsmen all along the road in a show of protection, then took up her own position flanked by Maddy and Crystal at the doors. Many of the people making their way up the road looked relieved to see a guard of protection, and smiled and gave nods to Treen as they passed her to enter.

Robbie with Rune made his way inside, where he was guided to the long rows of chairs that had been set down the centre and reserved for the members of the church. The poor divided and made their way down either side along the towering side windows. Robbie slid in halfway down the Cathedral, and sat in his seat with Rune at his side. Rowan and Jade sat behind them and leaned over the backs of the seats to talk. The rest of the Specialists in their robes separated, and filled the seats around Robbie waiting for his cue. Jett made her way to the front with Blades where she could be close to Alice, who wove her way forward and stood at the side of the rows of chairs at Jett's shoulder.

The cathedral soon filled up, and Rune closed her eyes and sensed the many monks sat within the place. Robbie peered out from under his hood as he watched the faces of those in front who had turned sideways on to talk with their respective partners. It took just a few minutes and Jett alerted Rune, to a group of monks dressed in black who sat on the opposite side three rows in front of Robbie, Rune whispered quietly to Robbie as Rowan and Jade leaned in.

"Three rows ahead dressed in black on the opposite side, Jett says they have weapons under their cloaks." Robbie turned his head slowly and spotted them. There were four rows of seats filled with the same black clad monks; all of them were leaning into each other talking. He noticed quite a few brown clad monks leaning over the backs of their chairs and making comments. Stood a few feet away he noticed the two taller brown clad monks who stood in amongst the poor with their arms slipped up inside their sleeves, the hood of the tallest lifted and Robbie noticed the keen eyes of Smokes underneath as he gave a slight nod to Robbie, Robbie nodded back and watched as Smokes leaned into the figure beside him. Rune leaned in.

"Bear is with Dad and Harry, and my mum is also over that side with them, I think she is on the other side of the pillar."

"Ok so we know where they are and we have eyes on them, tell your mum to keep close, and try and find out what they are saying." Rune gave a nod and then scratched at her arm.

"Ok Robbie... How are you guys coping with these bloody awful clothes, my arms are red raw?" Rowan gave a giggle, and turned to view the Brethren.

Outside Jay gave the signal and it passed back down the line, Maddy came down through the archway onto the remaining street and looked out across the fields to the road, where she saw a long line of black clad Cutters who had come to a halt as they had obviously seen the large show of woodland forces. Jay came up at her side.

"What do we do?" Maddy watched intently.

"We wait and see what they do, Rune and Robbie are aware, and we have a good force here if we need it."

The last remaining people heading for the cathedral, hurried as they saw the Cutter forces behind them, trying to get to the sanctuary of the church's protection. Maddy watched as a lone rider came forward, she moved down the road a little further to meet him, as Jay took up position behind her, and the woodsmen fanned out and took up a defensive stance. The black cloaked soldier came slowly up the road and stopped twenty feet in front of Maddy, behind her from within the large Cathedral the music began to play as the service started; Maddy smiled holding her long white bow with an arrow fitted to the string.

"Good morning Commander, you appear to be a little out of your way, I believe the forces of your master are south of here behind the large ugly wall."

His horse appeared restless as its owner gripped tight on the reigns and leaned forward. "I was not aware that there was a guard of the woodland this far south, this is neutral territory is it not." Maddy gave a warm smile.

"You need to consult your map Commander, the divide line runs from Lincoln north, even though all church premises are considered neutral, this particular one is on ground under the protection of Lord Loxley, and therefore we ensure the peace. If you would like to partake of spiritual guidance, we would be more than happy to let you pass and partake with safe passage, once you leave your weapons beyond those trees. As I have already said, we are here to ensure the peace and safety of all on Loxley governed territory."

It was quite obvious he was not happy at the revelation that Lord Loxley had placed a guard there, but there was little he could do, he thought for a moment. "We were given the impression there would be an announcement of the new Church Council today, I have been instructed to relay the information back to my superiors." Maddy gave a nod.

"As stated, you are welcome to disarm and join the service in peace, we will give entry to all who bear no arms and you will have safe passage, you are all more than welcome to take part, but my orders are very strict Commander, I cannot let armed men into the cathedral. You have our word, no one who partakes of their religion peacefully will come to harm on Loxley soil. If you and your men remain armed, I must ask you to withdraw to the treeline at the end of the road, or we will have no option but to take action, the decision is yours."

He looked past Maddy to Jay who stood surrounded with bowman, all of whom had their arrows fitted and raised. Down each side of the road and on the roofs of the small remaining street, woodsmen sat with their weapons trained on him. He pulled his reigns and the horse turned. "I shall inform my superiors of your terms."

Maddy smiled and watched as he galloped back down the road towards his men,

Jay lowered her bow and walked slowly down to the side of Maddy. "That was a little awkward for him."

Maddy smiled as she watched his men turn and head back up the road to the trees. "He will be back, although I feel he will not be in a rush, he has seen we have a good size force here, I would imagine he will wait for Mason to strike before returning here."

Rune relayed the moments with Maddy as the service for the poor continued, Robbie gave a breath of relief, although he was starting to get a clearer picture of what had been planned, knowing the Brethren expected backup gave him the edge, because as of yet, they had no idea they had no reinforcements coming.

The service was far longer than expected, there were many prayers and hymns, of which Harry appeared to delight and sang all of them with great vigour, much to the amusement of Jade. Slowly the service came to the offering of food, and Robbie watched as young women dressed in all black carried large baskets of bread and cheese out, followed by young men who carried baskets containing vegetables. The poor cued patiently as they all were handed out the food, as they shuffled in a long line past the bishop who blessed them one by one. All of them crossed themselves and then shuffled down the central aisle and out through the back doors, as the monks sang yet more hymns, it all felt like a very curious ritual to Robbie who was more used to celebrating outdoors round a large fire with his friends and family.

Slowly the service came to an end, and as the bishop offered his final prayers, Robbie prepared. The service ended and everyone stood up, chairs moved and the hum of anticipated conversations began. Robbie moved quickly with Rune, making his way followed by the others down the cathedral and through the side door. Moving as fast as he could down the long corridor, he reached the room set up for the meeting, and placed the Specialists along the front two rows of seats to ensure he had a clear line of space between the new council, and the rest of the gathered members of the church. Father Warren waited by the side door for the arrival of the bishop, as the other members of the church came talking down the corridor at the back of what was usually the large dining room and filed into their seats. Smokes, Bear, and Steph, came in last and stood at the back with quite a few who also had to stand.

The room was noisy and filled with the long intense conversations of the members, Robbie stood with Rowan in front of their seats and watched as they faced each other in mock conversation, the black clad members of the Brethren were sat mainly towards the back scattered in amongst a large proportion of the brown clad monks who he assumed were the main delegation of Argus, all of them were in deep conversation as they leaned over the backs of their chairs with their heads down in small huddled groups talking very quickly.

Behind Robbie, there was a staged area, on which there was a long table covered in thick blue cloth, Jett and Blades stood either end next to the long row of chairs with their heads down and their slender female hands hidden from sight slipped up inside their baggy sleeves, the moment was set and ready as Robbie felt the tension in the air and waited for the bishop to appear and give his announcement of the new council.

It had been around twenty minutes, when Father Warren gave the signal, and in the room filled with the loud hum of busy conversations, Robbie braced himself as he sat in his seat at the end of the row, and turned slightly so that he had a full view of the stage and also of the gathered members. The door opened and Bowman Jersey entered and stood to one side, followed by John Stevens holding a thick bunch of papers. He turned and walked over to the small steps at the side of the stage and walked up behind the table covered in the royal blue cloth.

Robbie watched the seated monks and clergy, especially at the back of the room. Very few appeared to have noticed the entrance of Bishop Stevens, and continued to talk in a heated fashion. The sound of a gavel banging loudly brought everyone's attention to the front of the room and the stage, where the silent grey haired figure of John Stevens waited patiently. The hum in the room settled as John Stevens shuffled his papers and then lifted a glass of water to drink. From his place high up on the stage, there was no sign at all of any of the woodland forces; his only reassurance had been that they were there. He looked to his side where Jett stood just behind him with her head down where she could just about see most of the crowd without them seeing her. Rune sat on the front row with her hood of brown pulled over her head, connected to Jett and watching the group behind her, as the two of them held a silent conversation. Outside Treen prowled close to the doors with Maddy and Crystal, and they watched the street ready and prepared just in case Mason decided to deploy more troops. John Stevens swallowed hard.

"Good morning Ladies and Gentlemen, I bid all of you welcome, and offer my thanks for your attendance here today. I know a great many of you have travelled far to be here today, and I am pleased to see such a high number gathered to aid this church during times of such troubles in this country."

He lifted a large brown bound book off the table and held it up for all to see, and then in a loud voice he spoke. "THE BIBLE!" He let it go and it thumped to the table with a loud thud, there were gasps all around the room, and John Stevens leaned forward onto the table, as he looked out at each and every one gathered before him.

"The most sacred of books... A book of hope, courage, and the sacred words of our lord and god." He continued to stare out at all of them. "It is a book of love, for it is the teachings of our lord, and it is this book that binds all of us." Robbie looked round and noticed the attention all clearly focused on John Stevens, the room was so silent it was almost possible to hear the bishop breathe. John Stevens continued to stare.

"Without this book we are nothing, for we have sworn on it to dedicate our whole lives to it and in these the darkest of times, I have only one thing to say to all of you... Do you really still believe this to be a book of truth?"

The murmurs lifted into the air and the hum in the room grew almost instantly, John Stevens stood up straight, and raised his voice above the loud hubbub. "IF YOU DO NOT BELIEVE IT TO BE SO, YOU HAVE NO PLACE IN THIS CHURCH, SO LEAVE NOW!"

The room went instantly silent. Rune gave a snigger; she was watching from Jett's point of view and she could clearly see the look of absolute shock on the faces of many in the room. John Stevens waited for a moment and then lowered his voice to speak.

"My brothers and sisters, we are here today in a world torn apart by the violence of a deadly disease that has wiped out a huge amount of humanity, and we alone have survived to continue the work of our lord. Today we stand on the edge of a new beginning and we have the chance to change this church, and make it better than it has ever been. The old ways are over, and I get down on my knees every night and I thank God for it."

There was an instant rise all around the room as many of the gathered members of the church gasped and spoke out in anger, as they could not believe what their Bishop was saying. A few of the older monks scowled and shook their heads, the protests and angry exchanges were deafening, and yet within the ranks of the gathered crowd, there were a few who sat back in their seats and smiled. John Stevens banged on his gavel, and slowly the room began to settle as he waited patiently before continuing.

"I am sad to say that whether you agree with me or not, let all of us be honest here today, the church of old became tired and worn by political agendas, money, and the corruption of many who did not survive the Red Death. Our flock diminished as the church became riddled with in fighting and scorn, as it sat in judgement of the world and forgot the reason it was there. We lost our way and watched as the world overcame us, and sadly my friends, I fear many of us became that which we despise as we preached. We lost our humanity and treated those around in a very unchristian manner."

The silence in the room was total, and some of the gathered members even lowered their heads, Robbie felt the smile on his lips and found he was rather enjoying what had become a very rousing sermon by the old Bishop. John Stevens shook his head.

"This wonderful book tells us to be loving and tolerant, it teaches us compassion and kindness, and yet so many forgot that in the days of old. Yet today I fear there are many amongst us who like them have learned little and continue to seek power and self gain from their positions of authority. There are some I fear who would even return to the days of ancient times, where we tortured women and oppressed many to protect the wealth and riches of our comforts. I fear for those members of this church, for they have learned nothing." Robbie watched as heads nodded approvingly in the crowd, and yet the room was again as silent as the grave. John Stevens took a sip from his glass as he let his words settle on those they were meant for.

His voice was softer as he began again. "My friends, we are so lucky that we have the wisdom from those times to learn from, and in this world that is so torn apart at the moment, we are best placed to bring aid, comfort, and compassion, for it is my belief that this church, which has been spared from the destruction of the Red Death, should now take the lead, and play its part to the fullest as a strong force for the good of everyone in this land. That is now the direction I wish to take and lead this church, back to a place where it will be in everyone's heart as the power for good our lord and saviour meant it to be, and it is with that purpose in mind I have formed a new council of twelve to help in this task." Quiet muttering broke out around the room, Robbie noticed the scowls from the black clad monks at the back of the room, where there was a very hushed but rapid conversation going on.

An elderly monk stood up. "But where are they, I was led to believe they would be here in person, and yet I see only yourself? I was also informed we would have some idea of where their loyalties would lie." John Stevens gave a smile.

"Indeed, Farther Hill, have no fear they are here today, and you will all get to meet them, as for loyalties I would say they are loyal to the Christian Church."

Father Hill looked confused, he looked round at the others and then back to Bishop Stevens. "But are they supporters of Knox or Loxley?"

"Is that relevant father as long as they administer the duty of this church?"

Rowan nudged Robbie and giggled. "This is far more entertaining than I expected." Robbie gave a smile under his hood.

"I agree, I think there is much more going on at the back though, keep vigilant."

Father Hill stood in the centre of the room looking at those around him; it was obvious he spoke for many of those seated close to him, but for the moment he found himself at a complete loss for words. Robbie tensed as from the centre of the group of black clad monks a tall figure stood up and stepped out into the central aisle of the chairs. The room fell instantly silent as Brother Maynard took several steps forward.

"If it pleases My Lord Bishop, but that is not the answer we were seeking." His stern faced looked slowly round the room, and then back to the front where the bishop stood watching. "You are aware I know that there are many here who support Lord Knox and his valiant efforts to rebuild and transform this church.

Many of us here have gathered today, to gain assurances that you will follow in the footsteps of our previous council and aid him in that role. There are also many amongst us who favour the work of Lord Argus and his efforts. I am certain all of us are aware of his work of late to raise this church to even greater heights than previous days."

Five rows across a monk stood up, and Robbie recognised his face. "Argus sold us out; he made a deal with Knox and then left us to the butchery of his soldiers at the so called new mission. If that is what dealing with Knox is to be for us, then I say we bring aid to the Lord of Loxley, who I might add is the reason many of us still have our lives and are here today."

Across the room other loud comments could be heard. "Argus is a traitor... He lines his pockets for his own needs and forgets the needs of others." Rumbles of agreement broke out across the room, Maynard looked angry as he scowled at the standing monk.

"Sit down Thomas you know nothing of the affairs of this church, Argus has done wonders towards the glory of this faith."

"And yet he sends assassins paid for by the money he has bargained out of Lord Knox, hidden within the ranks of your party, to murder those who would build this church to the benefit of everyone." All eyes shot back towards Bishop Stevens, he gave a nod and lifted his hand to point right down the centre of the room.

"I see The Brethren, who bring swords into our sacred place of worship with intent in their eyes to use them."

There were gasps everywhere as the gathered members of the church turned to look back at the closely huddled group of monks in black. Rowan shuffled on his seat as he prepared just in case, Robbie pushed his hand back as if to assure him all for the moment it was fine. John Stevens spoke.

"It saddens my heart to see that in the last twenty seven years since the end came we have learned nothing, and still squabble against those who seek greed to profit and stoop so low that they would justify cold blooded murder in the name of our most sacred Lord God." John Stevens lifted his voice.

"Is this how you repay the church that has educated you, fed you, and provided you with a home and the support of our entire loving family? You arm yourself paid for by a monk who as we speak, is packing his bags and fleeing you all with his profits and gains?" Maynard walked forward and lifted his voice.

"THAT IS A LIE!" Bishop Stevens shook his head sadly.

"No, my foolish friend it is not, as you have planted your spies in my church, I too have done the same at Wells. It gives me no pleasure to tell you that fearing the reprisals of failing Mason Knox, Brother Argus has deserted all of you, and he is indeed making his way out of this country. By the time you return Brother Maynard, you will find Wells empty of all its silver, and your esteemed Brother Argus." Maynard looked defiantly at the old bishop.

"It changes nothing, you still have the problems of Knox and the treaties made by this church with him, they will not take kindly to you backing the woodland heathens, and he will come looking for you Stevens, and you will pay for your disloyalty." John Stevens gave a sad smile.

"Please Brother Maynard return to your seat and allow me to finish what I planned for today. I do not fear a lack of loyalty to Lord Knox; indeed, I wholeheartedly intend to pay him a visit." There were more exasperated gasps.

"My loyalty, and as I see it the loyalty of this church is to neither side, as it has only ever been to the preservation of this church, and the lord for which it stands in praise." Maynard gave a snort, turned, and walked back to his seat; Robbie relaxed in his own seat as John Stevens continued.

"It was because of the church taking a political stance in the times of old that it became embroiled in scandal and corruption, and I feel this church should have no part in the running of the affairs of state. We own land and have the resources to stand alone, and that I feel is the position we should take, after all at this moment in time none of us are sure of the outcome of affairs as they sit between the Woodland Realm and that of Lord Knox. Our place and loyalty is not to those leaders, but to those who suffer through this drawn out conflict, of which I can assure you a small number passed through this very place today in need of our help. That is and should be the place for this church, is it not our duty to care for the physical and spiritual needs of the people of this country? We should not be taking sides to influence the outcome, we should be looking at the reality and the truth of all that has been said and done, and so as my first task as leader of the new council, I intend to visit both Lord Loxley and Lord Knox to look at their evidence for who they both feel they have a strong case to support a new heir to the throne of this land."

It was a huge surprise to everyone including the members of the Brethren, John Stevens lifted his glass before he continued.

"Last night I spoke with Lady Knox, and later I spoke with both Lord Loxley and his wife here within the walls of the Cathedral. I have listened carefully to their views and I have also worked until the very early hours of this morning having discussions with the council, and we are agreed that we must see it as our duty to listen to the representations of both sides of this conflict, before providing aid to either party in the crowning of a future king. Until such time as we have heard from both parties, this church will continue to aid the poor and those caught in the middle of this conflict. So to my next part, please welcome the members of your new council who have been selected on their merits from both sides of the walls, as many have served the forces of Knox, and also those of the woodland peoples. And before you meet them, I will leave you with one more thought. All of you appear to think that all of the woodland is filled with Pagan heathens, well I can assure you the woodland contains many members of the Christian and also other faiths, and likewise the forces of Lord Knox who also has many Pagans and other faiths who have chosen to work for his cause, so I hope we can refrain in future debates from such distasteful generalisations of each other."

He paused momentarily; his tone softened. "My friends I see your loyalties divided, and that is my greatest concern. I understand that Mason Knox has indeed done great good in many ways for the country; his efforts alone in the south saved many lives, he leads a campaign to rebuild this land as it was once, and in all fairness the Lord of Loxley has been to the aid of many people, and again he too has saved a great many from death. He chooses to lead the rebuilding of a simpler more sustainable life, one that would lead peace back to this land where free men focused on their families and communities, don't you see as the church we have an obligation to both men to aid the recovery of this land and help broker a peace? We cannot choose to back one or the other; our part must be the centre where we work as a force for good to bring a positive change for all." From somewhere in the centre a voice shouted out.

"Yeah, but what about this bastard king of the heathens, would this church kneel before a heathen?" John Stevens looked round to try and find the source of the comment, but no one claimed it.

"If this king is truly the heir by right, we have a duty to work with him for the sake of everyone in this land, as with the claims of Mason Knox, if he too can prove he has full right to the throne, again we should support him in doing what is right for the sake of everyone. That is precisely why I feel this church cannot and should not align itself to either camp, we must seek out the truth and act accordingly, and that my friends will be the first task of the new council, for they are charged with aiding in the resolve of this matter to the satisfaction of everyone, which brings me to my final duty on this day. Ladies and Gentlemen the new council."

The side door opened, and the new council walked in, as young novice nuns distributed printed leaflets containing all the details of the council. Rune and Robbie stood up with the others and moved into positions of protection, as the gathered members got up and came forward to meet with each of the new members. Jett stood still on the stage and watched the Brethren, as they got up and scowled up the room at the new council. Brother Maynard snatched several flyers out of the hands of the young novice, and then turned and stormed out of the room followed by the rest of his black clad monks. Jett gave a nod to Steph who slipped into the door frame and made sure they were heading for the way out.

Robbie stood and watched the new members as they lined up and the old monks and vicars approached them. It was true many like Father Warren had served in the large stone cities, but that was no longer the case, most of them had been removed by Mason for not obeying his strict rules, although in the eyes of many of the church members there it was clear, they understood all sides of the conflict, and contrary to earlier belief, all of them found themselves welcomed.

John Stevens sat at the long table with Simon and two of his most trusted aides as Runestone walked up the steps, he expressed his belief in all of them and asked for their help, as he knew that he had to leave and keep his word of meeting with Robbie at Loxley to examine the documents of Leenard Rimmer, and then travel on to meet with Mason Knox. He knew that the word would travel fast, and hoped his letter despatched earlier that morning would reach Mason long before Brother Maynard and his group of assassins.

Rune sat down, being careful to keep her hood up and stay out of sight of the other church members. Robbie had made it very clear that no one must reveal themselves whilst on the cathedral grounds; she gave a nod to the bishop.

"I feel my Lord Bishop that went much better than you expected." He was a little surprised to realise who was sat beside him and he gave a smile of relief. Rune noticed how his hands still shook slightly. "I am pleased for you, and I am glad to know that you had protection at all times, for this room has many of the Specialists of Loxley, we felt it more prudent to remain out of sight." He gave a long sigh.

"I am very thankful; my hope was that you and your people would be here with me, yet I must confess when I walked out and was faced with just clergy, I felt a little uncertain, your good Father Warren gave me his guarantee you would be here protecting me, and in his word, I have great faith."

Jay sat on a low wall watching the road and the tree line where there was still a great deal of movement, she felt nervous and not completely certain that the Cutters had left. Many of the small camps along the side of the road were being dismantled as the visitors moved on back to their homes, two woodsmen came down to her side, one of them gave a salute. "Excuse me miss, General Du Luc has asked for you to return to the main doors, we are taking the watch here from now on." She slipped off the wall.

"Will you guys not be returning to Loxley?" He smiled.

"No Miss, Lord Loxley has asked if we will stay on and keep the church protected after the bishop leaves. We will take this watch and then return when a full battalion arrives tomorrow."

Back in the meeting room it was getting late and the kitchen staff were waiting to prepare for the coming meal of the day, Robbie and Rowan moved into action rounding up the members of the Council, so they could leave to visit Loxley. Slowly they shepherded the members from the room and took them down a long corridor to the back offices. Within seconds the group ripped off their itchy garments with relief, much to the amusement of the clergy. Rune smiled as she opened her violet window, the members of the church were not that sure as to what was happening, Jade gave a giggle.

"It's a doorway look?" She walked through and vanished and they all jumped back with surprise, her head came back through, and she smiled making them jump again, Blades giggled and took the Bishop by the hand.

"It is quite safe My Lord see?" She gently pulled, and he walked through into the lobby of the Hotel at Loxley where Jade stood smiling.

"Welcome to the Woodland Realm, enjoy your stay here in Loxley." The bishop was lost for words as he looked back at Rune's pulsating window. He shook his head in disbelief.

"Remarkable, absolutely remarkable." Jade gave giggle.

"That is just the tip of the iceberg, believe me my sister has far more tricks than this one."

Robbie stood guard as Jay reached the door, further down the corridor behind her John and Bear stood still dressed in their robes, as they watched the doors that led back to the meeting room. A large figure in a black robe came through one of the doors and looked up the corridor past the two monks to Jay Stood watching at the end room. He walked into the corridor, his eyes fixed on Jay as he moved swiftly up the corridor towards her, completely ignoring the two stationary monks in brown. As he walked, he slipped a long dagger from out of his baggy sleeve, Bear winked to John and as the black clad monk came past them, Bear stuck out his foot and the monk when sprawling forward onto the floor, the dagger sliding up the corridor towards Jay.

He scrambled quickly to snatch the dagger back, but a black boot stamped down onto the dagger, and he looked up to see the long black hair and pale face of Jay. There was a sudden grip on his hood and he found himself being dragged backwards and up, he tried to wriggle but Bear had him held firmly by his hood.

"Now why would a man of the church have such an elegant possession?" Bear lifted the monk up high as John bent down and picked up the dagger with a long silver blade.

"Nice, good quality" He looked at the monk who stared at him with hate. "Give that back it's mine you filthy heathen."

John shook his head. "Tut tut, such words from a man of the church." Jay lifted her hand to John.

"Let me."

As the monk scowled and looked at her as if she was filth, Jay clenched her fist, and before John or Bear realised what she was doing, Jay brought up her fist like lightening, and struck him hard on the chin, the monk jerked, blood and several teeth spurted out of his mouth landing on the floor, and he went limp in Bears grasp.

John gave a nod of approval as Jay stood resolute and smiled, he looked at Bear.

"Hanging with Jade and Blades has been good for her." He patted Jay on the back. "Nice one girl."

Bear dropped the lip bleeding monk on the floor. "Well, we did say no blood would be spilt, but hell, he will live so I guess we done good." He patted Jay on the shoulder. "Nice job... OK let's go Robbie is waiting."

Bear and John walked off up the corridor; Jay stooped and picked up the dagger and slipped it into her belt, turned with a smile and followed her friends up the corridor to meet up with Robbie.

For Robbie it felt like a great relief, as slowly he moved all the Specialists back into Loxley and left Skip and Steph to help settle the bishop and the council into the hotel. He walked back to the farm with Rune to see Jess and collect their buggy. Jett and Jade walked behind with Blades, Rowan and Rafe. Rune looked at Robbie. "What do you think?" Jett answered.

"As I said you cannot trust them, he should have chosen to back a real heir, but he chose to hedge his bets and walk the middle ground, believe me Robbie, I watched those Brethren, they are not the kind of men who give up, they know who was in that room and support Loxley now. Just you watch they will start turning up dead and before we know it Mason will be back in charge. I would get Will on the throne and fast, because if we don't, there will not be any one in the church supporting us left." Rune looked back at Jett.

"There were many there today who believe in Bishop Stevens, maybe your thoughts are clouded a little because of your feelings towards Argus and his friends." Jett shook her head.

"I don't think so, I understand men like that, my mother challenged many in her life and won out over them. Argus wants money and power, and whether or not you want to admit it Rune, that is the force that will drive the weak minded, it's the reason the old ways of modern man came to an end. If you don't believe me talk to your grandfather of the forest, I am sure he would agree with me." Rune looked to Robbie, who was listening, and yet he made no comment, but she could feel the depth of his thought, he had taken account of Jett's opinion and whether or not he agreed, she could see he was turning it over in his mind.

Rafe slipped his arm round Jett as they walked off down the street towards their cottage, Rune watched for a moment, Rowan and Jade stood close, it was Rowan who spoke, as Rune turned to continue walking up the hawthorn lined lane. "She has changed in her time away, I feel a little more Scarlet in her."

"She is adjusting back to how things work here, do not forget for Jett it was just over a year away, whereas here only one and a half months have passed, Jett has had a lot of time to sit and think, and has grown more accepting of her position." Jade looked at Rune confused.

"How do you mean position?" Rune slipped her arm back into Robbie's arm, she noticed he too was waiting for her reply, she started to walk again.

"In the realm where Jett was she was taken in by a small group, they too had a fight for their freedom, but they were little more than farmers, Jett joined them at a very important time, and in her attempts to prove herself, she took up the task of training them." Rowan started to understand.

"So she allowed everything Scarlet had taught her to come to the surface and she used it?" Rune gave a nod.

"Yes... She opened the doors and her true destiny showed, she was right in the camp the other night, she will be the Queen of Caerleon one day, and I think up until recently she had not realised how much her mother had trained her for the role. Jett is changing as she accepts the mantle of her future; she now understands what it is to rule and she is taking her first steps towards establishing herself in a bid to fill her mother's shoes." Robbie understood.

"Those are big shoes to fill Rune."

"They are indeed, but somehow I think Jett is the one person who will do it well."

CHAPTER TWENTY THREE

CLOSING THE CIRCLE

Across the Mere all was still, apart from the ripples across the water, as a gentle rain drifted over the woodland sprinkling tiny drops of water over everything, and dressing it in sparkling droplets like tiny gemstones. Robbie was at the Village Hall with Rowan discussing York, and young William was sat beside Steph as she ran through the family tree and the evidence of Mason Knox that her father had hidden at Kirklees with the bishop and his new Church Council,

The two small children were out with Jess and their two Fae handmaidens and the house at Robbie's Mere was silent, apart from the quiet mutterings of a strange language, deep below the house where Runestone sat at her table sweeping her hands across the cool surface as she placed the final pieces of her realm together.

The surface of her table turned and intense deep green and a soft fog like vapour funnelled from the centre of her table and slipped eerily across the whole of the table. Runestone gave a slight smile and sat back a little as she gave a satisfied gasp. "It is complete, now the tricky bit, showing her how to use it."

Rune lifted her hand towards the centre of her table, and through the green pulsating mist, a long shiny dagger rose from within the centre of her table. It was a plain looking dagger, apart from the hilt, where the top was round and smooth, and contained a design bearing the green round disk, on which was a white five pointed star, and in the centre of the star was a circle of green. It was not a solid circle; it looked more like it had been made of millions of tiny dots, and gave the appearance of a hazy green ring. Runestone stretched out her hand and grabbed the hilt, and as she did so, a small flash of green light leapt out of the dagger and skipped across the table, the fog instantly cleared revealing the large deep violet twenty pointed star of the Table of Runestone.

At the very same moment as Rune lifted the dagger from her table, Hearne turned from his watching place at the very top of Hearne's Rock, his eyes crossed the surface of the treetops in the direction of the house and Robbie's Mere, and he gave a slight smile. "Finally, the moment to end eternity, her circle is complete, the time of the hart and the wolf is upon us." With a swish of his cloak, like the falling of soft brown leaves, Hearne turned and made his way back towards the entrance to his cave. "Green to brown and brown to red, the circle ever turns towards the fates we face, and the destiny we follow."

Rune sat back and examined the dagger. She was pleased with the result, this last task to complete the Violet Circle, had taken some time and given her much to think about. She slid her hand down to the side of her seat and lifted a long green leather holster into which she slipped the bright shiny new dagger. Standing up she turned quickly, and headed for the stair up to the ground floor of her home. Lifting her patched bag, she dropped the dagger inside, lifted the bag onto her shoulder and headed for the back door; she had barely taken two steps outside, when her face broke into a large smile. "Grandfather?"

The old lord of the woodland gave a hearty smile as he pulled her into his arms. Rune stepped back with a smile as she then noticed the colour of his cloak. The long green robe that had been a combination of every shade of green for as long as she had known him was now fading to yellow and pale brown. For a moment she was puzzled, and then she realised and felt a sting of pain pass through her. Her words were quiet as she understood and she lowered her head with huge sadness. "You too are leaving me."

Hearne gave a long sigh that sounded like the wind across the top of the rocks on a cool autumn night. He lifted his hand and lifted her chin to raise her face where he saw the tears forming in Rune's bright sapphire blue eyes. "My Child, we both knew this time would come, you are Runestone, and all that has been written upon you, and you know this. Long ago we swore to give this realm to that of the line of man, and today you made the final piece and closed the circle of violet. My time here is done, for things will now turn away from the old powers and walk hand in hand with the new, and that My Child is the fate you will now carry."

Small violets appeared on the floor, as Rune looked into the bright dark eyes of her grandfather and lord of the woodland realm. The soft bark like skin of his face seemed darker, and his long beard that had always shone like the soft lush grass of the meadows was now pale and turning a soft buttery yellow, giving him an almost autumnal appearance. "Why must you leave me too, I don't want you to go, I love you so deeply?" For a moment it felt like her heart was about to break, and he felt the pain within her.

"You are now the lady of this realm, the time of the stag is done here, and now the wolf will walk and guide the Lady of the Woods, although as you see, the eyes of the hart will forever be watching."

Rune turned in the direction of her lord's gaze and saw within the trees a tall white stag of power. Hearne gave her a soft nod. "I will be watching over you wherever I may be, you can never truly be parted from me most precious of children, for you are the line of my blood, and because of that we can never be parted for long. Go to your sister and complete what I began all those years ago with my beloved Eve, and then come back to me at dusk in the hall of the council, for we have time yet and there is much to be done."

The old lord pulled her close again, and kissed her softly on her forehead, her eyes exploded with violet light, and flowers of green interwoven with oak leaves appeared in her braids around her hair, which gave the appearance of a delicate crown. "Go now daughter of the woodland, and bring the gifts destined to the new Green Circle, for it is now her fate to shape the land around us, and care for all at your shoulder." He released her with a smile and stepped back, and Rune gave a nod of acceptance.

"I will Grandfather, and then I will come to you one last time." He smiled

"Until then My Child." Hearne turned and walked into the trees, and Rune saw the stark difference from the colours of summer that surrounded him, set against the autumn yellows and browns of his clothes, she gave a deep swallow as the sadness surrounded her, and yet just being close to him once again had filled her with great hope. As the mists swirled in and he disappeared within them, she wiped her eyes and turned to the path that led towards Jade and Rowan's place.

Jade was alone at the house, which meant only one thing, she was busy in her workshop making jewellery and other assorted items for her home or the shop in the village. Rune heard her humming as she pumped on the bellows of her small furnace, and took the path away from the backdoor towards the door to the workshop at the side of the house. When she walked in Jade was pumping away bringing up the heat, on what looked like a long pole with a bright glowing orb on the end of it. She was dressed in a green vest and some very short shorts, which looked like they were an old pair of her woodsman's pants with the legs, cut off. Her skin glowed bright with sweat and her hair hung lank as she pumped harder twisting the pole to get the heat evenly across the red glowing orb.

Rune silently watched as her sister worked with a smile, Jade was completely oblivious to her as she took the pole out of the fire, and then lifted the pole to her mouth and blew. Rune realised she was glass blowing, something she had never seen Jade do before. Jade turned slightly and noticed Rune, she gave a smile as she pulled the pole from her mouth, and Rune stepped into the room. "Hey Sis, always fancied glass work, thought I would give it a try."

Rune gave a smile back. "How is it going...What are you making?"

Jade gave a shrug. "Not really thought about it yet, I thought I would try it and see if I can do it, I did think I might make some more chimes for the tree." She put down the pipe with a much larger round clear orb on the end of it and wiped her hands and face on a cloth. "It's pretty hot work, I thought metal was hard going but this is just as bad... So, what can I do for you?"

Rune was quite fascinated and for a moment she had forgotten her reason for visiting. "Oh yeah, I have something for you." She opened her bag and slid her hand inside, as Jade swept her damp hair back off her face. "The circle is complete Jade, or it will be once you have this."

Rune lifted the dagger out of her bag and handed it over to Jade. "Here is your table, it is time you learned how to use it." Jade looked a little confused as she slid the dagger out of the sheath.

"It doesn't look like a table; how do I use it?"

Rune gave a smile as Jade slipped the dagger out of the sheath and spun it in her hand. "Nice work, did you make this?"

Rune gave a nod. "Hmm... I have thought a lot about it, Rhiannon has hers on a ring, and Saff now wears hers round her neck, both work well, but I thought a dagger was more in line with your dress, after all you do carry quite a few, and it will be important you keep it on you and close, I thought a dagger would suit better, although you really have built up quite a large collection Jade."

Jade gave a cheeky grin as she saw Rune glance at the rows of daggers and knives laid out on her weapons table, having all been cleaned and sharpened. She walked over to the table and looked down on her deadly collection. "Yeah, they have grown a bit, although if folks want to throw these things at us, I am gonna grab em and keep em."

Rune noticed the dagger from Mordred and also the one the captain at York had used to try and stab Robbie, she felt a shudder run down her back at the thought of it. Jade turned her.

"So how do I use this?" Rune took the dagger out of her hand.

"This cap on the hilt with the star and circle is actually your table. To use it simply plunge the dagger into the floor and your table will appear, it is not as big as mine, it is about four feet across, but it is powerful as it holds many of the gifts of our line in it. In your basement you will find a slot in the floor, so when you are home, you can sit at the table like I do. All the tables are connected through mine, so with time and some practice you will be able to learn more of our line, and what things you will be able to do. Jade this table is very important, so please study it, all you have to do is close your eyes, and lay your hands on the surface, and then ask it to show you, and it will begin the process of teaching you."

Jade gave a nod of understanding. "Cool."

Rune was not entirely sure she was taking it very seriously. "Jade you are pregnant, you do understand don't you that a time will come when you will not be able to fight with everyone?" She looked surprised, and her voice faltered for a moment.

"What? No, I've not even thought about it." Rune patted her arm.

"Using your table, you will still be by his side always, it's just you will be here and he will be wherever Robbie is. I know it's hard to understand, I mean it drove me nuts when you all went off without me, but that time will come, and so you must practice with your table every day to be ready for when you cannot go into combat.

The skills you learn will help you join with us and fight in other ways." She gave a nod, but Rune could see it was something she had given no thought at all too, her tone softened.

"This is your link to Rowan; this will help you protect him always Jade." She smiled a soft smile and Rune could see a little relief wash over her.

"I guess I have not really thought about it all, since we got back from Avalon I have just been getting on with stuff, I don't think it has sunk in yet that I will have a baby in eight months."

Rune gave a happy giggle and linked Jade's arm. "Come on let's go down stairs and have a look at your table in action, I will walk you through the first steps and then you can start using it."

Jade gave a giggle and the two of them made their way out of the workshop, and back along the back of the house towards the kitchen door. Inside the kitchen they crossed quickly to the door that led then down the stone steps to the basement, and there in the centre of the room, Jade saw the neat oblong slot in the stone floor. It felt odd as she had never noticed it before, but she wondered if Rune had added it at the time of building or had somehow made it appear when she made the dagger.

Rune gave a nod and Jade slipped the dagger out of its sheath. "Ok now just drop it into place and stand back." Rune gave an excited giggle, she had spent a long time thinking it up, and she was very excited to see how it worked. Jade slipped the dagger into place and stood back watching, the floor gave a burst of green light, and then they both watched as a fine line drew itself in the stone floor.

It formed a perfect circle and then a star appeared in the centre of it. Slowly the circle began to turn, and Jade realised that just like the table in the crypt of Lancelot, the stone table would grow out of the floor.

There was a loud crack, and slowly a table four feet across rose up from the floor to waist height. As it ground slowly to a halt, colour flooded into the stone creating a bright white five pointed star on a green background, the edge of the table was smooth and edged with a fine violet edge. Rune pushed Jade in the small of her back to edge her forward, and as she did a round smooth seat rose out of the floor at the side of the table.

"Introduce yourself." Jade looked a little nervous.

"How?"

"Sit down and place your palms on the table and tell it who you are."

Nervously she rested her hands on the smooth cool surface. "Hi I am Jade." Rune gave a giggle.

"You are Jade Opal, and Lady of the Green Circle."

"Oh yeah... That too." Rune saw the jerk in Jade's arms as her palms stuck to the table, Jade looked panicked and tried to pull back but her hands were held tight, Rune rested her hand on Jade's shoulder.

"Relax and focus your mind on the table."

She felt the deep intake of breath as Jade tried to calm herself. Jade's eyes gave off a sudden burst of green light, and then she felt her hands release from the table, she gave a sigh of relief and then watched as small sparks of green flashed around the edges of the table. Jade smiled as she watched them jump like small fireworks, and they multiplied in number each time they hit each other. Slowly they increased around the edges of the table and then with a burst of white light from the star, they all hopped across the table towards the centre and began to spin.

Jade loved it and giggled more as she watched with fascination, the circle of spinning sparks shrunk inwards until they formed a green hazy circle in the centre of the white star, then without warning they dropped to the surface and sunk into the star leaving the impression of a green circle made from thousands of small dots. Jade turned and looked up at Rune; she gave a smile and shrugged.

"I thought you more than any would want something a little more entertaining." She gave a giggle and looked back at her table.

"I love it... Hey can this table find Harry?" Rune frowned.

"Is it not bad enough his life is terror filled when you are around him? Give the poor man a little recovery time in between your torments." Jade gave a giggle.

"I just thought." Rune smiled.

"Hmm, I know what you thought Jade Opal. Ok try not to create too much havoc, I have things to do so I will leave you to play, no doubt Jett will be visiting at some point? Remember, if in doubt ask your table, and it will reveal your abilities to you, practice Jade and become one with the table, and remember never leave without it, keep it on your belt and out of sight of others. Have fun." As Rune turned Jade jumped up and pulled her into a big hug.

"Cheers Rune I promise I will work hard to learn as much as I can."

"I know, enjoy yourself while it's quiet, no doubt Robbie will have new tasks for all of us soon. I will see you later I have errands to run."

Rune left, leaving Jade alone with her table, and walked slowly through the woodland, she still felt the sadness, but had not mentioned it to Jade, although she was not sure why. Something within her made her feel she should be quiet about the fact that the Green Lord would soon leave Loxley woods, she had not expected to have to say goodbye, and yet as she now saw, with the coming of new heirs, it made perfect sense that the lord of the woodland would leave as had been written thousands of years before.

Knowing did not help; she had lost so many since her moment of gaining power, and it felt unfair even if she did understand the passing of powers, would she too one day have to say goodbye and leave her children behind, it was something she felt she would never be able to do and it gave her a sick feeling in her stomach. Lost in thought Rune wandered through the trees completely unaware that she was taking the long route home, and by the time she arrived back on the steps at the front of the house the morning had slipped passed and it was already mid-afternoon.

Robbie was sat in the kitchen with Rowan and Smoke's; they talked as they ate cake and drank. Rune heard them as she entered and headed for the kitchen, she gave her father a hug, sat down sliding the plate over to herself to grab a piece of her mum's slab cake. "What are you guys talking about?"

Robbie swallowed and took a drink from his mug. "York... It appears stranger things are happening, Rayne has reported odd noises from behind the large walls, we were discussing travelling up and having a look at it if you are interested, thought we might case the place a little." Rune gave a nod.

"How long will you be there?" Rowan shrugged.

"Not long, we want to have a chat with Rayne in person, and then take a quick look at what he is doing. I don't suppose you can see what he is up to behind those walls?" Rune shook her head.

"No she has veiled it, I would assume he is doing pretty much what he was at Scarborough, building up his army and storing up his weapons ready for the assault of Loxley." Smokes gave them all a strange look.

"I hope so, because that we can deal with, let's just hope he has nothing more sinister in mind, after all, his mother has been very quiet since Avalon." It was a sobering thought, one which had crossed Rune's mind several times since they had returned.

Two hours later, joined by Rafe and Jade, all of them slipped through Rune's window to the outskirts of the woodland at York in front of the large grey wall of concrete erected by Mason Knox. Rayne stood with Gwinne waiting, his violet eyes watching as Rune's window flashed behind them and disappeared.

As soon as Rune stepped out, she felt it, and Rayne knew instantly as he watched her walk towards him. "You feel it don't you?" Rune's bright blue eyes shone as she sensed the world around her trying to find the source of the feelings passing into her. Robbie stopped and looked at the ground.

"Is it me, or are your feet also sort of tingling?" Rowan gave a nod as he looked at the floor stood to the left of Robbie.

"I feel it, it's like the earth is vibrating, what is it?" Jade was stood still her eyes flickering green beneath her fringe as she stood below the towering beech trees that filtered out the fine rain falling above her. Rune moved slowly through the trees and thick dense bracken, as she walked towards the high grey walls.

"It is energy... A lot of energy and it is coming from the other side of the wall."

Robbie felt a shudder run down his spine as a cold memory touched within him. "Never mind the vibrations; do any of you smell that smell?"

Rowan looked puzzled. "What smell?" And as he said it the strange odour of decay seeped into his nostrils. "God what the hell is that?"

In less than a second Robbie felt the memory and smell blend in his mind, and a deep desperate coldness swept down his spine. Rune picked up on it immediately and turned towards him, her voice rose a little as she made the connection in her own mind. "The dream... It was in the dream as the trees died and the rot took hold, it's her she is using that same power."

Robbie took two steps back and shook his head, his eyes locked on Rune's. "No, it cannot be happening... It was just a dream Rune; this is the real world."

The rest of the group stared at Robbie and Rune not understanding what Robbie was talking about, at the time of the dream when Robbie was held prisoner none of them had fully understood what had gone on, Robbie and Rune had said little of the experience of what they had seen. Rowan understood enough to work out it was somehow related to that incident, but he had no idea of what Robbie was actually talking about as he watched Robbie take two more steps back from the wall. Rune crossed quickly to his side and grabbed his arm, as he stepped back even further a look of abject fear in his eyes. "Robbie she cannot wield enough power to do that, she is using it on the other side to kill what is there, she cannot cross our defences with it, I will never allow it." He shook his head as if only half believing her.

"We need to get out of here; something horrible is going to happen." Rune Squeezed his arm.

"I am here you are safe." He was not sure; the feelings of helplessness from that dream were seeping quickly into him, as he felt the floor vibrate a little faster.

"Rune... WE NEED TO LEAVE!" He shook his arm free and walked a few more paces back away from the wall; Rune looked back to the others, who seeing the fear on Robbie's face were visibly unsettled. Jade's eyes turned instantly green, and Rowan snatched at her and began to pull her away, Rafe and Jett were hesitant but stepped back to level up close to Robbie, Jett pulled out her sword unsure of why in an empty woodland, but she too sensed danger and was going to be ready for it.

A violent crack sounded above them, and the colour ran from Robbie's face as he saw the large branch that had been touching the wall splinter and fall quickly to the ground, Rayne pulled Gwinne by the arm dragging her out of harm's way, and began to walk backwards to get closer to the others. "Rune what is she doing?"

Rune felt shocked and a little panicked. "We have seen this before but she cannot enter here I have placed protections on it."

Two more thunderous cracks echoed to their right and the huge limbs of the trees fell to earth with a mighty crash, Robbie retched as the same feelings from his dreams surfaced, and the smell washed down inside him. Rayne moved quicker towards them with Gwinne as the floor began to shake and vibrate even more.

More trees on the outer edge against the concrete walls splintered and fell, and they quickened their pace.

Rune was unsure, she could not believe the Dark One could gain such power as to infiltrate her defences, her eyes scanned the canopy expecting to see the same run of yellowing leaves and rotting branches, but the canopy above her was lush and still very green. Her eyes wandered along the edge of the wall. "It's the trees against the stone... Look the trees where they touch the wall are dying." She pointed up and several larger top limbs of the biggest trees gave thunderous cracks and fell to the earth, exploding on the ground revealing their inner decay. "Robbie we are safe, but nothing from our realm can touch hers unaffected SEE?"

He had walked several yards back his eyes fixed on the canopy as the coldness inside him flowed back from that fateful night, he could hear her words and understand what she was saying, yet the dread in the pit of his stomach grew even stronger. It was as if he was waiting for something to happen, and as Rune gripped his hand tightly and he felt the warmth of her enter into him his nightmare came shuddering and roaring out of his dream and into reality.

The ground shook violently and the group staggered grabbing onto each other, and the trees at their sides for support. Robbie's eyes widened as the thunderous roar came over the wall, and he knew before seeing what was going to happen. Suddenly understanding Rune snatched him tight into her arms as the floor pitched again and they all went sprawling into the undergrowth and landed heavily within the ferns.

Robbie lay on his back with Rune clinging tightly to him as his eyes looked to the wall and the uppermost canopy of the trees, and to his horror he watched as the smooth black damp walls of a castle thundered upwards out of the floor behind the tall wall of grey concrete. He felt a sharp tug on his collar and his head snapped back to the violet eyes of Rayne.

"GET OUT OF HERE... NOW!"

It took less than a moment to shake free of Rune, and he was up on his feet pulling at her arm. He dragged her up on her feet as her eyes exploded with violet light, and he heaved at her hard, pulling up and dragging her behind him as he broke into a run. The whole group fled backwards except for Jade. Rowan noticed she was not with him and slid to a halt to look back for her.

Jade stood five yards from the wall; her eyes were burning with bright green light as she looked to the trees above her. Her arms were extended in front of her as if she was holding back the wall, and streams of faint soft light danced around her and along the wall. Rowan turned to return but felt the warm soft hand of Rune as she took his hand and pulled him back. "She is safe have no fear, she is Green Circle and protector of all that is green, do not fear Rowan, go to the others and wait, I shall go to her."

She let go of his hand, and slowly Rowan walked backwards as Rune walked on towards her sister. Robbie watched through the trees seeing a larger black smooth inside wall that had risen over one hundred feet into the air, he felt nauseous and shaken, not really understanding how something that was just a nightmare, could step out of his dreams into the real world, Gwinne walked to his side and spoke softly.

"She is contained, have no fear, for this is not your dream, but it is her power and in that your dreams showed you the truth of what she is capable of. The green and violet of the circles work side by side and she cannot hurt the woodland you hold so dear, for that is your dream and it will be victorious mark my words." He swallowed hard feeling the vibrations running beneath his feet.

"You know of my dream?" Gwinne smiled.

"I was there remember?" He turned to her.

"You were?" She gave a nod.

"All of us were, we connected to Rune as she strove to help you, all of us saw the dream where the woodland rotted and fell, and you faced up to the Dark One. It was a remarkable feat that you faced her; one I think she will still remember. Have no fear she will not walk in to face you until she knows she has what it takes to face you again." He swallowed hard.

"I hope so." Gwinne patted his shoulder.

"You are safe here, although I feel this is not over yet, she is waiting for something, and then she will complete her task on that side of the wall." Robbie gave a frown.

"What could she be waiting for; she has control of everything over there?"

"I am not certain, but I feel the power building beneath the floor and she appears to be holding it back, I have no idea why Robbie, I just feel it. I thought it was Jade and Rune's power protecting the trees, but I think only the trees that have contact with her power from touching the wall suffer, and everything else is protected."

Robbie turned and looked back to where Rune and Jade stood side by side their minds focused on the canopy high above the trees. "Then what is she waiting for?"

Many miles away south under the canopy of Loxley Woods, a tall brown stag turned and looked back at the tall pillar of Hearne's Rock. The breeze in the trees lifted as if some soft whisper ran through the woodland kissing the trees and saying goodbye to all that lived there. There was a gentle sound like the rushing of dry leaves across a dry stone floor, and the large pillar of white that had been a part of the woodland for a thousand years crumbled to dust and was lifted by the breeze and scattered across the woodland, Hearne's Rock was no more, and the tall stag turned and bounded with huge speed into the trees and out of sight.

Rune gave a gasp and turned south, as she did there was a thunderous roar, and the forest shook violently shedding loose leaves from the trees to mix with the rain and fall to earth. Gwinne grabbed Robbie's arm. "NOW!"

Robbie already knew what was to come, he had seen it before. Tall towers of black smooth stone lifted out of the earth and raced into the sky. Battlements grew along the top wall and windows from which to shoot carved themselves out of the stone. His eyes fixed on the sight as the giant castle of black towered into the sky blotting out the sun across the canopy of the tall beech and oak. He had not remembered falling, but as he lay on his back and watched, he saw the very same castle he had seen in his dreams built to withstand one hundred armies and glistening black and wet in the fine rain. The Dark One had built her son a castle to defend his hold on York, and he knew then that from here Mason Knox would unleash the combined powers of the Dragon and the Raven with the soul aim of destroying his home.

It felt like an age but was a few short minutes before the earth shook still, and the strange vibrations from the floor ceased. He sat up and turned to see Rowan staring at the huge castle, sensing him Rowan turned to him and shrugged. "Well at least there is no bloody Raven on the top of it, looks like we have another bloody castle to defeat."

Robbie gave a slight smile. "We do not defeat this one, we wait for it to empty out and try to defeat what comes out of it, time is short, we have to prepare, the war is closer than any of us thought."

CHAPTER TWENTY FOUR

THE TIME CLOSES IN

The order was given to Rayne to pull back everything to within one mile of Loxley's outer limits, Robbie had seen the huge castle, and instantly knew this had been something Scarlet had not seen coming. He spoke quickly to Rayne and told him to start a complete withdrawal to the outer defences in order to ensure he met whatever Mason and his devious mother had planned on familiar soil. Robbie knew every inch of Loxley, and he held the firm belief that on his own soil he would wield the greatest advantage, he returned swiftly to the Village Hall and spoke with Fuse and Skip. War was going to come far faster than he had realised, and he was certain that he would not let Mason catch him unprepared.

As Robbie gave the call to assemble the Specialists, Fuse went to work tripling the guards and doubling the woodland forces placed around the five square miles of the Stockade. Letters were drafted, as the staff were asked to work late hand writing out each new set of orders to be despatched across the entire Woodland Realm. The lights would burn bright into the early hours of the morning as they reached the last day of July 2039. By dawn, Rags had prepared thirty riders ready to move the moment all the communications were ready.

Robbie headed back to the Mere with Rowan, he sat at his desk and shuffled through his papers as Rowan watched. "So what are we doing, I know what everyone else in the Woodland Realm is doing, what do you need the Specialists for?"

Robbie looked up from his papers. "We have the swords and the sceptre, we also have the Destiny Stone, what we don't have is the arrow that holds the crown." Rowan gave a nod.

"I thought so... You do know we will be expected?" Robbie gave himself a moment as he thought.

"This is not Avalon, he knows we are coming but this time he knows we will be ready for him, if I learned anything from Avalon it is that he thinks like I do at times and that gives me an edge as I can predict him. Canterbury will be well defended, but if the reports we have are right, it is also a space shared by our green lord, we will have an edge even if I am not sure what it is yet." Rowan gave a nod understanding Robbie's thinking.

"What about Hawk, we could use his keen skills?" Robbie thought for a second.

"Is he sober?"

"Treen and myself have been keeping an eye on him, and David and Henry have been helping him, he is clean and needs something to do, to be honest being stuck here is not good for him." Robbie gave a nod.

"I must admit we have missed him, OK give him his bars back, but I want no drama between him and Rafe, we have to be smooth fast and as sharp as ever." Rowan smiled.

"I will let him know he has been called for duty; he wants to prove himself again so I think we will have no problems."

"Call Mel up as well, we will need eyes in the sky and even though she wants to be close to David, this time round we will really need her, we are already down Saff."

"She won't be with us then?" Robbie shook his head.

"She is off doing stuff for Rune; although I am assured, she is watching out for us all." Rowan got up from his seat.

"Ok I will get right on it." He turned and made for the stairs as Steph came up, she smiled as she passed him and he carried on as Steph took his warmed seat.

"I take it we are all off on another adventure?"

"It's time to bring the crown here, we need to move and move fast, how has it gone with the bishop?" Steph gave a long sigh and relaxed in the chair.

"He is OK, his council needed some convincing as they did not understand the papers, but I think finally I have managed to get across the facts of my father's work. The bishop seems convinced we are right, but he insists that they now deliberate on everything before he gives us a response to our claim that Will is the rightful heir. I assume at some point he will require an escort to see Mason." Robbie sat back.

"Mason will kill them and put the Brethren in charge."

"I did tell them that, but these people live a completely different life to us, they still think there is good in Mason, they do not see him for the slimy cold son of a bitch I do. I hear today was eventful, I see his mother has finally arrived in the neighbourhood."

"Yeah, the question is what has she got hidden in her bag of monsters for us this time?" Steph gave a laugh.

"Well, we have faced some pretty vile things; she will have to up her game to impress us this time." Robbie smiled.

"Yeah, we have tested her resolve a little." Steph got up and patted his shoulder.

"I need coffee and to see my daughter, I take it she is down below the ground as usual?" He laughed.

"She said something about checking things out and her table, so I would think so."

"Ok I will go chat to her, talk to you later."

Steph made her way down the stairs leaving Robbie alone with his paperwork, and headed for the room of Rune's table, where she found her daughter watching the many images that flashed from her table and into the air. Rune sat back as her mother walked in and gave a smile as she stretched her arms. "Hi Mum."

Steph sat down next to Rune and lowered her voice. "We need to talk Runestone." Rune looked at her; there was something about the tone of her mother's voice that seemed to alert her.

"What about exactly?" Steph smiled.

"You play innocence well my dear daughter, but not as well as you think, we need to talk of bridges and Avalon." Rune knew where this conversation was going.

"You know then? I wondered if your connection as guardian to the Whitelines would at some point let you remember, sorry I didn't want to say anything unless I had to." Steph gave a nod.

"I can understand that... So, it's all true then, the wiping away of what was written to be written again? That is a dangerous thing you did Runestone, what if you had made a mistake?" Rune shrugged.

"I am the stone on all that is written, I realised that the bridge was not the myth it had been made out to be, but it was a deep Fae secret, a secret only made known to a queen of the Fae. Shortly before Sapphire became centre of her circle, and I had received the red stone, I knew that in time Iona would learn the secret. I started to plan to return Jett using it." Steph gave a nod.

"But neither Saff nor you saw the trap of the Dark One and Robbie's death." Rune gave a shudder and shook her head.

"To be honest mum I knew Saff would train Iona in the deep secrets she learned from her table of sight, it was only in those last moments when I tried to get through the tunnel to Robbie that I realised what was really happening, but by then it was too late." Steph nodded understanding.

"Ok so tell me this, when exactly did you take your pendant off, because without that Sapphire could never have freed you, did you see something before it happened?" Rune gave a smile.

"There is no hiding anything from you is there?"

Rune took her mums hand in hers. "The night I created the table in the circle of Avalon, I had a strange feeling. At first, I thought it was because I had just been given the red stone, my mind was so busy with things rushing through it, I was finding it hard to focus on anything. I spoke to Opal as I stood on the edge of the circle and everything in my mind stopped. It's hard to put into words, but maybe it was because I had to focus so hard to create the circle combined with the fact, I was at the centre of Eve's power I am not sure, I just knew there was more danger than we thought. That night my dreams were filled with visions of Sapphire searching for me with Iona, call it intuition if you want, but I knew if something went wrong, they would look for me and so I left them the means to do so by putting my talisman containing my essence within it in my bag." Steph smiled and squeezed Rune's hand.

"You always were too smart of your own good." Rune giggled.

"I had my bag with me always, so when everything came to an end and Amethyst was safe, I didn't worry too much, I just thought leave it there until we are all home safe, luckily for me it was a good instinct, because it was my lack of true essence that kept me safe all those years in her glass box."

"But why wait so long Runestone, why wait thirty years?" Rune shrugged.

"I had no choice."

"What...I don't understand?" Rune gave a giggle.

"Sapphire had to learn to master her abilities, and then teach Iona how to harness the power of the Fae. Iona had to grow up and mature before she would have the strength to match Sapphire. You see mum while I was lay there in her keep, I realised that Iona had to be able to use the power of the Fae to jump time, she became the key to everything because Gwendolyn and Opal between them helped her do it when she was just five years old, and she appeared in the cave to help Robbie." Steph gave a big smile.

"Sapphire could use the bridge to travel across realms, but she was not permitted to use it to travel through time, that is a privilege only for the use of a queen of the Fae."

"Exactly, Iona could use the bridge to send her back in time, Saff could not do it alone, it also helped that I had a guardian of the Whitelines on the other side with Jett to help with a little guidance, and not forgetting the last queen of Fae was coupled with Una and her grandfather's staff, which sort of made her a temporary Guardian of the Whitelines."

Steph gave a gasp. "Wow that is brilliant, I must admit sweetheart it was a massive undertaking." Rune gave a nod.

"It felt like it at first, when I first got free, I had little memory of everything, it took the connection with the table to fully restore everything that happened, at first I just wanted to run away, as I thought I had lost Robbie forever. Coming back here and sitting at the table brought everything back into focus, and it was then that I knew I could erase all that had been written to a certain point and start again. I won't deny it's the most frightened I have ever been, and I was scared that I might not calculate everything precisely. I was lucky to get our lord free with me, his strength and belief in me really made a massive difference."

Steph leaned over and gave her a massive hug; you did a wonderful job. Does

Sapphire remember?" Rune gave a nod.

"Most of it, I am not sure she is aware she had to die to do it, or that all that time alone she was never whole, but everything else yes she remembers it now, her table has filled in most of the missing parts for her."

"I take it that it was my mum that allowed Sapphire to run around as only a half human?" Rune gave a giggle.

"Grandmother is grandmother, she knows far more than she ever lets on and has learned more Fae secrets than I think the Fae would be happy to find out, but thank Hearne for her quick thinking because without her the whole plan would have fallen apart."

Steph sat back and gave a chuckle. "My mum was always poking around where she shouldn't, although she has saved the day on more than one occasion. I miss her, towards the end we had less time together, but growing up she was a great mum."

"So go see her." Steph turned not quite understanding Rune.

"How do you mean?" Rune gave a loud laugh.

"Mum you are the guardian of the Whitelines, you can now walk in any realm you want to, just go and pay her a visit, she would love it."

Steph started to giggle. "You know I never realised, all this guardian stuff it does take a bit of getting used to you know." Rune gave a loving smile.

"Welcome to my life Mother."

The evening was moving on as the Specialists began to arrive at the Mere. The rain was light but still falling as they gathered in the house, there was the usual loud noise of good cheer and laughter, as Robbie came down the stairs to meet them all. Hawk arrived a short time later, and as Rowan had reported he looked a little more like his old self, if not a little hesitant. He stepped in through the door with his bag shouldered and turned to face Rafe. Hawk looked a little nervous as he stared into the soft brown eyes of what had been one of his best friends.

"So, you made it back?" Rafe carried a stern expression, Hawk gave a nod.

"Yeah, they have called me back in." Rafe give a smile.

"Bout time, look mate..." Hawk cut him off in midsentence.

"Don't say it mate, it was all me I was well out of order and I really am sorry Wolfie, I just got lost for a bit." Rafe patted his cheek.

"I am sorry too, glad you made it back, it don't feel right without you." Rafe patted him hard on the shoulder and he smiled, Jett rolled her eyes next to Jade.

"God guys get a room will you?" Chuckles erupted everywhere as without noticing the room had gone completely quiet, and now everyone started to laugh and joke in their usual spirits. Blades looked up as Robbie watched from the bottom step.

"So where are we off to Robbie?" He stepped down onto the living room floor.

"We seek to crown a king, so we need the final part of our puzzle, we are looking for an arrow that holds a crown, we will be briefing in about an hour, so for now check your kit and make sure you have plenty of arrows, we are expecting a welcoming committee."

Robbie wandered round the room chatting with the others as Jade and Jett helped Una get the drinks together. He felt a little more at ease as many faces were now back in the ranks, and seeing Woody, Mel, and also the newly returned Hawk gave him a reason to feel a little more relaxed than he had previously been.

Rune made her way back up the steps from her basement and headed into the kitchen where she spoke with Jade, Robbie noticed her and wandered over towards the kitchen, as he came in through the door he caught the tail end of their conversation. "Are you sure you will be OK?" Jade gave a nod.

"Yeah, I will be fine, I do get a little off the mark occasionally, I think it's my hormones or something, but I know the place, it won't be a problem focusing on it Rune." Robbie looked at the three of them.

"What won't?" Rune turned to Robbie.

"Rob, I have something really important to do for the Green Lord, I won't be too long but I have to go soon as it's almost dusk, so I have asked Jade to open a window near Honey Hill to get you all there unseen." He gave a shrug.

"Yeah Ok, will you be alright, nothing is wrong is it?" Rune smiled and slid her arms round his waist as she pulled herself close to him.

"Everything is fine, but as always I will worry about you until I am back at your side. I have this task to do, it's not dangerous, but it is very important to the Green Lord. As soon as I am finished, I will join you at Canterbury to help out with getting the crown OK?" She stretched up and gave him a long slow kiss.

"Oh Man you two as well, get a room next to Rafe and Hawk." Rune giggled as she slipped free.

"Oh dear, someone not getting enough attention from the wolf man?"

"Yeah, right in your dreams girl, the wolf and me is well ahead of all of you." Jade gave a giggle as Rune turned and laughed at Jett's cheeky smile.

"Ok I am off, I will be as fast as I can, Jade, any problems and let me know, I will literally be there in a flash." She turned and gave Robbie another peck on the cheek, and then headed for the door. Robbie smiled.

"Weren't we getting drinks ladies?" Jett shook her head.

"Wow one snog and he is cracking the whip, won't keep you waiting sire, us mere underlings are on it." He started to laugh as he turned and went out of the door to prepare with Rowan for the group briefing.

CHAPTER TWENTY FIVE

THE CENTRE OF EVERYTHING

Rune walked quickly down the long meadow to the edge of the water, and then she opened her window, and stepped through into the meeting chamber of the ruling council. The Green Lord stood by the large round stone table and gave a smile as she walked. Rune was surprised to see how quickly the colour had faded from his green robes that were now a combination of hues of yellows and brown. She walked quickly over and embraced him. "Grandfather are you alright, your garments have changed as if with the seasons?"

His eyes still sparkled like summer berries as he gave her a loving smile. "Dear Child I am fine, I am of a great age, and as has been the saying of many men of the past, you can clearly see I have reached the Autumn of my years, as with all things in nature, I too show my age. Fear not, for I have much to do and many years to go before my old sticks are beyond life." He gave her a loving smile and she felt a little of the pain in her heart ease knowing he would continue.

Hearne turned towards the table where there was a bundle of heavy violet fabric. He lifted it carefully and turned back to Runestone. "Take this my child, for it is the same as the one I made for Eve, and it has protections within it that will aid you in times of need." He opened the bundle revealing a long violet cloak decorated with the leaves of the trees around its edges, it was a double of the one that Eve had loaned her when she had left Avalon briefly, only Eve's had been red.

"Oh Grandfather, this is so beautiful." He gently lifted it around her shoulders, and pulled up the large hood, for a moment he stood and simply looked at her, almost lost for a moment in time. Rune gently took his brown lined hand in hers.

"Grandfather are you alright?" He gave a jolt as if waking from a deep and wonderful thought.

"What... Oh dear, yes My Child I am fine... You are so like her at times I quite forget, and here wearing a purple version of her cloak, you brought back such happy thoughts, you must forgive this old man for his reminiscence." Rune smiled knowing of the bond and the love he held for Eve.

"What are we doing here, is there something you need to tell me?" Hearne took a long deep breath.

"It's not so much something to tell as it is to show, you are now the one on which all has been written, if you put your mind to it, nothing can be hidden from you, and so I feel it is right that you travel with me to the place I truly call home, for my journey is back to the centre of everything." Rune felt a little confused as the old lord turned, and began to walk across the room to one of the archway's that she knew led out of the chamber.

"Grandfather I thought the Forest of Time was the centre of everything?" He gave a small chuckle that sounded like water skipping over the rocks of a fast flowing stream.

"It is, but you see Runestone Sapphire and Daughter of Life, your forest is far greater than you ever could imagine." He walked straight through the archway and Rune hurried to keep up, as the bright white light flashed and she found herself stood in a forest of enormous trees before a huge wooden gate set between two cliffs. She hurried along the pathway to where Hearne stood before the gates, and much to her surprise Fagan knelt before his lord and master.

"I bid ye welcome lord of all forests and mountains and deepening seas. I say welcome and feels the honour of ye before a humble young servant such as I is."

Rune watched quietly as Fagan lifted his head whilst still on his knees, to be addressed by his lord. Such was his excitement Rune could almost see his ear wiggle below his massive bush of bright white hair. Hearne gave a smile as he viewed the large gates.

"You have done well Keeper, the centre land is safe due to the efforts of many of your years, I am grateful to you for the love you have shown in the care of your duty."

"It is I who is honoured my Lord of Green, twas my privilege to have been able to serve ye."

"Have you the keys?"

Fagan rose from the floor, and Rune knew he was tall, yet compared to Hearne he looked just average as his lord towered above him. Fagan slipped out a small ball from inside his shirt pocket, and Rune watched with fascination as Hearne spun the ball in the palm of his hand. She caught her breath, as a dozen small what looked like blue striped bees, flew out from the ball and headed towards the gate, they buzzed loudly as they made their way to the large gates, and the heavy golden lock that hung from the centre where the large gates met. There was a loud click and the lock fell to the floor, and the gates silently swung back.

Rune was not prepared for what she saw. Beyond the gates was a deep valley filled with plant life. The pathway they were on appeared to weave and twist downhill towards the bluest lake she had ever seen, flowers of every shape and colour grew in vast drifts, many of which she had never seen before. The skies were filled with thousands of birds and insects, and there was a hum to the whole world before her that just sang out of life and creation. Hearne turned and held out his hand.

"Come my lady of life, come and see the true roots of your kingdom."

Fagan gave her a cheeky wink, and stepped back with a low sweeping bow, and Rune walked forward and slipped her hand into the warm soft palm of Hearne the lord and creator of all things.

Walking along the path it was hard to know where to look, there was so much to see, most of it never seen in the human world as life exploded everywhere. Plant life covered everything, and she could see in between all the trees and bushes, animals she had no name for walked happily around feasting on fruits and berries that she could not name. Her mind reeled as she saw endless statues and sculptures of unknown things, and as she walked, Hearne spoke to her of the wonders of his home and of the life he shared with Eve who had blown life in almost all he had made.

No words could adequately express the joy and excitement that flowed through her as her eyes constantly darted from side to side, and slowly they descended into the deep valley that looked like it stretched for a thousand miles. Her grandfather was not wrong when he had told her the Forest of Time was far bigger than she had realised. After what felt like an age, they came to a halt at the edge of the clear blue waters of the lake, and before them stood an old shelter that covered a long table of heavy cut timber. Hearne turned a look of happiness on his face. "This is my home, where Eve came to me, and together we worked for the good of all we created, it is the perfect centre of everything we have built, and where I spent the happiest of times in my long life, here I will reside until the end of my days."

The briefing at Robbie's Mere was short. The Specialists sat as Rowan and Robbie both explained that they wanted to recover the crown pinned by the arrow at Canterbury as quickly as possible. They spoke of how they expected a welcoming committee to prevent them recovering the crown, but until they were close enough to see what they were against, they would be going in blind to do reconnaissance, at which point they would work out their best way in. Jade was a little nervous as this would be the first time since becoming pregnant, she would be using a window. Her hormones had been a little unstable and a few of her attempts at using her skills had gone slightly off target, something Jett found to be highly amusing.

As the day wore on and the moment arrived, she took a deep breath as the group gathered round, and she focused on the woodland at the base of the hill just below Magg's old cottage. It had not helped that Maggs had not left her alone for the last two hours, once she had learned she would have a chance to return back to the farm that for her was home. She had rattled around her gasping like an old donkey with her large horsey smile, constantly telling Jade of the joys of her farm and the cosmic energy that flowed through the heart of the earth, considering technically Jade was now the lady of the Green Circle, it appeared more than obvious to Jade that the earth was filled with energy, as she could tap directly into it.

Jade closed her eyes as Maggs jewellery tinkled a tune as she danced excitedly on the spot, and a fine green line drew itself in the air in front of her, Jett gave her a nudge and she opened her eyes to see it. "So far so good girl... Go on open it and let's jump through." Jade took another deep breath and the line expanded out like the doors of a lift opening to reveal a bright glowing green light. Jett could not wait much longer as she was dying to see where they were, and she leaned forward and pushed her head through the light and into the darkened woodland. She popped her head back and winked at Jade. "Well we have woodland that's for sure." Jade gave a big smile and turned to Robbie.

"We are ready off you go." The Specialists moved quickly through the window and spread out into the trees, and Jade came through last and up to the side of Robbie and the window snapped closed behind them. Robbie peered round in the darkness.

"What direction is the farm Pebbles?"

"What?" He turned and she could see his eyes shining in the dim light.

"I said which way?" Jade gave a hard swallow and shrugged.

"I am not sure... Ooh Robbie I was so worried it did not dawn on me to think about which way we came out, I just thought of the woodland and here we are." He gave a chuckle as Rowan slid up close to them.

"Ok not to worry Pebbles, we are here close by, we will work it out." Rowan leaned in and quietly spoke.

"Anything look familiar?" Robbie gave a snort.

"Not a bloody thing, but saying that it's so dark I cannot really see that much." Rowan chuckled,

"We had Rune and Ruby last time to guide us; I think we forgot how much we used their skills." Robbie tried to peer through the gloom.

"No moon, but there again it's not raining here, where the hell is Harry?" Rowan peered round in the darkness.

"Why Harry?"

"Well, I just figured he knows these parts, and if there are soldiers here there will be alcohol, and you know what he is like for sniffing out his tonic?" Rowan gave a giggle.

"Seriously Robbie?" Robbie started to laugh.

"Hey don't laugh, when I was a kid, a bottle fell off the cart and rolled down a steep embankment into the scrub. Harry discovered it missing when we got back to Loxley, and then walked eight miles back to search for it. I am telling you he can sniff the stuff out, there was no way on earth he should have found that bottle, but he did, he walked right up to it and scooped it off the floor as if it had a marker above it. Believe me when it comes to booze, he has powers to rival Rune."

Rowan gave a snigger in the darkness. "The sad thing is, knowing him as I do, I can believe it. What say we send Harry and Hawk for a quick look around, Hawk has keen eyes and with Harry's ability they might find soldiers, at least we will know we are heading the right way if we come across some?"

"It makes sense let's do it, pull everyone in close, with the dim light and thick trees I don't want to lose anyone in this darkness." Rowan grabbed Hawk and Harry and filled them in while Robbie and Jade made sure everyone was close by. Twenty minutes passed as they waited in the ever increasing darkness, until suddenly to their left they heard the snapping of twigs and branches.

Suddenly out of the darkness Harry appeared covered in sweat and breathing heavily, he ran right up to Robbie panting hard. "Run they got Jade hounds." He then sprinted past as Hawk came dashing up behind him.

Jett looked confused as she turned to Jade in the darkness. "What the hell are Jade hounds?" Jade shrugged in the dark.

"No idea." Hawk slid to a halt in front of Robbie and Rowan panting hard, he took several long gasps.

"Follow Harry, they got them big horrible dogs from the caves... Don't think they have let them off the leash, but if they do, we have problems they have about ten of them." Rowan gave a gasp.

"Shit Marsh Hounds, God I thought we had seen the last of those vile things, although it's probably a good thing Steph is still at Loxley with the bishop, not sure she ever wants to see them again." There were giggles in the darkness, Smokes voice echoed behind Robbie.

"Probably best we follow Harry, Jade and John have been looking hungry all day and this is no time for a picnic." Giggles broke back out, as Robbie turned to the group.

"Ok follow Harry but stay close together; I don't want to lose anyone. If we are lucky some of this cloud will move and we will get a little moonlight. Behind Robbie he could hear the sounds of the hounds barking and snarling. "OK come on, let's move with purpose."

The sound of the dogs was growing louder, as they dodged their way as quickly as they could in the darkness. Not all of them could navigate the trees like Robbie could and so even at a good pace they were far slower than normal, no matter how fast they tried to go, the sound of the hounds were getting louder, and Robbie knew that at some point very soon he would have to turn and make a stand. Rowan panted with Jade at his side. "Any new ideas for this particular adventure?"

Harry skidded to a halt and screamed out just ahead. "Whoa dudes it like totally ends here." Robbie raced ahead of the others to catch up with Harry; he slid up at his side and saw the steep drop towards what looked like a river in the depths below.

"Water is definitely out." He grabbed Harry and pushed him sideways. "Follow the edge and find a route through and down."

The others arrived in groups as Robbie swung his bow off his back and fitted an arrow, Jett and Blades came sliding up gasping for air and pulled out there swords, Blades pushed the others onto the rough path being ploughed through the undergrowth by Harry. Robbie lifted his bow as the hounds grew louder and the others passed him. "Get everyone down the track Blades, I will hold off what I can." He pulled back on the string and waited as the Specialists flowed past him. His listening intensified in the darkness and he heard Jett regulate her breathing at his side.

"They sound spread out Robbie, I got them coming from all around, it might give us the edge." He swallowed hard as he tried to catch his own breath back.

"We will need it, these vile beast are big hairy and carry the smell of death, don't mess with them, go straight for the kill if one comes at you, they are powerful." Blades called out behind them.

"It's clear let's move it." Robbie and Jett turned and headed onto the edge of the steep edge and followed Blades in the dim light, they moved as fast as they could to catch up with the others as the sound of a hound grew louder behind them. Jett moved quickly glancing back at Robbie.

"It's got the scent we will have to turn and face it soon."

"I know, just keep going until I say so, then we defend and go for a kill."

The group moved quicker along the edge, Harry ploughed through everything slashing and cutting with his swords as he ran. The hill was steep and his momentum fast, and without realising he ran off the top of a retaining wall and dropped with a shocked scream down six feet onto rough stony grass covered land. He landed with a thump as John and Hawk came blindly over and fell head first towards him. Harry yelled and the others slowed their way finding the spot where Harry lay moaning under the heavy weight of John and Hawk. Treen and Skip laughed as they dropped down and helped the three up, and Harry looked quickly round as he rubbed his ribs.

Magg's, Jay, and Judy dropped followed closely by Mel, Maddy, and Will, somewhere in the darkness above they could hear the snarling of the hound as it moved closer, and the others dropped from the wall, sliding out their bows and fitted arrows. Blades and Jett came quickly over followed by Robbie and as his feet hit the floor the huge snarling beast lunged into the air.

There was an instant volley of arrows, and the hound squealed in pain, Smokes ducked as the huge beast fell like a stone and crashed into the floor just in front of him, Robbie was already alert and ready to move. The smashing sound behind him, told him there were soldiers with other hounds not far behind, he saw the long flat plain and pushed the Specialists onward. "That way...Go!"

The group ran as fast as they could behind Robbie and Harry, as Robbie did his best in the darkness to identify shapes and find a way through. His lungs felt like they were burning as he gasped in yet more air, when suddenly in front he heard a sharp whistle, there was a faint pulse of blue and he swerved heading straight for it, as he made out the slight frame of Sapphire, he raced as fast as he could towards her, and came gasping up in front of her, and she pointed to his left. "That way and stop at the glass."

Robbie simply swerved glad to see her, and turned into what felt like a narrow corridor, he felt the grass leave his feet as he ran onto stone, and slid gasping for air up to what looked like the tall windows of a huge foliage covered old building. He leant back against the glass, his face covered in sweat and took as much air as possible into his lungs as the others arrived gasping for air. The sound of dogs grew louder as Sapphire appeared.

"Ok all you go through as quickly as you can and get out of sight." A bright blue orb opened and they all darted as fast as they could into it. They came out of the window into total darkness and stood gasping and panting as the window snapped closed behind them. Outside they could hear the dogs growling and snapping as the dogs lost all traces of their prey, everyone stood completely still not daring to move in the darkness as sounds of the dogs howled outside. Robbie felt a pat on his back. "You OK?"

He coughed a little to clear his lungs and get yet more air into his lungs. "Yeah, I am fine... Thanks Saff that was a close one... Where are we?"

"To be honest I have no idea, well I know you are three miles off Canterbury, I just don't know what this place is, I saw it in my table and jumped here, it looked secure so I got ready to get you all inside it." Robbie lowered himself to the floor to rest his legs, Bear groaned as he lay back on the cold floor.

"I have done that twice now, I will not do it a third time, the bugger will die by my hand or eat me, either way if I face one again, I will not be running."

Gradually the howling outside grew fainter as if the handlers unable to find any traces of entry or any living soul withdrew.

Sapphire had disappeared into the darkness and using her eyes to flicker she found her way around and came back with six small candles. "Here they are pine scented, it's not much but it's light and it smells sort of homely." She smiled as she placed the lit candle on the floor in front of Robbie. "Rune should be here in a little while, she is out of reach at the moment with the green lord, Fagan asked me to aide ye, he sends his best and told me she was safe and well protected, and he would send her on to you when she got back to him. Ok I gotta go now, so use the light to explore, there is all sorts of things here although some of it is kinda soil now, but you will all be safe from those dogs in here. Catch up with you later guys take care."

Robbie stood up and looked round as he wiped the sweat from his face. "Thanks Saff we owe you." She smiled.

"I'm still part of the team don't forget." She turned and in a flash of blue she was gone, Robbie looked round and spotted the sad look on Hawks face, he gave a nod and then moved into the group to get a lay of the land. Smokes was up with Jade squinting through the darkness at the edges of the candle light, Robbie walked up to him.

"Any idea of what this place is?" Smokes turned looking a little uncertain.

"Without lights it's hard to tell, but if I am not wrong, I think this place used to be a Supermarket." Jade looked at Robbie and frowned.

"Don't look at me, I have no idea what that means." He gave a smile.

Deep in the centre of everything Rune gave a satisfied sigh as she sat with her great grandfather in what was his true home. The light in the sky was fading and a deep orangey glow came across the lake turning the crystal clear waters to fire. Hearne sat at the large table beneath the shelter and talked of times long since gone when his beloved Eve walked the realm with him. Rune sat and listened, filled with awe as he revealed the truth of his life with Eve, sat on a large smooth rock with her head on her knees, she smiled feeling content and at peace, as the deep gruff voice of Hearne surrounded her.

Hearne pointed to the large rock face in the distance across the lake, which he told her was the back of White Steps Rock, the sacred burial ground of the Fae, and the place where Una had entered the valley that took her along the Bridge of Intention. Across the other side of the lake, he pointed out a very tall mountain, which rose into the clouds, Rune gazed at it as Hearne spoke softly. "That my dearest of children is The Seat of Hearne, for it is there that my journey will end, and I will rise to the top of the mount and take my rightful place in the seat. From there I will watch all the realms and have the company of my oldest friend and companion, the White Lord himself."

Suddenly it all made perfect sense to Runestone, she began to see that Hearne had brought her here to show her he was not leaving her behind to be forgotten, he was returning to his rightful place. This was the land where everything began, and yet for a time he had moved to the tall column of stone in Loxley Wood, Rune now saw the bigger picture and understood how he had left his home, to be a watcher and protector over her and Robbie, but with the completion of the Violet Circle, she could see that he had to return and allow the others to be the forces that aided her. Jade would take on the mantle of the Green Circle, and in doing so she would be the eyes and ears of nature within the woodland that surrounded Robbie's Mere.

"I love this place, and I can see why it is so important to you Grandfather, but

I am going to miss you terribly, somehow knowing you were so close to me has given me strength, I will find it strange to walk in an empty woodland that you have vacated." Hearne gave her a strange look.

"Why?" She did not understand him.

"Because you will no longer be there, and close to me." He gave a laugh.

"Dear Child how can you say that? There is no Woodland in all of the realms that are absent of my touch, I am in everything that surrounds you, I as your kin, am always with you; I know that you know this. Runestone you are Life, there is no realm that does not know your touch, you can walk freely throughout every realm, look to your cloak and tell me what it is that you see." Rune gazed at the violet cloak trimmed with golden leaves of every tree known.

"I see the cloak of Eve coloured violet." Hearne gave a resounding nod.

"Exactly... you see the robe of life, tell me, do you not see life in the woodland that surrounds you?" She understood and he gave her a smile. "You can come to me whenever you feel the need, all you need do is close your eyes and think of me, I will be waiting to greet you with the love of family."

Rune gave a smile, but deep within her there was still the feelings of sadness, to her it felt different, as if in some way she had lost a part of her life in Loxley. Hearne sensed it within her and his voice was soft.

"I know that times are growing hard, and I know that you have lost those who you have grown attached to, but this is the way of life and the circle it turns." She lifted her head to the kindly old face of her grandfather, and her eyes shone with the brightest of blues, he smiled a loving smile that filled her with his love. "Life has always been a struggle, and beside your Bowman you have seen this, I sense the doubt he sometimes holds deep within him, but look to the arrow which is the symbol of his life and you too will understand the life you both share."

Rune blinked not quite understanding her grandfather. "How is the arrow the symbol of his life?" Hearne gave another large smile.

"In order for an arrow to fire, you must first pull it backwards, I see how he feels at times like he is going back instead of forward, but you see my dearest child, that is the purpose of life, for once you have been forced back, like the arrow you can only travel one way, and that is forward at pace and with force. Trust in him, for he will overcome his doubt when the hour arrives, and then like the arrow he will force his way forward to meet his destiny."

Rune understood. "Avalon felt like everything was pulling us back."

"The first realm was hard but also necessary, it was good that the burden you faced was met at that time, for now your Wolveshead has been pulled back enough to understand what is required, and soon will be the time for him to fire with the power he holds forward against the Snake."

All she could do was hope, she had felt Robbie's doubts and it had worried her, yet she saw the faith that Hearne held in him, and that gave her deep reassurance as she sat in the fading of the day lost in her thoughts and let the peace of the realm wash over her, enjoying just being there alone with the peace and serenity of her grandfather.

The sun washed to red and sank below the lake, and as the day came to an end, happy and contented she slid slowly into a deep and restful sleep. He lifted her up and carried her gently to a small moss covered bed and laid her carefully down, he gave a smile as he looked at her resting peacefully. "Sleep well my most precious of children, you are and always will be the most fragrant flower of my realm, go now to the world you own, and be one with your Wolveshead and happy." With a wave of his hand, Rune sank slowly through the moss and disappeared, and Hearne lifted an old brown hand and wiped the tears from his eyes.

Turning on the path, he looked to the lake and the tall mountain in the distance. "I will be the eyes of all of you now my precious children." And with a heavy sigh the old figure walked off onto the path to continue his work in the land that held more of Eve than any other.

CHAPTER TWENTY SIX

STOPPING TO SHOP

Robbie looked at the group huddled on the floor within the circle of candle light. "Harry, Smokes, you know about these Supermarket things?" Harry gave a resounding nod.

"Oh yeah man we have knocked a few of these over in the past, we totally could be on to some funky vibes here." Robbie was not that certain he understood, but felt his trust in these two made the greater sense.

"Ok have a look round and get the lay of the land, looks like we are here for the night, check this place out make sure it's safe, and try and find a good place to set lookouts, if those soldiers are about, we will need to keep eyes on them." Smokes got up and lifted a candle.

"No prob's, we have scouted darker ones than this out, leave it with us." Taking a candle Smokes and Harry disappeared through what looked like two doors and into the main shopping area, to seek out possible places to watch. Robbie settled back with the others who sat quietly talking and wiping their faces down after the long run. Rowan slid in close to Robbie with Jade.

"So what do we plan now?"

"Well to be honest I don't want to go back in the dark with those hounds on the prowl, I would feel better in daylight facing them, at least I can see what to shoot at. I think for now we sit tight, Jade sorry, but you are not on your full game at the moment, I think it's best we wait for Rune or Sapphire to return before we head back to Canterbury. The good news is we are about three miles off course so with good fortune we will get there tomorrow." Jade looked really mournful.

"I am so sorry Robbie, honestly I was thinking of Maggs Farm, I have no idea how we ended up so far off. I am sure it's this baby thing, honestly everything is going all odd and off key at the moment, and my boobs are feeling really tight." Robbie gave a cough.

"Hmm, well, yes a little too much information Jade, but don't worry it's not as bad as it seems, we can still make good time. Let's get organised and then see what Smokes and Harry have to say."

In the twenty minutes it took for Smokes and Harry to return, Maggs managed to pass out cake and some lemon juice she had brought along. Smokes reappeared closely followed by Harry pushing a metal cage on wheels and looking very excited, he emptied the contents of the cage out in front of Robbie.

"Ok we got these torches, ten of them are working pretty well, we found a stash of batteries so these will be fine for a good while, these are wind up torches, just squeeze them like this and they will keep going all night. We found a box of them so at least everyone can have one. The store looks like it was barricaded in the early days and it's really stacked with some useful stuff, I think a group were living inside it for a bit, we found a stack of used tins and empty food packets all rotted away in the back rooms, they are pretty grim so stay out of them. The store itself has loads of stuff we can use; it's a pity it's so far away we could sack this place good if it was nearer home."

Robbie gave a nod. "Ok so are we secure and is there a place we can watch?"

"Oh yeah... we found a back stair that goes up to the roof, it took a bit of forcing but we can get on the roof to use lookouts, there are all sorts of plants and things growing up there so we have good cover to keep us out of sight."

Rowan seemed pleased. "Jade and me will take first watch." Robbie agreed.

"Ok we will scout round this place and see if there is anything we can use, we might as well as we are here for the night." Harry's eyes twinkled as he lifted up a set of spanners and a pocket knife from his cart.

"Oh man this place has loot all over the place, we can use tons of it man, it's like cosmic happy times in here." Robbie looked to the group.

"Ok we have some free time, follow Smokes, and go and have a look round, stay in pairs and keep alert; we still have no idea where the soldiers went or if they have reported this."

It took a few minutes to prepare and the Specialist moved out into what had once been the largest local supermarket in the area. After over twenty years of lying locked up, the mice had been to work and the dust had settled, although it was obvious that most of the store remained intact, if not a little dirty. The freezer units were filled with empty bags of decay and there was a strong lingering musty smell in the air, but all in all it proved to be a place of great adventure for those who had never seen the age of modern man, and the convenience of life at those times.

A bright pulse of white light brought Steph into the midst as she completed her work with the bishop and had spoken to Sapphire, like her father she too could use the long white tube to transport herself, something Robbie was relieved to see. There was still no word from Rune who was deep in the Forest of Time with Hearne, so while Rowan and Jade took first watch with Steph on the roof, Robbie decided to wander the huge store and get a first hand look of what life from an early age could possibly have been like.

Jade sat in the shrubs with her mum and Rowan up on the roof, her bow leant across her knee with an arrow loosely balanced across it. "What is this place supposed to be anyhow? Dad seems really excited about it?" Steph smiled at her daughter, in many ways she thought it was a good thing to not know about the old ways of modern man, and yet sometimes she realised that some knowledge could be a great help.

"It's a supermarket sweetheart... It's a place where people came to buy goods."

"You mean like the market we have at Loxley but bigger? That's silly there will be no one here in all these trees." Steph gave a small chuckle.

"No sweetheart, back in the older days, these were built at the edges of the towns, there were massive buildings filled with everything you would need. Hundreds of people would travel by cart to these places to load up for the whole week, or if they lived far away for the whole month, back then there were not as many trees as there are now." Jade considered the point for a few moments and looked back at her mum.

"That is just like home; Rowan and I go once a week to the market for all our stuff." Rowan nodded in agreement with Jade. Steph gave a smile.

"The market at home has traders from all over selling the things they make or grow, it's a market of many traders, and supermarkets were owned by just one company. There are no stalls inside, just rows of shelves with every kind of product."

Jade scoffed. "Sounds greedy and not fair, what about people like me and Rune we sell only our own stuff, not everything?" Rowan gave a nod and took Jade's hand in his.

"I have heard of these places, although it was said the Cutters raided most of them and burned them to the ground. There are stories of rings of guards and long lines of the carts from the Cutters taking the last goods out." Steph leaned back against the small tree.

"They didn't find all of them, just after the outbreak when everyone fled the towns, your dad and Harry made quite a job of finding quite a few of them. You would be surprised how many were locked up when the red death came to prevent looting. The army moved in and tried to regulate them, but the virus moved so quickly that many fled the towns, and cities to the country as others died. In our younger days, we found quite a few, Maggs and I used to sell the food in tins and bottles on the markets until Knox started raiding the markets and seizing goods. Where do you two think Harry gets all that black denim from, and those fine cotton shirts?"

Jade looked at Rowan, and then back at her mum. Steph gave a smile. "Your Dad and Harry have more than just the one cave piled high with goods at Loxley. Believe me those two cleared out most of the big ones in our area. They have quite a stash between them. Harry and your dad fed and clothed a lot of people in the early days as rogue traders."

Jade seemed surprised. "I thought they were spies?" Steph gave another laugh at the thought. She shrugged.

"They were, but you have to have a cover if you're spying, why not one that builds trust with everyone? As underground traders, they met all types of people and it gave them the chance to find out more of what was going on. Why do you think Knox went after them, they were selling the stuff at half the price Knox was and putting him out of business?"

Below them in the store the group were starting to enjoy themselves, as they explored and set up for the night. The café was filled with long lines of tables and chairs that were bolted to the floor. It amused Blades who thought it was silly, and could not work out why no one would want to move the furniture to mop. There was plenty of floor space free and it was here that the bedding roles were placed in rows. Harry returned with another large box of candles, which delighted Maddy and Mel as they gave off the most wonderful scents.

The others moved around the store in small groups using their torches and extra candles to lift the gloom on the dust and cobweb covered shelves, which silently waited to reveal their prizes. Beams of light hovered through the darkness all round the massive store, lighting the vents in patches across the large ceiling. Muffled excited bursts would penetrate the air. Through the darkness, the small group wandered giggling and chatting happily to each other, to most of them, this was a strange and alien dust covered world.

The men had gathered the candles and the tool section was the brightest place in the whole store, as Todd, Keith, Smokes, and Robbie with Bear, and Skip checked out the large arrangement of tools for every job. Bear had a long crow bar slipped in his belt, and Smokes was delighted with the several sets of spanners that had now found their way into his bag.

Robbie found a very useful pair of wire cutters and small axe, which he slid down the back of his belt. Todd loved the tools as did Keith, yet they were looking at them more in the way of using them as weapons. Bear had a small can of oil and a long grey wet stone; his dagger glinted as he slid it down the stone with a heavy stroke. He gave a satisfied smile as his slid his worn old stone out of his tunic and replaced it with the new one. Happily, the hours passed as Maggs assisted by Woody managed to open a vent, and light a fire in a large oblong metal container, it was not long before the café was a central base and the smell of Maggs cooking wafted across the darkness of the store.

Steph returned with Jade and Rowan having done their turn, and Jade got a chance to roam free with Jett around the store, there were many dark corners and stacks of shelves filled with an assortment of strange and unusual objects from the past. Jett found a set of stainless steel bar-b-que tools which she stuck in her belt, Jade gave a frown. "What are they for?" She gave a cheeky smile.

"Rafe loves violent foreplay and I have some great ideas for this lot." Jade stared, looking at the shiny tools of torture stuck in Jett's belt.

"Whoa you guys are way more freaky than Rowan and me... Here give me a set too." She grabbed a set and slid it into her bag with a cheeky smile, Jett appeared to approve.

"Awesome, go for it girl."

It was approaching midnight when Rune woke with a start in her bed at home. She sat bolt upright and looked round the room. "Robbie?"

All was quiet apart from a clinking sound in her kitchen below. Rune slid out of bed and found she was still fully dressed, she pulled on her boots and headed downstairs to find Sapphire sat at the table. "Oh good you are up, I wasn't sure whether or not to wake you, but you looked so peaceful I thought I would leave you a while longer. I love the new cloak it's beautiful."

Rune felt a little groggy. "How did I get here; I was with my grandfather in the forest?" Sapphire shrugged.

"Judging by the power I felt in the air as I got here, I just thought he brought you home, I sensed you upstairs and came up to check on you."

"How long have you been here?"

"About a couple of hours, I sensed you just after leaving the guys and so came straight over." Rune turned having poured out a drink.

"The guys, you mean Robbie?"

"Yeah, Jade went a little off track and they ended up lost, I think her hormones are in control at the moment. Anyhow I helped them find a safe place and they are holed up until morning about three miles out of Canterbury, so don't panic he is safe."

Sapphire filled her in on the full story before heading back to Callanish, and after checking the children and saying goodnight to them Rune grabbed her new cloak and opened her window. It was several long minutes sat in the café as Robbie recounted his side of the story before she settled and realised they were all safe.

She was glad to find her mother had also arrived and took her into the darkness with a torch to tell her of her day and the leaving of Hearne, something she had not yet mentioned to the others. Both of them walked and talked and their conversations turned to supermarkets and the old ways of Modern Man. Rune like the others was very curious about this place that had remained unchanged since those times.

It was not long before Una and Mel appeared and then Maddy tagged on as they all walked along what was left of the clothes section. Rune stopped as she looked at the dust covered clothes hung in long lines on the dull silver rail. The garments before her fascinated and confused her; she turned to her mother holding a small item of black lace. "This is underwear, isn't it?" She looked unsure at the black lace and then back to Steph who smiled.

"Yes darling, it's a thong, it was somewhat trendy back then." Una leaned over Steph's shoulder and frowned at the thin garment in Rune's hand.

"Has it rotted away?" Rune lifted it back into her torch light.

"I don't think so." Steph gave a long chuckle.

"No, it's intact; I must admit it was not the most comfy thing in the world to wear." Una gave a wide grin.

"You actually wore these?" Steph nodded.

"As I said they were once all the fashion." Rune hung it back with the long rows of others all in differing dust covered colours.

"Glad I don't wear any, not really much point in them is there?" She wandered on as Una gave them a sly look. Maddy giggled.

"I have bigger handkerchiefs." Una gave a sly grin.

"Shall we try them when we get back; let's face it we have missed out on so much, let's be daring?" Una slipped three pairs in her bag, all black. Maddy gave an excited chuckle and grabbed two deep red pairs, which she quickly stuffed inside her pocket.

Harry hummed to himself as he slowly walked along the shelves in the dark at the far end of the store. His pockets jangled with several bottles of pickled onions and gherkins. He stopped as his eyes caught the dull red from below the dust covered jars of the cocktail cherries. "Oh wow man, that is like totally cosmic and very radical." He reached his hand up to the top of the shelf and lifted the small jar off and gave it a wipe on his cuff. "Whoa this is very cool."

He unscrewed the golden top and peered inside at the jar full of bright red cherries with a little chuckle. "Whoa man I love these little dudes." He stuck his finger in and gripped the sweet cherries in his fingers. With a look of delight and a contented happy little giggle, he placed his most beloved treat into his mouth and savoured the taste. "Ohhh man." His eyes rolled with enjoyment as he lifted out more in his wet fingers, and placed them with reverence onto his tongue.

He swallowed down his sweet delight and raised his hand up for the next jar. Harry froze, as two green eyes looked down at him out of the darkness above the shelf. His eyes widened as the jar he was just about to lift rose into the air and the lid unscrewed. He wanted to scream, but his throat suddenly had lost its ability to make sound, as his eyes widened and his torch hit the floor.

Harry took a step of fear back as he watched cherries float out of the jar into mid air below the bright green eyes. A small squeak came out from somewhere inside him; he raised a shaky white finger in the dark. "That ain't cosmic." The cherries floated under the green eyes and then suddenly disappeared. Harry swallowed hard and then let out an almighty scream; he turned and fled into the darkness leaving his torch on the floor.

Rune spun as the scream echoed in the darkness followed by an almighty crash of metal. Steph froze her hand on her knife in her belt; Rune listened and then shook her head. "Jade." Steph relaxed.

There was the quietest of patters, and the green eyes dropped to the floor and lifted the torch. There was a soft giggle, and the torch floated into the air and then switched off. "Yummy, cheers Harry."

Robbie and Rowan came silently and swiftly through the darkness. The torches flashed on and Harry screamed with wide eyes as the light illuminated his deathly white face and wide dark eyes. Rowan gave a long sigh.

"Harry what the hell are you doing running about in the dark?" Harry relaxed shaking as he lifted his finger from under the spinning pile of brightly coloured tins. He swallowed hard as he pointed behind him.

"Oh whoa dudes it's the evils, they found me, and pinched all my totally radical and cosmic cherries man." He gave a gasp and swallowed hard. "They ain't cosmic man, they should leave em alone, they is for happenin dudes."

Robbie slid his sword back into his belt, as he quickly worked out Harry's dark terror. He offered his hand and Harry placed his sweaty hand into it shaking nervously as Robbie pulled him up. Harry looked back into the darkness with a frightened look. "I tell you Robbie dude, I will never be like free of those uncosmic eyes man. They like totally chomped on my cherries man, I am like cursed." Rowan put his head down as he patted Harry on the shoulder and smiled, Robbie gave a little giggle as he lifted Harry's hat from under the Macaroni cheese in tins. Harry saw the labels in Robbie's torch light.

"Whoa man, now that's what the evils should eat, that is like none cosmic food that is, it rocks your karma and makes you do uncosmic things, don't eat that stuff dudes, it's like karma chompers in a tin."

Robbie patted him on the back. "It's Ok Harry, we will leave it for the green evils." Harry gave a nervous nod, and looked back up the dark isle, he walked slowly back with Robbie and Rowan casting looks all around the tops of the shelves.

Jade turned at the sound of movement. "Hey Jade, look what we found?" Jett's eyes flickered as she took a long swig from the bottle of Rum in her hand. Blades came into view with a bottle of something blue in her hand.

"Hey this stuff is way better than that stuff of Joe's." She handed it to Jade with a big smile. Jett gave a devilish wink in the torch light.

"There are loads more over there." She nodded back to behind her. "Come on we got quite a stash well away from everything." Jade took a long swig of the blue liquid and then took the bottle from her lips, as Jett raised her eye brows and smiled. The torches headed away down the aisle to the sound of quiet giggles.

Robbie and Rowan guided the pale faced and clammy Harry into the café and sat him down in a chair. Harry reached into his inside pocket for his hip flask. Smokes placed a tall bottle on the table and two tin mugs.

"Thirty year old single malt my friend, let's revive the old days." He slumped down in the chair at the side of the very visibly shaken Harry, and unscrewed the top with a smile. Harry watched the top open and gave a smile back as Smokes poured a very healthy measure into the mugs. "Fuel for the rider my friend." The mugs clunked together, as Harry smiled.

Two hours later the rain was pounding down outside the door, as Robbie walked onto the roof. Jay stretched under her cloak as Hawk took the two hot herbal teas off him. "It's all quiet Robbie." He gave a nod as he watched the heavy rain drops beating onto the plants.

"Maggs has some food ready, go and get something to eat and some rest, Rafe will be here in a moment, we will take the next watch." Jay nodded as she lifted her bow and sipping her tea, she headed into the darkness with Hawk in search of food.

Maggs wiped the steel surface down as Mel and Maddy helped dry off the last of the pots. She rolled the cloth in her hands and placed it down feeling tired. Harry and Smokes were already sat smiling with a rosy glow on their faces as they remembered the exploits of their younger days and the supermarket raids. Rune lay back on her bed roll and closed her eyes, as she thought of her day with her green lord. Maggs stroked back her mass of bushy curly blonde hair filled with beads and feathers, and wandered out of the serving area into the café area that was now the sleeping quarters of the Specialists. She sat back in one of the bolted down chairs and relaxed with a long gasp.

Rowan wandered in from the darkness with a bag that showed the shapes of many small boxes contained within. He walked up to Maggs and rested it on the table; he gave her a smile as she looked up at the worn chiselled features of Robbie's number two.

"Rune asked me to look out for this; the packaging is a bit dusty, but it should be good, she thought it might come in handy back at home." He pushed the bag across the table as Maggs dropped her eyes to see what appeared so important to

Rune to send Rowan in search of it.

Rowan watched as Maggs opened the bag and peered inside; she gave a loud squeak and looked up. "Oh Rowan darling, oh Rune, Oh how so positively groovy and totally cosmic, you are both such darlings." Her beads and bangles rattled a tune as she leapt out of her seat and pulled Rowan into a big hug. He caught his breath a little taken back by the sudden lurch of Maggs into his arms, but he gave her a big smile as she jumped out of his embrace and scuttled with her bag down the café towards Rune.

Rune opened her eyes and saw the cheery face of Maggs heading her way; Rowan sat down and gave her a nod. Maggs dropped to her knees pulling out a box of custard powder and showing it to her, as her eyes danced with delight.

"Oh Runestone my angel, you are such a totally cosmic darling, I feel like I could cry my vibes are so lifted with this utterly radical gift. Oh, my child you are so sweet and delightful." Her head shook back and forth as her teeth parted and her distinct horsy gasps of laughter reverberated into the air. All her beads and bangles rattled in tune and her hair filled with feathers fluttered in every direction.

Rune gave a big smile and placed her hand on Maggs hand. "You have done so much for us Maggs; I thought it would be nice for you to have your favourite recipe back for a short while. Just promise me one thing?"

"Oh Rune darling anything, just tell, and I will see it done in a most cosmic and groovy way." Rune giggled as she looked at the delight on Maggs face, she leaned forward and whispered.

"When we get home and we come round to visit, save some for Robbie and Me."

Maggs gave a loud horsy burst like a donkey in pain. "Oh my precious child, I will make you the most wonderful trifle you have ever tasted and reveal the secrets of my most karmic recipes for the both of you. My darlings you will feast on delights of cosmic wonder and your vibes will soar in a most happening way."

Harry who sat several rows up with a red face smiled in a dreamy way, and lifted his thumb to point behind him. "She is so right man, believe me your taste buds will exude pure cosmic bliss." Rowan gave an appreciative nod.

"I can hardly wait Harry." Rune smiled as she gave Maggs yet another big hug.

Robbie sat a few feet away from Rafe, as the rain poured down. "How is Hawk doing?" Rafe turned slightly in the darkness.

"He is dealing with it, he is hurting but glad to be here and doing something useful, don't worry about him, John and me have his back." Robbie smiled below his hood.

"Thanks Rafe, he is a good man, but this has knocked the steam out of him."

"He was a bit shaken when Saff appeared, but he is on the road back, to be honest it has probably done him good to blow off steam and get it out of his system. He will be fine Robbie; I would imagine if we meet a fight, he will focus his anger in the right places."

"Keep him safe for me, he used to tag a lot with Fish, but with him gone he needs to work out a good place to fit again."

"You just focus on the job; we got Hawk in our corner."

The air above gave an almighty crack and lightening streaked across the sky, moments later the deep rumble echoed in the distance, it was the early hours and would soon be dawn, and Robbie felt the impatience of having to wait, he wanted to get moving and get it all over with and return as quickly as he could. The pictures of the large castle lifting out of the floor and into the sky at York were foremost in his mind; he knew it would not be much longer now before Mason struck at the heart of the woodland realm. The moment he had spent two years preparing for was almost upon him, and he felt the pressure growing, suddenly almost overnight, he felt the cold finger of his destiny stalking him.

CHAPTER TWENTY SEVEN

A RETURN TO THE PAST

Fabian De la Roche had benefited a great deal from his association with Mason Knox and his mother. For many years he had played them off against each other to his benefit, and after ten long years of living a life in extreme luxury in Normandy, the time was approaching where soon it would be his part to repay them both.

The docks at Le Harve had been completely rebuilt, and once again they rang to the sound of goods and supplies for the massive army that De la Roche had been secretly assembling to unite with Mason in his bid to overrun England. The port was filled with large cruise liners and converted containerships, all to be loaded with soldiers and supplies that had been raped from the rest of the country in order to serve the needs of Mason, before he moved to French soil and began again his task of domination and control.

Most of it meant little for De la Roche; his primary concern was himself, and the gains he had hidden in secret to ensure his life of luxury and comfort. He had grown fat and lazy, but his mind was as sharp as ever, as he assessed each move he made to the greatest of political effect. On many occasions it was his greed and cruelty that ruled the day in ensuring he benefited more than any in all that he did. One such deal was the one he had made with the fleeing Brother Argus, a man similar in many ways, who shared an equal lust for wealth and the finer things in life.

De la Roche gave a smile as he saw the monk walking briskly towards him, followed by two soldiers who pulled the carts of cases and packing boxes behind him. The old monk gave a slight nod of recognition as he held out his hand to greet his new protector. "My Lord Fabian, I am greatly relieved to see you, it has been a rough sea and I thank the lord for my safe arrival on your soil."

De la Roche took his hand with a smile of conceit. "Abbot, I am pleased you made it safely, come I have a carriage that awaits you, let us remove ourselves from such distasteful and crude surroundings and find accommodations more suited to your position." Argus gave a sigh of relief and happily followed the direction of Fabian's gaze to a carriage that waited, decorated with all the trimmings of a man of great means and standing.

It was several long minutes before the carriage was loaded with the strong boxes and crates that were the possessions of Argus, and together they sat facing each other in the carriage, as it began its journey away from the port in the direction of more fitting surroundings set out of the town in a more picturesque landscape. Fabian smiled his immaculate moustache and goatee twitching, as he lifted a decanter of cut crystal from a small plush case attached to his seat. "Could I offer you some refined refreshment? This is a particularly excellent claret; it will aid our discussions of business."

The old monk gave a nod of appreciation; he rubbed his hands together releasing his tension. "I am very appreciative of your aid in this matter My Lord Baron, I fear things have not gone as I planned across the water, your protection means a great deal."

Fabian gave a slight snort of humour. "You are safe now, Mason will simmer for a while, but I find he loses interest, and moves on to other things quite quickly. Fear not he will not learn of your whereabouts." The monk took the glass appreciatively; Fabian felt the shake in the hands of the old monk and smiled to comfort him.

"Relax my dear Abbot, Mason wields great power there is no doubt, but even he cannot see everything, I have everything well in hand, there are places even his eyes cannot look, by morning he will have no idea at all where you reside, it will be as if the earth swallowed you up without trace."

"I appreciate your help; I will be forever indebted to you." De la Roche gave yet another reassuring smile and sat back in his seat to sip from his glass.

"Mason lacks in many ways, there are times he fails to see the true value of a good business relationship, whereas I have a deep understanding of how men of authority can benefit each other on many levels."

The face of Brother Argus turned purple as he dropped the glass, Fabian smiled as Argus gripped his throat and gasped for air, his eyes bulging as he began to cough and splutter. "As you see Abbot, you offer me a third of your value, when I can easily have it all."

Brother Argus retched and convulsed as he shook in the seat, and with his eyes staring in hate and shock, he gave one last almighty shudder and slid down the seat. De la Roche banged on the back wall of the carriage and it gave a lurch as it came to a shuddering halt. He stood up and opened the door, and walked calmly down the step onto the floor. The driver stayed the horses as he looked back to his master; De la Roche closed the door.

"Get rid of the body and then return with the carriage to my estate, have it unloaded into my private rooms, so I may account of the worth of our dear Abbot." The driver gave a nod as a second carriage arrived, and whipped the horses to move them on, and his master walked slowly toward the second carriage to return to his estate.

Sapphire watched from her table alone in her basement. "Well, I won't say I am sorry, one less man like Argus can only be a good thing." She waved her hand across the table as other pictures appeared and she continued on, although the death of the brother had not given a great deal of joy, she had hoped that it would have been her task to seek out and despatch the fat sadistic monk, and that moment had been taken from her.

Robbie walked slowly in the dark towards the huddled lump between the shelves, holding up his candle to avoid kicking the empty bottles on the floor. He gave the mound of blankets and loose articles of clothing a prod with his foot, and he heard Jett moan below. "Commanders, we move out in two hours."

The blanket moved and the tired bleary eyes of Jett appeared from below, he dropped her pants in front of her. "You will require these, I found them four rows back hanging, tell your Wolfman his shirt is still hanging from the ceiling, he will require it shortly to report for duty." Jett blinked and moaned.

"Yeah Ok... God Robbie keep the noise down my head is crushing my brain." He smiled.

"Hmm... there appears to be an outbreak of it around the whole place, I take it you and Jade found it and distributed it?" The blanket moved slightly.

"Actually no, which is sort of weird, this time we are innocent, it was Blades who discovered it in a back room." Robbie gave a nod.

"Well, that explains her condition, although innocent, is a word I just cannot associate with you or Jade. Get dressed there is coffee waiting, I want to head out as soon as all of you are capable of experiencing daylight." He gave a laugh as he turned. "You never learn, do you?" He walked back through the store towards the café area where the others were gathering.

Steph turned looking outraged. "What the hell were you thinking!?" Jade physically shrunk and closed her eyes; Rune gave a giggle as she saw the pain inflicted by the loud voice of her mother. Jade stood silent, unable to think as she tried to find some way to explain her strange appearance in the bright torch light. Her voice was almost a whisper.

"We thought it would look good, but it was not meant to be like this, it was supposed to have darker streaks." Rune was finding it hard to hold in her laughter, as were most of the others. Melanie tried to calm things down.

"Steph I am sure it's not permanent, I think with a little work we can put it right."

"RIGHT! HER HAIR IS BLOODY GREEN; HOW THE HELL DO WE PUT THAT RIGHT?" Jade almost fell back with the blast from her mother, even Mel looked a little afraid of her, she turned to Rune.

"Is there nothing you can do, there must be something?" Rune shrugged.

"I don't know, I have never used dye, I mean I know girls who use henna, but this is old world stuff, I have no idea what it is even made of." Steph again turned on Jade her eyes glaring with rage.

"Why the hell did you even try this, for Hearne's sake Jade, you are going to be a mother, what the hell possessed you to go and try dying your hair?"

Blades and Judith who were feeling equally as hung over stayed hidden behind the bottom tables, although the fact that Blades had green hands had a lot to do with it, as she could see the rage in Steph, and was panicked at how she would be able to explain that they thought during their drunken state it would be fun. After all she had bleached her own hair a hundred times, she had no idea the old world stuff could go wrong and turn green.

Steph turned on Smokes, who could not understand why she was picking on him, as he had been on the roof doing his watch. He stood still absorbing his wife's anger and trying not to smile, he somehow thought she was not going to see the funny side at all.

Jade felt her brain rattle and throb as her mother's voice bounced around in her head adding to the pain, any thought to explain why she had long curly green hair this morning escaped her, as her brain felt like it had exploded removing all attempts at any explanation. Harry tilted his head to one side as he looked at Jade from his seat at the table. "You know Stephy Baby it sort of looks funky and spacey; it reminds me a little of that time when you like dyed yours blue."

"What?" Rune's head snapped round at her mother. "You did yours blue?" Smokes gave a chuckle as Steph went on the defensive.

"SHUT IT HARRY!" She turned to Rune looking a little wrong footed. "That was different, it was a long time ago, and it was just for a party it was not permanent." Rune gave a giggle.

"How exactly is that different?" Steph stumbled as Jade opened one eye to watch her mother go into defence mode.

"As I said it was a long time ago, I was just a teenager and things were different back then."

"I am a teenager; I am only nineteen." Everyone turned to Jade who even though she was fighting the pain of her eyes in the bright light; she also wore an expression of questioning under her long green fringe. Steph was caught in a trap.

"Harry, you have a big mouth." She grabbed Smokes by the arm and dragged him off up the café. "We need to talk."

"Hey hang on a minute." But as fast as her temper had exploded on Jade she had gone, leaving Jade with green hair looking a little perplexed. Giggles and chuckles erupted as the women crowded in on Jade to examine her close up, Blades bobbed up to see if the coast was clear, and somewhere out in the darkness Steph could be heard fuming at Smokes, who appeared not to be answering her, and for Robbie it was yet another distraction that slowed things down as he wanted to get on and move out as quickly as possible.

The thunder overnight appeared to have cleared the air, and in a bid to clear his head and deal with his rising frustration, Robbie headed onto the roof to look around at the land around him. Skip and Treen were both on watch as he walked through what was quite a dense collection of trees that had seeded into the flat roof, to get a good look around. He came up at the side of Treen, as she viewed what was a vast forest in front of her, she turned slightly and smiled. "It ezz beautiful, ezz it no?"

She was right, the sky was a dazzling blue, broken only by the fragmented soft shapes of snow white clouds, and the sun streamed down on to the canopy of a vast area of green that rose before him to the top of what he knew was the steep incline they had followed down at the side of the river. "There ezz no signs of the beasts, I think they will ave taken them back last night in the rain." Robbie gave a nod.

"I was on watch and it was pretty heavy, not many would have been out last night, although they will have reported a group in the area, so maybe they are aware we are here."

"Maybe, but I think they would ave thought us just the thieves in the night, no, they would no be thinking it was you, they expect you to be closer than this place, we ave time to prepare, and then make the move on them." He gave a sigh, he was not that sure, and his voice was low, and almost just a thought.

"I hope so... I no longer have the time to deal with trouble, we must get William's crown and get back to Loxley as fast as we can." She patted his arm.

"We will, you need to ave a trust in us, even with the green hair, we will no let you down." She gave a giggle and smiled at Robbie, it was hard not to see the funny side and he giggled too.

"You heard then? Pebbles never ceases to surprise me." Treen gave a chuckle.

"She has the wildness of spirit, I think the colour must suit her, after all Robbie, it would no do for the rest of us. It will wash away at time, you will see, it is like my red, I ave to do it many times or it washes away." She lifted a lank of her hair where he could see some of the red was fading away and her natural golden blonde was starting to show again. "My Skippy as a liking for my red, so maybe I will do it many times."

"It does suit you Treen, I think it shows your spirit, which I think is something Skip really admires."

"I think so too." She watched the trees and he could see the smile on her face, it was clear that his comment about her and Skip had made her happy. He had seen Skip change a great deal since they had last visited Canterbury, and both Robbie and Treen knew that in some part it had been because of the way that Treen had added great happiness to his life.

It was almost eleven when the group was finally assembled in a condition that had them as alert as Robbie could expect considering their secret night on alcohol over twenty years old. There were many jokes in the air as the core of the group packed their bags, which Robbie noticed appeared to be fuller than when they left Loxley. Rune gave a nod and they all prepared with their bows ready, and then with a swipe of her hand, her violet arch opened and Big John and Hawk ran through to take up cover.

Robbie and Rowan came last with Rune and the window closed behind them. They were stood in a circle of trees surrounded by the Specialists, as they took up their places to ensure all was safe. Robbie noticed the line of green birch and knew just beyond was the old tree covered road separated by moss covered walls, and beyond that was the farm cottage that was the property of Hilda, Maggs mother. He took a long breath as he prepared, and then with a fast set of hand signals, Robbie gave the orders and they all began to move forward as quiet as the trees.

Slipping over the walls and onto the edge of the farm property, Robbie stopped for a moment and the group sank low to the floor taking cover, Rune looked over from two feet away. "What is wrong?" Robbie peered through the trees.

"Cabbages?"

Rune frowned. "What do you mean cabbages? That is where Rags hid; it is supposed to be a cabbage field." Rowan slid over to join in.

"Rags was lay down in them remember? We almost walked over her." Robbie gave a nod.

"Yeah, but that was because Hilda ran the farm, she died as we left, so who has planted these?" He noticed Maggs was listening at the side of Harry. "Maggs who planted cabbages for your mother, did you have any farm hands?"

He could see for a moment a look of hope in her eyes, but he knew Rune had felt Hilda leave the realm, so he knew it was not her, in his mind if Hilda had died and the farm burnt down, why would someone continue to work the land, it was making no sense at all. Harry was quietly muttering to Maggs, Robbie felt that Harry understood his point, Maggs looked back over.

"My mother was very radical, we paid the locals to do the plough and seed work, then we gave them some of the crops as payment to keep them fed through the winter. Mum had very cosmic vibes and believed in paying it forward to help folks." Rowan gave a shrug.

"It makes sense; maybe they have kept it up." Robbie was not sure.

"Ok here is the way we play this. Rowan Jade, Wolfie and Sting, you sweep round and come in from the top of the hill. Hawk, Blades, Skip, and Treen, cover the lane and front. Rune get a window ready to put Woody, Una, Crystal and us in the barn area, everyone else hold here until we give the all clear. Rowan you have ten minutes to get up and round, get going."

Ten minutes later there was a faint flash of violet under the barn doors. Robbie looked round inside the old wooden building which he remembered with fondness, and nothing had really changed. He had always thought the farm had been burned to the ground and he had expected to walk out into a ruined farm, but he was happy to see at least the barn had survived. Outside they could hear the chickens, and Rune smiled as she moved towards the double doors which were closed. Robbie moved to her side so they could whisper to each other. Rune peered through the gap and looked confused, Robbie expected the worst and waited for her to confirm it as she looked out on the scene.

A scruffy figure walked slowly along the path pushing a wheel barrow filled with chicken droppings. He came up the side of the barn, and was about to turn the corner, when he felt the tug from behind and a long silver dagger pressed into his throat, he froze instantly and closed his eyes and gave a long deep sigh. "Not bloody again… and looking at those red ties I cannot believe you done me again Lord Rowan." He heard the long gasp and then Jade's voice.

"Stan… What the hell are you doing here?" Rowan moved the dagger and Stan let go of the wheelbarrow. It was a strange moment when Rowan spun Stan round and pulled him into a tight embrace.

"Never in my dreams did I expect to find you alive." The old man smiled and he slid his arms round and gave Rowan a mighty pat on the back.

"I never thought I would be caught twice, but I must admit My Lord I am very happy it was you." Rowan released Stan and held him back to look at him, there was a happy expression across Rowan 's chiselled and normally stern face. Jade ran up and threw her arms around Stan, giving him a mighty squeeze, somewhere behind was a deep belly laugh as Bear came out from behind the wall wearing a huge smile.

"Well, I will be buggered. I am happy to see you, my friend."

For the next few minutes there was a tearful reunion as Rune ran out from the barn and dragged Stan into a huge hug. The old man was quite overwhelmed, and was soon in tears, the noise alerted those in the house and soon Bob was outside being swept into hugs and dragged into the crowd of the Specialist that had spent a week on the farm at Honey Hill over a year ago.

Bob introduced his wife, two teenage sons and a daughter, and there was a very rapid round of introductions which also included the new members of the expanded Specialists, that had grown in number since their last visit. Outside in the farm yard there was a great deal of celebration, which suddenly died as the group parted to reveal Maggs as she walked into the yard looking stunned to see her farm and home intact. Stan's eyes filled with tears as the shocked Magg's stared at him, and he opened his arms and walked towards her. Maggs burst into tears and snatched him into her arms as he spoke softly to her.

"Mistress Margret, I am so happy to see you, we have often hoped you were safe and have done all we can to keep the place safe and in good order just in case you came back home." Bob came up at her side and she jumped from Stan's arms into his as he squeezed her hard. As he pulled her back from the hugs with tears in his eyes he smiled at Maggs.

"Come with me, there is something you need to see."

Maggs was so upset she was unable to speak, Harry gave Stan a huge hug and thanked him for his cosmic vibes, as the others turned to see Bob walk Maggs into a small Rose filled garden at the end of the yard, and there surrounded by flowers was a beautifully well-tended grave marked with a white head stone.

Maggs fell to her knees and wept as she saw the grave, with the white stone that bore the words. 'Hilda Pickles. Lover of life and loved by all life.' Around the grave were small statues of small pot animals that showed each of the animals in the farm she had loved so much. Maggs wailed as Rune knelt down beside her with tears in her own eyes. Robbie gave a smile at Bob and patted his shoulder.

"You have done a nice thing here Bob, thank you for taking good care of her, I am indebted to you both for your kindness."

Maggs spent a long time at the grave of her mother. Rune spent some time with her and spoke softly to her before withdrawing and giving her the time to be alone. Stan took everyone into the house and Bob's wife Juniper, or June as she insisted, made drinks and prepared food for all of them. Stan soon joined them and together at the table they gave the events of what had happened as the group sat quietly and listened.

As Robbie and the Specialists had left, Bob and Stan had been at the small camp site clearing up, it was Bob who noticed the Cutters coming over the hill and down towards the farm, so together Bob and Stan piled all the leaves and debris they had collected onto the large fire. The result was a massive column of smoke rising up above the clearing within the trees.

They put their black vests back on, grabbed some weapons and ran out of the tepee camp, and started waving at the soldiers to say they had destroyed the camp and the Hooded Man had gone straight down the hill towards the woodland. They had hoped to protect the farm and Stan filled up as he told them of how another small group had come down the lane and attacked Hilda in the yard. Hilda had hit one of them several times with a spade, and refused to move or tell them anything, which had resulted in her death. Bob shook his head bitterly expressing how he blamed himself for not being fast enough getting down from the camp to the farm.

Once they got to the farm, they dragged all the hay bales into the yard and set fire to them to create a huge smoking fire that looked like the house was burning, and then ran out to the front to wave the soldiers on down the road in pursuit of Robbie, who they knew was too far ahead to be caught. Once the soldiers had lost the chase, they returned walking right past the house heading back to the barracks at the cathedral, and it was then that they took care of Hilda. A few days later when all had calmed down Bob left to go and get his family, and Stan stayed on to care for the animals, and they had been there since doing repairs and keeping the farm running to the best of their ability. Stan looked up from the table at Harry.

"We have kept things just as they were for her. You will find we only used the two spare rooms, and we have left Mistress Hilda, and Margret's rooms locked as they were. The boys have used the barn; we don't own much so we have no need of a lot of space." Stan turned to Robbie and Rune. "We hoped you would return seeing as you had to leave that arrow and the crown, it's still there hung in the leaves, it appears Mason made no attempt at all to get it, he left after a week or two and headed to London we heard." Robbie gave a nod.

"Thank you, both of you and your family, it means a great deal to us, and especially Maggs, there really are no words to express our full gratitude." Bob gave a nod as Stan sat back in his seat, his face which showed that times had been hard at moments in his life, was stern and resolute.

"I gave you my word we would aid you and your party, I knew you would have to pass by here at some point, so we prepared for you all the best we could. You gave us both a second chance My Lord, I hope you can see we were grateful for it and have tried to prove our worth." The Specialists all gave a nod of acknowledgement and Rune smiled.

"I once questioned your honour Stanley, and you have proven beyond question that you are indeed a man of deep honour, I am happy to apologise to both of you, for the kindness you have shown to Hilda shows great respect not just to her and her family, but also to you and your own family." Rune gave a small curtsy and Stan looked a little lost for words.

Over two hours later and after some very detailed discussion on the cathedral and the surrounding area, which Bob and Stan had been logging, Robbie sat inside one of the tepee's back on Honey Hill, surrounded by soft cushions and throws of many different colours. It almost felt like coming home as he had walked back into the camp, and seen the old pine table and benches with the round fire pit surrounded with huge logs to sit on. The two carts filled with large barrels sat idle under the trees, and he had felt a deep stirring within him as the memory of that week a year ago came rushing back into his mind. He lay back on the pillows and cushions and gave a long sigh as Rune lay down next to him and snuggled up. "It feels kind of odd and homely at the same time, doesn't it?"

He lifted his arm and slid it round her pulling her closer. "It does a bit... It was just over a year ago, and yet at times it feels like it was years, and now here it feels like only yesterday. I never thought for a second this place had survived, and in a way that always saddened me because this place is special and is filled with good and bad memories."

"Good and bad how do you mean, I thought you had a special feeling for this place?" He turned to face her and his eyes met her bright blue sapphire eyes, and he smiled.

"I do have wonderful memories of here, but it was a hard time of fear and doubt for all of us, remember how it felt knowing Alice was pregnant by Billy and she made me promise here in this place to kill him. There are so many moments here Rune, all the doubt, Scarlet and Ruby, Hog and his funny little ways, and feeling the death of Eric on my mind all the time. I suppose that it was this place that helped me find my way, I had been a lord for just over a month last time I was here and I was fighting so hard to handle it all, and then there was Billy's betrayal as well." She smiled and leaned in to kiss him.

"We were so new to each other, and I loved you so much and wanted so desperately to help... We made love here and our love grew deeper and deeper inside this tent, I have never forgotten our first times together Robbie here in this place. It is such a special place from a very special moment in time, and from here we really started to take the war away from Mason, and build a resistance against him. If you think about it, this is where it all really started in earnest, it is a very special place." His arms tightened and pulled her close.

"Yeah, you are right; this is an important place to all of us, because in here I became the Hooded Man returned for real, and maybe that is why it feels like coming home, this is the start of everything." She snuggled up and kissed him again.

"Make love to me; let's make more memories at the start of everything." He smiled and she gave a giggle. "You know Jade already has Rowan locked in their tepee?" He gave a laugh and pulled her closer, knowing he had a few hours of free time, because considering Jade, Jett, Treen and Una were all in the camp, he knew at least four of his men would be out of action for some time.

CHAPTER TWENTY EIGHT

IN DARKNESS

It was shortly before dawn two miles off the south coast of England, and the captain had just returned to the deck having had a meal and a short sleep. The first mate stood attentively to his left as both of them looked out of the windows, watching the bow as it rose and fell, cutting through the waves as its engine thudded below their feet. The spray coursed upwards over the bow, caught in the spotlight and sloshed over the deck, only to roll back over the edge below the metal rail and back into the sea. It had been a normal straight forward journey, if not a little boring, as the precious cargo and troops were ferried from France across the channel and up the coast to the new landing station built by Mason Knox at Hull.

The captain watched looking east for dawn when he would chart his way along the coast and into the new dock. It was quiet and peaceful as he lifted his cup and sipped the lukewarm tea, they had made good progress and he was relaxed and at ease, and looking forward to the three days break he would have as they unloaded the soldiers and all their supplies, and then restocked the ship for the return voyage to Normandy.

The First Mate leaned forward and peered into the darkness. "What the hell is that?" To suddenly see a light a short way in front of them was unheard of, as the only vessels they encountered were usually those of Mason's, but none were scheduled to return yet, as they were supposed to be the lead ship.

The captain turned and lifted his binoculars, he could see little but the bright spotlight that had just appeared out of nowhere. "It is probably just some fisherman, they look small, we are well lit up they will see us."

The First Mate continued to watch. "He does not appear to be changing course; you don't suppose he is in trouble, do you?" The captain dismissed the idea.

"No flare, so he either moves or we run him under, there is no way he cannot see us with our main lights on, it's as bright as day on deck."

The First Mate reached for his jacket. "Best get out there and see if he is signalling."

He pulled on his thick black coat, slid his binoculars over his head, and lifted a megaphone off the console, then made his way out of the door and along the deck to the front of the cabin and the white metal railings. The captain watched feeling a little relief from the boredom as the mate lifted the megaphone and shouted out across the water. "Ahoy... Ahoy!" Four more lights illuminated on the approaching vessel allowing the captain to see the shape of what looked like a medium sized trawler, he gave a smile.

"Bloody reckless fishermen, I might have known." He reached for the wire and gave it a yank, and the deep bellowing horns erupted in a deep bass tone that echoed across the water.

Leaning into the rail the First Mate lifted his binoculars and tried to see if anyone was on deck, his vision rose and fell with the motion of the sea, as he steadied himself and focused in on the small vessel, it was then he noticed the crew on the deck as they primed the small cannon lashed to the bow of the trawler. The trawler responded with a high pitched droning horn, and it took a few seconds for everything to sink in to the First Mate as he watched the scene unfold, and a black flag went up the mast. "You cannot be friggin serious?" His words almost a whisper as he put two and two together.

Across the darkness on the lead trawler, Captain Val Andre of Houat, stood at the side of his cabin giving his orders as his men ran round preparing. His vessel was on a dead line to contact the side of the bow as he watched with care instructing his wheel man as the vessel raced towards the large ocean liner. "Keep her steady Marko; I want this shot right on her nose as she falls into the waves." Marco nodded with a large smile on his face, as he watched the front of his ship, and saw the men setting the sights on the brass cannon that pointed over the bow.

Val Andre swung on the rail as he gave his next commands, shouting down the vessel to the two men who looked back towards him ready for his command. Andre gave a large smile and shouted. "For France... For Houat... For Freedom!" He lifted his arm as the First Mate on the huge liner turned and screamed at his own captain through the windows.

"PIRATES!" The captain frowned as he heard the roar of the trawler's horns and then a bright flash followed by a deep resounding boom. The First Mate staggered in panic as he grabbed for the wheel house door, and it suddenly became apparent to the captain that he was under attack. As he started to fully grasp the situation, there was another almighty flash, and as the explosion hit with a deafening crash, the ship shuddered and listed to one side and then gave another shudder as the bow crashed back down into the waves. The shock hit him as he staggered, and the First Mate fell in through the door, the captain grabbed at the console to prevent himself being thrown backwards, as the First Mate scrambled to his feet and screamed at the top of his voice.

"Sound the alarm."

Marco spun the wheel, and the trawler swung away from the approaching liner. Val Andre smiling as the roars went up, he continued to shout down the vessel to his men. "Reload and swing round, fire at will and hit them low."

Across the water red lights flashed as bells and horns rang out into the night's darkness. The two men worked fast with precision and swung the loaded cannon round, there was another large boom as the trawler turned followed by the deafening explosion as a second hole was pierced in the side of the large liner. Captain Andre watched through his field glasses and saw the flames inside the hull lighting the damage on the water line; the large liner was taking in water fast, as men flooded up from below onto the decks. Marco with one hand on the wheel, swung the floodlights round to light the side of the huge liner as they came alongside fifty yards out, the hole was just under the waterline and the ship was taking sea at an alarming rate.

The Pirates fired their third shot, and Andre watched as it hit the large vessel just under the centre point along the water line as they raced on passing it, Marco swung the wheel and they turned away, the lights went out and the trawler was thrown into darkness as it raced away leaving three large holes in the side of the liner, that was starting to list. On board there was panic as the lower half of the ship filled with ice cold water. The soldiers and the crew had been caught off guard, as they slept in their bunks; Val Andre took the wheel and swung the trawler to circle back around as the engines slowed and the crew gathered alongside to watch as the large vessel sank quickly in the water. Captain Andre stood beside Marco.

"It's one, but it does not feel enough, many of our people lay slain, and many no longer have their homeland. This is the start, and before I am done, Mason Knox will pay with the souls of many." Marco turned.

"They have lifeboats, what do we do with them?"

"Leave them to fend alone as they did our people, there will be other ships after this night."

Captain Val Andre entered back into the wheel house, and gunned the engines, the trawler turned and in the slowly appearing sun of a new dawn, the ship raced away, the large black flag flapping at the rear, and Mason now had Pirates to deal with, the sea was no longer his alone to rule.

Throughout the night Sapphire had walked through the woodland of the Hidden Realm in search of Opal. With Cal by her side, they had finally met up and walked through the quiet forest of tall trees until they had arrived in Opal's circle, where they sat quietly talking as they ate a meal that had miraculously prepared itself as if expecting the two of them to arrive. Sapphire had been stronger in her powers connected to her table, as slowly she gained more knowledge, her fears and doubts had finally begun to subside within her. Opal was pleased to see Sapphire was becoming more and more like the centre she had been destined to be. Opal could see Sapphire's mind was clearer and more focused than she had ever known it to be. She smiled at her, as she watched Sapphire eat.

"I see there is calmness within you not seen before, I take it you have remembered much of what happened and have come to terms with it?" She swallowed and gave a nod.

"I find having a table to be a blessing and also a little bit of a curse, there is no place to hide when the truth is revealed, but yes, I feel more at ease than on some of my previous visits." She gave a giggle as Opal smiled.

"That is good Child, and I am pleased to see you such, for the old powers have walked into blindness, and you are now the eyes of us all." Sapphire looked at her.

"Have you lost your abilities; I think that would be a huge shame as you have guided me so well?" Opal gave a cheeky wink.

"There are many ways to watch a road, and not all of them come from within, I still have eyes others are blind to." Sapphire somehow expected Opal to have more tricks up her sleeve, if anything else she had come to see that Opal was if nothing else more than talented when it came to bending the rules.

Sapphire finished her meal, and Opal handed her a tall glass of pink coloured liquid. "What news do you have of the others, I would imagine you miss not being with them in the south?" Sapphire smiled.

"So you can still see much of what is happening? I miss it and I don't, I have been so busy with the table and helping out Rune that to be honest I have not had much time to think about it. I watch them and try to help where needed, but apart from that I have been looking into a few things for Rune." Opal gave a nod.

"Walk that path slowly, she can be dangerous if she finds out you have been looking into the shadows cast by her family." Sapphire gave a laugh.

"There really is nothing that you do not see is there?" Opal gave a slight chuckle and then took Saff by the hand, for a moment her voice had a very serious tone.

"I mean it Child, be very careful, that family has hidden powers none of us have been able to fully comprehend, take it slowly and protect yourself at all costs. Morgan will not take kindly to you seeking out the skeletons of her past." Sapphire gave a nod of understanding.

"I am being very careful; Rune has warned me and knows at all times where I am." Opal gave a reassured nod.

"Good!" She gave a wink. "So what have you learned to date?"

Sapphire frowned. "Not that much really, apart from the fact that Igraine was taken against her will to Saxony shortly before the birth of Morgan, not a great deal really. I am not sure if it is important or was just some sort of family thing, you see it appears Morgan's parents were very deeply Saxon. I think to them it was important that all the children were born there, Mason was born there also; in fact the only one so far who was not born there was Raven Merle. I am hoping Rune will understand it all."

Opal gave a nod as she thought about it all. "It is true we knew little of Cornwall, we were all so busy with Uther and then Arthur, that we did not pay a great deal of attention until Morgan struck her first blow with Leenard. Of course by that time Cornwall was dead and Old Maud had been back in Saxony for a long time, I know Gwendolyn tried to look that way but Maud covered her tracks well and there was no trace of her or her family line."

"Hmm, I am finding it difficult at the moment to get anything about Saxony." Opal gave it a little thought, and Sapphire watched as she felt Opal trying to bring something to mind, Opal frowned and shook her finger.

"Oh what was it... hmm I am not sure if this helps, but if I am right, I seem to remember Gwen saying something about trying to look in and seeing areas that were just blackness. I seem to remember at the time her talking with Rhiannon, both of them seemed to think it was a type of veil none of us had ever seen before, if I am right, and I think I am, at the time they thought it was some form of power they had never seen before."

Opal turned to Sapphire. "I have often wondered if it was not some crude mixture of our powers with the Merle, but Gwen dismissed any talk of Fae magic and so no one really figured it out. Once Morgan fled the country, they all seemed to sit back glad she was gone and nothing else was really done as by then the largest part of the council had been trapped and imprisoned." She gave a smirk. "We were very busy with other worries trying to get out, and of course as you know, Morgan was actually down here torturing Gwendolyn and trying to steal her powers. So much happened at that time that I suppose we just forgot her past and tried to deal with her present, once we all escaped our focus was trying to undo the evil of her and Mason, everything else just escaped our minds for a while."

Sapphire understood. "I think no one has really thought about where she came from, except Rune, I think she plans to trace back everything, because she thinks it is in the heart of Saxony that we will find her greatest weakness and fear."

It was not something that Opal had given a lot of thought to over her long years, but as she sat with Sapphire in her circle of protection deep below the tall trees of the Hidden Realm, Opal saw the deep wisdom in Rune's thinking. "It will be hard Sapphire; do not let her go alone, she must have aid at her side. I know little of that place or what lies hidden below the darkness cast over it, but having studied Morgan for most of my life, one thing I know is how tricky she can be."

She stared out at the trees for a moment as Sapphire watched her, and then suddenly she turned to Sapphire so quickly it made her jump, she spoke almost excitedly. "Dreams my girl we all have them, and that might just be the key to your success, have you added Cal to your table?"

A combination of surprise and slight confusion flooded her mind. "What... No...

Why do you think I should?" Opal gave a burst of laughter.

"My Dear Child he is a part of you, of course you should add him, he is a dream spirit, he can walk anywhere where people have dreams or desires." She suddenly appeared to be very excited, and her bright blue eyes danced in her pale wrinkled old white face. "The Sandling's are invisible to all, Cal will be able to sit amongst any who are there without ever being detected, and then he can return to you and let you know what he has seen and heard. My Dear Child this could be a very important breakthrough for Rune and yourself, through his eyes you can watch from your table, you must add him straight away."

Sapphire gave a giggle as she saw the excitement on Opal's face. "I will, I will add him as soon as I get back."

Rune lay in the darkness of her tepee next to the sleeping Robbie and smiled to herself. "Thank you, Grandma, you always find the most obvious answer to my problems." She closed her eyes and rolled over pulling Robbie close to her, she had known all along that Opal would look at the subject in a completely different way to either herself or Saff, and she felt a little relief in knowing she had been right to advise Saff to pay her grandmother a visit. Outside in the darkness on the edge of the trees Jade sat with Rowan as they watched the camp.

Jade gave a long contended sigh as she leaned on the tree her face turned to the dark silhouette of Rowan and not really on the camp. "This is nice, I am so happy the camp was not destroyed, this place is special to me, do you remember last time we came here?" Rowan gave a giggle, and he turned in the darkness, the light glinted in his now darkened slate grey eyes, and yet Jade knew him so well that his chiselled features appeared to her even in the darkness.

"How could I forget, you held me captive in our tent for most of the time?"

She chuckled. "I was so in love with you, and I really thought we would die together in that big church thing, I wanted so badly to live Rowan, I really wanted us to live and be together." He smiled in the darkness.

"I must admit, I trusted Robbie, but when I saw how many soldiers, they had waiting I was not so sure. I wanted to live as well." He stretched out his arm in the darkness and felt her small warm hand slide into his; he gave it a squeeze as he relaxed against the tree. "We have seen much in this last year, sometimes I forget how short a time it has been, so much has happened that it feels somehow a lot longer, does that make sense?"

Jade gave a nod, and then giggled remembering it was pitch black and he could not see her. "I was thinking of the others, it must be hard on John here, he was good friends with Martin, and he fought beside Hog and Fish last time."

"They were good men, I think we all miss them, especially Martin and Hog, I must admit I didn't really get to know Hog as well as I did Martin, but I remember him in the Cathedral, he fought with great power, none of us would have made it to the stairs without him watching our backs, we will miss him when we go back for the arrow." Jade felt a little quiver run through her.

"It won't be as bad as last time; I mean Mason has left this place, hasn't he?" Rowan was not convinced.

"Mason knows we have a king to throne, and he knows we need that arrow Jade. If I was in his shoes, I would leave a good force here to ensure the arrow stays right where Robbie put it. Don't forget his blood is on that arrow, I very much doubt a day has passed since, where he has not thought about that arrow and how Robbie destroyed his plans. Mark my words, Robbie is no fool either, he knows Mason will have something there to try and surprise us." Jade gave a shudder.

"I just want to grab it, and get out and home as fast as possible."

"I think we all do Jade, Loxley is at risk and although no one is saying anything, I can feel it in the air around them, all of them want to stay close to home now and protect everything that has been built there."

"I could not bear the thought of them burning Loxley. Oh, Rowan if they burned down our house, I am not sure what I would do, I really think I would lose it." He squeezed her hand again.

"It's a long road from the farm to the gates of the Mere and our house, no Cutter will walk that road and live, they will face the wrath of Destiny and Honour side by side each step of the way. I promise you Jade, none shall meet and match the measure of Robbie and Me in defence of our homes, not even the dark witch will pass my anger. Have no fear, our children will be raised in that house." She gave a giggle, it was rare that Rowan showed his feelings, but his words held iron, and whilst she found it sweet and endearing, she also felt the warmth of safety run through her.

Martin Jarrod, with the small figure of Ben sat high on his shoulders, waded through the cold water towards the beach, where the Sage had removed his long green hooded coat, and was wringing it out on the mass of shale and pebbles. Not that far out to sea, but as close as the small boat could go, Toby watched from the Northwinds, making sure his passengers made it safely to land. Martin came up the beach and slipped Ben off his shoulders, feeling the relief as the young boy who was also carrying their two bags stood looking at the tree infested shoreline.

"Where are we Martin?"

The Sage lifted his rolled up coat onto his shoulder, and turned towards them. "If Toby is as good at navigating as he says he is, we should be near a place once known as Kingsdown, not far from Deal, although to Mason Knox, this place is known as Section Twelve." Martin appeared to recognise the place and Ben noticed as he lit the small candle in a jar at his feet.

"Do you know this place, Martin?" Martin gave his head a shake.

"No, but I have heard of it, cruel deeds befell the people who lived here not that long ago." It gave him a shudder to think of it, Ben watched as he stood up and lifted the small jar with the candle in it.

"Cruel, in what way?" Martin ruffled his hair.

"It's best you don't know this close to sleeping, let's just say the Cutter Brigades passed through here after the thwarted coronation of Mason, there will be little in the way of villages left for us to scout."

It took a few moments, but then Ben began to understand, even on the other side of the country in Wales the stories of the clearing of the east had found their way to the ears of everyone. Ben gave a shudder as the stories he had heard of rape and the slaughter of women and children came back to his mind. He looked up the beach to the trees, where suddenly he realised that somewhere ahead hidden below the plants were the burned ruins and scattered dead of what had been small fishing communities. He took several steps and got between Martin and the Sage, any ideas he had of exploring when the sun came up had suddenly vanished, he felt he wanted to keep as close to his friends as possible.

The Sage began to walk towards the trees. "We will stay just inside the trees for tonight, it is far too dark to do anything, let's make a camp and light a fire, don't be afraid Ben, this place is pretty deserted, it's why we chose to land here."

CHAPTER TWENTY NINE

NIGHT TIME REVELATIONS

The large room at the top of the castle that loomed in a circle of black scorched earth at the centre of the Hidden Realm, had changed much over the last few weeks. It was almost as if Morgan le Fey had changed her entire way of doing things, as she instructed her Houlen to completely rearrange everything. The long wooden heavy tables had been moved to form a large square, which formed a working space that surrounded her permanently raised table containing the red seven pointed star etched within a disk of black. Two slightly shorter tables had been brought into the room to complete the enclosure she had made, that provided a wide space for her to enter the enclosure, and she had forbidden everyone including Ursula, her assistant to enter the space.

Much to her surprise, the corner at the top of the room that had been Ursula's working space, had also been completely rearranged. A small wooden bed had been placed with a small set of draws, and a small cast iron stove had been set next to a table with a smooth grey polished marble top, for her to prepare food on. Even Salem the tatty cat which Morgan appeared to hate so much, had been given a large reed basket filled with soft rags for a bed, next to the new red plush chair and small candle stand for Ursula. At the bottom end of the long room, new shelves were built, and filled with glass jars containing many new ingredients that Ursula had never heard of. The long rows of coloured powders and strange leaves gave off a pungent, yet surprisingly pleasant smell. All around the castle change was happening as armies of Houlen in their more graceful form, opened windows and swept with brooms to clear the place of dust and decay, the atmosphere felt almost lighter than it had in previous years, except for the familiar sounds of torturous screams and wails, and the barking of caged dogs deep below the castle floors.

The last two weeks since the return from Avalon had been very busy indeed, and even though there had been a great deal to do and the work had been very hard, Ursula had found her spirits lifted greatly. It had a lot to do with the fact that Morgan had given her consent to the pairing up of Ursula with her escort Tom, and she was now able to leave the great room of the castle two nights each week to be with him. Morgan had felt that Ursula had earned the privilege via her actions in Avalon, where she had if nothing else proven her loyalty beyond doubt.

For Ursula it had felt life changing, her heart skipped a beat whenever Tom entered the room, and she found herself smiling for no apparent reason as she copied the notes of her mistress down in the new large ornate black book. Her days had become filled with the watching of the sun above the trees through the open window, as she secretly waited for the moment where she could be relieved from her duty and scurry off to spend her nights embraced in her love making with Thomas.

The tortured years of toil locked in the old crone's body were over, and now she felt like her life was changing for the better. The heavy polished door handle gave a creak, as she scratched at the paper and she turned to see Mason enter the room, he glanced round the newly refurbished room and then his head turned and his eyes met with Ursula's as she turned to face him. She jumped from her seat and gave a small curtsy. "My Lord Knox, I did not expect you at such a late hour." He gave a slight nod and flicked his hand.

"Please do not get up, this is an unplanned visit." He appeared to wince, and she noticed his hand slip across his stomach. She moved from her table and walked round towards him.

"Is the pain starting again? Come sit for a moment and I will get you some more tonic." She noticed the paleness of his skin as she approached to lead him towards the fire, where the two familiar old and tattered padded red seats sat on a thread bare rug. "Sit awhile My Lord while I mix it up for you."

Mason walked slowly, and she thought he had become very frail as she guided him towards the seat and gently aided him as he sat down; he relaxed back with a gasp and smiled. "Thank you my dear."

It felt odd to see him this way, she knew he was of a great age, but he had always appeared so strong and robust, almost youthful in the past. To see him this way felt a little startling, and she quickly crossed back to her long work table and began to mix together the ingredients, she looked back across the room to see him sat back with his eyes closed. "I will mix you a stronger batch; it appears that the last one does not appear to be having as long an effect."

Mason opened his eyes and watched her as she expertly mixed up the fine powders and mixed herbs; she lifted the tripod over the lamp oil burner and placed a small cast iron pot containing a pale green liquid over the heat. The whole room instantly filled with a bitter sweet scent, and Ursula added the mixture of herbs and powders. The liquid changed colour to a deep blood red, and she looked back and smiled as she observed Mason watching her. He was impressed with the skill she showed in the way she handled the equipment and measured the herbs, never once looking at the potions book, although he was not aware of how many times she had brewed it in the past. In the castle the potion of life was frequently used to enhance the lives of her mistress and also the old man servant

Hesketh, this had been the first recipe Ursula had been taught, it was in many ways her mistress's fail safe, as it ensured she could always be revived to full health should she suffer a life threatening mishap.

Mason gave a sigh of relief. "I don't suppose she has any scotch laying around does she?" He sat back in the chair, and Ursula gave a slight giggle.

"I am afraid she does not approve of it, but if you promise not to tell, I have a little." He gave a roguish smile towards her.

"Marvellous."

Ursula wandered over towards her small bed, and crouching down she slid out a small wooden box containing the bottle and a few other precious possessions. She lifted it up and grabbed the cup from the table and carried it over towards Mason and handed them to him. He looked at the bottle label and gave a smile. "Only the best for Hesketh I see." He winked and she gave a smile.

"He visits sometimes for a chat when our mistress is away, and he always brings me a bottle." Mason gave a nod.

"Hmm... He always brought a bottle when he would visit me, I miss his visits, he was very kind to me as a boy, I often wondered why he stayed here all these years?"

Ursula was already half way back to the table to check on the potion, she turned. "You do? That surprises me if you don't mind my saying." Mason turned as Ursula lifted the potion from the tripod with a thick rag and set it to cool.

"Why does that surprise you?" She poured some of the contents in a steaming cup, and turned to head back across the flat grey stone towards him, she could see the look of surprise and intrigue on his face, Ursula was very matter of fact as she spoke.

"She is his wife, and he raised you as a son, why would you be surprised that he wanted to linger on to ensure you were all taken care of?"

It was a question that had never crossed Mason's mind, but now he thought about it, he could see that Ursula made perfect sense, he gave another slight smile as Ursula crouched down in front of him with the steaming cup. She took the cup of scotch from his hand and handed him the tonic. "It's still a little hot so take care." She looked at the scotch in the cup. "I am not sure you should be mixing this with the tonic that is quite a powerful potion."

He gave a chuckle. "Ursula when you have lived as long as I have, you will find boredom sets in and you take little pleasure from many of the things that gave you joy in youth. Although there are a few things in this life that endure and bring greater appreciation with age, and a fine scotch is most certainly one of them, regardless of whether or not it is good for you." She gave a smile and stood up and handed him the cup back.

"Go steady; the potion will take a while to kick in." As she turned he swallowed the potion and gave a gasp, and quickly took a large mouthful of the scotch, then he gave a little shake.

"Brrr... I hate this stuff, believe me the scotch makes all the difference." He gave another little shudder. "If you are not busy, sit awhile, I have to wait until this vile concoction kicks in, and we have spoken little in the past, I would be glad of the company."

Understanding that he hated weakness, and yet here he was having to rest up for a while she took the seat opposite, he poured a small amount of Scotch into the cup and handed it to her, then he took a long swig from the bottle and settled back in the chair. His face was still very drawn and pale, yet his pale blue eyes sparkled, he seemed more approachable, and in a way a little vulnerable as he smiled at her.

"My mother has praised you highly recently, if it wasn't so unbelievable, I would hazard a guess as to say she has even grown a little fond of you. I must admit Ursula, it pleases me to know she has a companion, she has spent a great age alone, your company has improved her situation."

Ursula was greatly surprised, she was not even aware that her mistress would mention her at all, let alone pay her a compliment, but she too felt a deep bond for the old sorceress and she smiled. "My mistress has been very kind to me, there are times I know I did not deserve it, but we have grown to work well, and I am grateful for all she has taught me over the years. I know she has what appears like harsh ways, but I too am very fond of her, I hold nothing but the highest respect for her."

Mason gave a soft nod as if he understood her. "She was actually a very good mother when I was a child, I suppose most people do not see it. I may even forget at times, but she made my early years very happy. I suppose considering she lost her parents so young, she felt she wanted to make up for what she lost with me, I too owe her a great deal, it has been so long it easily slips my mind, but she has achieved great things and been the rock from which this family has grown in strength."

Ursula took a sip of her drink. "Family are important Lord Knox, even those we feel we have lost, at the end of the day it is all we have. I am lucky because I lost my family, and my mistress has taken good care of me, I feel at times she treats me as she would a daughter, and I am grateful for it."

Mason gave a knowing smile. "You were young when she found you; you know little I take it of your roots?"

"I have the power of sight, I have seen little, but it has enlightened me as to where my roots lie, and my mistress did let slip that my Grandmother Ariel worked for your great grandfather, although little is known of what happened to her." He gave a nod.

"So you are aware you are not from these shores, and your roots lie back in the old world of Saxony?" She gave a nod.

"Yes... I am also aware that Ariel was the Romany who tried to kill your great grandfather, and although she fled, she was caught several years later and imprisoned by him." Mason gave a sigh.

"Otto was a vile and sadistic old bugger to all of us, I must admit I hated him, and for the record I have to confess that I felt like killing him a few times myself. He treated your grandmother terribly, and to her credit she took it and remained faithful for many a year, I don't blame her for trying to kill him, I know my mother wished it many times in her youth. He never forgave his son for marrying a Celt, and having a half breed as he called her for a granddaughter. He was short sighted then and still is now."

The colour appeared to be running back into Mason's face as the potion took effect, he appeared to rise slightly in his seat, and looked physically stronger as he took yet another nip of his bottle.

Ursula looked surprised. "He is still alive?" Mason scoffed.

"That old bastard is unkillable believe me, it's the reason I stay the hell out of that land, and he still spouts off his vile mantra of Saxon blood. Last time I was back in the homeland which is an age ago, the whole family gathered and they were so interbred they all looked identical, it was hard to tell who was father, brother or son, I hate the place, if you ask me my grandfather showed great wisdom to leave and marry Igrane, he knew for sure he would not be marrying a sister or aunt." He gave a wicked laugh as his humour returned and Ursula could not help but giggle.

Ursula looked down at her cup for a moment and then back to Mason, his pale blue eyes met with her brown, and he could sense she was looking for the right to ask a question, he smiled. "What?"

She shuffled the cup in her hand slightly. "I don't wish to pry, but speaking about family I have to ask, if you would permit me?"

"Ask away... tonight you have done me a great service and helped with a terrible affliction, which has subsided as we have spoken, so call this my repayment, and ask me anything without fear."

She shuffled in her seat. "Will you really kill your own son, is it true you have put a warrant out for his capture and death, I mean he is your first born, doesn't that count for something?" Mason gave a broad laugh as he sat back and relaxed, Ursula was not completely sure if he wasn't laughing at her.

"My dear girl if I know anything for sure it is that William has the same heart as myself, whether or not he accepts it, he is a Knox, and he will endure no matter what comes his way. That boy will cheat the devil until his last dying breath as an old man." He chuckled as he leant towards the surprised looking assistant of his mother. "Look William is a survivor, and never forget he was trained in Loxley, as much as I hate that pile of old logs, I am not so stupid as to underestimate the power of the skills they have when it comes to woodcraft." He sat back in his chair as he saw Ursula understand him; he gave her a gentle nod.

"One of the main reasons we put him in there so young was so he could be taught and trained by old Jake, who even I have to admit was one of the best woodsmen of his time. But I will say, things got a little confused, I had always planned to pluck him out when the time was right and then use what he had learned to train my men. In that he showed me he was a true Knox, because rather than follow my line, and be the dutiful son, he decided to go off with his adopted brother against me, and that showed me he was more like me than even I ever expected. Have no fear there will never be a time that I am faced with the order to commit him to death, in that I am 100% certain. William is caught in the centre of two huge forces, both of whom want him dead, and as a true Knox he will survive as I expect him too." He gave a giggle and Ursula smiled.

"So, signing the order was all about saving face?"

"It was... Do not forget the army I command; I cannot show the slightest weakness as Loxley did when he allowed him to escape. The order is worthless without him caught, and in an ironic twist, my enemy has trained him so well he will never be caught. Odd as it sounds, I want him to live, I owe him that much." She gave a sigh of relief.

"I am happy to hear you say that, I only met him a few times, and I know he made my mistress so angry at times, but he was nice to me and he did make me laugh at the time." Mason gave her a wink.

"See a true son of mine... so it's not only my guard Thomas who caught your eye, I see you too are a darker horse than I thought." Her cheeks suddenly felt very hot and she could do nothing but smile.

"You have a very handsome son if you don't mind me saying so." Mason gave a roar of a laugh as he rose from his seat feeling much stronger.

"I do not mind at all, I am sure he will turn many a maidens head before he is through, well I must say I have enjoyed your company a great deal Miss Ursula, and I offer my thanks for your skill, but the hour is late and as with all things I have a wife to please and an empire to build." Ursula got up and headed across the room to the table where the large flask of the tonic was much cooler, she pushed in the cork bung and handed it to him with a smile.

"Remember it's a little stronger so try and make it last longer."

"And no Scotch?" She gave a giggle.

"And no scotch if you can avoid it?"

He gave her one last smile and turned towards the doors. "I will nip up and see Hesketh before I leave, I shall tell him you need two bottles next time, and I thank you for sharing... Until next time." He swung the door open and he was gone, she gave a smile and walked back to the chair and collected the cup and the bottle, then headed back to her desk to continue her work for a while longer.

Silence fell around the castle as the cool night air flowed in through the open window, Ursula lifted her nib and dipped it into the ink bottle and began to write in her neat script. High above her a green moth with pale patches and pointed wings, let go of the brickwork and flapping it's wings, it sailed out into the night above the trees.

Swooping low, closer to the cover of the canopy, it fluttered with purpose until after a long flight, it flew into a cleared circle. Sat in the centre perfectly still, the white clad figure of Opal concentrated as the moth flew down towards her and landed on her shoulder. For a few moments her concentration intensified and the moth wandered up to the side of her face and began to gently flap its wings, she gave a slight smile, as she listened and then opened her bright blue eyes and stirred stretching out her legs.

"Thank you, my small green friend, you have done well indeed and we all are very grateful... Oh yes indeed that is very useful, I am certain it will aid Runestone and Sapphire a great deal, fly free with our thanks for the night is still young enough for you."

The moth fluttered back into the air and was gone; Opal closed her eyes for a moment and thought deeply. "Hear me Cal, for I have great need to speak with you."

Through the trees the sounds of the waves could be heard crashing up the shingle beach, Ben was fast asleep rolled up in his blankets close to the fire. Martin now in dry clothes dozed against a tree as his clothes hung on a small line at the side of him to dry, and the Sage tossed and turned as he felt a great unease rising inside him.

Martin watched as he stood up and walked quietly off into the trees, he knew something was bothering him and so he stood up and checked on Ben, before he silently followed him.

The Sage wandered through the trees of this very overgrown strange part of the country, he had never walked here before, yet he felt his feet were being guided by some unknown power, it was only a few minutes before he walked out into a clearing and was confronted by a tall white stag, in front of which he saw his strange little dream spirit kneeling. The Stag looked him directly in the eyes, and he fell to his knees beside the small crouching figure with reverence. "My Lord."

The light around the stag intensified and the Sage closed his eyes, after a few moments he opened them to find the light had faded, and he saw on the grass in front of him two long bark like feet. The soft sound like grass swaying in the breeze filled his ears as he looked up at the large imposing figure of his lord in the form of a man. "Rise up young tree, long have you been in the back of my thoughts, and so I must apologise for not speaking to you sooner."

The Sage felt the dryness in his throat as he turned and saw the small shabby figure of his companion who wore a broad smile of love, he was sure some of the faded colour had deepened in her clothes since he had entered the clearing. He turned back to looking up at the high lord of the woodland, his voice croaked as he spoke. "My Lord, I am not worthy of such a visit, and I feel I should leave for I have dishonoured the code taught me in Loxley."

The Old Lord gave a nod, and his deep voice softened. "Yet you remain true to the words you swore to my daughter, and you have fought hard to undo much of the pain caused by the line of your kin. Is not the time for penance over, stand before your lord as the man you wish to be, and let your heart and actions be judged as a man of Loxley should be."

The Sage shook his head slowly. "My lord I was judged by the lord of Loxley and I am not worthy to stand before you, I shall remain on my knees as is befitting for a disgraced woodsman."

"It was not a request young tree, I command all in this realm and when I say stand, you will obey, now stand before your lord and be the man you were born to be." There was a slight rumble in his voice like thunder, and the Sage rose slowly to face his lord. Hearne gave a nod. "Good... now come and sit with me, for I have things I wish to discuss with you." The Sage bowed.

"Yes My Lord."

Martin watched through the trees on his knees and lost for words, he had heard many tales of a stag appearing to Woodsmen, but never had he heard of the woodland lord appearing in man like form to talk to a woodsman. He cowered feeling afraid in the trees, and holding his breath in case the large powerful figure would spot him and attack. Hearne creaked like old bark as he lowered himself down onto an old fallen trunk; the Sage waited respectfully and then seated himself opposite on another slightly fallen tree. Hearne looked at him with eyes that sparkled like dark succulent fruit, his face was old, and yet the Sage could see the wisdom and life in his eyes, and somehow, he thought of Leenard.

Hearne lifted his arm and pointed at the worn flaky mask of birch on the face of the Sage. "The time of hiding behind old wood is finished." The mask gave a sharp lurch and cracked, it fell to the floor in two pieces, revealing a red swollen face where the mask had rubbed away some of the skin leaving it rough and worn and looking very sore. "You have paid for the wrongs you have done, come kneel before me so I may look on your true form and tend to the cuts and sores of your penance."

The Sage, afraid to speak slid off the trunk and knelt in the deep grass before Hearne as the old man looked at the sores across his forehead, nose and cheeks. "You pay a high price young tree, I see the pain you have suffered, and the damage done by your act of repentance, but I feel you have tortured yourself far greater than was the need."

The Sage stared at the old face of compassion, but was resolute that it was his burden. "I disgraced the oath I made as a woodsman, and worse than that I betrayed the one who called me brother, even though you command it My Lord, I will not remove the mask that hides the face of shame until I feel I have redeemed myself in the eyes of the one I betrayed."

Hearne gestured to the small Sandling to come forward, he looked at the face of the small sad creature and he made up his mind. "This I will tell you young tree as it appears to me." He looked at the small creature knelt on the grass beside the Sage.

"This creature loves you deeply, for she alone took the choice to bond with you, and as such she had joined with you and she too carries your burden as you can see from the sadness around her. It is unnatural for such a sweet and delightful creature to look so sad and dull, and yet under the burden you have set for yourself, she too suffers without complaint and has remained loyal, even though you have not lightened her load by naming her."

The Sage looked down at the pitiful creature that he had grown very fond of in his time connected to her, and he felt her sadness. He had not realised that she had become a reflection of the burden he had imposed upon himself, and he felt guilty knowing she had guided him faithfully and shown great loyalty towards him. Hearne gave a smile.

"Finally, you see yourself in the guise of your own creation... Listen to me young tree and I will offer you a deal that will lighten your load, and relieve some of the burden from this poor creature who is devoted to you." The Sage turned and looked back at the old lord.

"I honestly had no idea, Opal told me she would cheer up, but I had no idea that I was the cause of her pain, I would not wish for anyone to carry my load." Hearne gave a nod.

"The honour you learned in Loxley shows in you... Let me create your mask, a mask worthy of his lord and one that will wear on the body less, yet will keep your true identity hidden until such time as you are released from the debt you owe to the Lord of Loxley. This I will do if you agree to name the child of dreams, and keep the oath you swore to my daughter."

"If this will ease her burden, I would gladly accept your terms, for I will never fail in the oath I swore to your daughter to aid the Woodland Realm."

"Then it is settled, give her the name you feel fitting, and release some of the burden from her shoulders." The Sage turned and smiled at the small figure; her large dull eyes blinked up at him.

"You are so small and delicate, and yet I see how resilient you are in the burden you have carried. Both of us serve the woodland and its cause, so if it is OK with you, I will name you Leaf, for they are fragile and yet equally as resilient."

The Lord Hearne smiled as he saw tears flow into the eyes of the small creature, but it was not sadness he felt emitting from her but great joy. He leaned forward with a kind smile and collected her tears as they slipped off her cheeks in the palm of his hand.

"So shall it be known by all in my realm, that Leaf is bound to you, and has my blessing." He rubbed his hands together and the fine skin on his palms peeled away and was washed in the tears of the small Sandling. The Sage watched as the skin turned a silvery white flecked with veins of black, Hearne faced the Sage and lifting the pieces of broken peeled skin from his hands he spread it onto the face of the Sage and pressed it into place.

"So bark becomes skin, and skin becomes bark, may this mask remain and bring ease, until all below is healed and your heart is set free by the will of the lord you betrayed and called brother."

As he moved his hands away, the Sage could feel his face burn for a few moments, and then he felt the relief as the pain faded and his skin cooled. He now wore a face of skin not unlike that of the Lord Hearne, except it was white and Birch like as his mask had been. Hearne gave a smile. "This I feel will be less likely to irritate and should ease some of your burden, now return to your seat as I have a task for you to bring aid to the Hooded Realm."

The Sage slid back and almost jumped with surprise as he saw Leaf. Her hair had turned a deep vivid blue with soft streaks of a paler blue through it, her eyes were as red as raspberries, and her tunic was a pale apple green. She wore small mustard brown leggings and soft green shoes, and in many ways, he felt she had all the colours of spring summer and autumn in her appearance. She gave him a huge smile and blinked at him, he smiled back and ruffled her long blue hair. "I am so sorry, if I had realised, I would have named you sooner, I have thought about it for a long while now, please forgive me Leaf."

She scurried up to him and leaned over and hugged him, and he felt the pulse of love run into him, and a little of the guilt he felt subsided. Hearne gave them a moment and then spoke.

"On to business, the wheel is turning and things change with each passing moment, your task as you know is to gather many in the cause of the woodland and take aid to those who support Loxley. Go into the trees and find everyone who lives here, take them to Canterbury and tell them to gather the fruits of the trees that grow there. Take these fruits that contain the seeds of this realm and distribute them to every area of the south where you find stone, spread the seeds of rebellion and allow them to take hold, for they contain something no magic of the Merle can ever defeat. Use this weapon of life to shelter all who oppose the snake that was your father."

The Sage gave a smirk. "Well technically he still is, but I doubt he will admit that now. It's probably a daft question but we all thought this area was empty, the Cutters cleared it and killed everyone a year ago." Hearne gave a chuckle.

"The power of the green is it hides many things well; you know this son of Loxley. But there is one north east of here who I wish you to seek out, for your example may be of benefit to him."

"Ok so what is he called?"

"He has many names, but let me say he was once a woodsman who swore an oath as you have, and has in turn betrayed the trust of his people and abused the power of his position. I wish you to meet this man and convince him to change his ways, for he has many captives who he has exploited for his own needs under the guise of protecting them. Young Tree, there are many there who will fill your new army of green, for these men and women are capable fighters and will aid your cause well. Go to them and release them from the lies of their leader and use them well."

Hearne rose as the Sage nodded understanding. "Remember young tree, when the Lord of Loxley commands it your mask will fade, when it does take the example of your sister, and walk as the man Bill Hargreaves, for in that name there is still some honour." He turned to leave and stopped and pointed behind the Sage.

"You will find supplies for many days next to the place where your companion hides over there, take them and may your trail be lightened by the flowers of the woodland trail, go with speed my children." The Sage looked behind not at first understanding, and then spotted Martin as he rose up from the bushes looking a little embarrassed.

"I wasn't following you; I was actually worried about you." He shrugged. "I did not think he would notice me this far back."

The Sage gave a smile and turned back to see an empty glade, he felt a little sadness and had hoped to thank the lord as he made his goodbye's. He swung his legs over the old tree and looking at Leaf he smiled. "Come and meet Martin, he is a good guy you will like him."

CHAPTER THIRTY

A STORM BREWING

Runestone lay in the darkness next to Robbie as he slept, her eyes were closed, and yet a slight hint of violet light flashed across her cheeks. *"Yes, Mother, Saff is right, it may be dangerous, but we must find a way to get under the veil they have cast around them."*

Sapphire sat at her table below her kitchen floor, as strange images rose out of her table. *"Cal will leave shortly, now I have placed him within the protections of the table, I should see everything he sees, if you are right Steph, then this Otto must be the father of Victor Duke of Cornwall, and her grandfather."*

"There is little I understand from my father's notebook, but Yes, I am sure he was Maud's husband, the fact he is still alive is news though, after all it's amazing Morgan is still living, let alone her grandfather, he must be as ancient as the mountains he hides in." Rune listened quietly thinking about what she had learned, she knew her task of defeating the Dark One would be difficult, but now her mind moved towards facing the fact that she may have more family than she had first thought, her thoughts moved back to the conversation.

"Mother, Saff, both of you must look as deeply as you can to find out what you can about her family home, we must locate a way to enter unseen, and then find our way into that castle, only then will we know how to stop Morgan and her vile family."

"I will Rune, and don't worry Cal will find us a way inside I am sure of it."

"Be careful Saff, you are on your own, if she finds out you are looking into her past, she might not take too kindly to it."

"I will Steph, I have the veil and a few other Fae tricks I have learned to help me."

Robbie disturbed in his sleep and Rune opened her eyes for a second, his face was bathed in soft violet light. *"Ok Saff, just stay alert and keep in touch at all times, I have to get some sleep now, I think we will have a busy day tomorrow, so I will say goodnight."*

"Yeah, no worries, Night Rune, Night Steph."

"Night Girls."

Rune closed her eyes and snuggled into Robbie, it was not that far off dawn, and yet she felt sleep was still some ways off. There was a great deal to think about, especially now she knew there were other members of Morgan's family, the sound of her mother's voice still echoed in her mind, they hated Victor for marrying Igraine, and saw Morgan as a half breed, it gave her a little hope, somehow it appeared that her family disliked Morgan equally as much as she did, there was a great deal to think about before she ventured into the realm of the past of Morgan le Fey.

As Runestone drifted into sleep, watched over by Hawk and Smokes, many miles away on the east coast, thirty nine miles from Lincoln, at Gibraltar Point, Lieutenant Scott Parker sat beneath the dead twisted figure of an old Elder Tree, surrounded by the thick emerald green of Gorse. It was almost sun up, as he knelt down and scanned the area through a battered pair of binoculars, ten feet behind him stood a low ram shack shelter made of long branches covered with grass and twigs. Sat inside, wrapped tightly in his cloak the young teenage recruit, Andrew Taylor, chewed on the last of the stale bread and cheese, as he shivered having only been awake for ten minutes.

Scott scanned along the coast where several small fishing boats had set out across the choppy water for a day's fishing. As the light in the distance drew a pale white line across the sea, Scott noticed something dark on the horizon as he panned left, and swung back slowly to check what it had been. As he lined it up and focused, he made out the dark shape of what looked like a large ship. "Hold up, what do we have here then?"

Andrew leaned forward still chewing as he looked at Scott. "I hope it's whatever is taking the fishermen, because three more days of this and I think I will freeze to death." Scott smiled still holding the binoculars to his eyes.

"Think this is more important than the loss of a few small boats lad, I am not sure something that big would worry much over a few crab hunters."

"How big?" Andrew crawled forward to the open front of the shelter, and raised up on his knees to try and see if he could see whatever Scott was looking at out to sea. Scott watched intently as he saw a series of dots on the water start to move away from the ship.

"Whatever it is, it looks like they are launching vessels." Over to their right on the long stretch of darkened beaches five huge fires lit, Andrew saw them first and peered over the gorse to see if he could make anything out.

"Looks like whatever they launched is going to land over there, Scott turned to view his partner and noticed the roaring flames in a long line across the beach.

"That's interesting, looks like we have a landing party." He turned and raised the binoculars to see if he could make out any of the figures close to the fires. "Two

Monks." He laughed. "I never expected that."

Andrew was confused. "Why would monks want to kill fishermen and steal boats?" Scott gave another laugh as he turned back to view the boats coming across the sea towards the beach.

"I am not sure they do Andy; I think we have stumbled onto something entirely different." The young recruit still was not grasping what was happening.

"Like what?" Scott lowered the binoculars and turned to face him. "Like we know that the church has nothing to do with ships, but that out there is a very large vessel, although we do know Knox has a lot to do with the church, remember the Cathedral?" Andy nodded. "Well it looks to me like there is some kind of landing party heading towards those fires, and if it's monks that are there to meet them then this must be something to do with the monks at the cathedral who oppose the bishop, I say we wait until they land and then get the hell out of here and report it fast, this is something the boys at the top will need to know about."

Andy gave a relieved nod, he had just about had enough of sitting out on the edge of the coast in the freezing winds, and the thought of getting back to the barracks and some warmth lifted his spirits. "Aye, I will get packed up ready."

Across the long beach as the darkness lifted, Brother Gideon waited as the wind blew in off the water's edge tugging at his robes and making them flap around his legs. He watched as the flames of the large fires roared behind him, and what looked like forty craft came slowly across the waters towards him. He was young for a monk, at only thirty one years old, and was heavily built; it was clear from his stance that he had lived a life that involved heavy work. "Be ready Cuthbert, as soon as they land, we head to the farm and saddle up for Lincoln, aide the men off the barges as fast as you can, and show them the way through the dunes avoiding the silt."

It took a further ten minutes before the roaring engine of the landing craft drove it hard into the beach ten yards off Brother Gideon in the shallow water. The huge metal front door of the craft crashed into the water revealing the host of heavily set monks, and one in particular who stood tall with his hood down. Gideon smiled as he saw his brother walk calmly down the platform and into the water; he opened his arms and smiled as the figure came towards him. The tall monk gripped his shoulders hard wearing a large smile. "Gideon, it is good to see you again my brother."

"Likewise Bart, tell me how have things gone in the north?" The tall monk watched from his brother's side as the host of monks walked off the craft and gathered as Cuthbert showed them the direction to walk.

"All is well in the north, although life was far too quiet, I crave a more active pastime and I am happy to be here and being of more use than in Scotland."

They turned together to follow the others as more craft crashed onto the beach, and more monks began to disembark. Further up the beach on higher ground Lieutenant Scott Parker had seen enough.

"I will tell you this lad, they might be wearing monk's robes, but I know fighters when I see them, and whatever that lot has in mind I will bet my last bit it ain't peaceful or Godly. Come on we better move and fast while it's still dim, we have a lot of ground to cover and important news to report."

As the empty landing craft revved their engines to leave the beach and return with yet more troops and supplies, Scott Parker and his young recruit moved quickly keeping low until they hit a small cops where two more woodland fighters and the horses waited. Without explanation he mounted up with the others, and charged at full pace to the outer post set on the divide line of the no man's land they were in, to pass the news of a landing of Knox forces 40 miles south east of Lincoln. As he rode through the trees, he knew that the moment every woodland soldier that held the long divide line had been waiting for had arrived, Mason was planning to hit them, and from what he had seen, he planned to hit them hard.

For most of the day the Specialists had been in high spirits, Robbie had risen early and visited Stan at the farm, Maggs appeared better and was tending the grave of her mother under the watchful eyes of a semi naked sunbathing Harry, and Mel and Rags accompanied by Mother and Smokes had walked up the high hill, where Mel sat quietly watching the cathedral through the eyes of a large seagull she had befriended, seeing as her eagle had returned home to the stones at Callanish.

Rune slept in late, as did Rowan and Jade, and even though Jett and Rafe had not been seen yet, judging by the sounds of passion coming from inside their tee pee, it was obvious it would be some time before they would appear. Camp life was a series of tasks from cooking, to cleaning weapons or sparring for practice, something Bear and Big John took a lead in with some of the others. There were many smiles in the relaxed atmosphere, but there were also many thoughts of what was to come. The Specialists had shared their first encounters inside the cathedral many times around the camp fire over the year, but to Robbie as he appeared back in the camp in early afternoon, it was easy to tell it was on the minds of the others.

Rowan sat with a heavily sweating Big John by the fire talking, as Robbie came up and sat with them, Rowan gave a nod to Robbie and lifted a cup and the bubbling pot off the fire. He poured a cup of black coffee made from Dandelion and handed it to him. "It's going to rain."

Robbie looked up at the dark cloud gathering in the east. "Probably, some rain at twilight may help us." John pulled his shirt over his head.

"So we go at twilight... why then, it's not like we have seen any of their men since we arrived?" Robbie took a sip of his drink.

"Yeah John, that is the problem, considering we are expected, why haven't we seen anyone around here?" Rowan had been thinking about it ever since Stan had told them of the few patrols and the emptiness of the cathedral square.

"Darkness is wise Robbie, Mason must expect us soon, and yet it appears he has something else in mind." Robbie gave a nod.

"Rune has Saff digging around to try and find out what. To be honest I expected this place to be overflowing with his men, so if they are not here, where are they?" John stood up and lifted his heavy black belt with his sword hanging from it.

"You ask me they are hiding in wait; I reckon we will get in with no bother, the question is will we get out as easy? I reckon that is when he will attack just like last time, he had thousands of the buggers waiting for us, and this time we ain't got Scarlet and her handy lads to watch our rear ends. Take it slow on this one Robbie, let's feel it out as we go." Robbie gave a slight nod.

"We will John, I have something in mind, and I will let everyone know as soon as they are all gathered.

Brother Gideon and his brother Bart, which was short for Bartholomew, had not lingered on the beach, and had made their way half of a mile inland to a small farm. Behind them on the beach with soft sand and silt, soldiers bearing the crest of the red dragon heaved and pulled, as the final landing craft arrived filled with carts packed full of weapons and supplies. From the beach down the narrow lane, a long line of soldiers stretched towards the farm.

Gideon with his brother and 150 members of the Brethren assembled at the farm, where they disrobed to reveal heavy leather fighting jerkins covered by a bib, which bore the crest of a golden elaborate cross on a burgundy red background. The monks had not come to pray or preach, they were no longer commanded by Argus, their orders came from Mason, and they were given the simple task of rooting out those who had taken the side of Lord Loxley, and bringing the cathedral at Lincoln down to its knees.

Mason was angry at what he perceived as a betrayal by the church, who were supposed to be supporting him whole heartedly, the middle of the road stance taken by Bishop Stevens was not as agreed, and so he intended to show his wrath, and had sent one thousand of his best fighters to join the Brethren, and take the cathedral for his own as he intended to assume full control of the church against Stevens.

As the soldiers of Mason, gathered at the farm under their Captain's on foot, Brother Bartholomew, on horseback, road with his brother on the long ride to the outskirts of Lincoln. There they would meet up with the rest of the Brethren and Brother Maynard, and await Cuthbert and the rest of the monks, as well as the large army of Mason. Bartholomew wanted as much time as possible talking to

Maynard, and planning what would be a fierce assault on a cathedral he knew was under the guard of the men of Loxley.

Somewhere in the dense and overgrown woodlands off the southeast coast, the Sage stopped as the rain began to pound down, and took shelter under a large sprawling Beech tree. Ben looked out on the thick wood before him, it had felt like a long hard day clawing through woodland that was as dense as a jungle. "Where are we Martin, are we lost."

The Sage stood just in front of him, turned and gave him a warm smile. "I knew someone once who always said, if the leaves are above your head, you are never lost." Ben smiled.

"Really?" The Sage gave a nod and winked at Martin.

"Really Ben, he believed that if you were under the trees, you had already found the perfect place to be, and I think he was right, this is so much nicer than the horrible stuffy tunnels in London."

"Well Yeah, but what I meant was where are we going? I mean we have been walking for hours and everything looks the same, how do you know where we are exactly?" Martin gave a smile at the Sage and shrugged.

"The Lad has a good point." The Sage crouched down and opened his bag.

"Ok I tell you what Ben, we shall take a break here and eat, and I will fill you in on what I know."

He lifted out a round baked loaf and broke off a chunk which he handed to Ben; he took it as the Sage pulled a lump off a block of fresh cheese and lifted out some chunks of white meat from his bag. Ben sat down and began to eat as Martin took his share and sat beside Ben. The Sage flicked a large chunk of the meat into his mouth as he looked around at the trees that encircled them.

"Ok Ben, judging by our pace and the hardships of the day, I would say we are about thirteen to fourteen miles away from Canterbury. What I am looking for is some sign of a well used track or the scent of charcoal, because I know somewhere in this thick woodland is a man of many names, and he has an outpost that is hidden, but he must have trade, and around here there does appear to be an awful lot of Birch." Ben nodded.

"And Birch makes charcoal when you burn it."

"Exactly, just like Wales, charcoal is a good form of currency to those who want smokeless fires to remain unseen, and if this so called man of many names is in charge round here, well, he will be the one controlling the charcoal burners, and he will need to transport it, probably to the coast, because we know that there are a lot of soldiers around Canterbury, so he must be using boats to move the stuff."

"So if you find the track and head inland, you will find the man of lots of names?" Martin gave a giggle, he had not considered how the Sage was going to find the man they were seeking, and suddenly to him everything made sense.

"As always Ben you're right on the money, the way I see it we must be close, the problem is we will not find it until we walk right on to it."

"Why does this man have lots of names?" The Sage gave a chuckle.

"That young Master Winters, I have not worked out yet, so for now all I can say is I do not know, maybe when we find him, I will ask him." The dark clouds rolled in and the light around them began to fade as they ate, what had started as a light shower built up over the hour, and the Sage stood to look at the sky, the rain intensified and a bright flash of blue light streaked across the sky, followed shortly by an intense rumble. "Get the sheet out Martin, we won't get far in this, it is probably best we stay here for a while."

On Honey Hill all the Specialists had gathered in one of the large Tepee's. Standing or sitting in a big circle as the lightning flashed outside, Robbie rolled out a plan of the cathedral and began his briefing. "As you can see, since we were last here there has been a lot of changes. Firstly, last time once we bolted the doors, we only had those inside to worry about, but as you can see on both sides of the main building walls have collapsed leaving large sections open to the outsides." He looked up from the drawing at looked at all of them slowly.

"If Mason has prepared a welcoming committee we will be exposed on all sides. Stan tells me the only really protected area is here behind the wall of leaves that holds the crown up next to the altar." Rowan leaned over the drawing.

"Hmm, yeah, it is covered on both sides, but if we get caught in there then we will be trapped with no way out."

"There's a way out Rowan. It's a small door, but the problem is you will be blind as to what is on the other side until you open it." Rowan looked up at Jett and remembered the small room at the side of the main altar with a door that led to the outside, Jett smiled. "If you're gonna open it, go slow and look before you run."

"Yeah, I got you Sting." Robbie continued.

"Ok, so we all know to stay as alert as possible, I am hoping the last of the days light will give us some cover, I want at least six to remain outside in the trees, I will need eyes all over the place, but unlike last time, I am not selecting people for the task, I want you to decide where you want to be. Will, you have to be there, in that we have no choice as it is only your hand that can pull that arrow, Rune, Rowan and Jade you guys will be inside with us too, everyone else let me know after what your preferences are."

"I am not leaving Will's side so I am in." Robbie smiled as Hornet looked around at the group; Jett gave her a slap on the shoulder.

"Me and the Wolf will be with you Hornet." Una spoke.

"I would rather be inside, but I can contact Rune quickly if needed, so I will take a watch in the trees and keep you all up to date." Maddy stepped forward.

"I will be with her, my arrows are better out in the open, I can hit more that way." Robbie nodded.

"Thanks ladies, anyone else got a preference?"

"I will take the roof if that's OK?" Robbie turned to see Blades, she shrugged. "I'm a fast climber and can drop down fast if needed; even in the failing light you will need eyes up high." He nodded.

"Good thinking Blades, anyone else got a preference?"

"Well, if Bear and Treen do not have an objection, I think a little sword play in the open may be required, after all it won't take too many inside to get the arrow out Robert, so count me as your protection on leaving, I take it we are going in via the doors?" Robbie smiled. "We are Skip, and I will breathe easier if you are out there waiting to guide me home."

"I am in it, or out of it with my Skippy and the Bear, I like plenty of room to stretch my arm on the heads of his Cutters, I like the space to move." Bear gave a nod.

"Yeah me too."

"Ok anyone else got a preference?" Jaz leaned over from behind Rowan.

"I would say take my mum inside, she can have eyes far out with her bird, and Fox you should go high with Blades and take Crystal in the tower, she proved a big help at the black rock. I will hang outside with Bear and Skip." Steph stood at the side of Rune.

"Pete and me will hold up at the doorway to keep it clear, John your place is beside Rune and Will, and I would say that Milly you would be best served outside with Jaz, if we get injuries inside Jade and me can deal with them, you keep everyone outside cared for."

"Ok Mother." Robbie gave a smile.

"Ok then, this is how we will play it."

"Whoa hold up dudes, what am I doing man?" Everyone turned to see Harry polishing his purple tinted glasses.

"You are not coming this time Harry, you will be holding the fort here with Maggs, Stan and Bob. Maggs is still shaken by her return and I don't want to leave her alone, but I will also need someone here to hold the fort if we get soldiers heading this way. I would imagine we will be coming here fast and hard on our return, so have everything ready to go, including Maggs."

"Aww but man you will need me like up top with my Baby Girl, this ain't too cosmic Robbie."

"Maybe, but you don't do birdie stuff either Harry, so you cannot be up on the roof either. Look Harry things have been hard on Maggs and I need you to help her get ready, we cannot return without her, so I need you at the top of your game using your cosmic charm to convince her to be ready. I would ask another but they do not have your gifts Harry, please don't let me down." Harry gave a frown as he thought for a moment.

"If you put it that way man, I am like whoa, how can I refuse, after all hey I am the dude with the cosmic touch man." Hornet gave a titter with Blades, Robbie smiled at Harry.

"Cool Harry, go do your thing." He stood up and stretched his legs as he looked round at everyone.

"We go in slow and quiet as a group, five on the grip and one on the string. If we encounter anyone, we take them as quiet as possible and at speed, once we are there we will break into cover and the main group will head inside, stay in sight of each other so you can all read the signals. With luck we will be in and out in no time. If Mason brings a party to the meet, we group back together and come out as one unit from the doors and back via the same route in. Alright people we leave in two hours go get your kit ready and travel light, just weapons, we will head back here before Rune takes us home."

They started to break and talk; Mel gave a frown at Maddy. "Five on the grip, and one on the string, just what the hell does that mean?" Jade leaned over.

"You hold five loose arrows in your grip hand on the bow, and you rest one on the string ready to fire, it makes it easier and faster to load, as pulling from your quiver will slow your firing down."

"Oh right... yeah I see that now, thanks Pebbles."

"No Worries."

Rowan hung back with Rune as the others made their way out of the tent, Rune slid her arms around Robbie and rested her head on his shoulder. "Stay close, I will be sensing the area the whole time we are in there." He smiled and turned to kiss her softly, Rune slid out of his arms and smiled as she turned to Rowan who was already packed and equipped to go.

"This could be our most insane or our most boring adventure yet." Robbie gave a chuckle.

"Mason knows we will return, unlike Avalon I am ready this time, it will be a lot of things Rowan, but boring won't be one of them."

CHAPTER THIRTY ONE

THE UNKNOWN FACE

The rain was pouring down, drumming on Robbie's hood as he wove quietly through the trees leading the group. In a change to his previous visit a year earlier, he moved the group to the east before entering the thick bands of trees that had covered the area around Canterbury. He guessed Mason would expect him to use the same route and try to use the sewers again, which would actually make things a lot easier, but just to be safe he took the group in the long way round.

Rune was close to his shoulder sensing all the area around them, with the pounding rain and the fact it was late evening, the darkness was drawing in a lot faster than he expected. The pace was a lot slower in the rain, and what he had expected to be somewhere around an hour's journey, had crept closer to two. Finally, he began to recognise parts of the surrounding area, and he was surprised at what he found.

The tower of the cathedral was as ever the focal point of the area; however, the wide cleared circle that had surrounded the building had gone. The whole area was covered in green, and trees had shot up everywhere. The clean neat buildings that had surrounded the area, were decayed and partially collapsed under the weight of the masses of plants and small shrubs that had grown over them, it looked as if the land had been left to nature a hundred years ago, not one as it had been. The air around him felt electric, almost as if Hearne would be stood there waiting, and as he crouched down and gave the arm signals to halt, Rune crouched close to him and whispered.

"The power of my grandfather's arrow is stronger than even I had realised; can you feel the air around this place Robbie?"

He nodded just staring at his surroundings; he had not been prepared for this at all. "We have encountered no one at all, I don't understand it Rune, do you think they too feel the green lord's power and are afraid of it?" She shook her head and the water droplets jumped off.

"I am not sure Robbie, I sense nothing, but I must admit I have a strange feeling in the pit of my stomach. I know it sounds daft but no soldiers bothers me more than you realise, it makes no sense as he knows we have to come back."

"Yeah, I know, it's kinda creepy, isn't it?" Rune shuddered.

"Shush, you are giving me goose bumps, and not in a good way." Rowan crept up as Robbie gave a quiet chuckle.

"What's the hold up?" Robbie giggled.

"It's as quiet as a grave with no living thing to be seen."

"Well, that is a good thing, isn't it? I mean we want in and out as fast as possible, if there is nothing living out there then why are we waiting?" Jett leaned over Rowan.

"Yeah, we done nothing living remember, they have masks that freak you out, or they just slope towards you with a fixed dead stare." Robbie hadn't even thought of that.

"What you think she may use Darkmares?" Rune gave a shrug.

"Come to think of it, I did not sense them at all, and the army of the dead we saw them coming on the battle field so I was not aware of even if I could sense them, as we were all surrounded by living soldiers, there might well be something not living waiting for us."

"Or she could have thousands standing by veiled, let's face it Rune, you have a whole town veiled from her, and if she has learned anything at all from you, it is to veil everything." Jett made more sense, but none of it made Robbie feel any easier, the fact of the matter was that he knew he was expected, and that there had to be some form of trap.

"Ok we are almost there, so let's stick to the plan, and if she has something there unnatural, we will face it no matter what, after all what choice do we have if we want that crown?" Rowan gave a chuckle.

"It's probably a good thing we didn't bring Harry; his worst nightmare might just be straight ahead."

Robbie gave the signals, and with a few chuckles, once again they began to move forward towards what had once been the tall surrounding wall of the enclosure of the cathedral. As they made their way towards what had been the house of the old arch bishop, Rune sensed a life and lifted her arm to Robbie. The wall was a few feet in front and had crumbled and collapsed in many places, and through the gap between the old bishop's house, and what was now the crumbled remains of the barracks, Robbie could see the front doors to the cathedral, and they were wide open. Inside was a faint glow, and as Rune whispered. "Robbie there is a single life force inside." He realised the light was from the flickering of candles.

Rowan questioned Rune. "Life force... As in human?" Rune nodded.

"I think so... it feels distorted, but I think it is."

"Nothing changes Rowan, it's one person and we are many, we go in slow and silent and find whoever is in there, and then we take the crown." He nodded and looked back to give the signals.

The group broke apart and went into cover quickly and silently. Robbie watched as the outside group took up their positions to ensure they could see every angle was covered, behind the smaller group for the inside gathered. Robbie gave the signal and then broke cover, and headed through the low scrub and shrubs towards the steps that led up towards the open doors. He came up to the left side of the wide doorway clutching five arrows with his bow, and holding one on the string, Rune was at his side and across the doorway Rowan winked as he leaned into the stonework with Jade.

Robbie quietly slipped round the edge of the doorway and peered inside what had once been a huge entrance hall. In front was the wall with the doorway to the cellars and to the side he could see what should have been the long clear aisle, which led to the archway and the altar. Everything looked deformed as it was covered in plant life and moss, but far ahead inside the huge remains of the cathedral behind what he knew was the partition covered in lilac containing the crown, he noticed the line of candles that burned on the altar. Slowly he slipped round into the doorway with Rowan mirroring him on the other side, they moved in as quiet as mice, and walked slowly towards the moss cover pews and seats. Behind them the others slipped in and took up positions, checking every part of the empty cathedral just to ensure it was indeed empty.

It felt strange as the light faded even more, he knew every detail of the inside, he had after all sat for hours just over a year ago waiting, and taking in every single aspect of what at the time had been an eye opening experience for him. He recognised many of the features, the statues of saints and the high roof, which all appeared to be intact. He glanced for a second across to the tall line of pillars that ran down the side of the cathedral, again they were intact and holding the central section of the roof up, but beyond that in the area where Scarlet and Skip had stood then fought, there was nothing but huge tree trunks and masses of leaves that led out through the broken down walls and into what had become a garden of woodland created by the green lord.

His cloak dripped as he slowly moved forward, on a carpet of rich deep moss, his eyes moved to the front and the dense wall of leaves that he knew contained a crown pinned to the partition with a long fine golden arrow. Behind the leaves there was no movement, just the simple flickering of the soft flames from the candles. His focus was fixed on the opening where lilac leaves hung down, allowing enough space for just one person to walk through. He leaned to his right and moved more into the centre of the aisle so he could get a better view, and to his surprise he saw what looked to be the kneeling figure of a nun.

He stopped and looked across to Rowan. Quietly he moved across to the centre of the aisle and Rowan did likewise, his voice was no louder than his breath. "Is that a nun?" Rowan looked up through the gap and then turned to him and nodded.

"I think so." Rune appeared between them both and whispered.

"Is she praying?" Robbie shrugged.

Slowly as a group of three they moved quietly forward, behind them on the balcony Fox appeared and raised his bow to cover, as Robbie had once done, Jett and Wolfie swung wide to walk in amongst the tall trees that had pushed down the large stone side walls ensuring nothing was lurking to surprise them, across the opposite side Mel and John were doing the same. Several feet behind them Hornet and Will walked equally as slowly holding their loaded bows and watching Steph and Smokes, as they took up their place at the main doorway. High up the tower Blades and Crystal were now on watch with Hawk, and far down below the rest of the group had taken up places in amongst the crumbled ruin of what had once been the cathedrals main square.

Robbie was ten feet from the partition covered in leaves when he froze, the nun had stood up, he held his breath as she moved closer to the altar and busied herself with the ritual, Rune felt the moment was right, and without warning she spoke. "Hello."

The nun gave a lurch with surprise and dropped something, both Robbie and Rowan jumped as her voice although soft, in the deserted dark cathedral sounded much louder, and Jade gave a titter. Rune stepped forward.

"I am sorry Sister, I did not mean to startle you, it's just... Well, there really was no other way to let you know of our presence." The nun smiled, although it was clear the sudden arrival of guests had given her quite a scare.

"No No... I am fine, a momentary fright nothing more, can I help you, as you can see the cathedral is not as was, and yet I find it an inspirational place to contemplate the teachings of our lord." She looked around forty years old, yet her eyes sparkled as though she was younger, her face was darker due to the fact that her back was now to the candles, Rune took a step closer.

"I am Runestone, and this is..."

"Lord Loxley and his party."

"Yes Sister, do you know of us?" She gave a slight chuckle.

"My Dear everyone around here knows of you, and the result of your last visit, in which you find yourselves once again standing." Rune felt a little embarrassed.

"Oh yes... I suppose everyone does, although this was not our intention, we were not aware that the arrow of the Lord Hearne would change your place of worship as it has."

"A house of worship is exactly that, fear not our lord remains here with us in these times of need. I take it you have returned for the crown to don your own king, after all you prevented the snake from taking it, we expected you would return to claim it one day." Rune looked back at Robbie feeling a little bit wrong footed, he came forward.

"You are quite right Sister, we have returned for the crown, but I must admit I am a little surprise to find the place so empty, considering we were expected, why are you here all alone?"

"I am all that is left, when that snake and his vile mother left, those of us who worshipped here had either fled in fear or been put to the sword. I managed to survive and now this is the only place I have; there really is nowhere else I could say I belonged." Robbie felt a little saddened and guilty, she reminded him a little of Sister Carla at the House of Good Hope.

"We will not inconvenience you for long, but if there is anything we can do before we leave, we would gladly assist in any way we can." She appeared to smile.

"You are very gracious Lord Loxley, but I am doing fine alone here, I have what little I need for life and I have all of my saviours house to comfort me. Please carry on and retrieve your crown, I have a few things to do and then I too shall leave for the night." Robbie gave a slight bow.

"Thank you, Sister, we shall not take long." With a flick of his wrist, John got the signal and came over towards them. The nun headed back to the altar to collect her things, as John slid his palms together and lowered them for Will to step into. "Ok Youngun up you go."

Will came forward and stepped into John's palms; John gave a heave upwards and lifted Will up into the thick dense leaves. "Can you see it?" Will was sliding his arms to either side as he pushed back the foliage to find where the crown was pinned.

"A bit over to left John, if you can?"

"What your left or mine?"

"Yours." John moved slowly to his left as he looked up into the foliage where Wills legs ran into it. There was snapping and loose leaves fell down, floating softly to the floor. Everyone eyes were fixed on Will, as he struggled through the tangle of plant life to grasp the arrow and retrieve the crown, he gave a gasp. "I got the arrow."

They stood motionless as they saw Will tug and his body wobbled slightly, it was if everyone was holding their breath just waiting, Wills body gave a lurch. "Got it!"

The crown fell out of the leaves, and Rowan caught it as Will grabbed the branches and steadied himself, before John could lower him down. Rowan pulled out the long golden arrow and handed it to Robbie. "I believe this belongs to you."

Robbie took the arrow carefully as the powerful memory of the moment he released it from his string came back into his mind, he could almost feel the power of his lord within it. Will dropped down with a smile as Rowan passed the crown back to Jade who slipped it into a cloth bag, and slung it over her shoulder. Rune was smiling as was Jade as Robbie turned back to John and Will.

"Good job Wi..." His voice died in his throat as he turned to see Will with a silver dagger to his throat, they had been so lost in the moment they had not paid any attention to the nun, who now had Will's arm up his back and the dagger at his throat, for a moment everything appeared to freeze as Robbie's world stumbled and he tried to understand what was happening.

"What is this?" Rowan had stepped forward and spoken to the nun. The whole cathedral flashed and then the air broke with the roar of the thunder above. The nun stepped back pulling Will with her, a scream behind Robbie alerted him to the fact that Hornet had only just understood what was happening.

"Judith stand still." Robbie took a step forward and found Rune at his side. "What is it you want Sister, this boy has done nothing to you, why hurt him? Tell me what you want." She took another step closer to the candle filled altar.

"He is mine, you can have the crown, but this one is mine, you shall not let her have him." Rune understood quicker than Robbie and took another forward.

"Let who have him, who are you and why do you want to harm Will?" The nun appeared to tremble slightly.

"I know you daughter of Eve, and I know of your fight, but you will not win her, and if she takes this boy all of us are doomed to an eternity of pain and suffering the like of which this and all the other worlds have never known. I cannot allow her to win, take the crown and go, but this last of a noble line cannot leave here with you, I earned the right to this moment through the loss of a mother and a child, I will suffer no more and take from her everything she and her vile family have built."

Robbie felt the mild panic growing inside him, Rowan looked white and Jade had her hand ready inside her jacket, he knew the dagger was in her hand waiting for the right moment, Rune was pale yet calm, he wanted to speak but felt she understood more of what was being said. Rune was as still as stone her bright blue eyes focused on the eyes of the nun.

"You are wrong, tell me your name and tell me of the wrongs you have been done by Morgan le Fey." The nun spat.

"Le Fey is that what you think she is called, you know nothing of the evil that has spawned in secret and has been wreaked on the lives of many. You are so blinded by her son and his weak ambition that you too have seen nothing, just like your grandmother before you; do you not see you have already invited her here this night? Before I leave, I will end her and the evil seed from which she grew. You know nothing of her and nothing of me, but I know all that has happened in the darkness Runestone granddaughter of Opal and line of Eve."

"How has she seen all that has happened? Tell me, for I can protect you."

The nun gave a mighty screech of a laugh, the whole of the inside of the cathedral lit up with another enormous flash, followed within seconds by an ear splitting explosion of thunder. "Protect me HOW! You have barely been able to protect yourself, you are blind child of Eve, and if you do not believe me look at the statues." Robbie instinctively turned to look at the statue of one of the saints, his spine turned cold as he saw the eyes watching him, and he remembered the cold eyes of Mordred as they watched him from the statue at Dunnottar.

"See she has seen everything and she is coming, but I will not let her take this boy, his life is mine and she will not have it."

"NO ENA!!"

Everyone's heads snapped round as they heard the scream, and the nun lifted the dagger away from Wills throat and thrust it down hard into his front. Hornet screamed as Robbie's eyes connected with the dark frightened eyes of Morgan le Fey as she stood motionless at the end of the aisle. Rune lurched forward and caught Will as he collapsed with a terrified frightened look on his face, and Hornet wailed as she ran up to him. His knees buckled and Rune took his full weight, behind Will the nun screamed with delight.

"He is gone, it is over, finally it over and the Ravens of Berengar will fall into dust, long have I waited for this moment Berengar, long have I waited to repay you for the evil of taking a mother and a daughter, your time is over and your ravens of evil and brutality will all die, the last true king is gone."

There was a bright burst of green and the nun disappeared, as Robbie turned to see Will slump to the floor, and slip out of the blood covered arms of Rune.

CHAPTER THIRTY TWO

THE LONGEST NIGHT

Judith hung over Will's limp body wailing, the lightening flashed again, and Robbie seemed to jerk as if he had been in a trance. He drew a long deep breath as if coming back to life, and the thunder gave another ear splitting crack above the cathedral. Suddenly everything around him seemed to be ten times louder than he remembered it. Rune was on her knees, her hands covered in blood, as she tried to push Hornet out of the way to get to Will. The front of his tunic was red as she screamed. "JADE, MOTHER I NEED YOU!"

She pushed Hornet roughly out of the way. "Judith, I need to help him, you are not helping him so move!" Jade appeared and went down on her knees, as Rune tore a large piece off Will's Jacket and screwed it up into a ball, her hands already starting to glow with violet light. All Robbie could do was watch almost stunned, unable to comprehend everything that had happened. He turned to see both Rowan and John just staring down like himself, still unsure of what had just happened, Rune looked up.

"Mother I need Milly's bag." Robbie hadn't even noticed her arrive, Steph turned and hurried past him, and then he felt the tug at his collar.

"Get out of the way leaf lover." He lurched backwards as Morgan le Fey forced her way in. "You do not have time let me help him."

Judith spun on the ground where she knelt and launched herself at her grandmother, there was a bright flash of bright white and Morgan le Fey reeled backwards as Hornet screamed.

"GET AWAY FROM HIM!" She landed six feet back on the soft moss floor and gave a mighty laugh.

"Finally, some Knox, it's about bloody time." She sat up and looked at the clouded angry face of Hornet. "Pout all you like, but you know as well as I do how important he is to both of us, now you either let him die here, or let me help keep him alive, what is it to be dear granddaughter?"

Rune and Jade both were pressing on his wound to try and stop the bleeding, bright violet light was flowing out of Rune's eyes, and she turned to le Fey. "How can you save him?"

Hornet shook her head. "No Rune she only wants to save him so she can kill him again during the ritual to save herself." Rune kept her eyes on Morgan, and Robbie felt helpless to do anything.

"Is she right?" Morgan stood up and gave a faint flicker of a smile across her pallid lips.

"Yes... I help you keep him alive and when he is recovered, we spar on, and eventually I will take him from you and take his life in a ritual I have been planning for many years. Any more questions, or shall I leave and let him die here?" Hornet shook her head.

"You cannot trust her Rune." Rune gave a nod.

"She cannot hurt him here, we are on sacred ground, to kill him will take her powers and she knows it."

Morgan gave a long gasp of air. "You are losing him, now what is it to be, am I in or out?" Hornet looked terrified as the tears streaked down her face, Rune gave her a soft smile and nodded at her, and Jett walked up and put her arm round her shoulder.

"Come on girl, step back and let all of them help him, my sword is ready, and if the bitch makes one wrong move, I will hand you her head as a gift." Jett looked at Morgan with utter malice. "You are the reason he is down there, so the way I see it you save his life or pay with yours."

Morgan rolled her eyes. "Dramatic, aren't we?" She rolled up her sleeves and placed her hand inside her pocket, and pulled out a crystal vial containing a rich golden liquid. "It's a good thing I was watching and prepared just in case."

Morgan le Fey walked back over to where Will lay, and got down on her knees, she looked at Jade with her dark cold eyes. "You are Green Circle are you not?" Jade looked terrified and nodded, she took Jade's hand and placed it onto Wills brow. "Focus on the wound, if you can, find the severed arteries and will them to heal." She turned to Rune. "Believe me Flower Girl no one here is enjoying this, you know what to do so keep doing it, hold his life while I work and keep him on this side."

Rune glared at her through violet eyes. "Just breathe a word of your ritual and sacred ground or not, I will take your life and give up my powers here and now." Morgan smirked.

"Testy little group tonight, aren't we?"

She placed two of her fingers either side of the wound and then stabbed them into the skin and forced the wound open. Will gave a lurch and sucked in a long drawn breath making everyone jump. "Focus Green Circle, and tell me if you think the arteries are closing." Jade blinked trying to avoid looking at her; Rowan stood close and watched them all around the blood soaked body of William.

"Relax Jade and focus." He could see her trembling and he knew more than most of Jade's fear of the Dark One. Morgan watched the wound and held the bottle over it, Rune focused.

"You are almost there Jade, just keep focused I can feel them through you."

Robbie held his breath, as did most the others, Smokes had appeared at some point and was quietly stood watching, although Robbie noticed his hand firmly on the hilt of his sword. Rune gave a gasp. "That is it, Jade has done it."

The Dark One gave a nod and poured the golden liquid into the wound, she pulled her fingers away and the wound closed. Then she slipped her hand into another of her pockets and pulled out a small silver box, she lifted the lid revealing a red powder; she pushed her index finger into it and coated it. Looking down at the wound she pulled her finger out of the box, and then pushed it into the wound and a strange pink coloured steam emitted as it hissed, the smell was disgusting, and Rune moved her head back. Morgan smiled.

"Release him back in there, that is all I can do, we will have to wait now and see if we have done enough. Now it is up to him to choose whether he will live or die." Smokes was curious.

"What was that it stinks?" She looked back at him.

"Nothing sinister I can assure you; it is something the mid wives of old used to do, nothing more, but if it works the boy should live and the game will be back on. You can let go of him now Flower Girl, you too young mother."

Jade looked up surprised and let go of Will's brow. "What?"

"You are with child I sense it, she is strong, even now she resists my influence, although I have not tried." The colour ran out of Jade's face, and she slid back away from Will; Rowan took her hand and lifted her up.

"Go stand with Hornet." He looked back at Morgan with cold hateful eyes, she smiled.

"The proud father I take it, fear not I have kept my end of the bargain, my only goal here is saving the blood that runs in his veins, any plans I have for you all will come at a later time."

She smiled and stood up, and then walked into the altar where the candles still burned. Rune gave a small gasp and Will jerked and drew another long laboured breath. Hornet moved quickly and fell to his side; Rune smiled and squeezed her hand as she nuzzled up close to him. Rune stood up and looked at Morgan as she stood by the altar wiping her hands on the altar cloth.

"What now?"

"We wait, you can send all your friends back home to that pile of logs they live on, but he must remain here until we know if he will make it, once he has gained some strength, you may take him away until he is stronger, but for now we must wait until I know he will live."

Robbie walked up to Rune's side. "How can we trust you Le Fey? How do I know the moment I step out of here you will not let your beasts free?" The question appeared to annoy her and she lifted her cold eyes towards him.

"I have no liking for you or any of your pets, but believe it or not there is a code we all live by, and I have stood on hallowed ground and given you my word. I called my beasts, as you call them, off the moment I entered here, for there was no sport to be had this night with the threat to the life of the only one I wanted alive. You can believe what you like Wood Chopper, but my word given on hallowed soil is exactly that, I find it questioned insulting, so either leave or stay, I care not, but as long as I remain here nothing will enter this place from my realm."

Robbie gave a nod. "OK I accept your terms with the grace given." He turned to Rowan. "Take everyone out." Rowan looked uneasy; Jett stepped forward.

"Wolfie and me are staying, I swore my oath to the king, so I stay with him." Robbie gave a nod and inside the altar the Dark One gave a snort. Jett pushed Rowan in the back and lowered her voice. "Get Jade out of here." Robbie agreed with a nod.

"Go she is too precious, I am here with Rune, get back to the camp and prepare for a fast departure, take Mother, she can make windows just in case you need one fast." Rowan gave a nod and patted Robbie on the shoulder.

"Stay alert; I won't relax until you are all at my side again." Robbie patted his shoulder.

"I will be there soon."

Robbie walked slowly down the centre aisle with Rowan, as Mother came up from the doors, Rune walked down to meet her and stood with Robbie, she looked at her mother and lowered her voice. "Take them back to the farm and waste no time, pack up everything and leave." Steph stared at the figure of the Dark One as she stood in the altar with her cold red eyes fixed on William, as he lay with his head on the lap of Hornet.

"I am not sure I should leave sweetheart; I have no trust of her, she is cold to the bone and her words mean little to me." Rune shook her head slowly.

"Mother I am not asking you; I am telling you as the centre of your circle, you must get back to the farm and take everything back to Loxley. I mean everything Mother, Bob and Stan and their families, all the animals and everything Maggs wants to save. Sapphire is already there with Harry helping to pack, but Maggs is resistant, you must take everyone and everything back as quickly as possible, we only have as long as it takes for her to be satisfied that William will live, do you understand me?"

Steph gave her head a shake and looked at Rune. "No, I am not sure I do Runestone." Robbie was starting to understand and so was Rowan, Rune looked determined and her eyes shone with life.

"Mother I am on sacred ground, it will hold her to her oath, but sacred ground stops at those broken walls outside, beyond that she is not bound to her word, and I am certain that as soon as she knows Will is alright, she will call on her beasts to track and kill every last one of us, so go and go fast, and save everything you can."

Suddenly everything made sense, Steph gave a nod. "OK I am on it, just be careful." She pulled Rune into a deep hug. "Watch her Runestone, never take your eyes off her, oath or not, she will try something I will bet my last bit on it. OK Rowan, Jade come on we have a lot to do, the others are by the doors."

Robbie walked with them down the aisle talking to Rowan as Rune stood and watched them leave. "Move fast, we have a cottage empty on the Orchard Road, tell my mother it is my wish it be used for Bob and Stan, they have served us well twice now. As soon as that is done head to the Village Hall, and tell my uncle what has happened here, her temper will be swift and she may come at Loxley, have the guard prepared. When you have done that, get Saff to take you to Rayne and Gwinne, fill them in and have them double the guard in the woodland north of Loxley, if she has contact with Mason, he may open his gates and come at us if he thinks we are preoccupied. We have a crown and we have a king and whether she has realised or not, she has made a great error tonight." Jade peered at Robbie from under her fringe.

"How has she made an error Robbie I don't understand?" Robbie stopped at the main doors and smiled.

"Will is not the only heir to the throne we have, we have Gaynor, and we also have Rowan, so go and go quickly." Rowan stammered.

"Hey hang on a moment." Robbie pushed him onto the steps where at the bottom Steph had opened her long white tunnel.

"Go and waste no time, we shall talk later."

Robbie turned with a smile and hurried back into the cathedral, where he saw the Dark One had come forward and was bending down over Will with her hand on his forehead. She turned and looked into the eyes of Hornet. He noticed Jett stood guard watching from the side, as she kept one eye on outside, and one eye on the Dark One, Rafe was doing the same on the opposite side.

The Dark One peered at Will. "He has a fever, but that is to be expected, for now his progress is good." She sat back on her haunches. "You love this boy?" Hornet spat back her at her with malice.

"What do you care, you just want him dead." The Dark One gave a nod.

"It is true his blood carries great power based in a magic older than time." She stood up and walked slowly back into the altar. "It is a power I greatly desire; I do not deny it. I feel though dear granddaughter, I have greatly under estimated you, for tonight I have seen a deeper side to you and tasted the bitterness of your temper, and I must say little Judith, I am impressed at the amount of Knox buried within you."

The hate in Judith's eyes was very apparent. "I am nothing like you, my name is Hargreaves, and William will live and together we will defeat you. I care nothing for what your family wants." The Dark One shrugged.

"His life is not guaranteed yet, and as for my family, never forget that no matter how many names you may give yourself, you can never hide from the fact that you are still part of this family whether you like it or not." She gave a little titter, Judith scowled.

"I am glad you find this so amusing, your smile will fade when your king forces you to kneel before him." The comment stung, yet Morgan remained smiling although it was clearly lesser.

"I smile dear granddaughter not from humour, call it more from irony."

Rune was sat with Robbie, a little way down from them on what had once been chairs; they were both now mounds of soft green moss. "I see no irony here Morgan, enlighten me."

She faced Rune, her cold white face still carrying her crooked withered smirk. "I find it very ironic Flower Girl, you see she denies any ownership of her true family, and it is no secret that we covert the throne you say is destined for this boy. Yet if she speaks the truth and really does love this boy and he lives, one day a Knox regardless of the outcome of this conflict will sit on the throne of England, tell me you do not see the irony in that."

Rune gave a moment of thought, her bright blue eyes fixed on Morgan, and she gave a gentle nod of understanding. "I am glad it amuses you Morgan, but you are forgetting one small detail, Judith met and had feelings for William long before she knew he was to be the heir to the throne."

The Dark One gave a slight shrug, her long black robes fluttered. "Yes, but you are also forgetting Little Flower, that my line has strong instincts and gut feelings that drive us towards our love of power." Rune smiled.

"And even so your gut feelings and instincts did not see the little trap our fairy guest placed inside your own trap tonight Morgan. Tell me, were they blinded by your greed for power?" Robbie gave a snort, and Morgan scowled at Runestone, even Judith looked down and smiled. Morgan walked towards the back of the altar her temper smouldering.

"That irksome little fairy will pay for her interference, you mark my words."

"Just who hell the is she, what did she call herself?" Everyone turned to look at Robbie, he shrugged. "Well, I've never heard of her before, and she sure as hell hates you... So, who the hell is she?" Rune turned to Morgan.

"Yes, you knew her, you called out her name as you arrived, it was Eh-na wasn't it?" Morgan paced more up the altar avoiding their eyes, she snapped out in temper.

"IT'S ENA!" She took a deep breath and lowered her tone trying to conceal her anger. "Her name is Ena, she means nothing, she is a runaway house servant from my grandfather's home. Forget her she means nothing, I will deal with her have no fear." Robbie smirked, she was obviously lying, and he could see how just her name had infuriated the Dark One. She stopped pacing and scowled at Robbie. "You find this amusing Wood Chopper?"

He gave another smirk and shrugged at Rune. "Well actually yes I do, I think I like her, I mean after all she caught us all out." He looked at Rune who gave him an odd frown. "What? Hey think about it, you with all your superior gifts, and her with her weird powers, and don't forget all the talent we have with the Specialist's, and yet here alone with no help at all she managed to almost destroy everything we have fought for. Come on you two you have to admit it was gutsy?" Both the Dark One and Rune stared at him with disbelief.

Robbie gave them both a smile. "Tell me I am wrong, apart from her trying to kill Will; I think we have a lot in common." The Dark One spoke before Rune could even mutter a word.

"Like what?" Which had pretty much been what Rune was about to ask, Rune looked at the Dark One and then back to Robbie and nodded in agreement. Robbie sat back and looked at the confused look on the face of Morgan le Fey.

"Well she wants your bony ass dead for starters." The Dark One threw up her hands and paced off across the altar muttering to herself angrily. Behind him Robbie heard Jett sniggering.

On the Farm at Honey Hill there was chaos. Sapphire had arrived very quickly and explained to Bob and Stan exactly what had happened. Bob got his son's as Sapphire opened a window, and between them they herded the pigs, cows, goats and several crates of chickens through to the farm at Loxley. Bob's wife along with Harry tried to hurry Maggs, but she was resistant and refused to budge no matter how hard Sapphire tried to convince her it was no longer safe at the farm. Harry ran up and down the stairs grabbing bags and throwing things in, as he did his best to collect up as many of Maggs possessions as possible.

In the middle of the chaos as the rain hammered down, and people ran in and out of the barn throwing bags on carts and lifting up furniture, Maggs stood resolute with her hands on her hips, her hair soaked with limp feathers and hanging limp, as her clothes dripped and simply refused to leave.

In a flash of white light Steph arrived with Rowan, who instantly took charge. "Maddy, Mel, Una, clear everything from the upstairs. John, Hawk, Jaz, head up to the camp site and grab the weapons cart and everything in the tents, and get it back here fast. Bear, Skip, Treen, grab as much of the furniture as possible, Bob and Stan have a new home to move into, so if Maggs cannot use it, they get it. Sapphire walked past Maggs towards Steph.

"She is impossible, we are stripping the place clean and she still refuses to leave. She is your oldest friend; you deal with her."

Steph gave a chuckle, she knew well how stubborn Maggs could be when she wanted to, she walked slowly across the yard and into the doorway where Maggs stood still dripping. Maggs lifted a finger a wagged it at her.

"I am sorry Stephy my darling but there is nothing you can say, I left once before and regretted it and I will not go again, I am not going to leave mother a second time here alone." Steph walked up and pulled her into a hug.

"I love you Maggs baby, you know that don't you? When I was lost, it was you who helped find me and awakened my soul." Maggs looked up with tears in her eyes, her voice was quiet.

"I love you too darling you know that?" Steph smiled and kissed her softly on the forehead.

"Then I won't say a single thing to change your mind." Maggs relaxed and softened as tears flooded into her eyes.

"Thank you Stephy baby."

John walked into the barn carrying a bed above his head; he lifted it up and placed it on the top of the cart. Steph smiled at Maggs, and looked to John. "John... Catch?" There was a loud resounding click, as Steph snapped her fingers together, and Maggs fell backwards, John swerved to catch her.

"Oh Shit!" He caught her safely and Steph smiled as she opened her doorway into the yard at Loxley.

"Take her through John and ask Beth to put her to bed if you don't mind."

He gave a nod as he cradled the tiny figure of Maggs in his arms. "Aye, no problems." Then he turned and walked into the long white tunnel. The air gave another bright flash, and the thunder hammered on the clouds, Steph gave another smile and turned to Rowan.

"Where do you need me?"

CHAPTER THIRTY THREE

BERENGAR AND BRETHREN

Jett sat and looked out into darkness as the rain bounced off the leaves and stone of the old Cathedral, several hours had passed and inside in the flickering candlelight, the conversation had died down, it was very quiet apart from the rain, and to her it felt unnatural. She knew there were soldiers or some sort of monsters hiding in the darkness, but so far there had been no signs of them, although there were so many trees and shrubs that had grown up in the ground since her last visit, it was clear that hiding an army would not be that difficult now.

Her eyes caught movement inside and she turned to see who was moving, gripping the hilt of the Sword of Truth that was laid across her lap. The Dark One was checking William again as Hornet slowly stroked his hair.

Jett's eyes gave a soft flicker of blue light. "Hey you... Dark One, why did that fairy laugh at your name Le Fey?" Her voice echoed in the darkness that surrounded the cathedral, as it wove though the sound of the rain. It had been on her mind since she had first heard it, and so she asked the question without even realising who she was addressing.

Morgan le Fey stood and looked across at Jett. "Oh yes the daughter of the Scarlet queen, I had forgotten you were still here." She laughed. "Le Fey is just a name I used when I moved incognito; to be precise it is Countess le Fey. As to my real name, why is it of interest to you?" Jett shrugged.

"Bored I guess, I heard her say something 'burger' and just wondered... no real reason really I figured a bit of chit chat might make things move along quicker."

Morgan scowled at her and turned to Hornet, who actually looked interested and also wanted to know. "I take it your father was remiss again in teaching you of your family line?" Hornet nodded. "Well, I suppose if you aim to attempt to marry this one and then change your name, you may as well learn a little of your historical past." Robbie noticed as Rune sat forward and stiffened slightly, Morgan took a breath and looked at Hornet.

"She called me Berengar; it is an ancient name that once was used by the Varisci tribe. As your dim witted friend over there pointed out, I no longer use my real name, so there we have something in common after all." Hornet frowned.

"I thought our origins were German?" Morgan gave a frown and looked like she had tasted something bitter.

"Dear lords in all the realms don't be so vulgar, we are Saxon, there is my girl, some difference I can assure you." Robbie giggled and Rune gave him a poke.

"Shush I need to hear this." Morgan continued.

"I shall slap your father when I see him for his lack in ensuring your good education. Saxons are high born, and the Varisci were the highest and the fiercest of all of them. I once used my true name which was Morgana of Berengar." Hornet nodded, she was actually quite interested and tried to show it, after all this was a part of her own history of which she obviously knew nothing about.

"So Berengar is a place in Saxony, and that is where our family come from?"

"No not quite, you have to understand that back in the old days, no one had a second name, people were often the son of or daughter of, and over time the successive family certainly within the high born lines, took the name of the head of their family. Berengar is my great grandfather, and as he is the head of the household, therefore all children born were named of Berengar, although in a way I suppose it is also a place, as I was born at Berengar Castle as were all my children and the family before me. It was my great grandfather's castle and so rightly had his name."

Robbie watched as Rune hung on every one of her words, he was not sure why, but leant forward and leaned into her, he whispered quietly. "Are you OK?"

Rune gave a soft smile. "I am now, nicely played Hornet, she got me the missing part of the puzzle."

"Are you talking to Hornet in your head?" Rune put her head down.

"I am, and Jett also, there are things I need to know and it felt like my best opportunity to find out."

"Wow Runestone Sapphire, you are far more sneaky than I ever imagined."

"No more sneaky than telling everyone to pack up and leave, if we want to win Robbie, we need to use every chance we can get, the time is moving and William has a much more regular breathing pattern, I think he will survive, which means very soon all hell will break loose."

"But she gave us her oath."

"I know, and I believe she will not kill us, but the five Houlen Jett just spotted have not given us an oath, and so I think when the moment comes, she will call in her beasts, so be prepared." He swallowed hard.

"Shit I knew it was too good to be true." Rune stood up and walked slowly towards William. "It is getting cold, should we cover him up? Rafe, give me a hand and get the cloth on the altar, it is thickly woven and will keep him snug." She knelt down by Hornets side; Jett moved from the window and came up towards them.

"Whoa girl are your legs not cramped up kneeling all this time? Here slip out and I will take him for a moment." Rafe walked past Morgan and across to the altar, he slid back the candles and pulled the long woven cloth from under them and slipped it off the stone table. Folding it in half as it was quite long; he walked out past the foliage covered divide and laid it carefully over Will.

"There you go buddy, keep warm mate." Rune lifted her hand over Will and it glowed with a faint hint of violet.

"He is growing in strength and his life force is getting much stronger." Rune looked up at the Dark One who now stood a few feet away watching, Jett lifted her arm and gripped onto Hornet, and Rafe leaned over Will. "NOW!"

There was a sudden explosion of violet light as Five Houlen screeched into the air, wailing like banshees, and Rune and the whole group fell through the floor and the violet light went out. The Houlen screamed into the cathedral as Morgan le Fey let out a wail of hatred and pain, and her eyes exploded with red as she turned to the howling masses of the Houlen and yelled at the top of her lungs at them.

"Well don't just stand there, get to the farm and join the others, kill them all, every last one of them and bring me that boy."

Moments earlier, Sapphire stood as the last cart was pulled through into Loxley by ten woodsmen her eyes flickering blue, standing with just Stan in what was an empty farm, they heard the first wails as the Houlen swooped into the small Ti pee circle. Within moments their rage intensified, and the flames could be seen through the trees. Sapphire took Stan by the hand. "Come on there will be nothing here by dawn, she will rip this place apart looking for us, and then burn it to the ground, your home now is Loxley, and it's a lot safer."

In the middle of five mature apple trees, Rune sat up and smiled at Jess. "We need a stretcher and to get him into bed. I cannot stay long I have things to do."

"It's on its way love, is everyone else alright?" Rune nodded as the others stood up and prepared Will for the stretcher.

"Everyone is fine Jess, especially your boy." Jess smiled.

"I worry less when he is with you; I know you will protect him always." Rune pulled her into a hug.

"You know us so well, and yes I never let him out of my sight." She turned to Hornet as two farm hands lifted Will onto the stretcher. "Get him settled then burn that cover and his and your clothes, I want anything contaminated by Will's blood destroyed, do you understand? Not a drop must remain."

Hornet gave her a nod as Sapphire walked through the trees from the farm. "Sorry guys but Robbie, we need you pretty urgently at the village hall."

"What's happening?"

"Come with me and I will explain." They started to walk through the orchard towards the farm house. "Everyone is out safe, and we recovered as much of Maggs stuff as possible, just as we left the Houlen arrived, there were plenty of them I can tell you. Rowan is waiting in the farm yard, he is just sorting out with Bob and Stan, but that is not the problem."

"So what is?"

"The cathedral at Lincoln is under attack, it looks like the Brethren called for back up and there is a load of them, we think over a hundred fighting at the moment. Mother and Smokes are already there with Treen and about five hundred men plus Louisa and the Outlaws. If reports are right further down the road there is a massive force of Mason's men coming to their aid. Mother is trying to clear out all the priests, nuns, and monks that want to come here, but there has been a lot of death in the Cathedral. A lot of the Brethren remained on the inside and they have slaughtered at least four hundred who they accused of being traitors to Mason, it's bloody chaos in there."

They came down the side of the large greenhouse where Rowan waited with the rest of the Specialists.

"They are tooled up and ready to go Robbie."

"OK what else do we know?" John Lox came out from behind the cart panting from his long run up from the Village Hall.

"Oh good you're back lad. Right listen up all of you, we got them Brether buggers kickin the shit out of everything at the bottom of the road from the cathedral, and it looks like there is a shit load of Cutters heading their way. Inside the church, which we know is sacred, Pete Lane has the Outlaws with Louisa beatin the shit out of the murderous monks, we need you guys on the road helping with them Brether buggers OK."

Robbie smiled. "Nice briefing John, we call them Brethers, Cutters with crucifixes it's easier." Rowan laughed, John Lox gave a big grin.

"Aye nice one, I will remember that in future. Ok now you know the score, off you pop." Robbie walked onto the path that ran down the side of the house, most of the farm yard was filled with fully loaded carts from the house at Honey Hill. Once everyone was assembled Robbie got ready.

"OK everyone, we face some mean buggers so get ready, make sure you have plenty of arrows and all your swords."

"Lord Loxley... Lord Loxley wait." A breathless young boy ran up with a note in his hand, he stopped panting for breath and handed Robbie the note, he took it and read the note, his face looked grim as he looked up from the note to Rowan and John. He handed the note to Rowan and John leaned in over his shoulder to read it. Robbie's voice was suddenly calm but stern.

"Specialist of Loxley, today we face our destiny. There is an army of two thousand on the way down the road to Lincoln, and messengers have arrived from

New Avon, the gates below Birmingham have opened and we have hundreds of troops on the march to Loxley, they are burning everything in their path. My friends we are now in a real war with the Knox Empire, may Hearne walk with us."

The window opened and Robbie led the group through into the centre of the cathedral at Lincoln. All around were the groans and moans of the injured and dying, many of them monks, nuns and vicars. Steph attended them with a group of nuns, she stood up as she saw Robbie approach, and she looked relieved.

"Glad you made it, it's utter carnage in the back rooms, they are lying the dead out in the gardens at the back." She gave a long breath and wiped the sweat off her brow with her sleeve. "Treen has taken command outside, hell Robbie it was like a slaughter house when we got here, those vile monks were at the doors, but Treen has pushed them down the street a little, I tell you if this is the Christian Church why are we so worried about crowning Will with their consent?"

Robbie patted her arm. "The people who did this are not really members of this church, they are hired muscle who wear the cloth of a cross for their own convenience, keep Jade inside she can help with the healing, I am going to take a look outside and see what can be done, Sapphire will be here shortly with more troops from Loxley." She gave a weak smile and he pattered her arm.

Robbie walked out onto the roadway that led under the arch and out onto the main street, Treen had used the little she had well and pushed back hard against the Brethren. She had made the bottom of the road and was organising her men, as they fanned out in ranks onto the wild fields below. The fighting was close quarters and brutal as a large swarm of men in dark red tunics bearing an ornate golden cross fought hard against the woodsmen of Loxley.

The ground was littered with the dead, some of which Robbie recognised from within the ranks he had used on his last visit; Rowan came up at his side as he viewed the battle. "The scouts say that there is a Cutter force less than an hour away, we will need a lot more men."

"They are coming Rowan, Sapphire has it in hand with John, they shall be here anytime."

"What do you want the Specialists to do?"

"Hold them back for a moment, I want to see what Mason has for us, two armies from the south feels wrong, he has something special in mind for us, and I want to know what."

Behind them the bright orb of blue burst open, and a long line of troops came trudging through and down the road to where Treen and her Captain's waited to direct them onto the field. Rune came slowly down the road and up to Robbie's side.

"It's finally started, I am not sure I believe it." He walked slowly down the road viewing the scene as he planned his next move.

"It is happening Rune; Mason has shown us his first hand. I want you to go back to Loxley with the wounded, take Jade, he has a lot of men, but we can deal with that, go and follow your leads on this Berengar family, there will be no crowning till all of this is over, so find me the means to kill her, I want her gone Rune, I want her out of the picture, so find me a way to kill her, and then all of Mason's cards will topple. No matter how hard it gets for us, dig deep and give me the means to end her, because if I have learnt anything watching her slather over Wills body, she is the key to everything, Mason is also her pawn, and if he wins, she will slit his throat and take it all."

Rune looked surprised as she watched his dark eyes dart across the field as he took the measure of the battle; she moved in close and kissed his cheek. "You sound like your father." He shook his head.

"No... He was to focused on Mason, like everyone else they think he is the one in command, I have learned from my grandfather's notes, he knew of her long before she appeared to the rest of us. I am not sure how, but he saw this coming and built the Stockade. This can only end with her, so go find me that fairy, because she knows everything we need to kill Le Fey."

"Ok Robbie, I will tend to the wounded and then head back with Jade."

Far up the road a long line of soldiers dressed in black appeared, and began to troop onto the wide open plain, Robbie turned to Rowan and smiled. "Prepare the Specialists, we will be joining the Outlaws and driving a road through black vests. Treen you have command of the Bowman from Loxley, we shall need a rain of arrows on black vests." She gave a smile.

"I am already in the thinking of it."

Rowan turned and gave his orders. "SPECIALISTS OF LOXLEY!"

They all snapped into rank, as the long lines of woodsmen from Loxley continued to pass them. Robbie pulled Destiny out and held it high so the sun glinted off the blade, he turned back to look at his faithful group and whispered under his breath.

"Stand by my men today My Lord Hearne."

With his sword held high, he began to walk the remainder of the road towards the battle field. The Specialist drew out their blades, and loaded their bows, and in file walked down the road behind him, as they entered the field, Robbie slid up his hood and the Specialist fanned out in a long row behind him and did the same. Robbie looked down at the blood stained grass and then back to the fight in front of him.

"SPECIALIST'S... CHARGE!"

High on the walls at Loxley the guard had been doubled. Woodsmen filled the trees surrounding the Stockade, and at the gates there was a heavy atmosphere of tension. David Williams stood his watch with his best friend and Sergeant, Henry. The sky was overcast but it was warm, and life appeared as normal as it had for years. In the distance there was a faint grumbling sound. "Looks like we may have some thunder Davie."

"Not really Henry look." Henry followed his gaze to the floor, where he saw the dirt and dust that had built up over the week vibrate and fall through the cracks in the floor. "Thunder does not shake the wood we are stood on Henry."

Henry continued to stare at the floor. "Then what the bloody hell causes that then?"

"What indeed my friend?" The rumble grew louder and the floor began to shake harder, David screamed down the walls to his men. "HOLD ON TO SOMETHING NOW!"

He grabbed the wall in front of him and looked out across the fields and trees, as the floor vibrated harder, Henry grabbed the wall as everything shook so violently he almost fell backwards. "Shit Henry look."

In the distance across the valley, both of them stared in disbelief as a wall a hundred feet high grew out of the floor. It slowly pushed upwards into the sky made of black smooth glistening stone, and David needed no one to tell him how far it stretched. As it came to a shuddering halt he knew. "Well that's it Henry, we are well and truly boxed in, his witch has cornered us, and for Mason, it's going to be like shooting fish in a barrel. Sound the alarm, Loxley is under attack."

Heirs to the Kingdom Book Eight: The Circle of Darkness.

The Final Adventure Unfolds.

Robin John Morgan. (Fiction/Fantasy/Slice of Life)

Heirs to the Kingdom.

Book One, The Bowman of Loxley.
ISBN: 978-1-910299-00-5
Digital ISBN: 978-1-910299-10-4
Book Two, The Lost Sword of Carnac.
ISBN: 978-1-910299-01-2
Digital ISBN: 978-1-910299-11-1
Book Three, The Darkness of Dunnottar.
ISBN: 978-1-910299-02-9
Digital ISBN: 978-1-910299-12-8
Book Four, Queen of the Violet Isle.
ISBN: 978-1-910299-03-6
Digital ISBN: 978-1-910299-13-5
Book Five, Crystals of the Mirrored Waters.
ISBN: 978-1-910299-05-0
Digital ISBN: 978-1-910299-14-2
Book Six, Last Arrow of the Woodland Realm.
ISBN: 978-1-910299-07-4
Digital ISBN: 978-1-910299-15-9
Book Seven, Bridge Of Sequana.
ISBN: 978-1-910299-17-3
Digital ISBN: 978-1-910299-20-3
Book Eight, The Circle of Darkness.
ISBN: 978-1-910299-26-5
Digital ISBN: 978-1-910299-29-6

The Curio Chronicles.

Part One, Abigail's Summer.
ISBN: 978-1-910299-27-2
Part Two, Curio's Summer.
ISBN: 978-1-910299-34-0
Digital ISBN: 978-1-910299-35-7
Part Three, Curio's Christmas.
ISBN: 978-1-910299-38-8
Digital ISBN: 978-1-910299-39-5

Other Works.

Rise Of The Raven
ISBN: 978-1-910299-30-2
Digital ISBN: 978-1-910299-31-9
The Countess Of Darkness
ISBN: 978-1-910299-40-1
Digital ISBN: 978-1-910299-41-8

Han's Cottage.
ISBN: 978-1-910299-36-4
Digital ISBN: 978-1-910299-37-1

Find out more about our authors and their books at
www.violetcirclepublishing.co.uk

www.ingramcontent.com/pod-product-compliance
Lightning Source LLC
Chambersburg PA
CBHW080726210726
48292CB00017B/2953